ALEX ROSA

UN
WRIT
TEN

ALEX ROSA

UNWRITTEN

Unwritten

© 2020 by Alex Rosa
Editing: Laura Perry
Proofreading: My Brother's Editor
Cover Design: Najla Qamber Designs

ISBN: 9798671478778

UNWRITTEN

ALEX ROSA

*This book is dedicated to all
the dreamers that never gave up.*

ALEX ROSA

1

———

Home sweet home… yeah, right.

I press my lips into a hard line and twirl my keys around my index finger as I examine the pristine condition of my childhood home, keeping a safe distance out on the dirt driveway. I didn't know it was possible to feel this much guilt. As I stare at the two-story cabin, I can sense the brick wall that I've built around myself over the years slowly start to falter.

I'd told myself I'd be strong settling my mother's estate, but staring at the lines of craftsmanship on the wooden details of the house hand-carved by my dad and remembering the days painting the teal-colored shutters that frame every large window with my mom makes me wilt. Every memory makes the hollowness inside me grow, until I don't feel like a person anymore. Just a floating form of guilt, ready to blow away in the mountain fog.

When my father died seven years ago, I at least got to say goodbye. Terminal cancer gave us months to prepare—which at the time I had thought cruel—but my mother died without warning. A heart attack.

The only thing that brings the slightest relief is the soothing scent of the pine forest surrounding the house—they don't call my hometown PineCrest, Colorado for nothing. That smell has healed me more times in my life than I can count.

I pull in a deep breath and let the mountain breeze roil over my cheeks.

But no amount of pines could cover the fact that my mother isn't going to greet me on the veranda. I wonder if she held it against me that I never came home even once after I bailed on this town for Los Angeles. My eyes drop to the ground.

What kind of daughter am I? Maybe I didn't deserve to see my mother one last time.

I peek up at the house, knowing that my heart never left—here, or this damned town. I'd never admit it out loud, but I couldn't deny it either. Not even to myself.

The corner of my mouth twitches; writing about this place was easy. A storybook cabin tucked away in the woods. I couldn't have picked a better setting for my first novel. Who needs an imagination when this place exists?

I tug my phone out of my pocket as a new worry shoves its way to the forefront of my brain. I check to see if Janet, my literary agent—and also my best friend in LA—has tried to get in touch with me. She's always supportive, but just like any job, she has deadlines to keep—my deadlines.

How am I supposed to come here and mourn my mother, take care of what once was her entire life, *and* write another book all at the same time? As if writing the follow-up to an international bestselling debut novel wasn't enough pressure. I gulp, realizing that writing book two here in PineCrest is either brilliant or the worst idea I've ever had.

One thing at a time, Hailey.

I shake my dirty blonde hair out of my face and stuff my phone back in my pocket. Right now, I have to focus on the issue in front of me. Entering the house.

Gravel crunches under my feet as I take my first steps toward the sweeping porch.

I squint through the bright rays of midday sunshine, trying to find a glitch in the home, but find none. How did my mother keep up with the constant, diligent care that the house always seemed to need?

Suddenly, I'm blinking back tears, knowing that I didn't have a hand in any of it.

Deep breaths.

Now that my mom is gone, I'll never get to ask all my unanswered questions, or have the chance to talk about my broken heart, or why I left and never looked back. I'll never get to admit it was all because of fear.

Her death also means I can't run away from my problems anymore. So here I am. And at twenty-three, it's time I make a change. I need closure.

My heart thumps in protest. "It's gonna be okay," I whisper, "Just stay strong and don't fail me." Her flailing beats are known to tangle themselves around lots of things, but especially stupid boys with electric green eyes. I worry that having to write about them was enough stress, but seeing them again might damn near send her into a panic attack.

Remember, one problem at a time... focus.

The wooden porch boards creak as I walk over them. I tighten my grip on my keys and repeat the motion I had made hundreds of times as I approach the door.

Meow.

Spooked and confused by the unfamiliar cry, I spin around looking for a furry four-legged creature, but find none. We used to have a dog. However, Sidney, our Belgian Shepherd, died of old age many years ago before I left. But a cat? We never had a cat.

Cautiously, I walk around the corner of the porch. My stomach knots seeing the worn wicker furniture lining the wall, along with my mother's easel, dusty and cobwebbed, leaning against the side door. No cat. Although, I smell something peculiar melding with the pine.

I wrinkle my nose as my eyes fall upon a food dish sitting on the white wooden railing of the porch. *Huh.*

The cat food is still wet, as if it's only been here a couple hours. How odd. Who put this here? I never considered my mom the cat-lady type, but maybe it got lonely in this large house. The nearest neighbor is almost a mile away. Actually, it's exactly .7 miles. I'd known the exact distance by age twelve, because my best friend lived there.

My chest tightens. Nope. I will not think of him right now. I thought enough about him on the flight.

I make my way to the front door. My hand jiggles the key to the right twice in the lock, knowing this old door has a trick to it—I can't help a small, gloating smirk when it works. The monstrosity of a house swells with the summer humidity; the door wedges open with a squeak, and I'm overwhelmed by the nostalgic scent, much more intense than the familiar pines outside. I bask in the fact that the wallpaper has absorbed the smell of fresh apple pie and my mother's floral perfume.

A tremor shivers through my heart as it hits me that my mother will not be exiting the kitchen to hug me, to tease me, to tell me I need to eat more. She won't poke my bum and apologize for not gifting me with her shapely figure. I picture her wide smile and the dainty shoulders that contradicted her large hips. She had a smile I envied ever since I was a little girl. When she smiled, you felt it.

I stare down the hall as the ghosts of memories float away and I'm left with nothing but silence.

My eyes slip shut. I knew this was going to be hard. Hell, I've been making mental lists of what to be prepared for since packing for my flight from LA to Denver. I went over them continuously during the three-hour rental car drive from Denver to PineCrest.

Home. Or at least it used to be.

I drag my fingers over the edge of the couch in the living room, my fingertips loving the feeling of the ivory crocheted throw over the back of it. I glance at the picture frames on the shelf depicting years of family vacations, the vase with fake orchids on the mantel, the overly detailed wrought-iron screen covering the fireplace in the corner, even the untouched piano against the window. Everything is so achingly familiar.

I try not to panic.

How long would I have to stay until I sorted things out? I hadn't been able to write in LA; the guilt had rendered me useless. But how will I get anything done here if I can barely breathe with all these claustrophobic memories?

The sound of wheels scraping against gravel makes my heart leap into my throat. Who the hell is that?

I jump next to the curtain, but then don't dare to peek outside. *Am I actually hiding?* I listen: a loud, rumbling engine cuts off. A car door moans open. "Oh, Baby Biiirrrddd… is that your fancy Land Rover in the driveway?" echoes from the front yard.

My heart releases its vise grip on my ribs. Only one person would ever call me Baby Bird, and that's Brandon Watkins.

There are only a few faces I wouldn't fear at this juncture, and he's is one of them.

I sprint out the front door and then try to take the porch steps more calmly, but my foot slips on the worn wood, and I stumble. I'm caught before I face-plant into the gravel.

The warm, woody laughter that barrels into my ears is nothing of what I remember of squirrelly Brandon Watkins, who'd pick a fight with just about anyone if they looked at him wrong just to prove that he could.

My eyes don't have enough time to catch up as they collide with a man I feel like I don't know. His arms come around my shoulders, standing me up straight with ease. If it weren't for his peculiar bluish-brown eyes, or the nickname, I'd have no idea who this is.

"Holy shit, Brandon!" slips through my lips. No matter how weirdly grown-up he looks, I'm comforted by the memory of him being one of only two boys who ever allowed me to be my tomboy-ish self.

I jab both of my fists playfully into his chest, encountering muscle. Wide-eyed, I do it again to confirm the firmness, taking the rest of him in. His shaggy reddish-brown hair is slicked back, and the short, fashionable mustache and chin scruff throw me for a loop, too.

"Brandon Watkins, are you in there?" I squint. Tattoos peek out from the long sleeves of his gray Henley. "You're all grown up! I barely recognize you!" When did he get so tall and… manly? This is weird. I try to hide a giggle.

"You still punch like a girl, Hailey." He looks me over, letting out a whistle. "And holy shit, yourself. Wait until—" He stops, as if quickly remembering tact. "—wait until CeeCee sees you."

My jaw locks in annoyance. I know what he was going to say. More like *who* he was going to say. "CeeCee, ay?"

The grin that spreads across his face melts the bit of protective ice encasing my heart. "Yeah, CeeCee. She can't believe you're back in town. None of us can. She works at the diner now."

My brows shoot up. "She does?" How did my mother not tell me this during our bi-weekly calls? Oh yeah, I never let us talk about home.

"She's the manager there, actually."

I release a long exhale. "Is it weird that home feels like the twilight zone?"

"Nah, it's all the mountain fog," he tries to joke before stuffing his hands in his pockets, sympathy washing over his face. "I'm sorry about your mom, by the way. I'm glad you're here, but I wish it wasn't under such shitty circumstances."

My shoulders slump, and he doesn't second-guess his next move, throwing his arms around me in a tight hug. He's been here five minutes, and everything already feels a tiny bit better. "I missed you, Brandon."

"I'd tell you that I've had a phone all this time, but I'll save the guilt trip you deserve for later. I'm just glad to see you here. Your mom was loved by this town, and even if you were gone, you were always the talk of it. Your mom wouldn't have had it any other way."

I squeeze him tighter. "Are you sure nobody hates me?"

He releases me and sets me back on my feet. "CeeCee might throw a fit at first, but don't let her fool you. She misses you like hell."

I tug at a wavy strand of my hair, twirling it around my fingertip. "We'd kept in touch for a while, but things died off between us. If I remember correctly, it was also because ..." My stare collides with Brandon's wide-eyed recognition.

"Oh, uh. Me and CeeCee didn't work out. We are... friendly with one another, now."

I shake my head. "I figured you two would make it since you couldn't keep your hands off each other since middle school."

He laughs, rubbing at his chin. "Who knew you'd get me to blush. If you must know, she dumped me, but it's for the best. I get in trouble when it comes to the women of this town."

I roll my eyes, throwing another goading jab at his arm. "I bet you do."

"Shut up." He jabs me back. "Maybe I'm here to tell you the real version of life in PineCrest before you get to face everyone. Save you from the gossip and horror."

I release a loud laugh, and it feels instantly good. I decide in that exact moment that laughter will be my goal when it comes to everything here.

"So, Baby Bird. What's your plan?"

"Plan? I wish I had a plan."

"Well for starters, there's the county fair. The memorial for your mom."

"What?" I gasp, rubbing my temples. I hate that my stress levels spike so easily.

"You didn't know?"

"I just arrived." I choke back a breath. "Sorry, I guess I didn't realize how hard it would be, coming home."

He nods. "It's weird for all of us, but know everyone can't wait to see you."

I try to keep cool as my heartbeat picks up speed. "Who's everyone?"

He squints curiously. "Are you just going to come out with it and ask about Caiden?"

My heart jolts from hearing his name. "Forget I asked."

"Bullshit." He laughs. "You both kill me."

What does he mean by that? I chew my lip, desperate to ask more questions, but I know they would give me away.

He laughs again, louder than before. "He's doing good, by the way—"

I raise my hands, halting his words. "Spare me, Brandon. I don't want to hear about Caiden."

"It's all over your face that you want to know."

"Let's change topics."

He looks like he has more to say as he bobs on the heels of his thick black boots. The squirrelly look in his eye makes me think he's teasing me.

"Fine, have it your way. We have more important catching up to do. I mean, let's not forget you're famous now."

"I'm not famous."

"Oh, yes you are. You're the talk of the town, as always. Big author. Movie deal. You're the most famous person to ever come out of PineCrest."

My face heat as I ask the dreaded question I've been wanting to ask. "You wouldn't happen to have read the book, have you?"

He pinks slightly, and it doesn't suit his burly build at all. "Uh. I mean, I love ya and all, Hail, but—"

"No-no, it's fine. I'm glad. It's better that way."

"You're not offended?"

I shake my head. "The fewer people who've read it in this town, the better."

His eyes tick with a sense of recognition I don't understand.

"What's that look for?"

He smiles, and I like the fact that his smile is still the dopey one I remember from our youth. He may be a man now, but he's still Brandon underneath it all, and it's a relief. "Don't worry about it. So, back to your plan…"

I look back at the house and huff. "Going back in there isn't exactly appealing at the moment."

"How about you treat me to a cup of coffee and a piece of your mom's famous apple pie?"

I try not to laugh. "I'm treating you to coffee and pie? How does that work?"

"Oh, that's because you own a diner, remember? Elwood's is all yours."

"Right." A shaky smile curves over my lips.

"Don't look so terrified. Plus, we need to discuss when you're going to be inviting your hot friends from LA to our humble town." He winks as he leads me to his black Ford F-150.

I expel a skirting laugh, running my fingers through my windblown hair. "Writers don't have many friends."

"What a shame. How about we go reintroduce you to some old ones?"

I freeze mid-climb into his lifted truck.

Chortles of laughter escape him. "Don't worry, Caiden is hiding from you. But you, Hails, I've never known you to shy away from a challenge."

I finish my climb as Brandon slides into the driver's seat with ease. "You have way too much faith in me."

"Nonsense, Baby Bird. You've got your wings now."

I don't even attempt to hide my smile.

2

When the truck pulls into the parking lot of Elwood's, my insides won't stop squirming.

Brandon is already flying out the driver's side door. I follow his lead, slipping out of his truck. My feet make hard contact on the asphalt, and I can't stop staring at the glowing sign that looms above the homely building. It's just as I remember it. Like my home, it's exactly how I left it five years ago. My eyes drag over the neon glow of cursive that forms not only the name of this establishment, but also my last name—it all begins to feel like a time warp.

My parents built this business from the ground up before I was born, a time when they had big dreams and moved their life from the east coast to this small town to open their own restaurant. This place is the evidence of their blood, sweat, and tears… not to mention, their happiness. It was their dream for it to carry on for generations to come.

My guilt is multi-layered, and Elwood's happens to be part of the foundation. It's part of the reason why I should have stayed.

"Gotta face it sooner or later."

I pull my stare from the building to see Brandon waiting for me at the double door entrance. "I know. I just—"

"Stop trying so hard and go with the flow. Has big city

living made you that uptight?"

"No!" I scowl.

"Then giddy up!" he replies, opening the door for me.

"What do I do when I go inside?"

"You start with hello."

That isn't what I mean, but I go with it as I put one foot in front of the other.

He presses his palm against the center of my back, forcing me to walk faster than my snail's speed. "C'mon," he groans.

"I got it."

The apple pie smell is ten times more pungent as it twists around the aroma of hotcakes and fried goodness.

I don't know where I belong when I reach the hostess's podium. There was a time I'd walk right behind the counter and straight to the back office. My name may be on the building, but after so much time, it feels unnatural.

A tall, striking redhead blindly approaches the stand, focusing on a notepad in her hand, as if recounting her most recent order. "Welcome to Elwood's, how many?"

She still hasn't looked up, and I can't help the involuntary arch of the corner of my mouth as I take in the sight of my best friend since elementary school. The prominent freckles that dot her nose are just as I remember. Her fiery red hair sits in a lazy but still effortlessly pretty bun on top of her head.

It was never a secret that Cecelia Baker was the prettiest girl in town—from the slope of her nose and heart-shaped face, to the sapphire blue of her eyes and her slim stature, she always had the boys in this town giving her double takes.

Brandon is on the verge of laughter. Having him here makes me feel slightly more confident than I would be alone, but I can't seem to speak. It forces CeeCee to look up at me. Her eyes widen as she dissects my face. "Holy hell," she chirps, "a ghost."

She drops the notepad and flings herself around the podium. She practically jumps on me as she throws her arms around my neck.

"Hailey-*effin*-Elwood!"

The eyes of all the diner patrons dart my way. Brandon snickers behind me. So much for going incognito. I hug her back, squeezing tight, and she squeezes right back. We practically suffocate each other before we pull away. "CeeCee, you're not mad at me?"

"Ha! I'm mad as all hell! But for right now, I'm too damn happy to see you! Look at you! Fancy city living has done you good." She places a hand on each of my shoulders, holding me at arm's length. "Oh, you look like your mama."

My smile falls.

She gifts me with a sympathetic one in return as she shakes my shoulders. "We all miss her."

"CeeCee, it's so good to see you!" I can't bring myself to talk about my mother yet, not when I'm standing inside Elwood's.

"So, what's on your agenda? Here to come check out the biz? Promote me? Or tell me you desperately missed me?" She winks.

I let out a second round of laughter, amazed by the effect my old friends are having on my soul. The dread I felt over the idea of encountering them drips away. "I can't believe you work here."

"Well, I never saw it coming, either. It's a pathetic story, really. You know I was never good at the school thing. I only survived high school copying off you. College wasn't for me. I lasted a year. Then your mom gave me a job. Turns out, I'm better at balancing books than I thought. I've been managing the place for the past two years."

When I was in high school, my mom told me she was always worried about CeeCee, who paid more attention to boys than her studies. I guess I shouldn't be surprised my mother swooped in to save the day. She was always the hero. "Wow, that's fantastic."

"Right?" a voice erupts deeply from behind me. CeeCee

flicks her eyes to Brandon, who bobs on his heels with a smug grin. "Hey, CeeCee, you look good."

Her lips twitch. "Look what the cat dragged in."

Brandon gives her a knowing smile, and I find myself grinning as I watch them stare at each other. A giggle escapes me, and then CeeCee is on me like white on rice. "Stop that. I know that sound. We have a lot of catching up to do! Brandon over there has a rap sheet longer than your book."

"C'mon," Brandon whines, but he doesn't seem too fazed by it as he bashfully sticks his hands in his jeans pockets. He almost seems proud.

The sliver of normality warms me. These two have been teasing each other since they could talk. Though, I'm more than curious to know what's happened between them. The scene sparks something I haven't felt for a long while, and I mentally file this situation away in my brain. *Inspiration*. The writer in me is pleased, which will in turn please my agent. I'll be sure to start my research with CeeCee, who has never been one to mince words, whereas Brandon has always had the tendency to omit the truth.

That prevalent question comes to the forefront of my mind. "Speaking of my book, did you—?"

"Oh-my-gawd, you're gonna ask me if I've read it, aren't you?"

Her frantic tone gives her away, and I pull her into another hug. My secrets continue to stay safe. "Don't even worry about it! I was just wondering."

CeeCee pulls away, blushing. "Sorry, we aren't much of the reading type around here, but I'm so proud of you. I should never have ever doubted you. When Hailey Elwood wants something, she goes and gets it, Miss Fancy Author."

Heat rushes to my cheeks. "It's just a stupid story."

"Whatever, we know you're a superstar. Thanks for coming to remember the little people."

"Oh, stop it!"

Brandon butts in. "Let's convince her to stay."

"Looks like I have a new project," she agrees.

My shoulders tense. "Jeez, one thing at a time. Let's not plan an all-out kidnapping."

Brandon puts his arm around me. "C'mon, Baby Bird. We ain't so bad."

He's right. This town—my friends—they're wonderful. But to stay? That seems terrifying. I've been home less than twenty-four hours. I have more to navigate, and too much to figure out.

"All right, let's not terrify her or she'll jump ship. Are you here to just say hi or to look around?"

Brandon answers for me. "She's treating me to coffee and pie."

"Is that so?" CeeCee looks at me with a crooked smile. "I know you probably want to catch up with this oaf, so I'll leave you to it, but I demand girl time."

I nod with a level of enthusiasm that feels like I'm overdoing it, but I'm so desperate for her friendship right now.

This town swallows you like an all-encompassing bear hug, complete with fuzzy feelings and all. For most, there isn't much reason to leave.

I was never really like everyone else, though. I had wants and needs that no one here could understand. Now that I'm back, it's funny to see people proud and in awe of my success. At the time, everyone openly told me my dreams were too wild to chase when I already had what most people called bliss:

Love.

It was never a choice I thought I'd have to make, but then again, I didn't willingly make that choice.

"Take a seat in a booth and relax." CeeCee's voice pulls me out of my reveries. "I have some stuff in the back to take care of—work and all. I know Elwood's is yours now, but let's save that for after you've settled in."

I welcome her words. I'm not ready to take the reins just yet, and I'm thankful she senses that. In a way, it's strange and comforting to have the people I grew up with able to pinpoint exactly what I need, especially during such a sensitive time. Time may have passed, but they seem to still know me better than my friends in LA.

They don't call it home sweet home for nothing.

She leads me to a booth. "Take a seat." She lifts her eyes to Brandon. "Not you. You know where the coffee and pie are." CeeCee winks, but it's most definitely an order.

She skips off in the direction of the kitchen, and I watch Brandon's eyes on her swaying hips as she disappears. "Well, glad to see who wears the pants in your relationship."

He grunts. "She only pretends to hate my guts."

"How curious…" I gleefully file another mental note, wishing I had a notebook with me.

"Pie?" he asks.

I shake my head. "I'm not ready for mom's pie yet."

He shifts his bluish-brown stare to mine. "Understandable. Still take lots of sugar in your coffee?"

"You know it." I exhale.

He walks toward the breakfast bar and helps himself to pie and coffee.

It gives me a moment to catch my breath, but as I scan the space, I notice that the half-filled diner seems to be focused on one thing: me.

The patrons try to hide their expressions behind forkfuls of food or mugs of coffee, but I feel them—little numbing pinpricks that send tingles down my spine.

I recognize some of them, and I'm tempted to wave. Instead, I try for a tight smile, too nervous to embrace the attention.

I attempt to focus on the vintage décor. The green vinyl booths and barstools. A neon Corvette clock on the wall above the bar. And the classic movie posters adorning the walls. Elvis hums in the background.

The waitresses still wear the same mint-green aprons.

Nope. Things haven't changed a bit—and they won't, as

far as I'm concerned. I want Elwood's to stay just the way my parents always wanted it. A clean, classy 50s home-style diner and local hangout to the population of 4,000. One of PineCrest's landmarks, I'd say.

Brandon reappears, placing two mugs of coffee on the table, and then retrieves his pie. He slips his roguish build into the seat opposite me.

"What's wrong?" he asks as he peeks up from his plate. "I mean besides…"

"Everyone is staring."

"Of course they are. You're fresh meat. I'd give it a day before the whole town is gossiping about you."

I perch my elbows on the table and place my head in my hands. "Brandon, you're not helping."

"Face the music, Baby Bird. You knew this was how it was going to be."

"I hate that you know me."

"Shouldn't you be thanking me?" he replies with a shit-eating grin.

"I wish I had something to throw at you."

He laughs. "It's so good to have you back. I can only imagine CeeCee just got her partner in crime back."

My heart swells as a smile spreads across my lips. "I guess we always gave you shit, huh?"

"More than my dear old dad."

"How is Mr. Watkins?"

"Still an angry old coot. He's retired now and just tends to the horses. Keeps him busy. He sold the hardware store last year and couldn't be happier."

"Who'd he sell it to?"

Brandon, who was in the process of lifting his forkful of pie to his mouth, flinches at the question. "Um." He chews. "This Palmer guy. He's bought up the hardware store and Martha's Market from the Cavanaughs. He's a small-town developer. He's been around for a few years."

You rarely hear of newcomers to this town. It's been nothing but generations of the same families for as long as I can remember. "I guess that's a good thing. This town needs some variety."

His eyebrows shoot up as he chews through the thought. "You say that now."

His response is odd, but the peeking ink revealed as he scratches his arm distracts me, and I can't cage my intrigue any longer.

"Let's see those arms. I need to see what's hiding under there. Last time I saw you, you were a scrawny firecracker with scars and bruises. Definitely no ink."

He smiles as he folds the gray sleeves up the length of each arm, revealing intricate art, extends both of his arms out to me and lets me drag my fingers over his tattoos as I examine them. A nautical theme marks his right arm, with ships, oceans, and a compass, complete with a scantily-dressed woman, while the other arm is more traditional with a rockabilly theme of skulls, roses, and hearts.

I can't help my gobsmacked expression. "Two full sleeves? In this town? They didn't get their pitchforks and torches and run you out?"

He laughs. "You should see the other guys. It's hard to hate us when we are, admittedly, the not-so-humble heroes of this town."

I roll my eyes but can only seem to focus on one sentence. "Who are the other guys?"

"Are you sure you want me to talk about it?" He raises his brow. "I guess Caiden is an inevitable topic."

Deep breaths.

He eats another forkful of pie and wipes a bit of whipped cream from his mustache, enjoying keeping me in suspense. "Guess who runs this town now?"

"Wait, are you a cop now?"

He nearly chokes on the last bit of his pie. "No, nothing like that," he sputters with a laugh. "We all work at the fire station. Some of the old grumps who refuse to retire are still there, like McPherson and Dalton, but now it's all of us boys you know and love." He winks. "We tried to go our separate ways, but you know how we can't operate without each other—"

"How cute." I sip my coffee.

"We followed Caiden's lead and joined the fire academy with him. There isn't much that goes on in town, so most of the time we end up getting sent away to fight the fires around the state during fire season. Brush fires and such, ya know?"

Fire academy? I nod my way through it, trying my damnedest not to show how floored I am by this new information. I had no idea that even interested Caiden. My guts start squirming again. "Wow. That's crazy... but awesome," I add as I try to unclench my jaw. "And the tattoos have to do with this how?"

His chest puffs out proudly as he says, "We all have them. Remember all those drawings I did in school? I bought a tattoo gun and sharpened my skills. Never thought being good at drawing would get me anywhere, but it seems it finally proved useful."

Now that's a cool fact. I can't help but beam with him, remembering the moments in high school when I would let Brandon wreak havoc on my notebooks with his elaborate creations and designs.

"What about your tattoos? Did you let the boys do yours?"

"Pfft! Hell-*fuckin*-no. I go into the city for mine."

My mind jumps to the tiny bit of ink that I have hidden among my other secrets. A blush rises to my cheeks.

"So, all the boys have tattoos done by you?" I ask, wondering about a certain person who shall not be named.

"Most of us. Oh, Adam moved to Denver to open his own construction company, but he's back in town a lot. His sister and parents are still here. Adam stayed away from the ink, but me, Tyler, Cameron, and... Caiden stayed to work the fire crew, and we all have them."

I heave in a leveling breath. "Where does that tattoo gun of yours live?"

"At the station, of course. Hailey, this is a small town. We need *something* to do."

I roll my eyes and let out a belt of laughter, which only draws more attention, but I decide I don't care.

3

Meow.

My eyes flicker open, and I can't figure otu what woke me up. Is it the sunshine from the living room windows, the lumpy couch, or that incessant meowing?

I stand up and stretch, my memories sliding back to all those overpriced yoga classes I took in LA as I attempt downward dog. I pull for zen, but the screechy meowing ruins it. Frustrated, I stand up straight, realizing the couch from my youth will not be the best option for sleeping.

I haven't allowed myself to walk upstairs. I don't know what I fear. I just know I'm not ready.

I adjust my shorts and tug my tank top over my waist as I walk toward the front door and yank it open. "Here, kitty kitty."

My bare feet contact soft, worn wood as I step onto the porch and look around. Patches of fog are lifting from the forest floor; the smell of crisp pine wraps around me. Well, one thing's for sure: Colorado is stunning in the early morning.

Meow.

Grr. I walk around the porch, expecting to see a cat, but instead notice a freshly filled bowl again.

"What the hell," I whisper. I lift my chin and attempt another look. "Helloooo?" I shout, walking the full length of the wrap-around porch. "Is anyone here?"

I make it back around to the front feeling like I've stepped into a Stephen King novel. Who is feeding this cat—if this cat exists at all? I rub at my shoulders, getting the creeps. I mean, I was on the couch just beyond the window.

"Hellooo-ooo?"

I huff, shaking out my body. As much as I love the privacy of this house, there's something comforting in the fact that your neighbor is mere feet away in LA It almost seems safer, but I know it's a laughable thought when I consider the city's crime rate.

The writer in me glances into the pine forest, and I can't help but think LA may be home to crime thrillers, but this could easily be the home of a horror novel.

RedRum, RedRum...

The thought propels me inside. I lock the squeaky front door behind me.

I need a mental evaluation. And coffee, stat.

In the kitchen, I help myself to the dark roast. As it brews, I swing open the fridge door to grab the milk, and the smell of rancid food hits my senses. I slam it shut, rattling the jars inside. I don't even want to think about how long it's been since someone last used this kitchen—and why.

I guess this means I'll be required to venture out. I'll be damned if I don't get coffee.

Which means I'll have to clean myself up first if I have to face the public.

I try not to glare with an unfortunate sense of nostalgic admiration at the glowing neon sign above Elwood's. Just like my childhood, my town wanderings always bring me back here.

In search of a purpose after my morning meltdown, I abandon coffee, hoping I can find a friendly face to soothe my soul. Maybe I can find some creative inspiration or sanity at the diner. Or maybe in a twisted way I hope to see someone I shouldn't want to. Sometimes I wonder if he's the remedy I need.

I think I'm going to need a lot of therapy after all this.

I hold my breath as I enter Elwood's, and what a shame it is because the cinnamon permeates the air so wonderfully.

"Hails!" is squawked from the kitchen before I can engage my plan of action—which I haven't created yet.

I open my mouth to respond, but CeeCee must have magical powers because she's in front of me in a flash. Her arms swallow me in a vise grip.

Ever since I moved away, I had to blend into big city living, and in LA, people don't tend to touch each other. Well, not so willingly and openly as they do here. So, on instinct, I flinch. She doesn't let go. I find comfort a second later; my shoulders drop.

"You look as pale as the moon."

I haven't said a single word before she takes my hand in hers and shouts over the counter, "Let's sit. Tiff, bring over two coffees and pie—"

"No pie!" I shriek. Forks and knives clatter onto plates around me. I shake myself out again, but CeeCee's hand tightens around mine. "I—I'm just not ready for pie yet." I hurriedly scoot into the booth beside us before I spontaneously combust into dust before her.

She looks at me with sympathy.

"Sorry," I stutter as she slips into the booth opposite me. "I'm being dumb. I'm being ridiculous, like, so insane, I'm sor—"

"Hails, if you apologize one more damn time, I'm gonna smack some sense into you!" She cracks her knuckles in front of me, but her smile tells me she's only half serious.

Two coffees appear before us. A sweet brunette girl gives me a tight smile before scurrying away.

"So, let's vent, Hailey. It's obvious that's what you need. I know we haven't seen each other in a long time, but I've never seen you so out of whack."

Out of whack—yes, that's exactly what I am. But venting? I don't know.

"What do you want to talk about first? Your mom or Caiden?"

A sputtering sound comes out of my mouth, and so does a bit of spit that lands on the table, which has CeeCee's face twisting in mock disgust.

"Spit it out, sure, but I didn't mean it literally."

A snort escapes me, and the corner of my mouth finally turns upward. "I just can't believe she's gone, ya know?"

She hums while nodding. "I know. It spooked all of us, but you know that everyone here at least has some idea how hard this is for you. She was an important member of this town. People are coming to Elwood's just to feel more at home now that they can't just give her a call. There's comfort in knowing how special she was, right?"

"It's… So. Hard being at the house." I grab for the napkin beneath the silverware, fiddling with it, folding it in half, and then folding that piece in half again before I finally find the words. "I haven't even walked around, Cee. I can't peek inside her room. I can't even look in my own old one. I'm supposed to be sorting through her life, and I don't know how to start."

She perks up in her seat. "Where have you been sleeping?"

"The couch, and let me tell you, it's awful. Not to mention the cat alarm clock."

"You lost me."

"There's this cat somewhere. I hear it meowing in the morning, and when I go to look for it, nothing. Then I feel like I'm slowly losing my mind like some Stephen King movie."

CeeCee giggles, and there's something about the way she doesn't ask any more questions that makes me feel like she knows something I don't. Like a private joke I'm not in on. I'm ready to berate her for details, but she cuts me off. "Do you need some help going through the house?"

"Yes!" The question floors me, because the idea of not doing this alone is a relief and an epiphany. "You have no idea how good help sounds, and I'd never admit that to anyone but you."

"Of course! From this point on, know that you don't have to face any of this alone. You never had to in the first place. Don't let your silly pride get the best of you." CeeCee whips her head back, making the red hair of her ponytail wave like she's Marcia Brady. She must be proud that she's helpful, and I support this.

Sitting across from CeeCee offers me that anchor I've needed since this morning, and I feel guilty again. "Sorry for leaving—"

"What did I just tell you about apologizing? Stop it! I know you keep beating yourself up over it, especially now, since your mom's gone, but you don't need to. It's crazy. You don't owe an apology to anyone here for leaving, not even Caiden."

My chest constricts. CeeCee is the only person I've told the truth. The only person who listened to me cry, and then talked me through my tears from a thousand miles away until finally I felt stable and confident. She never told me that my choice to leave was wrong. She always made me feel like what I did was right. Even if we stopped talking, she was always my voice of reason when things got tough in LA. I chased my dream, and I caught it. I can't regret that. She wouldn't let me if I tried anyway.

"Caiden…" I huff, and I don't know why saying his name feels instantaneously cathartic.

"Yeah, that jackass," she replies before daintily sipping her coffee

I fight a smile, fiddling with the napkin in front of me again. "Do we have to talk about him?"

"Hells yeah, we do. Are you kidding me! You're like a mopey teenager right now, and if I know you, your mind is working a mile a minute, and it probably leapfrogs from your mama to your ex-boyfriend and back again."

I throw my napkin at her. "When did you get so smart? I don't remember this."

She laughs and rolls her eyes. "At least you're kind of smiling now."

I have to do a body check. I realize the corners of my mouth have in fact risen. *Huh.*

"I don't even know where to start. I've been here two days, and I feel inclined to talk to Caiden, or at least, I don't know, *see him.* It feels like I need to be sure he exists or something. Like, I didn't make him up." Little does she know, the tip of my insanity iceberg begins with that exact thought. As a writer, sometimes you lose track of fact and fiction. The lines blur, and you worry what's real and what's not, even memories and emotions.

She huffs, "Oh, he exists, and he's as hilariously douchey and charming as ever."

I cringe. "*Charming*? Really, CeeCee? You think I need to hear that?"

"Did you not catch the *douchey* word before? So you haven't seen him yet?"

I look out the window in case he might be out there on the main road, but no, I only see the older faces of the people of this town I once knew well.

"No, but I'd be lying if I said I wasn't looking." I release a remorseful laugh. "Don't get me wrong, I'm terrified to see Caiden, but I'm not going to hide from him either." A fluttering exhale blows through my lips. "But who cares; he's nowhere to be found anyway. I bet you he's hiding. He's always been a master avoider."

She clucks her tongue. "Give him time. Maybe he feels the same. Ya know he's—"

I raise my hand, shaking my head. "No-no. I'm not ready to hear all about Caiden's life right now. *Douchey* and *charming* are about all I can stomach."

"You're no fun. I was about to tease you and tell you all

about his—"

"STOP!"

Her pink lips stretch devilishly, yet annoyingly prettily, over her freckled cheeks. Her Grinch-like smile is something she's had since the age of five; she's just perfected it now. "Are you sure?"

"None of it matters. None. Of. It."

"Aren't you curious?"

"Am I curious? Of course I am. Am I a masochist? No, I am not. So, carry on, Carrot Top."

"HEY! You know I hate that name."

"I'm aware. Let's drop the Caiden subject then, okay? It doesn't matter anymore."

She nods, squinting. She doesn't believe me, and hell, even I don't believe me, but she repeats it back, so we can cement it. "It doesn't matter anymore."

I could sing those words into a tune for her right now if she wanted, with how many times we've repeated them back and forth, and I'd make sure I sang the words to the beat of a Backstreet Boys song if that would sway the damned topic, but I doubt it'd help my cause.

Yup, I'm out of whack. It's official.

"I just… don't know what to do with myself. When will things feel normal?" I want to spit out *NEVER* in answer to my own question, but CeeCee beats me to the punch line.

"How about I put you to work?" she chides with a little swing to her shoulders, trying to be funny, but she's brilliant.

My eyes light up.

"I was kidding, Hailey. I'm not going to put you to work. Stop it. Just stop."

"What? Why? It's a genius idea. Has the menu changed much?"

CeeCee rubs her temples while fighting a bout of laughter. "Just the daily specials. You can't be serious, though? You need more time to chill out."

"You're wrong. I need something to do. It'll be just like high school when I helped Mom," I plead. "I was an excellent waitress then, and I was not above waiting tables in LA"

She looks up from her hands. "You waited tables in LA?"

Her shock is a bit disappointing. "Yeah, it was during my dark ages."

No one knows what my existence was like the first few years after I left. I survived on ramen noodles and the McDonald's dollar menu while I lived as a starving artist, harnessing my craft, a.k.a., writing a romance novel I didn't quite understand.

She rolls her eyes. "Are you sure you don't want to learn the business side first? I can start with the books. That's the part that you should probably know anyway."

I shake my head. "No, CeeCee. I want to get back to my roots here. I'm going nuts. I don't know who I am. I need to wait tables. I need to feel normal."

She grumbles as she gets up from the booth. I follow as she walks toward the kitchen. "Fine, but know this is not me agreeing. This is me pandering to your pathetic eyes. I can't say no. Let me get you an apron. The lunchtime rush will start in twenty minutes. Grab a menu and refresh your memory."

I leap up and fist-pump the air before snatching a menu from the counter.

"Good God, Hailey. Calm your ass down."

"I'm just excited to feel useful."

A mint-green apron swiftly hits my face.

Familiar faces come in. In a way, I think I prefer seeing old friends this way. Having to tend to their food requests gives me easy escape routes: *"Nice seeing you, but I have to check on that table. Be right back,"* or *"Let me go make sure we still have that pie..."* However, it also allows me to confront my demons bit by bit. The kind hellos and chitchat in short spurts are nicer than I thought they'd be. Most everyone who recognizes me seems happy to have me back, and every person I greet has the same sincere resolve, which lifts my heart just a smidge.

No one seems mad at me or resentful like I expected.

For once, hearing about my mom and our hereditary similarities from people who have known us most of our lives doesn't sting. They give me the sense of home I'd hoped to find. It's not a complete transition, but it's a starting point.

Though, there was one crabby moment when Mr. Reynolds, my old math teacher from high school, grumbled about me moving to a trashy city like Los Angeles. But his wife leveled it out with how proud they both are of me, and how my parents would feel the same.

Honestly, if I could be so bold, this lunch shift has shown me more love than I've felt in the five years I've been gone. These folks don't force sincerity, and each passing conversation is filled with natural kindness. And just like that, I start to get my sea legs back.

That is, until I hear Brandon's truck pull up. The loud rumble rattles the windows before the truck turns off.

I drop my stare to the counter. CeeCee's next to me. Damn it, and the afternoon was going so well. Her cheeks turn pink. "Uh, the boys get lunch here almost every day. Did I forget to mention that?" she chirps too happily.

My mouth opens, but no sound comes out.

"Including Caiden."

My mouth slams shut.

"Stop glaring at me like that."

"I told you earlier, I'm terrified to see him!"

"You also told me you weren't going to shy away from him."

The doors to the diner jingle open. I hold my breath. There's no avoiding this.

"Baby Bird! Look at you, the working girl! Didn't think

you had it in you anymore."

I heave in a leveling breath as I turn around, looking everywhere but at Brandon.

I look for a set of burning green eyes, but find none. Though, all the gazes that collide with mine are heartwarmingly familiar, now set into older, boyish men. Shakespeare wasn't kidding when he said that the eyes are the windows to the soul: all of them are instantly recognizable because of this feature alone. Deep blue orbs barrel toward me, accompanied by a shit-eating grin. I barely get his name out of my mouth before I'm encased in a bear hug.

"Cameron!" I squeal as he lifts me off the ground, twirling me once before letting my Chucks land on the linoleum.

"Hailey Elwood. You fuckin' sneak! Thinking you could fly under the radar!"

Cameron is only slightly shorter and less bulky than Brandon, but his thick shoulders don't go unnoticed as I give him the once-over, finding that his stark blond hair has always been his trademark feature. His arms are flawlessly clean of ink, but instead, I find a hint of some peeking beyond his collar. I'm more than curious to see what permanently marks my friends' bodies and why. My mind flies to Caiden again, but I shake my head, ridding it of the thought as quickly as it came.

"I'm no sneak!" I retort.

"Look at the fresh meat that hit town," growls another person in the back.

I leap up on my tiptoes to see Tyler weave his way between Brandon and Cameron. His burnished brown hair blazes brightly with his hazelnut eyes.

"Holy shit," escapes me. "All my best boys at once!"

I throw my arms around Tyler, who is just as tall as Brandon, if not taller. His long arms peek out from his navy blue fireman shirt, covered in the ink that Brandon talked about. He may be on the leaner side in comparison to Cameron, but his grip is just as tight.

"And who are you calling fresh meat!" I shout.

Brandon lets out a low whistle. "Without Caiden around, aren't we allowed to talk about how tomboy Hailey turned into a smokin' hot piece of—OW!"

CeeCee appears next to him, her fist colliding with his upper arm. "You will not finish that sentence! At the station, go ahead and act like Neanderthals, but not here. Get some manners!"

Brandon rubs at his arm as he fights off a chuckle. "Damn it, Cee. No need for violence."

She turns to me and winks. "Boys, Hailey will seat you."

I never let the boys manhandle me when we were kids, and even if I did, CeeCee was always there to level the playing field. It's good to know that that hasn't changed either.

"Quit it with that smile," Brandon says, eyeing me.

"What smile?" I grab three menus and head to a booth.

"You know," he hums. "Don't think I didn't notice your mini-freak-out when we came in."

Cameron appears at my side as we stroll down the aisle. He places a heavy arm around my shoulders. "Ya know, Hails, it takes a lot to scare Caiden nowadays. Who knew it comes in the form of your pretty little package?"

I swallow his words. Everything is in jest, but they don't need to know my insides are knotted. Except Brandon. He's watching me closely. He smooths over his hipster 'stache. His eyes tell me he can sense my inner turmoil. The jerk.

I shrug off Cameron's arm as I toss the menus on the table. They're all clunky as they clamber in. They're no longer boys, but foolish men. My lip twitches, seeing what they've become. I think I'm proud, but it might still be up for debate.

Cameron speaks up. "What's wrong with you?"

"Huh?" I ask, scrambling for a pen from my apron pocket.

Brandon laughs. "She's freaking out just like Caiden freaked out."

Tyler nods as he fights his laughter. "Figures. Five years is a long time. Does she—?"

Brandon cuts him off with a string of coughs before saying, "Do we know what we're ordering?"

Brandon peeks at me from the corner of his eye. I won't be fragile about this. Nope. "So, Caiden didn't come with you guys because I'm here? How would he have known?"

Cameron snorts. "You've got *Miss Town Gossip* as your head honcho, duh."

I roll my eyes and swivel around to find CeeCee already trying to hide behind the register.

Yup. Some things never change.

None of them need the menus. Apparently, they order the same thing every day.

When I'm done scribbling, Brandon is still watching me. Not that I know this for sure, because for some reason, I can't look him in the eye. He'll see through me if I do, but I can feel his penetrating gaze scoping out my weakness.

"I'm not a wilting flower, guys. So, Caiden just skipped out, then?" I lift my head with a smile, attempting to prove my point. It becomes obvious I'm prying, and I wish I could take the abrupt question back, but I own it. I square my shoulders and release a breathy laugh—like an idiot.

Cameron laughs and is the one to reply, completely oblivious to my need to keep some sense of control and dignity with this topic. But he's a guy. He doesn't care or see the signs. Must be nice being a guy. "Yeah, the idiot just called it a day. Headed straight home. What a pussy."

I grin and use the levity as my way off the topic. "Well, I'm happy to see you guys! We need to catch up. What have you been up to?"

Brandon finally jumps in, "Ya know, saving lives. Ms. Peterson called 911 the other day because she found a possum under her couch. Life or death in PineCrest, right?" He wiggles his brows. "All in a day's work."

I laugh, shaking my head, and the rounding hums in appreciation from the table have my laughter trailing off as I watch them inquisitively. "What is it?"

Brandon smiles, lifting a surprisingly gentle-giant hand to my elbow. "Your laugh. It's just the way we remember it. Nice to hear, ya know? Considering…"

He doesn't finish his sentence, and I realize that these people care far more about me than I ever realized. They're worried about me, and it doesn't matter how much time has passed.

In this exact moment, I decide I will be better. For them and for myself. Like I said before, I'm no wilting flower, and these boys have never known me to be one. It's time I start being me, regardless of the agony or heartbreak. Plus, I've never been in the business of worrying anybody.

My heart swells joyfully because maybe they can be jerks on occasion, but right now, they're wonderful. I'm only two days in, and I feel ten times better than when I arrived.

"I could totally go for a group hug right now, but ya know, it's not my style." I spin my pen in my hand, trying to exaggerate my coolness… of which I have none.

Tyler elbows Brandon. "Hailey's all grown up now, boys. She's too good for us; big city girl and all."

I reveal a full-toothed grin, and before I can mock them, Brandon grabs for my arm and yanks me over their laps.

Cameron rises from his seat to join us on that side of the booth. "I will NOT be left out of this group hug!" He wraps his arms around my waist, barreling his way into the bear hug, and I can't stop my hysterical laughter.

"I'm working!" I squeal, wiggling my way out of their hold. "Let me go! A group hug could've waited… or at least could've been more organized!"

They all laugh as my ass slides out of the booth, hitting the linoleum. I try to ignore the patrons in the diner sharing in some of the laughs.

Cameron is decent enough to scoot back out and help me up. Our laughter twists around each other as he plants me firmly back on my feet, and that starting point of home feels like I just traveled a few more miles. I'm that much closer to normal. Trying to regain control over my face and stupid smile, I busy myself with smoothing out my apron.

"Ridiculous!" I gasp, biting my bottom lip to restrain my smirk. "Regardless of what just happened, I'm hoping I get to spend some quality time with you guys soon. I'm guessing I'll be seeing you all at the fair."

They nod. Brandon adds, "We look forward to it. We're all going to come together to celebrate your mama, too."

Cheers erupt from the table in gratitude and memory of my mom. Even though she's gone, it becomes bearable to deal with knowing she was so loved.

"Awesome. Let me go put all of your orders in now."

I give them a sweet smile and roll my eyes at Brandon, who wears smug like a badge of honor.

However, I don't make it a few steps without overhearing Cameron whisper, "I don't know what Caiden's worried about. She's the exact same, if not better."

4

I plop onto my couch, equipped with a blanket and pillow I pulled from the downstairs closet, ready for sleep. Working at the diner has definitely been a good idea, but CeeCee refused to let me stay full days into the evenings. She tried to bring up something about labor laws, *blah-blah*. I reminded her that I own the place while in a caffeinated stupor, but I wasn't fooling her. She barked that I needed to find another distraction. She knows me too well.

PineCrest could never be considered an escape when every inhabitant knows you better than you know yourself. I'm not trying to distract myself so much, but more trying to solve the mystery of my missing sanity. Which will remain unsolved until I can lay eyes on the one person I shouldn't.

I've worked the morning shift two days in a row, and by lunchtime each day, I had hoped to see him, but alas, Brandon and the crew appeared sans Caiden. He clearly didn't want to see me. Surely a blessing in disguise, but I couldn't ignore the little ache in my heart.

Okay, I'm lying. It hurts a lot more than a little.

Honk-honk. Honk.

My chest nearly explodes—I peer down at my shorts and oversized shirt, not knowing what's appropriate and who's honking. I rise, opening the front door to see CeeCee already trotting up the steps toward me decked out in a short pale blue dress and legs for days, a feature I've been jealous of since high school.

"You're pathetic, you know that?"

"Excuse me?" I swing the screen door open, and a breeze wafts in with her. I love that summer nights are brisk.

"You. This." Her index finger darts all over the length of my body. "It's Friday night and you look like you've got a pint of ice cream as your date tonight. This is unacceptable."

I bite my tongue, because there's totally a pint of ice cream sitting in my freezer, along with booze in the fridge, and Doritos. Ya know? The essentials.

Okay, maybe I am pathetic.

"I'm fine," I lie.

"Get dressed. You haven't been gone nearly five years to reappear and not be my wing girl. Put on something hot, please. And by please, I mean now." She turns around to face the living room and stares at my open suitcase. "Still haven't made it upstairs?"

I shake my head, grumbling as I walk over to it. It's an industrial-sized suitcase I bought when I spent a month in Europe last year. I didn't know how long I'd be staying, so I packed as much of my life into it as it would allow, resulting in a hefty overweight luggage fee.

"Where are we going?"

"O'Sullivan's. So, be hot, but not fancy."

I roll my eyes. "Do I have to go?"

It's a locals' bar. I've never been there, seeing as I wasn't old enough to get in the last time I was here, but I know it. Anyone who's anyone in this town (and under forty) frequents O'Sullivan's. The older folks do the biker bar thing up the road. O'Sullivan's is as hip as this town gets, which will be a sight to see, I guess.

"You need a drink as much as I need a drink, just looking at you."

"Is that supposed to convince me?" Unfortunately, it does.

I dig through my suitcase. Drinks were on my agenda anyway, right?

I pull out a jean skirt that I might have packed for this exact potential occasion.

I remember my mother always making fun of me for being overly prepared for everything in life. I sigh, ripping the price tag off the skirt, then grab for a white crocheted top that hangs over my shoulder, and my combat boots. I never said I was conventional, and you'd have to bribe me to ever consider cowboy boots.

I'm dressed in record time and emerge from the bathroom. CeeCee releases a low whistle.

"I knew you could follow directions."

"So, I look okay?"

She giggles. "I hate to say this, but LA has done you good. Not bad, Hails."

"We need to work on how you compliment people."

"Whatever. Let's go. Everyone's waiting."

I'm barely out my front door before I'm back to a stuttering mess. "W-who's waiting?"

CeeCee grabs for my hand, tugging me along. "Ask what you mean." When I don't respond, she continues. "Apparently, Caiden isn't going to be there, no matter how much Brandon tries to convince him."

Ouch.

She turns to me. "Oh, Hailey..."

Damn my stupid face. "It's nothing; it doesn't matter," I squeak as I slip into her beat-up Jeep Wrangler.

"The hell, it doesn't." She sighs, shifting her car into gear and pulling out onto the road. "Just know it's not because he doesn't care. It's the exact opposite."

I know this. I've overrun my brain with the whys and the what-ifs that involve this elusive person. However, whether I like it or not, what I said before is still true: it doesn't matter.

"I think you owe me a drink," I reply.

She gifts me a tight smile and a nod. "Deal."

When I stroll through the double doors and hear the beats of a popular rock band over the hum of the crowd, I'm already nodding my head in approval. It gives me hope. And when I see my friends hanging around a pool table, I want to find a home among them.

Brandon catches my stare from across the room. He lifts his arm and crooks his finger toward himself, signaling me over.

CeeCee pushes me forward as she says, "It's good to have you here," and I want to believe her.

"Baby Bird," Brandon says as I approach. He taps his chin. "What are you doing wearing such a short skirt?"

"Since when do you care?" I quip despite his brotherly tone.

He grabs for his beer, sipping it before answering. "Uh, since I'm trying not to stare and keep this bro code in line."

My fist flies out and jabs him in the arm. "Don't be such a guy—and what bro code?"

"Thou must not covet thy bro's ex-girlfriend, bro code."

I laugh and then tense again. The fact that there are conversations involving Caiden and my name is unnerving, and infuriating.

"Where's my drink?" I ask.

CeeCee reappears with glasses clinking. "On it! I'm the best wing girl ever. Don't listen to a word Brandon says."

"Cee, have more faith in me than that," he replies with a wolfish grin.

She rolls her eyes but can't hide her smile. "I have no faith in you, but that's beside the point. When am I beating you at pool?"

"Whatever," he huffs while a new arm comes around Brandon's shoulders, connected to a dopey-eyed Cameron.

"Ladies," Cameron hums, apparently a few drinks in.

I laugh and sip the drink. The booze hits me hard and strong. "What is this?"

"Gin and tonic," she chirps, sipping her own.

"Where's the tonic?" I ask, but still take a large slurp, thinking I could use the liquid courage.

She giggles proudly. "Mission: Get Hailey Wasted is a go!"

Without missing a beat, Cameron walks between us. "On it. I'll get the shots."

"No, no, it's totally okay, guys!"

It's too late. Cameron is gone, and I might have reached the bottom of my drink already. I need to keep some sort of pace here to save my waning dignity.

By the time I'm back to paying attention, I'm catching the tail end of CeeCee berating Brandon, who's taking the verbal lashing well, both of his hands resting securely on CeeCee's hips. Interesting.

"You had one job, Brandon. One. And you totally failed."

He releases her with only one hand, grabbing the glass. "I tried. I told you. He was being a little bitch about it. He's all pouty and broody, and I can only take so much of that shit."

She huffs, pushing her empty glass against his chest. "I want another drink. Two limes… please."

"Yes, ma'am." And he's off.

The interaction is baffling and kind of inspiring. I wish I'd brought a pen, but then again, writing in bars would just make me even more lame.

She turns around. "I'm sure he'll get us both one." She gives me a double eyebrow raise, but I'm too busy scanning the bar. "Looking for someone?"

"Nope… just scoping the scene. You forget that this is technically my first time here. You may like to think of me as a local, but I've been gone a long ti—"

"Shots!" Cameron shouts, placing a full tray on the table

next to us.

I release a long sigh, finding the grungy darkness welcoming and the atmosphere far from stressful even though the bar is packed. I almost feel like I could hide among the crowd. As faces shoot glances my way, it occurs to me that I must have gone to school with some of the people here. They're all around my age.

I turn around at the thought. I don't think I'm ready for a high school reunion tonight.

CeeCee was right. Brandon returns with drinks for both of us, and I'm so curious what their deal is.

Brandon gives me a nudge. "Stop those cogs turning in that brain of yours right now."

"What?" I ask with a sly grin. "You and CeeCee, huh?"

"I told you, there isn't anything there. Just some fun."

"You are so full of shit."

He laughs. "And so are you. Now, drink up." He hands me my fresh gin and tonic in one hand and gives me a shot in the other.

This is too much, but then CeeCee shouts, "To Hailey! Welcome back to our daydreamer, our go-getter, and our friend!"

I shake my head back and forth, trying to fight their kindness, feeling my face go red, but I can't stop smiling. Everyone clinks their glasses with mine clumsily, and I can't help but laugh. CeeCee winks at me as she brings her shot glass to her lips, and I follow suit.

A chilled caramel flavor slides smoothly down my throat, and I'm greeted with the goofiest smiles from every one of my friends. My heart feels full, and my face feels warm. For a second, I feel like I belong again. Almost like I never left.

I like that we're older now. The memories I have of when we drank before were always us sneaking bottles out of our parents' liquor cabinets and avoiding the cops.

Times have changed, but we're still intact... kind of.

I sigh, realizing that something is missing. We're not

complete. Especially since we all have our other halves. You could assume CeeCee would be mine, but it's obvious she has Brandon as her other half, and Caiden was technically mine. He always had a place right under my skin, whether I wanted him there or not. He had that effect on me since we were kids. It's a shame he's being such a coward about—

"Well, I'll be dammed," I hear sputter from Brandon's lips.

I look at him first, but all my friends are already staring at the door to the bar behind me. I'm terrified to turn around.

Brandon and the boys disperse with secret smiles back to the pool table, beers in hand.

I swallow my nerves. They must be looking at Caiden, right? What else would spark such drama?

I turn around slowly.

My eyes lock on to a guy—I'm almost not sure if it's him— but my body knows. A vibrating hum starts in my gut and ripples like waves over the surface of my skin.

Caiden.

He walks into the bar with what seems like frantic determination. His eyebrows furrow, seeking out something, eyes darting from one side of the room to the other. My chest constricts, and I clench my fists while trying to fight for air. Five years has done him good, and I decide that maybe I should be mad at him for it. I hate that he fills out his jeans and his simple maroon thermal to near perfection. He drags his hands through his sandy-brown hair that's been visibly kissed by the sun, and I know it's only a matter of time until he finds what he's looking for.

"Leave it to Caiden to say no and then do it anyway," whispers CeeCee beside me.

I don't think I'm supposed to hear her, but she's right. It does sound like him. So much so that it makes his adult appearance a tiny bit more bearable.

CeeCee's elbow jabs into my side, forcing me to look away.

"What?" I gasp.

She smiles. "You didn't want me to talk about him before, but he's taken, you know?"

"He's what?"

CeeCee's smile only grows. "But it doesn't matter."

I squint. So, this is how she's going to get me to talk. "You're right. It doesn't. He can date whoever he wants."

She rolls her eyes, realizing her plan to pry information has failed. She retaliates by swiftly walking back to the pool table without another word, leaving me out in the open like a defenseless gazelle. *Damn her.*

I think I need fresh air. I'm not running; I just need oxygen and space… and whatever. I take a large pull of liquor from my straw, slurping the last bit from beneath the ice, and set it down with a clank.

When I turn back around, Caiden is already standing there a mere five feet away. His eyes are still the color of lush trees in the middle of spring, and all I can do is stare.

He's not smiling, but he's not frowning either. Do I know this Caiden anymore?

He's more like an actual man than I remember. His jaw is more pronounced, accentuating his striking features even under a layer of dark scruff.

His arms are crossed over his broad chest. I'd remember that chest; it's not anywhere near the slimmer stature it was when we were eighteen. In the darkness, I can make out tattoos on his right arm peeking out from his long sleeve. The sight has my heart winding up like a propeller to a helicopter. The only thing I recognize are his eyes. With each second of silence, his eyes seem to chip away at me, like they always have. He'd win arguments by doing this exact thing. My lips twitch, and so do his, as if he remembers, too.

"Hi, Hailey," he says in a dark-chocolate tone that I surely don't remember, but my heart seems to as it jumps to my throat. "It's been a while."

I nod. He nods. We nod, like utter, complete strangers. It's painful.

"I think I need another drink," flies out of my mouth, and I move past him.

This new version of Caiden still can't avoid his look of shock as he watches me walk toward the bar.

Sure enough, he comes jogging up to my side, and like a cosmic vacuum, he takes my breath away. I no longer think I need air; I know I do.

"Let me buy you a beer," he says, hailing the bartender.

I shake my head, scrunching my brows together, having no idea how to handle this. "No. You. Will. Not."

Someone snickers behind me, and I remember how much I hate small towns.

"Don't argue, Hailey. I'm sure we'll have more reasons to argue later, don't you think?"

More snickers.

My gut twists, and I'm forced to look at him. He's smiling. I sure as hell remember that smile. My mouth goes dry, and lucky for me, the bartender appears, setting two open beer bottles in front of us.

I grab for mine, needing to wet my palate. My eyes are glued to that half-smirk a little too long before swinging back to his eyes. "Thank you."

Forcing myself to turn around, I realize I don't have a place to run, *err*, I mean, go. I stroll back to the pool table.

I clutch my beer close as I approach. Brandon shoots me a supportive smirk as he leans against his pool cue. It isn't until I see his eyes shoot behind me that I know Caiden is following. Brandon gives him raised brows of recognition. He's apparently shocked that Caiden's finally revealed himself. This thought angers me, and made bold by my previous drinks, I abruptly swivel around. With Caiden trailing so close behind, he nearly runs into me.

I point the tip of my beer at him, squinting with one judgmental eye. "So, were you just going to hide out until I left town?"

He at least has the decency to look contrite. This time, he glances over to our group of friends, who feel more like his group of friends now that we're standing here. When his eyes fall back to mine, he takes a long chug of beer before responding. "Glad to see that mouth of yours hasn't changed."

It's almost like he's flirting, but then again, it also seems like an insult.

Caiden sees me trying to form a response and cuts me off. He knows better. "No, I wasn't going to. Was I avoiding you? Maybe. But I realized that was stupid."

My guts knot themselves into a pretty bow inside me, and I want to reply with *Maybe it wasn't*, but instead I say, "It's nice to see you."

He releases an exasperated laugh as his stare drags down the length of my body, and then takes another gulp of beer. "I find that hard to believe, but I appreciate your manners. Your mom would be proud."

He's the only person in this town who could get away with saying that, and I laugh, but as the sound escapes my lips, it makes my heart ache. It's too soon.

"I'm really sorry about your mom, Hailey." His hand lifts as if he's about to touch me, to comfort me, but he thinks better of it and retracts it.

I don't know what hurts more at this moment, him mentioning my mom or not wanting to touch me. "Thank you," I reply robotically.

He bobs on the heels of his boots, and I can't stop staring at him. The long sleeves of his shirt hide what I desperately want to confirm, and I'm so ready to chew him out, but I can't figure out what about. He's always been a lot taller than me, but now he's wider and more built. Now he's like a towering wall, but a cute one. Handsome, really.

His presence sends my mind into a daze I don't know how to manage yet. I set my beer down, because I don't think more alcohol is the answer right now. "How are you?"

"I've been good. Keeping busy."

"I heard you're a fireman now, with the guys. That's pretty cool."

He smiles smugly. "Yup. Took me a while to figure out what I wanted, but I do love the job."

"So, you like, rescue kittens from trees and stuff, then?"

He laughs, and I love the sound so much that I hate it. I'm aware that makes no sense.

Curiously, the corner of his mouth lifts. "No, not all the time."

"I see."

"So…" He mirrors my sarcastic tone, placing his beer down, too, and jams his hands into his tight jeans, shooting me a coy glance. "I heard your writing thing worked out." His smile tells me he's fucking with me. The bastard.

"Keeping tabs on me, Caiden?" I don't want to talk about my book with him, and alcohol makes me bold. "Have you missed me?"

He laughs, and shoots a grin to someone behind me, who I can assume is Brandon. "I heard you've been at the diner working?"

He's not going to answer me, and I hate that that makes him smart.

"I have." I nod. "I heard you've been avoiding the diner."

He grits his teeth. "I didn't know what else to do."

I don't know where to start, so my mouth flies open and words come out. "It's hard being there, ya know?" I don't know why such honest words emerge when I've only been standing in front of him for five minutes, but I can't stop. "It's just, I'm trying to figure this all out. The diner. Not having Mom. You. It doesn't seem like I'm allowed to deal with any of this the way I'd like."

"So, you missed me, then?" he asks, using my question. He reveals a full-toothed grin, and although it's knee-liquefying, it's not what I want to hear.

The rounding sound of laughter from a group behind me isn't either. My guts squirm at the realization that we're not alone, that I've said too much, and that people are staring. This is small-town life, and I can't assume everyone minds their own business like they would in LA. I don't like feeling so vulnerable.

I glance around to see people darting their eyes and eavesdropping away. My skin crawls, and I don't know what to tackle first: Caiden or our audience. I shake my head, feeling my pulse rise in my throat. His grin drops as fast as it had appeared.

"Sorry, Hailey," he responds. "I was just trying to make a joke; that was stupid of me."

I just stand there, enjoying watching him fumble when all I'm giving him is silence.

He scratches the back of his neck and ruffles his thick, unkempt hair. "I mean, I miss your mom, too. She was like my mom, ya know?" He lets out a growl of frustration, his eyes dropping to the floor as he says, "Ah shit, I'm fucking this up, aren't I?"

He is, although I don't know how to make this awkwardness any better. I don't want to talk about my mom. Not now that he's standing here before me, but he's rattled my emotions in another way I didn't see coming.

"I need some air."

And I'm gone, making my way to the exit, walking out the door he just entered, but when I hit the night air, I start to run to the opposite side of the parking lot. I love the cool wind against my skin, finding that I feel on fire everywhere and out of breath. I instantly remember how much I love the crisp summer nights in the mountains. When the rush of fresh oxygen barrels down my throat as I inhale deeply, it's a relief to my senses.

I hear the fast crunching of gravel approaching, and I know whoever is following me is inevitable, and that deep, dark place in my heart wants it, even though it shouldn't.

I thought I was prepared for encountering Caiden. Okay,

maybe I wasn't so prepared to see what he looks like in comparison to five years ago, but I had an inkling of what I'd be facing emotionally. But this is different. This life has an audience, among other things.

I exhale, closing my eyes.

"Hailey?"

I never doubted he'd follow me, but I don't want to turn around. Standing at the edge of the parking lot, I open my eyes, greeted with lush darkness. I can smell the pine forest that's in front of me even though the night shields me from it. I'm totally baffled by how green and forested it is here. How could I forget that my childhood adventures always lay a few feet beyond every bit of home? I'd only have to run into the woods to let my imagination run wild, or to seek a quiet moment, or even to let my heart fall hopelessly in love. I don't have this in LA I'm in awe of this escape route.

"Yes?" I reply, turning around. Caiden is so ridiculously grown up in such a heart-stopping way that I forget how to operate my mouth. "Five years did you unfortunately well, Caid."

He laughs, his eyes blatantly sliding up the length of my body again. He's opening his mouth to respond, but my heart and mind have another battle to score. "Don't respond to that," I blurt.

"We're not so good at this seeing-each-other-after-all-these-years thing, are we?"

"We're all over the map."

He nods. "Where do we start now?"

I lift my hand, and in my flustered state, I grab for his tattooed arm, pushing up his sleeve. "Show me," I whisper. It's a demand I shouldn't make.

He doesn't pull away; he just stares, pinning me with intensity and goading curiosity as he whispers back, "Why, Hailey?"

"I just need to know."

The curve to his lips makes it feel like he's achieved his own personal victory. I know I'm showing I care too much.

"This is where you want us to start?" he asks.

I just nod, liking how the soft skin of his wrist feels under my fingertips, and how he keeps staring at my hand on him.

"Well, it's still there. I didn't cover it up." He gently pulls his wrist from my grasp and pushes his sleeve farther up his arm to bravely show me the underside of his forearm.

There it is.

My initials, still there on his skin, but this time, the cursive letters weave around an intricate, stark tree tattoo, the letters wrapping around the branches. Almost like a secret among the woods that mark him now.

I blink a few times, not realizing that I would feel such an ocean of relief at the sight, but my frantic heart can't seem to catch up. "Oh," I breathe out.

His tattoos are a work of art. The wrist and upward of his arm have a forest, and a deep, purple night sky above it with artistic designs and swirls between the trees, including the letters H.L.E.

Hailey Lynn Elwood.

My eyes lift from his perfect forearms, strong and manly and sort of beautiful, and I can't believe my initials are still there now. I don't know how to recover from my poised freak-out.

"Does everyone know about it?" I can't even say what it is. I just raise my finger and point at my three initials that are on his skin so strategically that you wouldn't be able to notice it. It's clever and stunning all at once.

He chews the inside of his cheek, lifting heavy shoulders as he gruffly responds, "Everyone knows I have your initials tattooed on me except one person."

"Who?"

"My girlfriend."

There it is.

"Oh." It's like he's knocked my feet from under me. CeeCee mentioned he had a girlfriend, so I thought I was prepared, but I'm an idiot. I wasn't given the time to digest it properly. Hearing him confirm it stings more than I'd ever admit out loud. "I heard you had one of those."

It's like he's waiting for me to react, but I can't. I've reacted so much tonight that I might be reacted out.

"Of course you heard about that. Brandon tell you, or Cecelia?"

The question has the corner of my mouth twitching. It becomes clear what Brandon was avoiding during all those awkward moments with him and the boys.

"Cecelia," I smirk.

"Figures." He pauses, pawing the ground a second before he lifts his head up to say, "So, did you get all fancy in LA and remove yours?"

My face twists at his tone, but if anything, I understand. I feared the same when I heard Brandon say they all got tattooed. Caiden could have easily covered my initials, but he didn't, and I can't tell what it means, or if it means anything at all.

Note to self: dissect that one later.

My eyes focus back on his as I blindly fold down the material of my jean skirt on the right side of my hip to show him his initials.

Each letter of black script curling around the other.

C.L.A.

Caiden Lawrence Anderson

Untouched. Unmarked. Still in its pristine form, just like the memory of that crazy day when we were eighteen.

He stares at it hard, examining it as he licks his lips before bringing his eyes back to mine. "I was worried you'd get rid of it like you got rid of me."

"That isn't fair, and you know it." I shake my head, having to look away. This is one of those moments I expected but could never wrap my head around how to handle. "I had to make a choice, Caiden."

He stuffs his hands into his pockets, his eyes heavy. He

doesn't seem afraid; if anything, he seems determined. "And you chose to leave me."

"You didn't have to make me choose." I rake my fingers through my blonde waves. How do I explain myself?

His loud, disgruntled sigh catches me off guard, and when I see that his eyes are clenched shut as he tries to figure out what to say, I don't feel so alone in this.

He lifts his tattooed right hand to rub over the thick scruff covering his jaw, and I'm curious what it might feel like against my fingertips. I used to know everything about this guy, every curve, every smile, but now there's a level of unknown, and it almost feels like an adventure... a terrifying one, a ludicrous endeavor if there ever was one, because isn't it all impossible now? He's not mine. He's someone else's.

When his eyes fly open, I almost feel guilty for watching him so closely.

"I know—I know, Hailey. Hindsight is twenty-twenty, right? Your dreams were bigger than I could understand at the time. Is that fair to admit?" He kicks at a few rocks before trying for more. "At the time, I needed you here with me. You wanted me to go with you to a big city so you could be a writer, but how was I supposed to understand that? All I could understand was, I had to leave everything I knew."

"We could have made a life there and figured it out together, don't you think?"

"Ya know, it's almost cute how you still think it's so simple. Even when we were kids, you were always so sure of yourself. You always knew what you wanted. I couldn't run away with you to chase your dream when I didn't know what I wanted. I only ever wanted you, but I didn't know what I wanted out of life yet. I know it seemed simple, that I could just follow you, and we'd be fine, but it wasn't for me. I was terrified. You never even considered what it would be like for me to leave—it kind of killed me. Maybe that was why I made you choose."

He peers up, puppy-eyed and apologetic through thick brows, and the corners of his mouth droop beneath his scruff. "I know you kept telling me there was a life for me there, but my world was small, Hail. It still is. That wasn't the life I wanted. That was the life you wanted, and I figured if that was the case, then you were choosing not to include me in this dream of yours. It felt like you knew what was at stake, and you made your choice. You never asked me what I wanted."

My jaw hits the ground. It's too much. It's maybe the most honest thing he's ever said to me. Even when I left, he allowed me to leave in a cloud of silence. We argued, sure, but it never made sense. He was mad; he was hurt, but I never knew why. He made me choose, and I always thought that was unfair. Now, I realize it wasn't just about me leaving. It was about him needing as much help as I did to figure things out, and I never considered that.

He continues, "It was childish for me to make you choose. I know that now. We could have compromised. We probably had other options, but we were so young. Things just happened, and we can't take them back, but hell, I can't imagine you thinking you made the wrong choice."

Maybe he thinks he's complimenting me on my success, but I kind of hate him for it. It was never about right or wrong. Sure, I won the proverbial dream, but I also lost a whole hell of a lot, including him. I'm tempted to tell him but—

"Haiillleeeyyyy!"

Both of us turn around to face the entrance to the bar. I can see a stumbling CeeCee coming toward us with Brandon, whose arm is slung heavily over her shoulder.

I cast a glance at Caiden, who apparently doesn't seem to care what we're witnessing because he's back to staring at me, but he's fiddling with his bottom lip with his left hand again. This time I notice the tattoo covering his knuckles that spells "true." It's distracting. I try to make a mental note to ask what word comes before it on his right hand, but I'm too busy rolling my eyes at his gawking.

I turn to shout at my dubious friends. "I KNEW IT! I SO

KNEW IT!"

Brandon waves me off with his free hand and chuckles. "You know nothing, Baby Bird."

He offers no further explanation, and I'm still rattled by the man beside me. I can't seem to appropriately respond as I see them stroll toward Brandon's truck.

"Cee, what about being my ride tonight?"

"Whoops," she hiccups and winks. I shake my head disapprovingly. "Sorry, Hails. I drank too much, and strapping Brandon here is going to give me a ride."

I roll my eyes. "Or do you mean you'll be riding him?"

All of them erupt in loud laughter, including Caiden. I meant it as an insult, but a joke works fine, too.

"Oh man, you're clever, Baby Bi—"

I cut Brandon off with my head shaking in shame. I knew they couldn't have dropped each other that easily. It's all over their innate chemistry.

"How am I supposed to get home now?" I shout.

CeeCee giggles. "Caaaiiideennn," she sings drunkenly. "Give Hailey a ride, will you?"

Caiden doesn't seem to think twice about it as he replies, "Of course."

So crisp. Polite, even.

I want to punch him. I don't know why. It's irrational, I know. Maybe it's because, when it comes to Caiden, it's anything but easy for me.

"Have a good night!" Brandon chirps, and I swear if he had a hat, he would tip it toward us in all his dapper, jerk-like glory.

I'm fuming. I know my anger might be because of the gin, or the beer, or Caiden. Who cares? "I wanna go home."

"Huh?" Caiden asks, thrown by my words. We both leap at the sound of Brandon's truck turning on and leaving the parking lot.

"I can't believe her right now. It's like she planned this."

Caiden laughs, and I even hate how much I love the sound. It's so much deeper than when we were kids, and it causes my skin to tingle. I hate it. I love it. No, no... I hate it.

"She's a fuckin' trip. Her and Brandon aren't together, but they fuck around pretty often."

I shrug. Talking about someone else is easier to do. "I figured, actually."

"Yeah, but..." He leans forward, as if he's telling me a secret. "Brandon's in love with her, but he hurt her really bad, so she won't date him again."

My brows knit together, and it almost feels like old times when we would form our own theories about our friends while sitting on the edge of the lake.

"Newsflash, Caiden: CeeCee's in love with Brandon, too. She's just stubborn."

"How do you know?"

"Because CeeCee plays the slut card well, but she doesn't actually sleep around. She's getting her fill of Brandon, pun intended." I pause to watch Caiden look away to laugh, basking in it a second before continuing, "And she's just terrified. Brandon can come with a lot of false promises."

He straightens his posture in defense of his best friend. "He'd prove it to her if she let him."

I shake my head. "It doesn't work that way."

"What, are you a specialist in love now?"

I tense as I stare into the eyes of the man who's unfortunately taken permanent residence in my heart, whether he knows it or not. "I'm anything but. I just know my friends."

An awkward silence falls between us. We don't do so well with the love topic.

"You ready to head home?"

I nod.

"We okay, Hailey?"

He's already walking the opposite direction, as if scared of my answer. I trail after him, not having a clue what he might drive nowadays. His first car was a beat-up red pickup truck.

"Are we, Caiden?" I hum back when we're finally shoulder

to shoulder. I want to ask him how we could possibly be okay when we have each other's initials tattooed on our bodies forever, but I don't.

"I knew seeing you was gonna be... interesting. I just didn't realize I would word vomit everywhere."

I laugh. Oh, God, I laugh. Then he laughs. Then his deep laughter tangles around mine, and it makes my insides turn to goo. Sweet, delicious, syrupy goo. It's like I'm sixteen all over again.

I lift a suspicious brow as I clamp my teeth over my bottom lip. "We've covered a lot of bases tonight, don't you think?"

This time his laughter chokes off. "We've always been good at covering bases, Hails."

Lord, help me.

My cheeks pinken, and I must look ridiculous because his elbow comes gently colliding into my side. "Oh, come on. I was joking. You can't be the only one allowed to freely hand out sexual innuendo-laced jokes. That wouldn't be fair."

I wrinkle my nose. "I make the jokes about others, not about us."

We make it to a navy Ford pickup, shiny and new, but not as ostentatious as Brandon's monster.

Confidently, he chides, "Let's not deny we had some good times, Hailey. That would be silly."

He opens the passenger door, nudging his chin for me to get inside. I might be thankful, because I don't have it in me to appropriately respond with "That we did," and instead shoot him a wry smirk as I scoot onto the seat.

Caiden pulls into my gravel driveway. It floods me with memories of doing this exact thing repeatedly, but years ago when we mattered. We don't matter anymore, or at least I don't think we do.

By the time he cuts the engine, I'm so rattled by nostalgia that I feel another freak-out coming. "Don't walk me to my door."

When his eyes go wide, like I've just spoken in tongues, I know my freak-out is uncalled for. I shrug apologetically.

Something about Caiden terrifies me. Maybe it's because I know he holds all the cards, and maybe it's also the fact he doesn't necessarily know that yet. He suffocates me, he always has, and I didn't know suffocation could be so achingly sweet but still entirely hard to handle.

I reach for the door to leave.

"Hailey, wait—"

It's too late. I'm already out of his truck and power walking to my front door.

"Have you lost your mind?" he shouts from behind me as I hear his truck door slam shut.

Finally, a question I can answer. I turn around on the second step, my eyes colliding with his. "Actually, I have." I lift my stare up to the billions of stars that naturally illuminate this place, and the glow of his eyes. "I'm bat shit crazy, if you must know. This place does that to me. You do that to me."

The crunching sounds of his footsteps on the gravel stop.

"Let's just blame alcohol for that one, okay?" I grit my teeth, forcing a smile. "I know it may not seem like it, but it really is good to see you." He'd never understand how the relief of knowing he still exists is a remedy to my mind and nerves. "G'night, Caiden."

"Hailey…" He sighs.

I'm already approaching my door, trying to pull my keys from my pocket, staring at my hands as I reply, "Don't say my name that way."

"What way?" His wry tone is back. His footsteps sound again, then the clomping of his boots on the steps.

I don't want to look at him anymore. I've had enough for one night.

My keys tumble from my hands and clatter loudly when they hit the wood floor.

He leans down before I can, and instead of handing them back to me, he unlocks the door for me and opens it, waving me inside my home.

I huff. "I hate you."

He rolls his eyes and walks inside. "No, you don't."

"Hey! Who invited you in?"

All I can see is his broad back, the fabric of his shirt rippling with every heavy stride. He stops in the doorway of the kitchen and turns around. "It's weird in here without her, huh?"

I close the front door behind me, peeking at him through my eyelashes. "Tell me about it."

He's too big for my house now. He fills the frame of the door, and the room feels like it needs to expand to be able to contain his presence. He's always been larger than life; that's why him moving to LA with me never seemed impossible. He's the type of person who makes the most, if not better, of what's thrown at him. I learned at the tender age of nineteen that even he has a breaking point.

His eyes tense as he watches me, his lips twitching under his scruff. "There's so much I want to say, so much I want to talk about, and so much I think you need to talk about, too, but I want to be selfish. Maybe because I've been waiting for this moment since you released your book."

My heart constricts, and I forget how to breathe again. My diaphragm stops moving. "I don't know what you're talking about." I shrug.

"We need to talk about the elephant in the room."

"Caiden, there are so many elephants in this room that we could open up a frickin' zoo."

He laughs, and the sound triggers that natural pull of oxygen. I remember writing my book and how describing him the way I did was never a lie or an exaggeration.

"We need to talk about your book first."

"There's nothing to say." I turn away. I realize we're in my house, and I have nowhere to run.

"Stop it. Just because this whole town is illiterate doesn't mean I am."

It's supposed to be a joke, but my heart leaps into my throat, preventing speech.

He shakes his head. "Wait here."

What a silly thing to say. Especially since nauseating fear and embarrassment have me nailed to the spot.

He walks past me, flings open the front door, leaving it wide open as he rushes outside.

"What are you doing?" I ask, swiveling around.

He's fiddling in his truck for less than a minute before trotting back inside, closing the door behind him, and strategically placing himself a few feet in front of me. He lifts his right hand holding a book. *My book.* I recognize it as the first edition with the old cover, before my publisher revamped it after it hit the *New York Times* bestseller list.

His copy has my jaw dropping as I stare and examine it. It's not worn like a book you read once and place on your shelf to collect dust. No, this one is tattered in a cherished way. The corners and edges are bent and faded, and the spine is lined with many folds of repeated use. However, what shocks me the most are all the tabbed Post-it notes sticking out from all sides in different flagged colors. If the book was larger, you could mistake it for a textbook just by the sheer number of notes that it seems to hold, but no, it's my book.

Speechless. I'm speechless.

He's watching me again, and I still can't stop staring at that thing in his hands.

"Are we going to be honest, Hailey, or are we going to pretend that this book isn't about us?"

My mouth that was still hanging open slams shut. I guess I knew this was always a possibility. My big fear was that anyone in this town would pick up my book and find out that they were the foundation to its setting, but damn it, I had hoped that Caiden would never touch it and see it for what it really is. I thought in the edits I did a good job of covering my tracks. I changed names, locations, and appearances.

Though, staring at him now, it's those eyes of his. They've always been: piercing, expectant, honest, determined, and they can see right through me. They always have.

Nope. I can't. I'm not ready. Not for this.

Tonight has been too much. From seeing first loves, tattoos that tell stories, to missing Mom… I can't talk about this right now. I think I'm ready for another good cry, and maybe more beer. It's hard to tell.

"I don't know what you're talking about."

"The hell you don't. Did you think I wouldn't notice?"

I wish I could admit I have a lot I want to say, but it's just not the right time, and for now, denying everything sounds like my best option.

"It's not. You're just reading too much into it." I lie through my fucking teeth, and I know he knows I'm full of shit.

He grumbles, running his free hand through his hair, utterly frustrated with me, and I don't blame him. "I'm going to let this go for tonight, because obviously you're dealing with a lot, and we've really talked about so many damn things that I can't decide if we made any progress, BUT," he enunciates loudly, "don't think I won't make you accountable chapter by chapter. It might not be that obvious to anyone else, but I know this book is about us."

I stomp my right foot like a child, which only ignites his glorious smile. He riles me up. It's like he pushed me down in the schoolyard to show affection. And trust me, he did that a lot.

"I don't know what progress we have to make, but there's nothing to talk about, Caid. Just drop it."

He lets out an exasperated sigh, but reveals a comical crook to his lip. "Still stubborn as all hell."

I cross my arms over my chest, and nod my stubborn agreement.

He starts for the door, walking past me, but stops abruptly

before reaching it. He turns around, but his eyes aren't on me.

"Why haven't you unpacked?" His eyes drag over the couch, taking in the blanket and pillows before coming back to me.

"Uh… um…" I stammer. I shrug so hard it almost knocks me off-balance.

He sighs inwardly before taking two steps to reach me, and I don't know what to do, or what he's doing. But then he grabs for my shoulders and pulls me into a rough hug. It's abrupt, but it's also tight, secure, safe, and brief.

I hate it when he releases me, just like I hate his handsomely grown-up face, and his dashingly beautiful forearms, and his stupid, stupid eyes.

"It's going to be okay, Hailey. This isn't over. We'll talk more, all right? And for the record, I'm glad you're back."

He asked me a question, but the pain etched on his face, and the fact he's already turning around, heading out the door to his car means he doesn't want an answer to it.

What if I'm done talking to him? What if I have nothing more to say? What if I told him he can't come here and dust off my heart from the pile of ashes it's been sitting in and inspire everything that I thought I lost?

Instead, I pout, standing on my porch. He shoots me a sharply crafted smirk before climbing into his truck, as if he knows I hate him for all those reasons that I don't hate him for at all.

His truck skids out of my driveway as if he's running away from me as much as I wish I could run away from him, and I scurry back inside, hit with something I haven't felt in months.

I pull my untouched notebook from my suitcase and start scribbling words down.

Then I hear a meow outside my window, and for the first time, I don't care.

I think I just found my *eureka*.

5

————

Sipping my third cup of coffee as it nears noon, I listen to my agent, Janet Martinez, on the phone worrying about my focus. Little does she know I wrote nearly six pages in my notebook last night.

"Listen, Janet, I take back what I said before. I think this might be a good thing."

"Are you sure? How's everything going with your mom's... estate?"

Janet does not do well with feelings or emotions, even though she's an incredible friend, and a devourer (and cheerleader) for all things romance novel. I like to call her The Queen of Introverted Love. She's got a lot of heart, but she has a hard time verbalizing her emotions. When she tries, it's a big deal.

"Um. Mom *stuff* is as good as it's going to get. My mom wrote in her will that she didn't want a typical funeral, which is so like her. She hated anything sad—sad movies, sad songs, everything. She wanted a party, nothing more. Her ashes are supposed to be delivered this week, and I guess the memorial is happening at the county fair to celebrate her life. I don't even know what to prepare for."

"The fair? Dang, when you said small town, I didn't think you meant *Little House on the Prairie* small."

I huff out a laugh. "Yeah, you could say that. Overall, there's so much love for her that it's making it easier to handle, except this house. I can't seem to face this house at all."

"What about the diner?" she hums, and I know there's tenseness to her voice that she's trying to hide. Her biggest fear is that I'd come here and never want to leave, or write again, and instead work at the diner.

"It's great and in good hands." I smile, thinking of my red-haired, freckle-faced friend with a penchant for charming exes with mustaches. "And don't worry. I never wanted to run the diner when I was a kid, and that hasn't changed, but I'm not getting rid of it. I still need to work that part out. I don't know what to do with any of it. The house. The diner. All I know is that I'm not ready to let go."

I pull a pot out from a cabinet and set it on the stove, then grab for a can opener.

"Are you cooking?" I can hear the squeak of Janet's office chair and picture her leaning forward in disbelief, her dark brown hair falling from behind her ears and hazel eyes going wide.

"Don't sound so surprised. Plus, there aren't many options—no delivery here. I grabbed the essentials."

"What does the essentials mean to someone who survives on coffee and rice bowls from Panda Express?"

I sigh mournfully. "The essentials consist of coffee, soup, grilled cheese ingredients, and wine. But damn, now I want a rice bowl." We laugh together, and it reminds me that life isn't terrible in LA My life is just different there, and void of erratic heart palpitation problems that come with years of baggage.

"So coffee, a few cans of Campbell's, cheese, a loaf of bread, and a bottle of rosé?"

"Uh, yeah. The essentials. Your point is?" I chide, prying open the tomato soup.

"I'm just saying, I didn't get you a six-figure movie deal for you to be slumming it."

I roll my eyes. "Unfortunately, my slumming it is me working with what I know. I'd love to eat ratatouille, but I wouldn't know the first goddamn thing about how to make it. We all can't be professional Pinterest savvy cooks like you, all right?"

"Fine, but if and when I decide to come and visit, let me cook."

"Sold!" I crank the stove to high.

Our laughter dwindles, and she sighs. I already know what's coming when she lets the silence hang a few more seconds. "How's, ya know, the other thing?"

Oh, *the other thing*, that's what we're calling it now.

I pour the can of soup into the pot, letting out a grunt of frustration. "Are we talking about me writing the sequel or my ex-boyfriend?"

"Aren't those the same thing?"

I slam down the empty can in the trash like I'm Michael Jordan in the playoffs.

"Well, the good thing is, I'm writing."

"Oh—oh, that is good to hear."

"Yeah," I groan, walking into my living room, glancing at my suitcase. I really need a better place for it than the middle of the floor. "Except I'm going to be building this book more from a fictional sense, not that I need to live it for it to be true—Gah!" I slap my palm against my forehead. "What am I saying? My first novel is fiction, too, but written from real experiences with some finesse. This time, I'm winging it."

A tiny condescending squeak comes from the other end of the line. "I'm guessing you saw your ex."

"Is it that obvious?"

"Did you buy ice cream, too, to accompany that tone of yours?"

"No!" I lie. "It's whatever. He's moved on. He's got a girlfriend, and I wish him well."

"Bullshit."

"I'm just going to ignore you said that." I walk to the front door, swinging it open to get a glimpse of the midday sun over the sea of pines. I suck in a breath, and the scent is immediately calming. "It was weird seeing him, okay? Sort of awful and awesome. I don't know. Janet, the chemistry is so volatile that if someone were to ignite a match when we're in the same room, we'd explode."

"Ooo, write that down, would ya?"

I roll my eyes, realizing I already have. "More than anything, it was nice reconnecting, and we're working on it." I wrinkle my nose as I say it. I have no idea what there is to work on, and what the hell I mean. "Anyway, seeing my friends has also helped, and this town is filled with the kookiest people, too. I've got a lot of material to work with."

"I'm hearing a lot of really good news. Please tell me you have a plot sort of set up in your head?"

I nod, even if she can't see it or my puffy pout. "Actually, I kinda do."

"Fantastic. Well, when you've written a few chapters, send it over, and we can talk over the kinks."

It's a brilliant idea, and I'm glad it buys me some time to, you know, actually come up with a plot. I wasn't admitting that there's a mixture of fictional details and the nonfictional elements that I'd also like to get straightened out.

"Sounds perfe—"

BEEP! BEEP! BEEP! BEEP! BEEP!

"WHAT'S THAT SOUND?" Janet yells into the phone.

"I DON'T KNOW!" I spin on my heels, my eyes going wide as I see a large cloud of billowing smoke coming from my kitchen. "OH SHIT, CALL YOU BACK!"

I hang up my phone, throwing it onto the couch. I run into the kitchen while covering my ears.

BEEP! BEEP! BEEP! BEEP! BEEP!

The ringing is so loud, it's messing with my brain waves as I try to take in the sight of the kitchen currently filling with smoke.

"MY SOUP!" I scream. I rush to the stove, waving away the cloud of smoke. I can barely see, and now I'm coughing.

A small flame plumes from the burner. I fumble with the switch, blowing it out, and move the pot to the sink.

The fire is out, but the smoke detector is merciless.

That sound! "ARGH!" I shout, waving my hands to disperse the smoke. I fling the kitchen door open and run to the window above the sink, wedging it open, all while still flailing my arms.

"Mom would kill me," I mumble, trying to remember where the smoke detector is, but I can't catch sight of a blinking red light, and it's too loud and has been ringing too long that I can't pick a direction it's coming from.

BEEP! BEEP! BEEP! BEEP! BEEP!

I run to open the front door and all the rest of the windows downstairs.

That's when I hear not only the incessant beeping, but also the sound of a fire truck.

"Oh no," I groan. I consider trying to find a place to hide, but I can already see a red fire truck coming to a crunching halt out the open window. There's no avoiding this terribly embarrassing situation.

"They just HAD to be firemen, didn't they? And I just HAD to try and cook something!" I grumble as I scoot myself back into the kitchen to try and wave off more smoke, and maybe to also hide my face.

Thinking I'll have the whole crew, meaning my stupid friends, come into my house, I'm surprised when I hear only one pair of heavy boots enter my living room over the constant *beeps*.

I'm the color that my tomato soup is supposed to look like, not its charred remains in the pot. I want to crawl into a corner to never be seen again.

The nameless boots take a few steps inside, clonking around, and the anticipation is killing me.

"There's no fire. You can leave!" I shout. My hands fly

over my mouth, and I whisper to myself, "You are digging yourself the most embarrassing grave of your life, and when people come to visit you in your death, they will only point and laugh."

Suddenly, the beeping stops and the heavy steps move toward me. It's a relief when the throb in my head stops and the ringing in my ears slows. My brain can finally catch up with what to do.

I peer down at my oversized sweater and shorts with boots. I look homeless-mountain-woman-chic, which is not the cutest.

Caiden appears in the doorway to the kitchen with a crooked grin; a black and yellow helmet is set securely on his head. His appearance must be a joke to mock me, no gear other than the helmet. A navy long-sleeved shirt stretches across his chest and is tucked into navy work pants that are even tucked into burly black fireman boots with a yellow trim. He looks hot, and I add it to the list of everything I hate him for.

"Well," he chuffs, a fire extinguisher resting easily in his left hand. "What do we have here?"

"Nothing." My jaw locks as I try to think of an excuse. "I was cooking and—"

"There's your first mistake, I think."

I want to tell him that Janet would agree with him, but the comment would go over his stupid helmet. My chompers chomp shut in annoyance as I glare.

"What were you makin'?" he practically sings as he leans toward the stove.

"I know you're just here to dance around me being an idiot."

He grins, and his pearly white teeth appear blindingly under his dark scruff. So smug.

"Hailey," he tuts, taking two steps closer to me, and I hate that I think the permanent charcoal smell of his uniform is wonderful. "I take my job very seriously."

"Right," I reply, crossing my arms over my chest.

He laughs as he watches me, leaning in even closer, and I swear you'd think this guy just won the Nobel Peace Prize or something, he's gloating so much.

"Plus, I guess you were wrong. I don't always rescue kittens from trees, now do I?"

My jaw falls slack as he repeats my words from the other night. He lifts his large hand to my face to *boop* me on the nose in the most patronizing way he can manage. "But maybe I do rescue kittens from burning buildings, eh?"

I try so hard to hide my smile. I close my eyes and shake my head. My arms come jutting out, and my palms collide into his chest to shove him back. It doesn't move him. He's as solid as a rock, and I let out an audible grumble. "Gah! Get out!"

This time, he releases a belt of warm laughter that's most definitely at my expense.

"I'm not a kitten, Caiden, I'm a fucking lioness who's going to swipe that smug grin off your face with my claws."

More laughter, and his eyes do that heavy drag that I've witnessed so many times skimming every surface of exposed skin on my body.

Once his twinkling eyes meet mine, they spark as if he remembers something. "Speaking of kittens, I hope he's okay…"

Caiden turns around and hurries out the front door. Before I know it, I can hear his boots on the porch on the side of the house.

My eyes go wide. "Oh. My. God. The cat! You're looking for that cat!"

When I exit my front door, I can see Brandon, Tyler, and Cam leaning against the side of the fire truck, and they're all laughing… at me.

I slide my accusing finger their way. "You all need better things to do!"

"Why would we want to be anywhere else when you provide the best entertainment since you hit town?"

I don't have to look to know who said that as my feet turn

the corner. "Fuck you, Brandon!"

More laughter. I make a mental note to remind Brandon that my right hook is as good as it was when I was fifteen. "Caiden!"

When I round the corner, my face twists in mock disgust, and I run both hands through my hair. "Caiden, you do realize you're a parody of yourself, right?" But then my loins writhe in hormonal need when I see him holding a kitten. I can't tell what's happening to my lower half—my ovaries might be melting—as I watch him cuddle this white cat with little black paws, a black patch of fur over its nose, and wide green eyes that could rival its rescuer.

"What?" he asks, still scratching the underside of the cat's chin.

I'm still trying to pull the puddle of myself together while trying to be irate. "A fireman and cats? You've got Harlequin written all over you. You'd practically write my novel yourself."

His chin darts up. "Did you just admit you've written about me?"

My brows scrunch together as I realize what I've just said. "Uh, no. I just meant with your stupid, hunky fireman backstory and love for the annoyingly furry, you'd be—" he's watching me with that shit-eating grin again. Yup, my grave is much deeper than before. "What I mean is… *what are you doing with that cat?* Are you the one who's—?"

His grin calms as his eyes dart everywhere but to me as he realizes he's given himself away.

"I was just making sure *Soot* was all right, ya know, after you almost burned the house down."

I grit my teeth, mainly to hide my irrational smile. "First, I didn't almost burn the house down. Why is the alarm set up to alert the fire station directly? That makes no sense. The alarm is supposed to signal me to dial 911."

He shakes his head. His face is back to rugged and rigid as

he gives me a no-nonsense look under his brows. "I didn't trust your mom. Her hearing wasn't at its best. I had her alarm connected to her wifi, so if it went off, we'd be notified immediately."

From him holding kittens, to making sure mothers stay safe: ovaries initiate implosion.

"Oh…" I hate that with every reveal of new information, I seem to react in this dumbfounded way. "That is a good idea, and I guess I should say thanks."

The right corner of his mouth lifts. "You're very welcome."

I stare a few seconds longer than I should and then regain my composure. "Secondly, who is Soot?"

Caiden moves closer, not seeming to realize that I have a perimeter bubble that needs to be intact whenever he's near. He pops it into oblivion, almost putting us chest to chest, or chest to stomach, if you consider his height. He plops the cat in my arms. "This is Soot."

He moves him closer, and the cat lifts its head to sniff at my lips and nose before rubbing all over my face. When I blink up at Caiden, he's smiling dopily. He's smitten with this kitten. And I mean the one in my arms.

"Oh-em-gee. This is YOUR cat, isn't it?"

He shakes his head guiltily. "No. No, it isn't. He was your mom's."

He, interesting.

I shake my head right back, and I can't help my mouth hanging open accusingly. "You've been feeding this cat, haven't you?"

"Uh…" He bobs on his heavy boots, trying to think up an excuse, but the tight pout of his lips has me thinking he doesn't have one. "Okay. Yeah. Maybe I have."

Soot has taken up residence in my arms as he tries to nestle his paws into the crease of my elbow before setting his chin on my arm and purring.

"I can't believe you right now. You've been sneaking onto

the porch every morning, haven't you? You've been feeding this cat. I-I-I s-seriously cannot believe you right now."

"I jog in the mornings and do it then. I was gonna tell you eventually. A couple of times, I considered knocking just to say hi, but…" He clicks his tongue. "I wasn't ready."

"*You* weren't ready?"

He twists his lips as he scratches the top of Soot's head in my arms. "Yeah, I wasn't ready. Can we drop it, please?"

I smirk. "So, are you gonna continue feeding him?"

His mouth stretches wide. "I think it's time we share custody and you take your turn taking care of him."

"Did you just refer to this cat as our love child?"

He laughs. "Stop being weird. Also, Soot likes it inside at night, so I'd prefer it if you let him in."

"Are we delegating our child's needs and requirements for its living situation now?"

He grunts, rolling his eyes as he starts walking toward the front of the porch. I trail behind him without stirring the cat in my arms, although I'm reeling with giggles over his dismay.

The boys see us coming and take it as their cue to start climbing back into the truck.

"So, what does our child like to eat?"

"Hailey," he whines, and the tight curve to his lips tells me he doesn't mind reprimanding me. "He likes a can of wet food in the morning. Dry food during the day."

"Got it." I nod, still desperately trying to stop my laughter. "When do you get custody of our munchkin, then?" I find myself hilarious and like I'm losing my mind. The two come hand in hand, I think.

Caiden doesn't hesitate, swiveling around as if he's had an epiphany. "Oh, don't worry. I'll be coming around. We have lots to talk about, remember? We'll start with chapter one."

My laughter ceases as I pale. "There's nothing to talk about. We're starting new, Caid. Let's drop the past."

His eyebrows rise comically. "Not happening." He leans

forward, and I'm petrified again, of all the things he might want to say in regard to my book, because hell, I know I said a lot of the things I couldn't say out loud in the book. He probably knows that.

He places the fire extinguisher that I forgot he's been wielding on the porch. "Should I leave this here in case you decide to cook again?"

My scowl is back. "I suggest you leave. I'd hate for our child to witness our first domestic dispute."

He rolls his eyes. "You're something else." He turns around, carrying his fire extinguisher with him as he blindly waves at me. "See you at the fair, Hails. We'll talk there, yeah?"

Another question not requiring an answer.

He climbs into the truck, and the boys wave me off through the windows as they leave.

I scratch the back of Soot's head, his purring roars within my arms at the touch.

"Chapter one, indeed," I hum as I wander back inside my nearly smoke-free house in search of my notebook, a pen, and a glass of wine.

6

I've been sitting in my car in the dirt parking lot a lot longer than I intended. I'm too anxious to enter the fair knowing it's for my mother's memorial, and also because I know everyone from PineCrest will be here. It's such a public setting for something that feels so somber, but I try to remember it's a celebration of life. *Her* life.

I can see the glow of the white country lights strung among the trees and lampposts, along with the colorful gleam of the Ferris wheel and small carnival rides surrounding it next to the buzzing dance floor. I can even hear the hum of bass from the band.

My phone buzzes with a text message. It's CeeCee.

> I can see you in your car moping. I thought we already decided on no moping?

I tense, because for once I don't want to be accountable for much tonight. Am I going to cry when they say my mom's name over the loudspeaker? Or will I sit stoic and indifferent? Will people hate me for the latter?

I haven't showered in two days because I hate being in the upstairs bathroom. I cry every time I'm there, and I'm so sick of it. Especially the moment I walk into the hallway and see all the doors closed, including the one to my old bedroom and my mother's. The closed doors feel like a metaphor for my life, like each door represents a choice I need to make, but I don't know what the doors mean even though I know what lies behind each.

I should be studied in the name of science for "*insecure girl syndrome.*"

I climb out of the car, suffering from the diagnosis of myself as I smooth over my jean shorts and tug down my flannel shirt. I wanted to try and fit in, but couldn't say no to my combat boots. *Never.*

I follow the sounds of the band, knowing that's where I'll find my friends. I tell myself seeing them will make me feel better.

I had been running off the high of my interaction with Caiden for a solid twenty-four hours, but that soon faded, and I hate how it feels like drug withdrawal.

Strolling up to the open plaza, I run a hand through my blonde waves. I take in the throngs of townspeople dancing and the stage that sits about five feet off the ground with a band offering their own indie twang to rock and roll. I smile because I remember this cozy feeling. The one with the soothing evening warmth that hangs in the air and the buzz of the music wrapping around me every summer.

I suck in a breath knowing that my mom's favorite part of the fair was the dancing. I scan the dance floor and see faces I've grown up with, and some new ones, too. I gather little glances here and there, but being here a week now, I've gotten used to it. I never know why they might be staring, though. Is it my mom, or is it because of my book? I guess it doesn't matter.

"Finally you decided to join us!"

I turn to see CeeCee coming toward me. She loops her

arm around mine and tugs me toward the table.

"Brace yourself, all right?"

My feet shuffle a few steps before getting a grip again. "This sounds bad."

"Kristen's here."

There is a finality to her voice that implies I should know who Kristen is, but I don't.

Before I can go through a process of elimination, my eyes collide with not an emerald stare, but an arm slung around a brunette who is everything I'm not.

Got it. *That's Kristen.*

I dart my stare away quickly, and when my gaze lands on Brandon sitting on the opposite side of the picnic table, he's already mouthing *sorry.*

I shrug, molding my face into indifference. When he seems convinced, he winks. I want to go back to my car.

Caiden, who was in the middle of laughing at something Cameron said, suddenly stops, and that's when the stares from my friends are more unnerving than the townsfolk.

"Hi." I wave.

Mostly everyone waves, even *Kristen*, except Caiden. Instead, he's just staring. Trailing his vision, starting at my toes, then up my legs to my eyes, like he seems to do often. I tightly smile, but he doesn't relax his shoulders from up at his ears.

Cam comes around, wraps an arm around my waist, tugging me close, and it's so abrupt I squeal, slightly embarrassed, before he nudges me in my temple with his nose adoringly as he whispers, "We gotchu," and then turns to face the crowd to say, "Come sit next to me, you cute little *thang.*" I roll my eyes, but am relieved nonetheless as I fall into the rhythm of his friendly touch, trying to find comfort there. I do find it as we slip onto the bench, both of us squeezing between Brandon and Tyler. Tyler swings a heavy arm around my shoulder. With all this support—I can do this. I pull in a deep breath as I feel the dopiest smile spread across my face, even as I skim over the view of Caiden and his girlfriend, then to CeeCee who is watching me in awe as she perches herself on Brandon's lap. For not being together, they sure are chummy. So ridiculous.

"You must be Hailey!"

My head whips around, and I'm shell shocked by Kristen's bold approach, more because that's totally something I would do. Her hand is outstretched over the table, and I can't get my head around her wide, honest smile.

"I've heard so much about you. It's nice to put a face to the name."

Cameron's boot comes colliding into my shin under the table because I must be staring too long. I reach out for her hand and shake it. It's a soft but firm shake. "Hi, hope they were all good things because I've been known to get into trouble with this group. And you are?"

Wow, okay. That wasn't so hard. That actually sounded sane and cordial. One point: Hailey, Zero: insanity.

"Kristen Palmer," she nudges her elbow into Caiden's ribs playfully before adding, "the girlfriend."

It sounds like a label rather than a place within this group. But she's still smiling this bright-as-the-sun smile, and I hate that it's hard for me not to like its genuine gleam.

"Good luck with that," I blurt out, and everyone on my side of the table starts laughing.

Okay, maybe I could have kept my mouth shut with that one.

Kristin's grin shrinks to a smile, and Caiden's eyes are on me with a heavy, searing weight. I don't feel bad, and I won't. So I look away.

"It's nice meeting you, Kristen."

"Same. Your mom was always sweet to me. I'm sorry to hear about her passing."

She's still smiling, sticking her hand out again, and actually dares to touch me on my forearm in condolence. I pull my arm away. "Thank you."

I swallow down the hurt that my mom knew Kristen and the fact she knew she was dating Caiden yet never said a damn thing. Why does everyone in this town seem to think they're saving me from something by withholding the truth?

A glutton for punishment, I ask, "How long have you two been dating? We didn't grow up together, did we?" I don't know her face, but the name seems vaguely familiar.

She smiles, revealing cherub-like cheeks. Another annoyingly likable quality. "Um, we've been dating a bit over a year now, right babe?" She turns to Caiden, who actually smiles when his eyes meet hers, and I hate that they might even twinkle the way they used to for me. He nods, confirming it before she continues. I want to vomit everywhere.

"I've only been here about two years overall. My parents were looking to transition to more low-key living. My dad is a property developer and bought some businesses. We moved from Denver. It's been nice."

I nod, smiling back. "PineCrest has its perks."

She looks back at Caiden, grinning in admiration, then back at me. "It does."

Did I mention I want to vomit?

I have to swallow the rising bile in my throat, and scratch my forearms to tame the sizzling nerves that rise to the surface of my skin. This moment has turned to agony, and none of this should matter. I didn't come back to town for Caiden. The whole plan was to come for my mom, to conquer her business, and then to leave. Caiden was supposed to be nothing but an acknowledgment I knew I'd have to endure, but since seeing him, he's been consuming me more than I'd like. But witnessing his bliss has me feeling foolish for all the emotions that have flooded me, and has me wanting to flee.

"Let me get you a beer, Baby Bird."

Kristen chirps, "That's such a cute name," before turning to Brandon, "I want one too, plus some popcorn. Mind if I join?"

Brandon doesn't hesitate. He nods and waves her on with ease. I love my friends for being careful with me with the situation, but it's obvious that I'm the odd addition here, not Kristen.

She rises, turning to Caiden. "You want a beer, babe?"

He nods, and I pray to the sweet angels of my sanity they don't kiss—

She leans down, obliterating my hope at composure when her lips press to his.

Before I can plan my sudden escape, Caiden turns to me, his eyes blazing apologetically once she's out of sight, but I shift to look at Cameron, who wraps his arm around me, pulling me close.

But I shrug it off. Not because I don't appreciate it, but it's all too sympathetic for my liking. It's like the whole world knows my pain and heartbreak, and it fucking sucks. I'm not losing. When did everyone decide this whole thing is my loss? It's not. At least, I don't think so. Life happens, and I WILL suck it up and deal with it, even if it hurts.

"She seems nice, Caiden," I say, offering a small lift of the corner of my mouth as I release a pent-up breath. He nods, unsure what to do with my words. "Now," I nod. "Seeing as we've all gotten over that moment, does anyone know when my mom's thing is?"

Everyone is staring at one another as if dumbfounded. Are they confused that I want to brush the fact Kristen is Caiden's girlfriend under the rug? Or what?

I wish Caiden wasn't the one who responds, but he is. "I wanted to talk to you about that. They're gonna do the memorial at seven, and then I'm gonna go up and speak, and then, if you want, it'd probably be nice for you to say something, too."

"What?" I squeak, my mouth hanging open. This night is too much. Why is this town constantly testing my emotional limits?

I tug my phone from my pocket and take a look. "Oh my God, that's in fifteen minutes. Why didn't you say something about this before? You're speaking? I, uh, I don't know what to do right now. Where the hell is my beer?"

CeeCee is at my side in a moment, shoving Cameron out of the way, which has him rolling his eyes as he says, "What if I'm the one Hailey needs? It's possible."

CeeCee presses her palm to his face, pushing him away, causing him to erupt into laughter.

At least this has me smiling.

My eyes lift to CeeCee's. "I can't do this," I quip.

"You don't have to," she replies with a comforting shake of her head.

Her words have my face twisting tightly like I just sucked on a lemon. "Uh, yeah I do. If this jerk-off over here is going to speak, then I should." I pause, turning to Caiden, confused a moment. "What *are* you doing saying something about my mom, by the way?"

He shrugs. "I thought I was a jerk-off?"

"You still are. Why, Caiden?" I repeat.

"She's important to me." He shrugs.

My chin falls, and no one needs to know I'm staring down at my heart, trying to tell it to calm the fuck down. I have no words.

CeeCee's hands come around my face, squishing my cheeks together in the most unattractive manner as she lifts my stare to hers. "You got this. You're a writer. Words. All you need are words."

Did she not just get the memo that I have none of those, hence my silence?

Her compassionate glare has me considering she might slap some sense into me soon.

"Okay, okay, I got this," I gulp down.

The silencing music and the screeching mic has my head perking up. I see the old fire chief, Dean McPherson, walk up to the podium, and when he shoots me a smirk and a confirming head nod, I swivel back around to Caiden, who is feigning his own look that's almost a smile but a downright guilty one.

"So, McPherson might think I've already told you about speaking tonight," he blurts out.

"What! You had all the time in the world to tell me, Caid. This is really sudden, and it has to do with my mom. I don't appreciate this being thrust on me."

He at least has the decency to droop at my words. The realization that this isn't fair to me, hitting him. "Sorry. I should have said something about this earlier, but to say I had all the time in the world is a stretch. Don't forget I got distracted by saving your house from burning down."

CeeCee's head whips in his direction. "You what?"

Brandon appears holding two beers. I leap upward, hating the moment and the fact I'm overheating with embarrassment.

"I need!" I grab the beer and begin a hard chug.

Kristen is gliding, or walking, or *whatever* behind him. She sees me chugging and laughs, and I think she says something to me, but all I can hear is the gurgle of my own throat as I wave her off, needing this long, hard drink. She floats by, and her hair wafts this overly sweet smell that has me thinking that's what Care Bears might smell like, and how can you hate a Care Bear when they're so damn *nice?*

Chug. Chug. Chug.

"Martha Elwood touched everyone's lives. If she wasn't smiling at you across the street, or serving you her famous pie at the diner, she was always a phone call away to be there to help. But she won't be forgotten, and we hope her legacy lives on with Elwood's. She will be missed, but never forgotten." Dean sighs from the stage, taking off his baseball cap to wipe his forehead before turning my direction to say, "A face I'm sure you remember, a girl Martha couldn't stop talking about is also here, and we'd love to invite her on stage to speak."

I pull the beer from my lips, handing it blindly to

Brandon. Everyone's staring, and did I mention earlier that I could vomit everywhere?

Caiden rises from his seat and is at my side in a second, placing his hand against the small of my back, causing this electric current to ignite the movement of my body, like Victor Frankenstein to his creation. He lightly pushes me forward and walks me to the stage. I smile nervously and tell myself not to cry.

As my boots hit the steps, I remember I have no idea what I'm going to say, but there's no going back now. I don't need more reasons for this town to talk.

I left my mom and this town, and they probably hate me for it.

Okay, let's not think like that right now.

Dean walks over to me, wrapping his thick, burly arms around me, his protruding gut also slamming against me, tenderly hugging me close.

I will not cry. I will not cry.

I can still feel Caiden's hand at my back, but when I'm released and walking of my own accord to the mic, his touch is gone. I'm on my own.

From only five feet above, I realize that the crowd really is the whole town. I try to smile, but I can't tell if I'm succeeding.

Everyone is smiling back at me, at least. This gives me the boost I need.

I clear my throat as I lift my hand up to the mic, as if to test if it's real and tangible.

Okay, yup. It's real. This is not a dream.

"Hello, everyone. It's been a while, huh?"

A tiny hum of giggles swiftly moves through the crowd, and it's more of that comforting boost I need.

"I'm Hailey Elwood, I'm not so prepared for this, and ironically enough, I feel like that rings true for this situation and losing my mom." I lick my lips, finding my words more overwhelmingly honest than I intend, but it feels right, so I run with it. "A lot of you might know that I up and disappeared about five years ago, and it wasn't because I was running away, but instead pursuing a dream I had always wanted. If you knew my mom, she was always a curious sort of creature, and I totally credit her with my own mental wanderings. That being said, she may not have understood my dream, but she could see it was what I wanted, and without understanding it, she pushed me to go for it. For her, my dream was like her wanting to open the diner with my dad all those years ago. She saw it as happiness, as passion, as something I needed to do as a person. And I think anyone who knew my mom knew that she was a person of passion. You could see it in the way she ran the diner and interacted with each and every one of you. Leaving was hard, for many reasons, but to come back and see that she was so loved is incredible. And I know my mom would hate it if I got all mushy, but I thank all of you each and every day for being here and loving her as much as you did in person, because it was so hard to do that being so far away. She was in good hands, and I'll forever be grateful. We will all miss my mom. There's no doubt there, but to know that she leaves such a legacy of smiling faces is enough for me to think she left happy. Thank you."

Applause. Tears. Hoots. Hollers. I hear it all.

I smile. I cry. I think I even hear a "We missed you, Hailey" somewhere in the crowd.

I pull in a deep breath, wiping the corners of my eyes, getting a grip, thinking this wasn't bad at all. I feel this odd sense of relief embracing my mother's memory so openly. My heart feels raw, but the ache is sweet.

I turn around, and it shocks me when I walk into a rock hard Caiden, whose arms come around me in one swift move.

Whispers soon gather in the crowd, but I can't stop my deep inhale with my nose pressed against his chest, basking in the comforting squeeze. He's always made me feel safe. It's the perfect BAND-AID to my wide-open heart, and the fact it isn't stinging is a strange thing to wrap my head around.

My mind and body are so fickle when it comes to Caiden. Hot or cold, sweet or sour, regardless, it always seems perfect for whatever moment we share, and I wonder if that will ever go away.

When he releases me, my mind is fuzzy with feels, but soon clears as I rush off the stage, needing distance.

Reality is hard to define nowadays.

I rush back to the table, and like caring parents, Brandon and CeeCee reach out, pulling me between them, both their arms thrown over my shoulders. I have a picture of this exact thing when we were kids, and I think back on when life was simpler as I rest my cheek on CeeCee's shoulder, taking a deep breath in unison with Brandon's gentle, cajoling squeeze.

Caiden walks up to the microphone, and the whispers haven't ceased. I wonder what this town makes of me being back. We were high school sweethearts, but I pray that isn't front-page news for this place anymore.

Caiden taps the mic as if checking it's working, even though he knows it is. He towers over it, needing to lean down to speak. He tugs on his bottom lip first before gruffly starting with, "Hey folks. It's a beautiful night for a beautiful soul, right?"

I squint as I watch him career the crowd's emotions into full-fledged applause. My eyes examine his thick stature, and I think, *Where has the time gone?* And *Why does he fill out that shirt so well?*

"It's no secret that Martha was like a mom to me. When I was in elementary school and I had the sniffles, she made sure I had cup of soup to go for lunch, and even in the most recent years she'd give me hell about taking care of myself and still deliver soup to me at the station. She had too good a heart, and she cared about people more than I could ever understand. She talked me through my lows…" Caiden's eyes flicker in my direction for the first time and my gut plummets. "… but she was also always the first person to congratulate me on the highs. I'm not only losing a close friend, I'm losing my family and a piece of me with her. She'll be missed, and like Hailey said, her legacy lives on in all of us, and I'm sure we'll never forget her, especially with her pie becoming practically a point of celebration in this town." Solemn, understanding chuckles and giggles erupt from the crowd. "Thanks for showing up this evening. If I know Martha, she'd probably be smacking me upside the head by now, telling me you're all here to dance and not to cry. So, let's start up that band again."

More laughter and cheers erupt as the band starts up on command and begins crooning to the crowd with upbeat guitar riffs to a country-rock song that everyone seems to know. They dance in her honor, and I am in awe. *Damn him.*

Brandon and CeeCee lift their already linked arms over my head. CeeCee pretends to not want to dance, and it's adorable that it only takes Brandon's smile and a tug to get her following him.

My insides feel like goo as I watch nearly everyone get up from their tables and dance, and I want to believe it's my mom's memory that compels them to have a good time.

Caiden emerges from the crowd, but his eyes shoot over my shoulder and I realize that he's trying to tell me he can't come near me... or won't.

I force a smile through pursed lips even though my cheeks feel like the surface of the sun. I stick both of my thumbs up in understanding and in appreciation of the speech he made about Mom.

Like I expect, he smiles apologetically but moves swiftly past me to Kristen, extending his hand out to her, and I stare at his strong forearms emerging from his rolled-up shirt, my eyes reluctantly falling on the secret scrawling of my initials as he leads her to dance.

I sigh, turning away before he can see whatever emotion chooses to appear on my face. Right now, there is so much I'm feeling that I can't pinpoint the overruling one. None of them are good.

I feel too much here, it's confirmed.

I turn completely around, heading back to the table to find it empty of friends but holding my beer bottle. I'll take it.

Care to dance? I think as I approach the beer, rolling my eyes as my fingers wrap around the neck of the bottle, and I take a seat so I can watch from the most depressing perch ever.

I even notice Cam and Tyler, who must have picked out girls earlier in the night, twirling about on the dance floor.

Although I'm glad everyone is happy at an event that could easily be so sad, it feels like there's a huge drill making its way through my chest, and the painful hum vibrates out to my limbs as my eyes drag over the dance floor. I hate that it all falls in rhythm with the live band. Could this pain not have a soundtrack, please?

I rub over my chest knowing that it's my heart causing this mess. I was bound to have a moment like this. I had anticipated so many scenarios before I arrived, and this was just one of the many. Still sucks. I was working through how to cope with my mom, but then there was just no way for me to truly be prepared to see Caiden with another girl.

I sip my beer, mulling it over as I stare at them hand in hand, twirling, dancing, and smiling.

I just wish she wasn't so nice. It would be easier if she was rude to me, or mean, but she wasn't. She looked me straight in the eye and flicked her hair with an air I'd never be able to achieve, and a sincerity that I wish I could despise. Did I mention she's pretty, like, super pretty? Her perfectly straight brown hair gleamed against her skin and only brightened her hazel eyes. Goddammit, why couldn't she be hideous?

Maybe I could accidentally push her off a cliff in my next book. That would make me feel better.

"Hailey?"

I leap up off my seat as if being caught committing the actual murder.

Fiction, Hailey, you write fiction...

"Eep!" I squeak.

A soft but deep, unfamiliar chuckle hits my ears, and I watch a face I don't think I know sit across from me at the picnic table. He knows my name, but I don't know his. Or maybe I do.

"It's been a long time. You probably don't remember me."

I place my beer on the wood table, squinting as I scrutinize his clean-shaven face, but the lightest of dark stubble manages to show on his chin, my eyes only noticing because his long fingertips strum over it as he watches me with heavy blue eyes, and I want to say I know them.

He laughs again, and that pang of familiarity hits me once more, but I shake my head. "I'm sorry..."

He sighs, placing his elbows on the table, his muscular arms emerging from a faded Colorado State University t-shirt.

"Figures. I probably wasn't the nicest of guys, let alone one of your favorites in high school."

His eyes dart to the dance floor. I turn around, following his line of vision to see Brandon and Caiden already staring even though they're blindly dancing with their dates. They don't look happy, and for some reason I like that.

"Huh," I huff, eyeing him again, and I note that from Brandon's look of hatred and his natural inclination to fight ever since I've known him, and Caiden's loyalty to his best friend, it hits me. I scrutinize the man in front of me again. His slicked-back hair doesn't fit with his worn shirt, but his well-rehearsed smile that looks like he's been charming women, young and old, since being out of the womb, becomes clear. Because I remember his baby face getting into *lots* of fights, too.

"Gabe? Are you Gabe Samuels?" I laugh, covering my cheeks, because I sound terrible. "I mean. I'm sorry. I should know this. I just haven't been around for a while."

His belt of laughter causes delightful crinkles to appear at the corners of his eyes, and I want to like him even more. "Yeah-yeah, it's me. What gave it away?"

"I think I remember you fighting Brandon all the time, and Caiden, too."

"Oh yeah, too bad those are the only memories I've got left. A contact sport will do that to you, though."

I nod, flooded with memories at the comment. I lift my hand, pointing at him. "Oh, I totally remember you now. Quarterback, jock, cool guy… I was in the land of misfit toys—"

"You totally were not," he snorts.

I find my lips twitching curiously as I watch him squirm, and I'd go as far to say that he's almost embarrassed.

"I was invisible in high school, Gabe. You definitely were not."

"Since I've never been lucky enough to chat with you like this, even in high school, I'm just going to forget you said that. You're kind of a big deal, Hailey Elwood."

He even knows my whole name, and then I remember my family owns the diner, and that knowing my name isn't something I shouldn't like so much, but I kind of do.

"So Gabe, are you a resident of PineCrest still? I think I remember hearing about you getting a full-ride scholarship."

I'd never let him know that I remember this part clearly. Brandon wanted that same scholarship, but the Colorado State football scout chose Gabe over him, and I remember the fight that ensued at the homecoming game our senior year. The irrational oafs. I tilt my head, examining Gabe a little more closely, and see that he's naturally a big guy, but leaner than a football player would be.

His smile distracts me, and my thoughts must be written all over my face because he says, "I don't play football anymore. I ended up quitting sophomore year at State."

"But you had NFL all over you."

"Oh, so you do sorta remember me."

I laugh. "Only because my best friends loathed you." I smack my forehead. "Sorry. That's not a nice thing to say, either."

"You were always honest. I like that." He chews his lip a second before going on, "I don't think I have much time before your bodyguards come make me accountable for things I don't care about anymore, but I just wanted to tell you *thanks*."

He starts rising from his seat, and I feel bereft all of a sudden, and I rise, too, which has him smirking curiously as he runs a hand through his gelled-back hair. He's clean-cut, skin empty of ink, and totally unlike my friends. He's like a blank slate. The difference is a nice switch up. He's even light with his words, and the way he carries himself and that smile.

"Thanks for what?" I ask.

"For getting up and out of this town. Your mom was good friends with mine, and I heard you had up and left PineCrest to move to LA to become a writer. I had already quit football at that point, but you sort of, I don't know, inspired me, I guess."

"Inspired you?" I'm choking on my words as he sticks his hands in his jeans, and I can tell he's on his way to walking away from me.

He shrugs, grinning. "Yeah. I was coming home every weekend from school, and it just wasn't enough for me anymore. I thought if Hailey Elwood could get out of PineCrest, I could. We kinda want the same thing, except you made it."

I reach for his arm. I'm too intrigued by his words. I've never inspired anyone.

His eyes drop to my hand, and I immediately let go. "I just don't know what you're talking about."

He laughs, wrinkling his nose adorably as if debating on divulging this detail but doing it just the same. My mouth goes dry as I watch and listen. "Do you remember in high school, that short story contest for the local paper?"

I nod, heat rushing to my cheeks, remembering how badly I wanted to win it because it earned me notoriety in a town that only knew me for the diner.

"You won, of course," he says. "Your story was far better than mine. I couldn't compete, but I was runner-up."

"What?" I ask through a befuddled giggle. "I don't remember that."

"Yup," he shakes his head, "I had aspirations like yours, except it wasn't so cool for the quarterback to write stories."

"You're blowing my mind right now, Gabe. Tell me more." And I so desperately want to hear more.

"I moved to New York City to become a journalist after college. It's not a bad gig. I'm working at it."

"That's amazing, Gabe. I'm just so—"

"Shocked? Yeah, I get that a lot around here. I'm no author, though." He winks, and the butterflies caged in my gut flutter. I don't remember feeling that in a long while, because this type of flutter is new, and God, something *new* sounds nice.

"Anyway, Hailey. It was a pleasure seeing you. How long are you in town?"

What a question. "I actually have no idea."

He laughs, his eyes shooting over my shoulder, causing his smile to vanish. "I better go. Your squad is coming, and I'd rather not hear what they have to say. It's been really great seeing you. If, uh, you stick around for a little longer, I'll be here for another couple weeks. Maybe we could hang out or something. It's a little unorthodox, but gimme a call, yeah?"

As if the piece of paper was prepared for this exact moment, he pulls a receipt from his pocket with his number already written on it.

He smiles once more before he says, "It's your choice."

He walks away, making it to the people I assume are his family at another table across the outdoor picnic area. I think I remember his mom and mine being friends. Her face looks like a diner regular, and oh my God, if that's his sister, she is so grown up.

94

"What's Gabe got to say to you?"

I swivel around, and Gabe was right. My bodyguards loom over me like overprotective brothers. Brandon, Caiden, Tyler and Cam all surround me. And I hate that CeeCee is talking to Kristen behind them, sweetly indifferent to the ruckus the boys are causing with me.

The brief moment of flutters disappears, and I turn as rigid as the boys in front of me.

"Is there a problem?" I ask, placing a hand on my hip.

Caiden grabs the piece of paper in my hand, and I get some serious satisfaction when his eyes go wide. It's quick, but I catch it. He hands it back to me instead of commenting on it. He knows he can't care and that he can't say a damn thing. I snatch it back, stuffing it into my pocket as Brandon begins his big brother speech. "He can't just stroll back into town thinking he runs it. He doesn't anymore."

My brows knit together. "Well, he doesn't *run* me, if that's what you're saying, Brandon. I'm not territory you can claim."

He rolls his eyes, looking at Caiden. "Dude, you want Gabe talking to Hailey?"

Brandon has put Caiden in a very strange spot, and I wish he hadn't, because when Caiden refuses to make eye contact with me and shrugs before he says in the harshest, most indifferent tone I've ever heard, "No, it doesn't matter," it hurts. It fucking stings. It feels like someone just dipped my heart in hydrochloric acid.

"Then fuck off, the both of you." I shove between them and wave a hand to CeeCee, who is ready to trail behind me, but I don't want her to. "I need a moment," I say.

"Hailey!" she whines.

"Please," I hiss. I need air. I need space. I need to be alone.

My life is not supposed to be at the whim of others. Caiden cannot dictate who I talk to. He doesn't *allow* me to talk to Gabriel Samuels, and it's as if Gabe knew that.

It's your choice, he said. And the thought is embarrassing and infuriating all at once that someone on the outside could see that Caiden and the boys have some say with what I do. I grew up, dammit.

It has me thinking about my mom. Everything always ends up coming back to her.

I remember when I was younger, my mom telling me that the boys don't own me, but they feel an obligation when it comes to my well-being. I hated it then, and I hate it now. Sure, it's all cute when your friends and your boyfriend are willing to fight for you, but not anymore. It's juvenile, and I'm over it.

I come to a stop at the Ferris wheel. My heart is working overtime as I heave shallow breaths in and out. I desperately need/try for calm. Too many feelings.

Smiling at the young kid running the attraction, I blindly hand him a five-dollar bill from my pocket. I shrug him off as I approach the open basket. The night is winding down and the Ferris wheel is near empty, so that five should give me more than a couple rounds.

As I climb inside, I can see Caiden running toward me.

"Caiden, don't you fucking dare!" I shout.

He shakes me off, approaching the teen who is having a hard time hiding his smile.

"Don't let him on!" I shout, but when Caiden hands over a crisp twenty-dollar bill, that most definitely trumps my five, all the kid can do is shrug.

"Sorry, ma'am."

Caiden walks over to the basket, smug and stern. "You gonna scoot over?"

I turn away, staring in front of me rather than at him. "There are lots of other empty baskets."

"Hailey…" he says, and I hate it when my name tumbles off his tongue like a steady drop of summer rain rolling over a leaf.

"What?" I reply, clipped, but I scoot over just the same.

Bittersweet, it's the only way I can describe Caiden. How can he go from heartbreaking, to supportive and charming, then rocket back to being an utter asshole all in the same evening?

"Stubborn, stubborn, stubborn," he whispers to himself as he scoots inside, locking the small gate, keeping us in.

I hate that the entire length of my body is touching his in the bench seat. It makes it hard to think.

The rickety metal Ferris wheel begins to move, lifting us upward, and I take in that crisp, leveling breath I so desperately need.

"What was that about?" Caiden asks.

"You're kidding me, right? Because this is your fault."

He snorts, sitting back as if he doesn't have a care in the world. I shake my head, wishing my existence was that easy. The jerk.

"Calm down, Hailey."

I'm anything but, and because of this I choose not to respond, staring off into the distance and letting out a not-so-surprised huff when the Ferris wheel stops with us at the top.

He lets the silence hang, too, and proving his point earlier, my stubbornness wins out when he loses his patience.

"So, are you gonna call him?"

My lips twitch as I try to hide my smile. "Who?" I ask.

He grumbles, and I know he hates this, and it serves him right. It's about time I get some company with this irrational hatred. "C'mon. Are you?" he asks again.

I turn to see his face set in a hard line, and I hate even more that that also pleases me. "Yeah, I'm thinking I might."

Wait, am I?

Before I can add more of an instigating caveat he says, "I don't even know what he's doing in town."

I guess I don't know why either, but I'll make it my mission to find out. "He was nice."

"Nice?" Caiden grumbles. "How can you say that? Do

you have any idea how many times my fist has met his face and vice versa?"

I giggle. "Yeah, I do. He isn't the same guy now." This is something I have no evidence for other than a five-minute conversation, but I roll with it.

"He obviously still has the hots for you."

I snort. "Shut up, Caiden. Gabe Samuels never had a crush on me. Now you're just making shit up."

"Well, I must have done a pretty good job hiding that one then, or it might have made it into your book among a slew of other things," he hums. "Why the hell do you think I got into so many brawls with him, combined with the fact Brandon hated his guts?"

I'm shell shocked, my mouth going agape as I stare at Caiden, who looks anything but amused. "I never knew that."

"I hated the way he talked about you in the locker room. I used to think it was just to get to me because he knew we were dating in high school. Ya know, thinking he did it to psych me out before practices? Guess I was wrong…" He pauses to stare at my mouth, and it has my heartbeat beginning a hard, heavy rev like an engine within my chest. "… Are you *smiling* over Gabe Samuels right now?"

"Are you angry right nooowww?" I ask, dragging out the tone of my words in defensive embarrassment.

"No." He looks away, out into the abyss of the night sky, his jaw back to that tight clench I remember seeing down at the picnic table.

"Where's your girlfriend?" I try my best to not sound like a snotty teenager.

He releases a sigh. "On the dance floor with CeeCee."

Oh, so she's with my best friend, I think, and then I remember that I've been gone a long time and that CeeCee and Kristen are probably friends, and that I might be the one interrupting the dynamics of the group friendships. This thought gives me a nasty taste in my mouth.

"She isn't wondering where you're at?"

He lifts his hand to fiddle with his bottom lip, like he's been doing since we were teens, the same maneuver he couldn't help when we were at the bar when he'd stare. This is Caiden thinking, while at the same time attempting to be considerate. It's a Caiden trait.

"She's self-sufficient," he replies.

I hate that the statement makes Kristen seem smart, independent, and not the jealous type. Self-sufficient means she isn't worried about Caiden, because she trusts what they have. I wonder if he loves her.

I'm hating this evening more and more. I try to change tack.

"Thank you for what you said about my mom. It was really great."

Ignoring the change of direction, he says with an annoying smirk, "You don't like me talking about Kristen, do you?"

"I like it about as much as you like the idea of me talking to Gabe."

He blows out a low breath between his lips. "Gotcha."

I bite my lip to stop myself, but like a bubbling geyser in my throat, the words need to escape. "Do you love her?"

I can feel his whole body tense against me. "Uh," he says, toying with the idea. "I might. Yeah. I think it's a possibility."

I consider leaping off the Ferris wheel in hopes the hay bales to the right might save my fall, but I refrain from such extreme stupidity.

"That's nice."

That's nice? Yeah, maybe I should jump.

"You not seeing anyone in LA?"

"No one seriously."

"But there was someone."

"Caiden. Stop."

"Stop what?"

"Stop…" I flail my hands between us. "*This*. Whatever

this is, we need to stop."

"I'm not allowed to know?"

"You're allowed to know, but you're not supposed to care."

He turns his attention back into the open air in front of us. We let the proverbial dust settle, and the moment drags for what feels like an eternity, but we need it.

"Do you care… about me?" he asks, his voice low.

My head drops into my hands as I let out a laugh. "Do you want me to?"

"I care about you," he says, his voice steady and anxious.

My heart melts. And I hate the desperate roundness to his eyes as he locks his stare with mine. Sure, he's twenty-four now, but in this moment he looks like the nineteen-year-old I remember, except this one has a beard. "I'd be lying if I didn't say I cared, but you're making things really complicated in my head."

"Right back atcha, Hails."

Nothing is resolved. He's not going to listen to me, but at least we cleared up one thing: we care. That's enough for me now, and I don't think I could handle much more.

"I'm glad you're happy, Caiden. It's important to me."

He smiles, the corners of his mouth reaching ear to ear. "Thanks."

His smile hurts, but I reciprocate, because regardless, it's stunning. "I'm sorry your mom passing away is what brought you back. I wish things were… different."

I gulp down his words. Different is an understatement.

"Yeah, me, too. But at least it feels like she was in good hands. Everyone loved her."

He peers over to his left, down below, before swinging his stare back to me. He nods, but seems in a rush now as he rubs over his bottom lip again. "You wanna know the moment I knew your book was about us?"

"No," I reply, letting out a skirting giggle, looking away

to hide my reddening cheeks. When his finger comes jabbing into my gut, I leap at the touch in such an intimate, squishy part of me. I squeal, "Caiden!"

His burly laughter rumbles between us, and he ignores my denial. "It was the first, or second chapter, I can't remember—"

"Why don't you go take a look at your notes to double check."

He gives me a wry smile and tries poking me again, but I swat his finger away. If he touches me one more time, I'm going to need to change my panties, and I will take that deep, dark secret to my grave.

"What I mean is, it isn't obvious. We've known each other since we were kids, but in your book, they meet for the first time their first day of school, but you made it *our* first day of sophomore year."

The fact he knows that gives me chills. "Did not," I lie.

"Can we just skip past your constant no's now? Because it's getting old fast." He doesn't wait for me to respond. "You wrote the character wearing this cream, lace, fitted dress, and when she stepped out of her car, the guy across the parking lot made fun of her. You said the character hated him then."

I nod and smile.

"She didn't hate him. You didn't hate me then, either," he says smugly.

He's blending the book's story with reality now. "Correction, the character in my book might not have, but I most definitely hated you in real life for it. You didn't need to be such a jerk the first day of school."

"You know why I made fun of you?" he asks. I nudge my chin for him to go on. "Because you looked hot in that dress. You never really wore dresses before. It was super short, and holy shit, I kept trying to deny that puberty hit you that summer. You filled out that dress better than you ever had. The only way I knew how to react was to make fun of you."

I giggle. "I know, Caiden. I know."

"You knew?"

"Boys aren't that hard to figure out, especially you."

He bites down on his bottom lip, and if it wasn't for his scruff, he might just be blushing.

"You chose an interesting way for their relationship to play out in the book."

I suck in a breath. "Yeah, I did."

"A lot of it was the same, but there was a huge section that was different." He says this last part slowly, his eyes reading me, and I know what he's referring to.

"I know."

"It was weird reading myself in a character. I mean, you nailed a lot of what I was feeling, which is kind of terrifying, but then again, reading what was going through your head was equally as scary."

"I know," I repeat.

He looks down at my hands in my lap, watching my fingers nervously fiddling with one another before swinging his stare back up to me. "There's also a lot I didn't know and…" He clenches his jaw. "… I wish I would have known then. Like—"

The sound of a phone going off bursts our bubble, and his face falls, not in surprise, but as if he knew our time would eventually be up.

He pulls his phone from his pocket and answers without looking. I turn away.

"Hi Kris… Yeah, I am… No, it's okay. I'm on my way… No-no, it's fine. Meet me at the car."

Ow. That also hurt more than I anticipated. When he hangs up, I release the breath I was holding.

"I have to go." He leans over the Ferris wheel, putting two fingers in his mouth, and blows out a loud whistle to the operator below. The Ferris wheel soon begins to swing downward.

I nod, forcing a smile through pursed lips, wrapping my

arms around my chest. "No problem."

"Me and you will talk more, but *we* gotta be up early in the morning."

We, he said *we*. He means he and his girlfriend.

They are *we*, Caiden and Kristen, and instead, he and I are singular, separate entities.

"It's okay. Early plans?" I ask, and I try not to say this through clenched teeth.

"Oh, uh, she has to drive back home."

I cringe when I realize she's staying the night, but then something else dawns on me as we make it to the bottom. "She doesn't live here?"

He shakes his head, climbing out of the basket, and I follow, tension riddling its way into my shoulders while my heartbeat picks up pace.

"No," he says, and when he stops his strides after five steps, as if struck with what might be going through my head, he says, "Her parents live here, but she lives in Denver for school." He swivels around slowly, the angles of his eyebrows pointing downward.

That's over three hours away.

I gulp down his solemn look. "You're in a long-distance relationship with her?" I ask.

There's no hiding the hurt in my voice. He might be pissed off that I made a choice he wishes I hadn't long ago, but I'm instantly damaged by the fact he's in a long-distance relationship that he didn't once consider having with me. Granted, a car ride versus a plane ride is very different, but still.

His lack of response is too much, and he's still just standing and staring. I shrug to fill the silence, as if to excuse my incoming behavior as I reply sternly, "Good night, Caiden." I turn around and walk the opposite direction, feeling like I need space. Lots of it now.

I think I hear my name, but I *choose* not to care.

7

———

I hurt.

There's no better way to describe it.

I cried when I got home, and I cried when I woke up this morning.

I don't remember crying this much since leaving this town.

Everything sucks. I feel sideswiped by the night.

My tears involve many things, including my mom. I moved a photo of her from the mantel and placed it on the coffee table so I could be closer to it as I slept. I might have even talked to it a few times.

Leaving is getting easier and easier to fathom. This time it almost feels like running away, but I convinced myself after a few pages of writing that I don't belong anymore. Last night made that clear. I'm the last Elwood in town, and maybe it'd be better if I left the legacy with my mom and vanished all over again.

The sudden sound of tires outside causes my body to propel off the couch as if caught red-handed with my thoughts. It's already eleven in the morning, and I run to a mirror in the hall worried my puffy, tear-stained face will give me away. I scurry to the kitchen sink, splashing water on my face.

I hear a knock at my front door, and I'm terrified who it

might be.

"Baby Bird, let's go swimming!"

I cringe when I hear Brandon's voice and then the tight giggle of CeeCee that follows.

"Go away!" I shout as I enter the living room, seeing both of them beyond the screen door.

CeeCee hates the immediate rejection and opens the unlocked door. "You don't mean that."

I nod. "Oh, yeah I do."

CeeCee looks over her shoulder at Brandon, both seemingly confused.

"What's wrong?" she asks.

"Everything. Last night sucked, and you both are a bit at fault."

"Blame Caiden," Brandon adds to the conversation.

"Why? Because he has a girlfriend? Newsflash: it doesn't matter anymore. I don't care. I know it naturally sucks, and it's weird for all of us, especially me, but I've been gone a long time. It would be weird if he didn't move on. Let's be honest."

Brandon's brows knit together. "Do you have a boyfriend in LA?"

"No."

"That's weird."

I screech a sound of frustration, but I can't tell if it's a sigh or a scream. Either way, I resemble a banshee. "No, it's not. I've been focusing on my career. Sometimes success comes with isolation. I'm okay with that."

Brandon's eyebrows expressively rise. "Are you sure about that?"

"Yes."

CeeCee jabs him in the shoulder. "Go wait outside!"

"What?" he whines.r

"Now. I need to talk to Hailey. Go wait in my Jeep."

Brandon looks pissed. He rolls his eyes, shaking his head as if this moment won't be forgotten before he treks out the door. It's then I notice his flip-flops and red swim trunks matched with a plain white shirt. Very unlike his normal attire. What time is it again?

"Hailey," CeeCee hums. "What's wrong? Why are you mad?"

Without Brandon nearby, I feel able to say what I need to. "Why the hell didn't you warn me that Kristen was there? It was really unfair of you to just throw me into that situation, knowing what I'm dealing with."

CeeCee places her hand against her chest, aghast at the accusation. "Do you think I would purposefully let you walk into that? I didn't know she was going to be there. I didn't even know she was in town. Caiden just showed up with her. He didn't warn any of us, probably because he knew we would have told him to fuck off."

CeeCee doesn't cuss often, but I love it when she does. "You promise?"

"I can spit in my palm, and we can pinky promise like we did in the third grade if that helps convince you."

My head falls into my hands, and I let out a sigh of relief. I walk over to the couch, taking a seat, trying to focus on my breathing.

CeeCee is at my side, wrapping an arm around me. I won't let myself cry in front of her. The realization that she didn't just forget about my well-being makes me feel ten times better.

"You handled last night really well, though. You have to know that. She's nice, but she's not my best friend. She's not you."

I shake my head, lifting my stare to hers. "I didn't have a choice. I never have a choice."

Gabe Samuels suddenly comes to mind, and my head spins.

"You've always been good at handling whatever the world throws at you, Hails. That's why moving away to chase your dream would only make sense when it's you."

I smile. "Thanks, Cee."

"What else is on your mind?"

"You don't even want to know. Tons of things. Like that oaf of a boyfriend of yours."

She goes wild as she rises from the couch, hands flying to her hips with a sway. "He is not my boyfriend!"

"Whatever," I laugh.

"I don't want to talk about Brandon and me right now. He's pissing me off and getting too clingy, like he always does. What has he done to you?"

"I was talking to Gabe Samuels and—"

"He's in town?"

I shrug. "I guess."

"What were you doing talking to Gabe? He's like our archnemesis."

I laugh. "Cee, we don't have an archnemesis."

"Uh, yeah we do. Brandon and Caiden have hated his guts since freshman year."

I roll my eyes. "We're out of high school now. Isn't it time we let those grudges go? And he was nice to me. Did you know he's a writer? Well, a journalist, but still."

A tiny 'v' appears between CeeCee's eyes as she stares at me curiously. "Are you crushing on Gabe?"

"Maybe. He gave me his number. He's in town for a short time, and so am I. Might be nice. I don't have anything to lose, right? Plus, Caiden is messing with my head." I rub at my temples.

"I think this is a fantastic idea."

My head perks up as I watch CeeCee pace my living room, tripping over my suitcase on her second round.

"Wait, you just scolded me for talking to him."

"I know, but..." She strums her pretty fingers over her pointed chin. "This might knock some sense into Caiden. I can see he's crossing lines when he's around you. He keeps staring at you, and he needs to know his place. I think this is a great way to make him jealous."

I shake my head. "No, no. You're missing the point. This isn't about Caiden; this is about me. I should be the one allowed to live and have fun."

"Of course. I hate to admit it, but Gabe is pretty cute. Plus, you're right, he's in town for who knows what, but a nice fling tonight might be perfect."

"What are you talking about?"

"Oh yeah." She wiggles her fingers at me. "Two things. Get up. We're going to the lake for the day. Shore day." She grins. "Tanning, drinks, and friends. It's exactly what you need."

"But you just said something about tonight?"

"Oh—oh, party tonight. Bonfire like the good ol' days. Your favorite. John Walden still hosts them on his property on the north side of the lake. He took over his dad's ranch and likes bringing everyone together a few times each summer to hang out. They've become staple get-togethers for everyone now. Also, John's been trying to get into my pants since senior year."

I giggle. "You never?"

"Good God no, but I like to make Brandon jealous. Anyway, you should tell Gabe to meet you at the party tonight."

I nod. "This sounds like a solid plan."

"Now go get a bathing suit on."

I grunt, "Do I have to go? I mean, I'm still really cranky over yesterday. The way Brandon handled the Gabe thing—"

"These boys don't know when to quit, trust me. He does it because he cares, even if it's misplaced. It's always been that way, Hails. You know this. I'll allow you to be cranky on the shore. Fair? Also, you need some sun. You're starting to look pale, and I'd hate for the Californians to get a bad impression of Colorado when you go back looking like a ghost. Or you could stay, of course?" She wiggles her brows.

I release a nervous laugh, rising from the couch. I don't

know how to respond and choose to just agree to go rather than face the fact I'm not sure when I'm leaving, because unfortunately, it's all a matter of *when*, not *if*.

Brandon is surprisingly quiet on the drive to the lake, which has me thinking their arguing lies deeper than CeeCee sending him to the car. I try not to break the tension since that's none of my business.

Instead, my eyes are glued to the scenery as CeeCee's Jeep careens off the main road, hitting a dirt path toward our group's favorite shore spot since we were preteens. I love that these things haven't changed, including the mention of the bonfire tonight.

CeeCee wasn't lying when she said it was my favorite. I loved the atmosphere of those parties. All my best memories lie in the dancing shadows of the fire with good friends, drinking, and laughter. Not to mention, all of those forbidden memories of sneaking off with Caiden. I tell myself I can appreciate the memories, but to not put misplaced meaning in them any longer.

As we come to a stop, parking in between two large pine trees, the shore only a couple hundred feet away in the clearing, I look around the open dirt spot.

"Where's Cam and Tyler?"

"Working the station," Brandon finally speaks, clambering out of the vehicle. "But Caiden should be getting off soon and heading over."

My good mood dissolves. I wasn't sure he'd be here, and the mention of his name rattles my nerves. I got to express my anger with CeeCee and cleared that up, but I haven't been able to check Caiden off that list, and I wonder if I ever will.

I need to remember to ask more questions when I decide to go places in this town.

"Oh," I chirp.

"Help me with the barbecue, will you?"

I agree, but CeeCee comes into view as if reading the shift in my demeanor. "Don't worry, Hails. We got it. Why don't you just go set up and lounge over on the shore? You could use a moment to chill."

I huff, peering up at the sun hanging in the middle of the sky, feeling the warmth over my skin and the fact I do so desperately need to chill.

"Okay. I'm gonna go be cranky over there."

She nods. "Fine by me."

I lay out my blanket and lie down. It takes only a few minutes until I feel myself nodding off to the sounds of the slow lapping waves of the lake twenty feet away, blending with the sounds of CeeCee and Brandon bickering over how to light the barbecue. It's my quiet chuckles to myself that keep me awake.

It isn't until I hear a truck and burly hellos that sound like someone I could do without today that my body goes rigid. I keep my eyes closed and let myself bake in the sun, hoping to be ignored for a little bit longer, but alas, wishful thinking.

When I feel a body lie down next to me, the thick bare arm of a man touching mine, I tense. I don't need to guess whose confidence knows no bounds, but I'm not in the mood.

I can even sense the heavy weight of his stare, and it has me feeling uneasy. I sit up abruptly, my eyes flying open. I'm about to speak, but a shirtless Caiden does something to the synapses in my brain. I wasn't ready for this.

He's all lean muscle and tan everywhere. The sprinkling of hair that trails from his belly button to below the waistband of his navy blue swim trunks renders me speechless. His arms are the only things tatted so densely with images of nature, stopping at the curve of his shoulders, leaving the skin of his abdomen smooth and inviting.

Normally, he'd probably gloat at my open gawking, but I

realize he's doing the same to me.

His synapses must have backfired, too, because he blurts out incoherently, "Tiny. Bikini."

I freeze and grab for my oversized knit cover-up, pulling the holey white material over my body in a frantic jumble. I might have chosen this black string bikini with that exact reaction in mind, but to actually get it *in the flesh* has me turning red everywhere.

"Stop staring."

"You're mad," he says, regaining his wits.

I release a sigh, wishing I could roll him off my blanket. "Mad?" I ask, toying with the word. "I don't know what I am. Please let me fester before I say things I don't mean. Today is not a good day to mess with my emotions, Caiden. I'm warning you now."

I keep replaying the events of the night before in my head and find more wrongs than rights.

He sits up, too, and I hate it only defines the ridges of his abdominal muscles.

"Is this about last night?"

I shift, my annoyance growing exponentially.

"Did CeeCee or Brandon send you here?"

He shakes his head. "No. For the most part I tell them me and you are an off-limits topic."

I wish I could say that to our friends, because they keep testing my limits, too.

"Then what is it?"

"I wanted to apologize for not mentioning the memorial thing. I've been thinking about it, and I feel terrible—but you handled it like a champ." His reflexive smile and nudge of my arm sends a confusing combination of rocketing electricity to each limb but also has my guts knotting.

I abruptly stand, letting out a high-pitched huff as I do. "I don't care if you think I handled it like a champ. I don't want to improv the memory of my mother in front of the whole town. I slept on it, and it was incredibly disrespectful of you."

He rises, his brows knit tight as he watches me like a cornered wild animal.

"I'm sorry," he says slowly. "I get how wrong that was. *I was wrong, Hailey*," he repeats for emphasis, as if knowing how much I like hearing it. "I meant to tell you the day before, but like always, I don't think so straight when I'm near you."

I hate that his words are caramel smooth and sincere.

I cross my arms over my chest, unsure how to respond because gratefulness is not an emotion I am capable of expressing right now, especially when his eyes keep trailing over my body.

This afternoon is off to a terrible start, and I feel a bit erratic, but I can't rein in these feelings anymore.

Unfortunately, Caiden finds the need to continue. "I know last night must have been a lot to handle."

I shake my head. "I handled my mom's thing, and as far as everything else, everyone needs to stop treating me like this. Don't apologize for having a girlfriend, and no one should be babying my existence when I'm around you. I'm stronger than that."

"I know you are. You've made that abundantly clear... at least to me."

It's almost a compliment. A smile tugs at the corner of my mouth. "Then just let me deal with all this on my own, okay? No more apologies now. I'm fine. Just give me space."

CeeCee and Brandon are not so stealthily watching our interaction from the barbecue, and I wonder what they think of this situation.

Regardless, I hate having an audience. This is when I heave in a deep breath and turn around. I just need to escape these claustrophobic feelings. I'm always doing this now, but it's the only thing that feels right anymore.

"Please don't chase me, Caiden. You always think you need to run after me, but let me explain that when I walk away, it usually means I don't want to be near you."

I head the opposite direction, my bare feet picking up speed on the shoreline sand. I have a goal in mind, and I know my goal makes me a sadist.

I make it far enough away that I can't hear my friends arguing any longer. My shallow breaths match my frantic steps. My eyes keep darting to the left in search of something very specific.

I have a favorite tree, and I've been gone so long, I worry I won't be able to find it. This only adds to my frustration, but my feet keep going in hope, until sure enough my eyes lock onto the very thing I'm in search of.

I inhale deeply, trying to gather my wits as I move forward, drawn to it because to my relief it's still wonderfully recognizable. But just like me, this town, and my friends—it's aged. The trunk is thicker, the branches longer, the tree taller, but one very clear mark distinctly shows on the dark bark.

I make it to the tree, running my fingers over my name and Caiden's carved into the trunk. Feeling that sticky sense of regret and longing all at once, but nostalgia, too, as my fingers dig into the carved wood. Five years did nothing to the clarity of our names that Caiden would repeatedly drag his pocket knife through in our younger, more carefree days. At the time this carving felt like a life promise, but now I don't know what it means.

This spot was ours, and I always liked that it was a far enough escape from our friends, but also a homey niche by the lake that felt like *ours*.

"Hailey…"

I leap around, feeling caught in something terribly embarrassing. He knew exactly where to find me. The curve to his lips as he approaches tugs at that heartstring that I wish someone could put scissors to.

"Please. I want to talk," he says.

I lick my lips, staring at him getting closer and closer until he's right in front of me.

"It's all you've been saying, and it's all we ever do," I

reply. My hands are flying everywhere as I heave in a deep breath. "And ya know what? I think I'm the only one who gets the short end of the stick here with our talks. You get to ask all the questions, as if you're the only one with a problem."

His brows are tense as he watches me. He looks almost mad, but then again, also a little sad.

"I'm sorry, Hailey. About everything," he says into the void, watching me.

A huff escapes me, my eyes trying to carve myself into him now as I turn to face him more completely. "I kept thinking being here was going to get easier, but it's only getting harder."

"I know. That's not what I want."

"What do you want, Caiden, because for the life of me I can't figure out what that is. Your sad looks, or funny jabs, or the way you stare at me like you want to hold me but push me away. I can't take it. None of this feels fair."

"Ask me," he says placing himself right in front of me; too close.

"Ask you what?"

"You're right. I'm the one with all the questions, but it's only because I never thought I'd get the opportunity to ask them, so I'm all over the place trying to get answers to things I never understood. Your book flipped my world upside down, and coping with that all these years has been hard. Ask me whatever you want."

Being put on the spot so suddenly, I lose my train of thought, and I try not to stare at the fact that his swim trunks hang effortlessly on his strong, perfect hips. The V dipping into the waistband of his shorts is as defined as much as our names in this stupid tree.

"I don't know where to start, other than with what I'm feeling right now."

"Then say it."

I don't hesitate. I'm sick of overthinking. I need answers

just as much as he does. "Why didn't you chase me then, all those years ago? Not that I needed to be chased, but why not try harder? It seems so easy for you now. You never once considered doing the long-distance thing for me. If you love Kristen more, then I understand, but just say it and I'll drop this whole thing. Just tell me the truth; you're not going to hurt my feelings."

Lies.

He lets out a long sigh, his eyes dropping to the ground. He runs a hand over his chin, then tugs on his bottom lip. His eyes are blazing as they pin me to the spot, so much so that I take a step back, stumbling into the tree behind me.

"I did chase you."

He doesn't go on. He lets the words hang. I try and process them, but it doesn't compute.

"You did not," I respond.

He steps forward, looming over me. Our bubble is back, and I hate that I feel safe and that I'm not afraid of the honesty that comes with it.

"I did," he repeats, but doesn't elaborate.

"I would have heard about it."

He shakes his head. "Brandon and CeeCee swore never to tell because it would have done more damage than help things."

"What about my mom, did she know?"

His face falls. "She did, but she was also there for the aftermath."

This fact stings. My mom never stopped shielding me from what she thought might hurt. Why does everyone have this need to protect me? Haven't I proven that I can hack it?

"Caiden, don't start a conversation you can't finish, because this information is going to kill me, so you better explain yourself."

He grits his teeth, and I can see the fear in the depths of his eyes. "After you left, I was a wreck. At first I was a hermit, occupying myself with staying home. I didn't know what to do with myself. Your mom was sorta lost, too, without you, and to busy myself, I was over all the time, helping her with menial stuff. It was this stupid way for me to feel close to you. You dropped me and never tried to reach out."

"We—I didn't leave on the best of terms. You made it very clear that if I left, that was it."

"I was an idiot. I thought about things more during that time than I ever have. I'd consider calling you, then back out. I was hurt and scared. There was always this lingering doubt. Then, I don't know what happened. I woke up one morning needing to see you. I needed *you,* and this whole letting-you-go thing felt like the stupidest thing I ever did. I didn't care about the rights or wrongs. I figured I'd make it work somehow. So I bought a plane ticket that morning."

Taking in a deep breath, I shake my head, too afraid to speak.

He nods in retaliation, going on, "I did," he confirms. "I was ready to chase you. I wanted you. You need to know that part. You had only been gone two months, and I was floundering. I thought that no matter what, I would make it work." He releases a long breath, turning away from me but placing his palm against the trunk to the right side of my face, leaning into me.

"I got to the airport, and all I had was this half-filled duffle bag. Brandon dropped me off, and I went to the gate to wait for my flight. But I started chickening out again. I had too much time to kill. I started to think about all the reasons you might have left all over again, because I knew what I was doing was a huge risk. I didn't want to hold you back, and suddenly it dawned on me that me making you choose in the first place was me doing that exact thing. I freaked out." He stops, his eyes flickering with the painful memory as he shifts his footing, trying to resituate his thoughts.

"I worried that if I ran to you, that I'd be part of something you needed to keep afloat, and I'd be holding you back in an entirely different way. We were kids, only nineteen, I know. We've covered that. But I wanted the best for you, and suddenly in that moment my rash decision to see you felt like such a selfish thing. I was selfish once with making you choose, but I didn't want to do that again. You knew where you were going. You knew what you wanted. The damage had been done, and you chose to leave. I understand now that it wasn't you *not* choosing me, but in that sad, sad moment, I loved you too much to let you destroy what you were already working so hard for. I felt defeated, but for once I felt okay with it. I did try calling you in the airport to tell you all of this. I half hoped you'd talk me into getting onto the plane, to tell me you were going stir crazy, like me, or," he pauses, "or you'd confirm what I was feeling. That it was better I stayed in Colorado. You didn't pick up your phone, and I don't blame you for it. I knew you were still angry. But… I returned my ticket at check-in. I only got half of the amount back and used that to take a bus back home. I took the bus and then walked from the station straight to your mom's house. She told me to go with my gut, and that she wanted what was best for the both of us. I didn't know what that was. So I just went with the flow, losing myself in the tasks of life, trying to keep busy all over again, knowing that you were on a path you wanted, and I had to try and find mine without interrupting yours."

"My mom knew how much I missed you," I blurt out. "So did CeeCee."

His free hand reaches out and strums against my forearm tucked tightly against my chest, and each little tap disrupts the rhythm of my heart. It's too much.

"They didn't talk to me about you. No one would. Your mom only said that if it was meant to be, it would happen, and that only time would tell. I got pissed off every time she'd say it, and then she'd yell at me for the string of profanities that followed. Then she'd make me do yard work to blow off the steam."

"I did need you," I respond, gulping down the words. "If I

had known you were—"

"No Hailey, as much as I wish things had been different, I don't know if I would change it. You got what you wanted."

I let out a huff, shooting him a glare, but getting lost in his eyes just the same. "That's so unfair of you to say. You gave up on me. I never wanted to let you go. It was never supposed to be about sacrifice."

"I know it seems like I gave up on you, but it was all about preserving my own heart, too. I had never dealt with that sort of emptiness. I stayed busy, Hailey, and I know this won't make sense, but staying close with your mom was the only thing that got me through. I got to hear the tiniest updates about you that she'd allow. When you got your first chapter written, when you finished the novel, the ton of agents you queried, to getting the publishing deal. I knew about it all. It was the only thing that kept me alive and kicking. I was so proud of you." He lifts his hand to brush a piece of hair away from my face. I hold still even though I want to lean into his touch.

"I drove all the way to Denver to buy a copy of your book. It was like this piece of you that I was allowed to have, even if I had to share it with the world. Believe me when I say I never forgot about you. I didn't date anyone for years, Hailey. Although, I was lost and reckless. I threw myself into finding a purpose. The rough and strenuous work of being at the station just fit me. I got to work off all this pent-up aggression I felt with life. Eventually though, being so angry at myself started getting old. I wasn't living, and you never came back home. I started to realize you might never come back. Also, it started getting harder for me to ever consider leaving PineCrest. Your life in LA was getting better and better, and I knew I was a reminder of a failure."

"You are a reminder of why my heart aches, not that we failed. You don't get over your first love, Caid."

"I know. But I had told myself that after four years it was

time to move on, but don't ever think I wanted to. It was never over in my mind."

"I'm so mad at you right now."

He shrugs, and it makes me angrier.

"I didn't have anyone to help with how I was feeling," I say. "You know how I fixed my heart?"

He nudges his chin up, telling me to go on, and I hate that he's so close to my face.

"I wrote a fucking book about it, that's how."

His eyes go wide, as if he never considered the book as a coping mechanism.

"That's how I moved on," I add. "We both had to find our ways to move on, and I did, and obviously so have you. And that's okay! It's hard for us, I get it, but we can forgive each other now."

I'm trying to find a way to calm my out-of-control heartbeats and to somehow stomach this feral look overcoming his features as he stares, but it's hard to multitask with him around me like this. I want so much of what I can't have. He must know it. He's got to feel it.

"You know, if that's the case, Hailey, then why write the book the way you did? If it's all about the fact I was such a dick and made you choose, then why write this alternate reality as the way to move on?"

My face is heating up fast, and I have nowhere to run with him so close. He's talking about the one topic I've been dreading. The ending.

"I told you, it was cathartic. That's the nice thing about writing fiction. You can write what you want."

"Is that what you wanted then, Hailey? For us to work out?"

He leans in, the humid heat of his breath skimming over my lips, and I so desperately want to see whether he tastes the same, or whether he'd kiss me with the same frantic need he did when we were teens. But I'm finding I can't breathe. Alarms are going off in my head. I'm not nineteen anymore;

I'm twenty-four, with five years of heartbreak experience.

I close my eyes. I have to, in order to go on.

"Don't you dare kiss me, Caiden Anderson. It's not fair to me, and it's not fair to your girlfriend." My eyes fly open, and he leans back just an inch, obviously perplexed by my outburst.

My lips are stammering, but I try to keep my words crisp, licking my lips, wishing he'd kiss me anyway, but I know that it's wrong. It's all wrong. "You were right before. We can't change the past, but what's done is done. You have a girlfriend, and I'm here for only one reason: my mom." My jaw spasms at those words, because that's not entirely true, but I'm so hurt from the night before, and him standing before me, and the wanting look in his eyes, that it kills me. "Don't forget, Caiden, I'm going to be leaving eventually all over again. So anything you might be feeling is only going to last a little while. I'd hate for you to do something you'll regret, like kissing me. You're going to go back to living your life that doesn't include me, and that's okay."

I keep saying things are okay, but why does my heart tremble each time I say it?

"It's not like that, Hailey."

"It has to be; don't you get that? I'm here now, but it doesn't change the lives we built for ourselves. We had our chance."

His face, only inches away from mine, tenses all over again, from the muscles around his eyes to the ones around his perfect mouth.

"Let's stop pretending that there's hope for us. I'm thankful for you, Caiden, I am," I add even though each word, and each inhale and exhale, feels like sandpaper against my insides. Sometimes doing the right thing hurts.

"I missed you. It's not supposed to be like this," he blurts out as if to salvage whatever moment we had, but it's not enough.

I shake my head, my eyes watering. I wish I could say the same because it would be true, but that's not how this can work. I wipe the corners of my eyes. "Are you listening to me? Stop missing me, Caiden. Go call your girlfriend."

He's staring at me solemnly, hurt and regret riddled into every tense muscle in his body now. His eyes are trying to tell me something he can't seem to say, and I'm too terrified of what it might be.

I sigh, finding the confidence I didn't know I had as I step out of his encompassing presence and away from him. "I wish it wasn't this way either," I say, responding to his look. "But we just have to deal with everything now, Caid. We're okay, please know that. We can be friends, but this whole emotional entanglement we have going on doesn't need to be there anymore. *Let me go.*" My hand comes up to my chest, clawing at my heart, because if anything is painful, it's those words. Telling him to let me go when I'd hate it if he did is excruciating, but I don't take it back.

I take another step away. "And I know you're going to hate this, but I'm bringing Gabe Samuels to the party tonight. Figured I should warn you."

I turn around, starting my walk back toward our friends, leaving him to think.

"Hailey!"

I shouldn't turn around, but there's something in his tone that strikes a chord, compelling me to swivel around. "What, Caiden?"

Tugging on that plump bottom lip that's as swollen as mine from being chewed raw with nerves, he says, "You asked me something earlier, and you need to know that it was never about wanting to be in a long-distance relationship. When I started to date Kristen, she was already living in Denver for school. I only did it because it was easier that way. Giving my heart to someone who I'd only see every couple weeks felt more doable than doing it all at once. I didn't consider it when you left, only because the idea of not having you every day seemed impossible. I think it's important you understand the difference."

I nod. He smiles. I walk away hating that I didn't get the last word.

8

My boots crunch onto the dry pine needles as I hop from my car. I pull in a deep breath, loving the smell of the raging bonfire I can already see in the distance. It's almost more nostalgic than the pine smell it twists around.

I smooth my hands over my ribs, remembering it took me the entire evening to pick out a dress. And by pick out a dress, I mean pick from the four that I brought.

I stared. I tried on. I threw it across the room.

Rinse and repeat.

Sometimes I'd stop to pace the porch outside, needing a gust of fresh air as the day wound down since leaving the lakeshore.

The words *let me go* have been ringing in my head like a gong.

Why did I have to say *those* words?

I reassure myself that it was the right thing to say by putting one foot in front of the other, counting my strides until I'm at the party's edge.

Peering down at my clothes, I tug down the hem anxiously, reminding myself that after the ruthless deliberation, I ended up choosing my strappy dark navy dress that cuts off on my long legs mid-thigh and fits snugly against my hips. I told myself it's the warm, humid summer evening that had me convinced, but I'm beginning to question my own sincerity.

It's like I'm playing with matches.

Which reminds me of the blazing bonfire, my eyes flying to the center, noticing the fire is lit from three large wood pallets piled upon each other, and around it the expansive area is packed with people. Music blares from speakers sitting on the back of a pickup truck next to another truck harboring the many ice chests of drinks. It's the large bonfire, with its tall pluming flames, that acts as the centerpiece to the party, like a beacon.

My vision scatters in search of either my friends or that face that I still can't believe I'm about to spend the evening with. And for once, I don't mean Caiden.

I don't know how it happens, because how can I spot Gabe first when I barely know him? But I do. He's got a beer clutched to his broad chest as he talks excitedly to a person of equal stature next to the fire. Must be an old friend. There are lots of those around here.

I pull in a deep breath, finding comfort in the burning wood smell as I stare.

Gosh, he's handsome. His t-shirt stretches over his chest and ripples with every chuckle or movement, each line more defined with the shadows from the fire. His baby face is long gone, like many of the men I've known in this town.

I nervously tug down the edges of my dress again. Knowing now who he is, I feel the same nerves I might have felt in high school, which is downright ridiculous.

I'm not a hormonal teen any longer who'd run in the opposite direction if the quarterback of the football team glanced at her.

That is, until he catches me staring, and I'm ready to do the exact thing I said I wouldn't.

I remember Gabe from high school, and I hated how stereotypical he was even then. I might have written about it in my journal when I watched him cavorting with the cheerleaders.

I might have even written about how I wondered why it wasn't boring being him/them. Because, wouldn't it be? To know you're a parody of yourself, and when you watch those old John Hughes movies, that their story has already been told so many times to the point of annoyance? Maybe not. Maybe when you're in the cool kid group, life is just good, and you really have no understanding how the other half lives. That being me. I wasn't the biggest outsider, but I remember feeling like it. Maybe it's because I never truly felt like I fit in, even with all my friends who proudly flaunted their attendance in the extracurricular.

Of course, I attended every homecoming game, and even every party, but the people never fit. Boys like Gabe made out with girls openly at parties and shot-gunned beers in the living room with an audience.

I, on the other hand, begged Caiden to get into trouble with me elsewhere, pulling him from the parties to somewhere private, away from the crowds and popularity contests. Of course, he never minded. I liked my own type of mischief, and if it involved Caiden, I didn't care what we got ourselves into.

"Hey, Hailey."

I smile reflexively at the sound of my name, realizing that my nostalgic reminiscing has distracted me and Gabe is now standing in front of me, smiling openly, his smooth-shaven skin putting his mouth on full display.

"Gabe, hi."

"You look… great." He grins, scratching the back of his head nervously as he says it, and I laugh.

"Thanks." I force my hands to release the hem of my dress and try to embrace who I am. Which is an adult woman, who this good-looking guy seems to be interested in. God help him.

"Let me go grab you a drink. You like beer?"

He's still smiling, and I can't tell if my cheeks are flushed with heat because of the raging fire only fifty feet away, or because I'm that giddy girl I desperately don't want to be.

"Beer sounds great."

"Perfect. Don't move. I'll be right back."

He winks before departing, and I'm most definitely a dopey mess over it as he turns around. Goddammit, I need to get a grip.

"Baby bird, I had higher hopes for you."

I swivel around to see Brandon finishing off his own bottle of beer.

Raising a brow and placing a hand on my hip, I retort, "I'd prefer you not spy on me. Plus, Gabe's nice."

He laughs very obviously *at* me. "Whatever. I just hate that dumb look on your face when he talks to you. I wish things were different, ya know?"

Well, *I wish* I could throw a fit. I want to. Only because I know what he means, and like an idiot I ask, "Where's Caiden?"

He grins like he just won a game I didn't know we were playing, and I have the urge to punch him.

"Oh, he's around." I don't like the way his lips toy with his words, continuing this game at my expense, all of it containing hidden meanings. "I don't like you in that dress either, especially not around Samuels."

I roll my eyes, and I'm ready to playfully insult him, but Gabe appears. His eyes collide with Brandon's before they make it to mine, and Gabe's smile isn't as confident as before as he says, "Here you go, Hailey."

I lift one hand to touch his elbow while grabbing the drink with the other. It's a deliberate flirtatious move that doesn't go unnoticed as Gabe cements his grin, regaining the confidence he lost track of only seconds ago.

"Whatever," Brandon whispers before turning to me to say, "I'm trying to find CeeCee. She's pissed at me again, and hell if I know why. I can't seem to do anything right." He pauses, his eyes darting between Gabe and me, and I can tell he thinks he's talking too much. "Anyway, I gotta go find her."

Gabe clears his throat. "Um, I saw her near the drinks. She might have been talking to John Walden."

Brandon's face shifts into brute anger, but for once, not at his archnemesis as he grumbles, "Sonuva—if she wants to play that game, *fine.*" He's about to stomp off in the opposite direction, but his heated stare shakily makes it back to Gabe as he reluctantly huffs, "Thanks," before leaving.

Once he's out of earshot, Gabe releases a long huff before saying, "You think he's forgiven me yet?"

I laugh an honest to goodness laugh, bringing the bottle to my lips, loving that the tension between my friends and him, and the reasons why, are not hidden away, but instead blasted for comedic relief.

"Doubtful, but I appreciate the effort."

He nudges his chin behind him. "Let's go hang out over there."

I nod, then take a large gulp as I begin my strides through the fairly crowded party. Gabe's hand comes to the small of my back, lightly leading me. His touch makes me nervous and excited, but also feels forbidden at the same time. I make a mental note to catalog these feelings later in my notebook.

We weave through the crowd, the crackling fire mixing with the bass beats coming from the speakers.

This party reminds me of all of those others I used to attend when I was younger. Especially when I nod a few hellos as we walk by people, and when they glance to see who's next to me, their looks of confusion afterward have me wanting to laugh hysterically—out of madness. Gossip still has a deep vein here.

We stop on the opposite side of the fire, on the side of the party closest to the lakeshore. I know the shore to be a few hundred feet through the thick forest.

So many memories.

Gabe picks a spot next to a large pine tree, the trunk

ginormously thick. He takes his own long pull of beer as he leans his shoulder against the tree. He's just staring with this funny crook to his lips.

"Gabe… you're freaking me out," I joke, staring back.

He laughs, "Sorry. I thought I would talk too much once I got to spend time with you, but the truth of the matter is, you scare the shit out of me."

I laugh again, and his own tangles around mine.

"Well, I really like your opener, Gabe. It's a real attention grabber. 'Girl invites guy to party, and guy admits he's terrified of girl.' I think you've got the beginning of your first novel, or your next eclectic exposé on dating in the modern world."

He laughs hard, snorting a bit while trying to contain his burly chuckles, and it feels like such a win.

I don't know what's come over me and where this confidence comes from. If I could be so bold with the over-dissection of my psyche, I'd say I get some sick pleasure knowing that the most popular guy back in high school can't stop staring at me. That can surely make any awkward girl feel a little more on her game.

"Have I told you how much I like you?" he says, smiling, but his mouth slams shut. He's embarrassed, but he doesn't seem to regret saying it.

I take a slow sip of my beer this time, eyeing him curiously until I'm done. He has me hopeful for the night.

"No, you actually haven't told me that at all. Did you have a crush on me in high school? You can say no."

To hide my own bubbling, bold nerves, I take another sip. He rubs at his jaw as he lets his eyes caress every surface of my exposed skin before letting out a soft chuckle. "Um, maybe some of junior year, but I definitely did senior year. Have you always known that I did?"

I gulp, taking a step closer to him, liking that he's on the defensive. "Actually, someone told me just recently."

"Which somebody is that?" he hums.

"Haileyyy…"

My heart leaps into my throat as my eyes lock apologetically onto Gabe's, knowing exactly who's crashing my fun so soon by the rumbling voice coming from behind me.

"*That* somebody," I reply crisply before swiveling around to see Caiden, hands stuffed in his pockets, grinning like an idiot, but he isn't alone. He has an accomplice. Cameron is smugly at his side, and it becomes obvious that they know exactly what they're doing, or about to do, at least. The bastards.

Gabe's abrupt chuckle catches me off guard as he says, "Oh, well that makes sense now."

And I can't help my own string of laughter, too, and I enjoy Caiden's look of confusion in response even more so.

"We were just talking about you," Gabe says, not missing a beat before taking a sip of his beer.

The tension rises a level as I watch the two men eye each other. It feels so silly, but I stay quiet, watching it unfold.

"It's been a while, Gabe. What brings you back to PineCrest?" Caiden asks, and I don't trust him one bit.

This is when my eyes dart to Gabe's. Unfortunately, I'm eager for the same information.

"Ah, well, my sister starts college soon. She got into NYU, so I thought I'd road trip it with her to New York. Ya know, since I live there."

I smile. That's kind of adorable.

Gabe catches my look and smiles back, but adds apologetically, "I was actually hoping to stay a while, but it turns out she has to be there earlier than we thought. So I'm leaving in a few days."

My smile falters. *A few days*?

Is it weird that not only am I disappointed by the fact that Gabe is only here for such a short amount of time, but I'm also suddenly more jealous that he knows his end date?

When am *I* leaving town? How long can I stay?

"New York is so far from California," rolls off the tongue of the infuriating man to my left.

I visibly roll my eyes, knowing Caiden's going in for the kill so quickly.

My mouth finally chooses to function. "But we can totally keep in touch. I mean, if you want," I fumble, adding a shrug.

"That'd be cool," Gabe responds, and I feel victorious.

My blood starts coursing through my veins with a little pop of adrenaline, and with an odd sense of exhilaration with this battle I'm knowingly participating in.

Cameron stays rigid and silent at Caiden's side, apparently only here to provide moral support to said douchebaggery shenanigans that are ensuing. Boys are so dumb.

"I don't know many writers," I add. "Writing is this sort of solitary universe."

Gabe laughs, "It's true."

Caiden reappears as he says, "That's right Gabe, you're a reporter, right?" I can't tell if his tone is condescending, but it's the corner of his mouth that lifts upward when he speaks that gets me so riled up. It starts a tornado ripping around inside me, as love and hate twist around each other, making it hard to choose how to feel. "Have you read Hailey's book?"

I'm tempted to look at my phone for the time, just to clock him on how long it took him to go in for the win so ruthlessly.

Gabe shrugs, eying me carefully before he says, "No, but it's at the top of my to-be-read list."

It's a perfectly acceptable answer that I would actually prefer, and I smile. "You don't have to read my book. Seriously."

Both men laugh, but stop abruptly at the sound of each other, which then dominos into my own odd burst of laughter. It's obvious that each are laughing for very different reasons, and I find the fact that only *I* know, hilarious.

I try shaking the moment off, but Gabe is quick to capitalize on it, noticing my nearly empty bottle before he asks, "You want another drink?"

Yeah, I could use some air too, I think.

"Yes, please."

He grins, turns, and strolls away. I release a long breath, letting my shoulders slump, not realizing how exhausting that just was. Regardless, I huff out a laugh as I turn toward Caiden, and shake my head. Cameron, the silent accomplice, scurries away as if he's done his job.

I lift my eyes across the party, through the flames to a truck parked on the other side with drinks and watch Gabe sifting through an ice chest.

I bring my sardonic glare around to face Caiden again, taking notice of his twitching smirk. "What do you think you're doing?"

He shrugs, dragging his teeth across his bottom lip before speaking. "Just being a friend."

Raising a suspicious brow, I finish off the rest of my beer before I reply, using it as an excuse to admire the glow of the bonfire in his eyes. "We need to work on your definition of friend."

"Why's that?"

"Because you're kind of being an asshole."

He laughs, and I hate that I love it. I shake my head again. This is not how this is supposed to go. I need to hate this stupid animalistic display of jealousy.

His smile turns into a dopey one. His boldness might be due to some solid amounts of consumed-liquid courage.

"You're drunk, go away," I test playfully.

He shakes his head but doesn't deny it. "I'm not drunk enough, really." He rolls his eyes dramatically, and the giggle that emerges from me is an accident, and I cough to hide it.

"Did you really just come over here to be an ass?"

He shrugs, not fighting it anymore. "He's so *into* you," he mumbles, and I realize he must have drunk a lot, because he's letting his words out too loosely. He wouldn't normally be this verbose when it comes to the *me* topic. Not now, anyway.

"You think so?" I hum, shamelessly taking advantage of it.

He nods, clenching his jaw. Our eyes shoot across the party to spot Gabe still busying himself with a drink.

"Unfortunately," he replies too quietly. Caiden's eyes are back on me as he asks, "You like him?"

I shrug. He grunts. I roll my eyes.

It's our cycle.

I hear a rumbling from across the party, and I can already tell it's Brandon probably getting a little too rowdy.

Caiden looks off toward the sound. "I gotta get back to best friend duties at some point. Brandon and CeeCee are in a rough patch."

I sensed this earlier, and it kind of irks me that Caiden knows and I don't. "Why's that?"

His eyes shoot back to me, smirking again. "CeeCee leads Brandon on, messes with his head, and he gets all confused when the lines get muddled. It sends them both into a frenzy. Usually, it ends up with them dropping each other for a month or so until they're back at it again."

"I'm sure CeeCee doesn't mean to lead him on."

Caiden snorts, "The CeeCee we know can be vindictive when she wants. Sometimes I think she does it just to torture the guy to make him pay for cheating on her."

"He did what?"

Caiden tugs on his bottom lip. "You've been gone a long time, Hails."

A wave of nerves tumble through my body. "I know." *I know. I know.*

I see Gabe heading back toward us, and that seems to be the cue for Caiden to leave as he turns away.

"Where are you going?" I ask, and I can't tell if I'm trying to instigate another battle or if it's because I care.

He doesn't turn around. He just shouts back with a waving arm, "To get another drink," before disappearing through the crowd.

"That could have gone smoother, I guess," Gabe says as he extends my beer to me.

I sigh, "It went as well as it was gonna go, I think." I feel eyes all around me, like little pinpricks against the back of my neck. I reach for Gabe's hand, tugging him toward the dark forest. "Come with me. Let's go talk over there."

He doesn't hesitate, not even for a second. We stroll through the woods. It gets dark and darker before any moonlight shines through the trees until we reach the clearing to the lake. I stop just short of the edge of the trees.

"That's awesome that your sister got into NYU, by the way." I say, trying to pick up the fluidity of the conversation. I take a long sip of beer as I watch him respond.

"Right?" he exclaims proudly. "I was never really home during college unless it was for a long weekend or holiday. Figured, now is as good a time as ever to try and be a better brother. I like the idea of her going to college where I am, too. I remember college and everything I got into. I don't even want to think of my sister going. But at least I'll feel better if I'm just a quick cab ride away."

I chuckle at the sincerity. "You're nothing like I remember you in high school."

He says two things, and both pluck different strings to my well-being. "We all grow up. Well, actually, you're kind of exactly how I remember you."

"How's that?" I ask, and my tone must imply something I wasn't aware of because he takes a solid step forward, putting him inches away from my face.

My heart thumps and I think: *yes, kiss me.*

I want to feel something, anything. I've felt empty too long, and Gabe, even for just getting to know him, gives me hope that this *thing* I can't seem to shake could be cured.

"You're still as honest, funny, and clumsy, but..." He

133

pauses, licking his bottom lip before going on. "You're a whole hell of a lot prettier than I remember. Which is crazy, 'cuz you were always really pretty."

His words teeter on cheesy, but I bask in it, letting a smile spread across my face as he inches closer.

I close my eyes, eager for the contact and still hopeful. I could make this work if I wanted. I can do anything I set my mind to.

He presses his lips to mine, and it's this lightning-quick yank that ignites in my heart—and then it pushes and pulls, like I'm fishing for that feeling. I'm almost there, but it doesn't come. It's like the hook I cast doesn't catch, and that empty feeling is still there when I reel it back.

It's always like this with everyone. I've kissed many men to try and cure me of this feeling, but none seem to stick. They don't spark or ignite much of anything inside me.

There was a second where I thought Gabe could be my chance. He has all the ingredients of home, yet all the excitement of something new.

Once, I dated a guy for a whole three months in hopes the spark would suddenly ignite, but it never did.

All of my attempts at relationships feel like this. An empty kiss that will never compare to what I had. Caiden's ruined everything. But I gave it my all.

Gabe's lips stroke mine, and the tiniest bit of spice hits my lips as his mouth gives way, coaxing me to open for him, allowing his tongue to explore and taste me. It's sweet, and nice, but my heart doesn't race, and the butterflies in my gut flutter, but it's not enough.

Ugh. Why is it never enough?

My heart deflates in defeat but gives me a beat of *hrumph* as if to say, *"We're trying."*

That we did, heart. That we did. And what a beautiful, handsome try it was.

I lift the corner of my mouth for Gabe as he pulls away

slowly.

He's smiling, and it's enough to have me wanting to scream how frustrating this is for me. Gabe could be perfect, but something inside me won't let him be.

"I'm sorry I'm leaving in a couple days. I was going to tell you…" he breathes out.

I lean forward, shaking my head, basking in his attention anyway. Maybe none of it is enough, but this moment can be mine. "It's okay. I meant it when I said let's keep in touch. I could always use more friends."

His lips twitch at hearing my words, and there is a comical curve to them. He must think the use of *friends* is sort of ironic now that we've just kissed, but little does he know that I'm a useless romantic attempt for him now, even if I wish I wasn't.

"Do you ever find yourself in New York with writing and stuff?"

I nod. "My publisher is there. I haven't been yet though, but it's possible I could find a reason to." My gut knots at this blatant flirting. I don't want to give Gabe hope, but the words flow too easily. I try to trick my brain into thinking maybe this is something I could try again, meaning him, but my heartbeat falls to a flat rhythm at the thought.

"That would be aweso—"

A loud sound of hollers and cheers breaks through Gabe's words. I shake my head a moment, dissecting it, and find a sense of familiarity to the sounds instantly. That's when another rounding "Yeaah!" rumbles through the trees.

A fight. Someone is fighting, and I have my money on who is involved.

Some things never change.

I lift my chin to Gabe and use this as my escape. "I—we have to get back. Something is happening at the party. I have to go check on my friends."

Gabe blows out an exasperated breath, and I don't blame him, but he must know what baggage I come with as he says,

"Okay." He doesn't hesitate pressing one last kiss to my lips before letting me walk away.

I force a smile as I trot away, leaving Gabe at the lake's edge. He isn't upset, or at least I don't think so. He's almost smitten as he smiles back, shrugs, and chugs his beer as he watches me break into a sprint toward the party.

When I'm a safe distance away, I heave in a heavy dose of oxygen, wondering how I'm going to handle what lies behind me, and how I'm going to handle what I'm about to face in front of me.

Another round of hollers and goading cheers comes from the crowd as I get closer, and I pick up speed.

My prediction is that I'm about to find Brandon in a fistfight with John Walden, the guy CeeCee uses to make Brandon jealous. It's the most logical scenario, but when my eyes collide with something I never saw coming, I gasp.

Caiden and Brandon are full-on throwing punches at each other.

I try for that leveling breath again, but I can't seem to pull in enough air this time as I make my way to them, shoving through the watching crowd.

Fights between best friends, Caiden and Brandon, are not unheard of, but it usually means someone got a bit too personal. And the only solution these oafs seem to find when it comes to a man-to-man issue is to get physical.

"Stop it!" I shout indignantly once I make it to the front, fuming at the fact that Brandon's nose is bleeding and Caiden's beautiful bottom lip is cut and swollen.

Both men… err, *boys,* stop their circling, but keep their fists raised high as they both turn to face me.

I must admit: I've never been able to stop a fight so suddenly in my life.

Brandon blurts out into the humming party silence with, "He started it."

CeeCee appears, looking as frustrated as I feel, her hair

flying as she shakes her head with each irate word. "It doesn't matter who started it, you're both idiots."

Brandon and Caiden both grunt, turning back toward each other.

Partygoers start to go back to minding their own business, going back to conversations and drinking now that all the action is over.

I even fling a look over my shoulder in time to see that Gabe has rejoined the party with the same guy I saw earlier. His eyes dart to mine once, but offers nothing for me to dwell on other than a handsome smile.

CeeCee brings my attention back to my idiot friends as she says, "I think you two have had enough party. I'm taking Brandon home. Hails, do me a favor and take Caiden home, too, would you?"

It's not a question; it's a polite demand. Brandon and Caiden must have ridden here together. She tugs on Brandon's burly arm, but it isn't enough to deter Brandon from pointing a deliberate finger into Caiden's chest as he says, "Get your shit together, man," before following CeeCee.

Caiden wipes at his lip, his eyes angry, but there isn't a fight there anymore. It's almost like he agrees.

I take a couple strides toward him. "Let's get you home."

He doesn't argue; he just follows me silently out of the party, far from the glow of the bonfire until we reach my rental car.

He climbs in, and so do I. It takes five minutes of heavy silence as we follow the dirt path to the main road before he says, "Sorry."

I jerk my head toward him for a quick glance and then back at the road. "It's fine. What were you and Brandon fighting about, Caid? It's not like you guys to be at each other like that—"

"—You. We were arguing about you."

The response stuns me, and I try to focus on the tiny white lines on the road rather than allow myself to ask more questions in regard to that.

"Did you have a lot to drink?" I ask, changing tack.

"I didn't get into a fight with him because I'm drunk, if that's what you're asking."

I'm not, but I choose not to speak anymore. I'm too scared of the truth. Caiden's frustration with me is building as much as mine is with him. The only difference is that when the frustration builds with me, I'm the one that wants to be more closed off, but with Caiden, he becomes more expressive with his words, as if he can't contain them. It was always those elements that balanced us. That push and pull that kept us level, him pushing me to talk when I needed it, and him learning when words aren't needed.

It doesn't take me long to pull into his long, winding driveway, seeing as he lives less than a mile from my house. The trees that line his driveway are more overgrown than I remember, but it's also hard to pick out the details in the darkness.

As we get closer, I can see that the porch lights are on, illuminating the front of the old rustic house: dark wood, one story, like a hidden haven in the woods, and once a haven for my mind.

"How are your parents?" I ask as we wind down the path.

"Fine. In Florida, doing what they do best by ignoring the world."

Caiden's parents retired to Florida right after we graduated high school. His family was always so different than mine. Growing up in my household, we were forced to mingle with each other and talk, but Caiden's family were the eat in silence types. His parents forced him to grow up too fast, and mine were always willing to feed into my imagination. He's the yin to my yang, really.

We're also both the only child. We understand what it means to need someone to be your best friend and your playmate.

In a way, it was almost inevitable how we both ended up so tied to each other. Since the age of six, I've never known a life without him.

It's also no wonder how it's become impossible for me to find someone to fill that void.

I slow onto his gravel driveway to the garage, remembering how his parents were always nice to me, but it was nothing to how my parents, or most importantly, my mom, treated Caiden. He was like one of our own household.

Caiden's parents always talked about wanting to leave PineCrest to be near the beach and live out their lives in the sun. Even then, Caiden never wanted to leave. I should have seen that as a sign.

When his parents left, they gave Caiden the house, nearly everything in it, and retired to Florida, leaving him to live his life.

No one had any doubt that he'd manage just fine, especially me. He had a steady job, and we were both attending classes at the junior college an hour away. Life was good. Life was simple.

Not anymore.

I pull the parking brake, turn the car off, and decide I better see Caiden inside. If I'm this rattled by the evening, then he might be, too.

"Let me walk you to your door. You okay?"

"How romantic of you to offer, Hailey."

I shoot him a scowl, but he's smiling.

"Stop looking at me like that," I quip.

I open my door, walk around the front, and watch him stumble more unsteadily out of my car than I'd expected. Yep, probably a good idea I make sure he gets inside safe.

I can still care, can't I?

I fight the urge to touch him or help him. Instead, I lead the way up the few steps to his porch.

"Caiden, where are your keys?" I ask.

I notice he's stopped at the top step, leaning against the

post, which puts him closer to me than I realize when I swivel around to face him.

"Did you kiss him?" he asks back, slicing the mood, his voice low and solemn.

He's looming over me, eyes pleading and hot, his body languid from his drinking.

"Caiden, stop. Just gimme your keys."

"You did, didn't you?"

I shake my head, trying to hide the burning guilt singeing every corner of my being as I stick my hand out, palm up while we stand on the porch that has haunted my dreams. We're nearly nose to nose as I look up into his bottomless forest-green eyes.

I want to tell him that it doesn't matter because *he's* ruined everything. That even if I did get a kiss from the jock in high school, and even though his kiss was warm and inviting, I felt nothing, absolutely nothing, and it's all his fault.

"Keys, please."

His jaw sets sternly as he takes a step back, pushing his pelvis forward, eyes dopey but pissed off again. "They're in my pocket, Hails. Help a drunk guy out, would you?"

The bold move throws me, and I wonder if this attitude shift is what got him into a fight in the first place. "You're being such an ass tonight."

"I can't believe you kissed him," he retorts.

I'm not ready for this conversation. I step forward, shoving my hand confidently into the front of his snug jeans pocket to grab his house keys. It's a quick move that happens so lightning fast, he can barely keep up before he's chasing me to his front door.

"Hailey, why won't you talk about it?"

I unlock his door, fling the wooden monstrosity open, angry all at once. "You don't get to ask me about who I kiss."

"I knew it. You did kiss him. I saw you walk off with him." His tone is soft and wanting, and more than anything, hurt.

It's entirely unfair, and what's worse about this interaction is that I don't know how I got here, but I'm leaning against the open doorframe, and he's suddenly towering over me with this defeated look. It calls to me on this deep level, and I try to fight it.

I hate that even like this, in limbo between misery and a beautiful chaos, I still feel satiated. I still feel content. As long as it's Caiden. It doesn't matter what I'm feeling. He fills the void just by being near me.

I reply quietly but firmly, "I don't know why you're acting like *you're* the tormented one, because you're not, Caiden, trust me on this one."

"Funny, that's what Brandon said."

I don't find this funny, but *something* cracks inside me, like a dam holding it all back at hearing his words. That *something* suddenly builds and gathers like a tsunami, and if I don't touch him in some way, it'll come crashing down. I need a little bit of contact as if to make sure he's real. That *we're* real.

I lift my hand to his face, brushing my fingers over the thick scruff of his jaw for the first time, basking in its roughness, my thumb falling dangerously close to his bruised bottom lip.

Watching me carefully, his eyes burn a path through mine and straight into my heart, like it's his lifeline. He shifts his face just enough to press a surprising kiss to the pad of my thumb and then takes it into his mouth to nibble it gently. The wave building inside me reaches its peak of momentum and crashes within, engulfing and amplifying all these feelings he elicits: pain, love, hate, lust, frustration; it's all there. And the calm of the crash, or lack thereof, nestles itself between my legs in a pool of warmth.

It's as if we share the same nerve endings, because the right sides of our mouths twitch upward in unison as we stare back in the silence. I suck in a breath, watching his teeth sit delicately against my thumb, not releasing it.

The urge to tell him the truth is ready to be unleashed. I want to tell him how I can't kiss anyone else without thinking about how they pale in comparison to his lips. I want to tell him my biggest worry is that there will never be someone else who can replace him, and instead this churning pain at the fact his perfect mouth isn't mine is just something I'm going to have to endure for eternity.

"This is what I mean. It's *torture*," I breathe out, hoping he's taking me seriously. Because I mean every damn word.

Caiden is a consuming person. We used to consume each other, and to know that even the lightest of touch causes the tiniest but most meaningful reaction kind of destroys me. This touch means more than that stupid kiss earlier with Gabe.

This is when I remember those three little words. *Let. Me. Go.*

"Caid, get some rest," I force through my lips in a whisper, trying to regain my bearings.

He blows out a defeated breath as his eyes sink closed while I pull away and walk back toward my car, leaving him.

When I pull out of the driveway, he's still frozen to the spot, standing in the doorway with his eyes clenched shut.

9

——————

I called CeeCee when I didn't know what else to do. Last night was a failed attempt at sleep, and I'm feeling it.

The morning took an awkward turn when I got a delivery that I should have expected, but my mind was somewhere else entirely. That's when I phoned a friend.

So when CeeCee walks through my front door without knocking, I don't budge. I'm just sitting on my couch, staring at the urn sitting on my coffee table as if it's staring back at me.

"Oh, Lord. Hailey, are you okay?"

I want to tell her I'm currently having an out-of-body experience that borders on overwhelming as my mind is continuously trying to manage all these emotions and thoughts that knot and tangle around each other forming an emotional ball of yarn. I snicker at the thought. My mom loved knitting. Seems ironic as I stare at her ashes.

CeeCee plops beside me on the couch. "Hailey?" she questions again.

"Yeah?" I ask, keeping my eyes on what is terrifyingly explained as my mother in a jar. I rise from my seat at the thought, hating it, wanting to cry, and losing my mind in the process. Then I plop back onto the couch. This time CeeCee's arms come around my shoulders in a hug.

But I don't cry. For some reason I can't. I just lean into her touch, wishing everything was different and that my heart didn't skip a beat for Caiden, yet weep with a slowing thump for my mother.

I'm a mess.

"Say something. Anything," CeeCee squeaks.

"I'll be fine. I'm just in shock."

CeeCee releases a breath of relief. "I was worried you were going to become an emotional mute. I know this must be hard."

I nod. "It is, but it's getting through the first wave that's the hardest. I don't know how I lost track of the days, but I somehow forgot that my mom's ashes were going to be delivered today."

"I'm sure there has been a lot on your mind."

Her tone implies she knows exactly what has been on my mind. I rise from the couch. "You want some coffee?"

"Sure," she says, getting up and following me into the kitchen, taking a seat on a bar stool on the other side of the counter island. "You wanna talk about it, Hails? I figured that's why you called me over. Unless you just need me to be a silent sounding board. Contrary to popular belief, I can do that, too."

I pull coffee grounds from the cabinet, turning my head to shoot her an honest smile. "Bit of both, actually. How did your drive with Brandon go last night?"

She sighs. "Not good. I'm about to tell him we need to take a timeout."

Needing a distraction from the urn sitting in my living room, I use this topic as my opportunity. "Why did you never tell me about Brandon cheating on you?"

She gasps, eyes wide as if I had just uttered the name Voldemort in Diagon Alley. "How do you even know about that?"

I feel guilty that I asked, and turn to the coffee maker,

filling it up and powering it on before turning to face her. "Caiden told me."

"Well, it's nice to know you two are at least talking." She rolls her eyes.

I shake my head. "We don't have to talk about it. I was just surprised to hear it. I noticed you and Brandon have been a bit... on edge lately."

She snorts. "Yeah, it always ends up like this. We can talk about it, I mean. It all happened at a really weird time for all of us." She pauses, chewing her bottom lip as if she's about to walk a precarious line with her words. "Ya know, just because you left doesn't mean that while you were gone you didn't still affect us. That's why having you back is so easy. Even if we missed you or wondered what you were doing, you were still part of us."

My brows twitch, my eyes blinking a little too rapidly to hold back the tears that want to appear.

She continues, "Caiden wasn't the same when you left, and although he was trying, he'd go through these constant peaks and dives that were rough. Brandon and Caiden have this way of dragging each other into their miseries... and joys, too, but mostly they like being there for each other for those extremes. Brandon and me dated for a little over a year after you left, but we hit this terrible rough patch. It was when I was failing all my college classes and Brandon was trying to figure out what to do with his life. This also happened to be during one of Caiden's emotional peaks." She grits her teeth a moment. "I don't know how much I should say, but Caiden was getting reckless. At first when you left he was pretty solitary when it came to girls. He never went out of his way to flirt or date, but then something in him snapped. He was the guy of extremes. He started fucking around. He'd find a new bed to sleep in every other weekend with a different girl. It didn't matter who."

I wince. I didn't expect this part. What's worse is, I'd be lying if I didn't admit that I went through the same series of experiences when I moved. When the empty kisses weren't enough, I'd jump into the beds of men I thought I wanted more with, but everything always fell flat. Not that there were a lot, by any means. I wasn't exaggerating when I said writing can be a solitary life. But I'd be lying if I said I didn't try.

Regardless of my own, what did CeeCee call them? Oh yeah, my *'emotional peaks,'* I still want to understand where Caiden's behavior came from, but the rational part of me wants to hate that I do.

"Caiden convinced Brandon and the other guys to enroll in the fire academy around this time, which in hindsight is of course a good thing. But at the time it also sparked this weird wave of a need for bachelor life, especially with Caiden leading the cavalry. And like I said, I wasn't the funnest person to be around. Because I was failing my classes, I was lashing out at Brandon in all the wrong ways. We got into a huge fight about how everything he does isn't good enough. We needed a break from each other, so he left to go spend time with Caiden, who was on a no-strings-attached binge. They decided to have a long bro's weekend in Boulder. All the guys went, and I was left at home. After a couple of days went by and not hearing from Brandon I started to worry, and I wanted to apologize for being so bipolar and mean—'cuz ya know, I can be mean when I want to be. I called the Sunday morning before Brandon was supposed to drive back. We hadn't talked since our argument, but when I called, a girl answered his phone. And then it was just over."

"Over?"

She shrugs, but her eyes darken sadly. "Yeah. There was no going back for me. The damage was done. And it was exactly what I thought it was. He got sad, he got stupid and drank way too much, and he made a stupid decision. But some choices are irreversible. We weren't broken up at the time. I just wanted some space. There's a difference, and the damage was just too much. What would stop him from doing that again when we go through another rough patch? I don't think I could take it."

"Why didn't you call me?" I plead, eyeing her in shock.

"It felt too complicated. If I called, I wasn't going to be able to hold back all this hatred I had for Caiden, too. I blamed him for feeding into Brandon's stupidity. He's still supposed to be a good friend to *me too*. He should have stood up for what was right, but instead he let his best friend cheat on his girlfriend, and all because he was still trying to get over you!" CeeCee stumbles over her next words, as if she wishes she could take the last bit back. I must admit, it does sting. "Anyway, I couldn't call and dump that on you. It wouldn't have been fair."

"You still never called," I say, turning away from her as I pour our coffees.

"Neither did you." She pulls in a deep breath and gives me a tight smile as she takes a mug from my outstretched hand. "We're both at fault. There's no grudge. Life moved on. But, just so you know, you have always been a part of what's here. Ya know, it's almost like you could *stay* if you want."

What a preposterous idea.

I sip my coffee slowly, trying not to freak out. Right now, there are so many reasons for me to leave, not to stay. Although, I acknowledge some of the happier moments so far have been an awakening to what it feels like to laugh again, even with all the rooted drama.

I shake my head. "Staying is a thought, but for right now there are other things on my mind. I just want to take my time with everything. There aren't any time constraints, and that's good enough for me." I can feel my shoulders tense, but maybe it's because my answer reminds me that my only time constraint is finishing my next novel.

Her goading smirk tells me she knows she's messing with my head. "How's everything else? I was right in assuming you're still sleeping on the couch."

"Yep. I'm just trying to get my bearings, that's all."

She laughs, leaning over the counter. "How's that working out for you?"

I throw my head back and laugh, too. "Terrible. Absolutely, awful." I giggle. "I'm a train-wreck and so is Cai—"

Knock. Knock. Knock.

My brows rise as I stare into CeeCee's eyes. She's forming a guilty smile that has my stomach doing a somersault.

I place my cup on the counter. "What did you do?"

She shrugs as my vision drops to my attire. I roll my eyes knowing that my jeans and white tank are just going to have to do, and as I walk out of the kitchen, I'm hoping my instincts are all wrong.

Unfortunately, they're not.

Caiden stands on the opposite side of the screen door, boldly staring at me, snuggling Soot against his chest. My knees turn useless at the sight. He's not what I need right now.

I release a heavy breath, shaking my head, which ignites his smirk. Shouldn't he be cowering, hiding, or pissed off at me somewhere? Why can't he just be mad at me?

"Hi," I say, just barely loud enough for him to hear. I gulp down my nerves. "What are you doing here? I can't say your face is one I particularly care for at the moment."

On reflex and in Midwestern hospitality, I open the door to let him inside. He scoots by me, careful not to touch me, clutching the cat close as he enters the living room. His eyes immediately fall to my open suitcase in the same spot he last saw it. It's his grimace that worries me most, but the involuntary stroke under the cat's chin that melts my heart.

CeeCee comes strolling out, her purse already slung over her shoulder. "I should probably be going."

"Going? Where are you going?" I swivel to turn to Caiden. "And you never answered me. What are you doing here?"

He shrugs as CeeCee continues to make her way to the front door. He says, "I heard you were having trouble going through the house and stuff, and... and..."

"And what?" I bark, putting the pieces together, realizing CeeCee must have told him how I've been doing.

"And to say..."

"—That you're sorry?" I question, cutting him off, and I can't help the sputter of a laugh that follows. Last night was a disaster. His lips still feel tattooed on my thumb, and even I can admit how absurd that sounds.

His lips tighten into a squirming smile. "Yeah, kinda."

"Well, are you? Sorry, that is?" I ask, letting my eyes scan the length of him, examining his fitted olive shirt and dark jeans, complete with an adorable white cat pressed against his chest. It's too much.

He shrugs, smiling at my expense now. "No, not really."

I snort, rubbing my face, taking in all the ridiculousness. "Please put that cat down. I can't take you seriously when you hold cute animals."

He laughs. I laugh. CeeCee even laughs.

Caiden releases Soot, who quickly heads back out the front door for his afternoon snack. CeeCee follows as she says, "Well, I'm going to let you two hash it out. Talk to you lovebirds later."

I could strangle her, and she must know it because she doesn't glance back at me as she scurries to her car.

When I turn back around to shoot Caiden a well-crafted glare, I'm surprised to see his eyes already glued to the rustic silver urn sitting on my coffee table.

My face softens because I understand that look so completely, and I can't tell if I love the fact that he might understand how I feel.

"Is that her?" he asks.

I nod, forcing him to glance back at me.

"It's so weird," he replies.

"Yeah," I breathe out.

"How are you doing?"

I feel more compelled to answer when he asks me. "With you messing with my head, and dealing with my mom, I can't say I'm doing fantastic."

We both release a chuckle, and I give in. I try to remember the days when we didn't have all the baggage. He was my friend before being my first love.

Reflexively, we stroll over to the couch from opposite sides, taking a seat next to each other in the middle. Normally, I'd put distance between us on principle, but there is this unspoken understanding that dealing with my mom's death is hard for the both of us. He doesn't hold my hand or put an arm around me, but with the length of his body just *there* pressed against me, it's merely his existence that makes the situation a little bit more bearable.

"I wish I had come home sooner," tumbles out of my mouth, and I don't know where it comes from. All I know is, staring at my mom's ashes makes me wish for all sorts of things, usually involving time travel.

"It's okay. Your mom understood."

The tension that I try the hardest to pretend isn't there resurfaces with a vengeance. Caiden doesn't know *this* pain. Being back makes me feel that regardless of all the success, I was still kept in the dark about so much. Who was my mom more partial to protect? Me or Caiden? With me so far away, how can I argue with her decision?

"My mom liked you more than me."

Why does saying that feel so good when it's such a terrible thing to say?

"Hailey, she didn't. She loved you, trust me."

I shrug, leaping off the sofa, unable to stare at the urn any longer. "She resented me for leaving, didn't she?" My lips sputter, and I fear it might be the sob I don't want anyone to see. I move around the couch, pacing the expansive hallway, back and forth, from the front door to the kitchen entrance.

"Why didn't she tell me about anything that was going on here? About *you*, about our friends?"

I yank my head around to stare at Caiden, who still gifts me a smile of reassurance. It's a remedy I remember all too well, and the sight is what keeps my voice level. "It's so wonderful to find out she was so talkative about me to everyone in town, and that she even mentioned my book." I release a sigh, rubbing at my eyes again. "Did you know she never asked me about my writing? It was always me feeding her news and updates. I felt like I was forcing her, sometimes even boring her with it all. Trying to convince her that I left for a good reason."

Really, I was probably trying to convince myself more than her.

He shakes his head, rising from the couch but keeping his distance. "That's not it at all. She probably didn't know how to express herself. It was obvious she missed you, but I could tell she wanted you to be happy. We were all fragile then, including me. She did support your decision. She was proud of you. I know that much."

"How can you say that?" I ask. I always wondered if my mom resented me for leaving, and I wondered if I resented my mom for not reading my book or caring enough to ask. She wanted me to stay, to keep the diner going, to keep our legacy alive. I was never supposed to run away and chase dreams.

On our weekly calls we'd only talk about the diner, random customer stories, how her doctor appointments were going, what new show she was into, or I would scold her for her long working hours. But she never gave up any relevant details to me. It felt like an unspoken agreement that we didn't talk about Caiden and our friends, and I never asked about them because I was scared it'd sound like I thought I made the wrong choice to leave. I wanted to show her I was strong.

He says she kept herself tight-lipped for our protection, but it was because of this constant lack of information that I was terrified of what this place holds for me. It made it hard to come home. It turned home into the land of the unknown.

"She's the only other person I know who's read your book," slices into my thoughts.

My jaw falls slack. "No, she did not read my book. She would have said something."

He nods, walking toward me. "Yes, she did."

"You're messing with my head, Caid." A sniffle sneaks out of my nose without my permission.

Now with my mom gone, I want to be able to let my resentment go, because it feels wrong, but I haven't been able to. Yet here he is, dangling emotional freedom from my mother in front of me.

He nods more forcefully this time and walks across the room to the corner bookcase near the stairs. It takes him a matter of seconds to snag a book from the third shelf before he's heading back toward me. He extends the book out once he's looming over me.

My hand shakes as I lift it to meet his. I pull the paperback from his hands and there it is, as clear as day, my first edition paperback. It's not nearly as battered as Caiden's copy, but it's still well-used. I blink back my tears. It's been here the whole time, and I never noticed.

"She really read it?" I whisper. "Why didn't she ever tell me that?"

"I think your mom didn't know how to talk to you about it. She figured out what I did, though. We only talked about it once. It was the moment I knew she had read it." His smile ignites a twitch to my mouth as I listen, enthralled. "One day, I was delivering a package that had arrived at the post office for her, and there I stood in your kitchen, holding this heavy box of who-knows-what; that's when she asked me something I'll never forget."

He pauses, watching me with a comical look as I eagerly ask, "What did she say?"

"She asked me if it was true I'd climb up the gutter on the

side of the house and sneak into your bedroom at night to tangle myself up in your sheets."

I screech a loud belt of laughter as my skin flushes everywhere. "She did not ask you that! What did you say?"

He laughs, too, and the deep sound releases in a relaxed rumble before he says, "Oh, hells yeah she did. I don't think I had been more embarrassed in my entire life. I almost dropped the box I was holding, but I looked her straight in the eyes and said... *Yes ma'am, I did.*"

My hands come up to my face, shielding it from him with one palm and my book. "You did not!" I giggle, knowing that he's enjoying this story way too much.

"I did. Your mom laughed, and then told me to mow the lawn. I didn't argue at that point."

We both laugh and laugh, and it's the best I have felt in such a long time.

I shake my head in disbelief at my own book, knowing now that she read it, even if she never told me. Maybe she was supportive. Maybe she was proud of me. It's enough to have me not beating myself up *as much* anymore.

Caiden watches me carefully, reaching out for my hand, and begins tugging me in the direction of the stairs. My good mood dissolves as I yank it back. "What are you doing?"

He chuckles warmly but turns around with a serious stare. "You asked me what I was doing here. Well, I'm really here to help you face the upstairs. I can't have you sleeping on that old couch anymore."

My brows knit together at his tone. "Caiden, I'm fine. Seriously."

"Then why don't you just go sleep in your old bed?"

It's a logical question. I strum my fingers against my bottom lip as I try to gather an explanation. I don't have one.

"It's complicated. Please, Caid. Let's just leave it."

He shakes his head. "No way. You need to face this now or you never will."

I hate that his words singe my pride. My eyes fall to the

floor; I want to move but can't find the courage to.

It isn't until I see Caiden's hand fall into my line of vision that I perk up.

"C'mon, Hails. I'm here to help you get through this. It's the least I can do."

I want to tell him that I do want the help, but I won't. Instead, I let my hand fall into his.

He leads me up the steps, and it isn't until we hit the hallway platform that we stop just short of my bedroom.

"Your bedroom first, then your mom's."

It's a cajoling request, but pretty close to a polite demand. It should piss me off, but the fact he cares enough to know I need to be forced lifts the weight of the world off my shoulders that little bit.

"Okay," I mumble, knowing I can't turn back.

My palm falls flat against the white wood of the door, and the icy chill that it throws back against my skin has me wanting to run.

"It's all right, Hailey." Caiden places his large hand over mine on the door and guides my hand forward as we both push the door open.

A stale, overly sweet breeze hits my face. When I step inside, it's like I've stepped back in time. The sugary smell is most definitely the residue from all of the half-filled bottles of body spray sitting on my vanity, untouched for years. I take another step inside, holding Caiden's hand securely. He's less than a step behind me.

I can sense him diligently watching me as my eyes scan over the room, taking in everything I walked away from, all of it right where I left it. The room screams of a simpler time, *a good time*.

My walls are plastered with happy photos of friends, the same five weirdos I've known since the beginning. My eyes dart to my bed, my powder blue down comforter haphazardly thrown over the mattress, dotted with white fluffy pillows. I gulp at the sight but find the memories of Caiden and me fumbling as teens under those sheets twisting around the new memory of Caiden's story about my mom asking about those sheets all too hilarious, and surprisingly calming to my thoughts.

"I can't believe my mom blatantly asked you about that bedroom scene in my book," I blurt out.

He chuckles, and I just love the sight of him in my room, even if he isn't exactly how I remember him. There's something about having him in this space with his laughter bouncing off the walls and delightfully dancing into my ears that feels like a slice of normal, or at least a *new* normal of sorts.

"I can't believe she did, either. It was the only way I knew she read the book," he jokes.

I squeeze his hand as I walk toward my vanity mirror, plucking a photo wedged in the frame. A laugh skirts through my lips as I wave the photo at Caiden's reflection. "I should have written this in my book."

"What's that?" he asks, walking up from behind, pressing his front to my back, realizing he's already staring at me in the reflection, his eyes curious and wanting, boring into mine.

"This photo," I quip, talking to our reflections, hating that my eyes love what they see and that my skin heats with his body brushing against mine. "It's from senior prom when my mom chaperoned. What a disaster. She caught you and Brandon trying to spike the punch." I laugh, and a sniffle tries taking advantage of the moment. I breathe it back, letting go of Caiden's hand to wipe my nose, my eyes falling back onto the photo. My prom gown was a dark purple sweetheart dress that stopped at my knees. My purple Converse sneakers matched my dress, and so did Caiden's purple tie. I try for a laugh again, because my mom is standing behind us with what I can now recall as a hilariously forced smile. This was taken moments after being caught, and we were escorted off the premises where Caiden and I got into our own trouble elsewhere. I pull in a deep breath to calm my rising blush.

Caiden laughs, "Holy shit. I remember that. She nearly dragged us out by our ears, but she kept the whiskey for herself."

My head falls back, pressing against Caiden's chest, releasing a string of laughter at the fact that is totally something my mom would do.

When I hear the sounds of our laughter twisting around each other after discussing one of my most favorite memories, my eyes begin to water. I tense, straighten myself out as I blink the tears back, wondering why this rush is coming over me. My sudden gulp nearly bounces back up my throat as a sob. I try to keep control. I try for a deep breath, and it must be noticeable because Caiden's eyes shift to worry as he asks, "What are you doing?"

There's no use lying.

"Trying not to cry," I breathe out shakily, still blinking while repeatedly wiping at the corners of my eyes. I don't want to cry in front of him. Not like this. I save these cries for my morning shower or the last five minutes before sleep. Not in front of people. They make me too vulnerable. They show the world the pain I'm trying to hide.

Caiden takes hold of my wrists, his grip gentle and reassuring. "It's okay to cry, Hailey." I shake my head, and he shakes his right back as he tugs me toward my bed, sitting us on the edge as he repeats, "Yes, it is. It's okay to cry. You need to cry." He pauses, leaning forward, gifting me a smirk when he says, "*I won't tell.*"

I want to smile, but it gives way to what I was holding back. The sob just beyond my lips escapes, freeing everything I've been fighting. I lean into his chest, releasing my tears as his arms come around me, encasing me affectionately.

When we were kids and just sandbox friends, I'd tell him my deepest, darkest secrets of playground gossip, and every time he'd say "*I won't tell*" with an adorable shake of his big head. Those same words carried into our teens when we finally confessed how we felt about each other; he had chided, *"It's okay to like me. I won't tell,"* as we sat in the bed of his pickup truck at our secret spot. Those words became a running joke in our relationship from that point on.

It's those three words that convince me that it's okay to be myself. It's okay to let go. And it's okay because it's Caiden that makes it so.

I'm crying and the tears sting as they fall, but the burning trail they leave is as painful as the tears are cathartic.

After nearly fifteen minutes of Caiden allowing me to cry into his arms, he helps me deal with my old bedroom.

Within a couple hours, we've sifted through different items, plucking them from the walls, drawers, and shelves, facing the memories rather than ignoring them.

As we talked through each one, we'd sometimes laugh, or even argue, and every time it felt effortless and fun. As we kept going through each memory, the next one became easier than the last, and even though this wasn't me directly dealing with my mom's death, it felt like the first step. It made the house less terrifying and more like home.

It makes it all easier to face.

As we sit on the floor cross-legged facing each other, nearly nose to nose as we argue over the details of where the stop sign hanging over my bed came from and who stole it, I realize it's the most comfortable we've been together in a long while. He's being the funny, charming, annoyingly witty Caiden I remember, and nowhere near the tempting asshole he was last night. It's enough to have me almost wanting him to kiss me, especially every time he tugs at his bottom lip. It's moments like THIS that make me want to give in, not tirelessly tense moments after parties. This is when he has me in the palm of his hand without realizing it.

Caiden's eyes have also been periodically darting to my lips, but it's as if we're both finally showing equal restraint. I think we're learning that maybe just being around each other is enough, that is, until his phone rings.

There's nothing remarkable to the sound, but his relaxed, carefree smile fades quickly with hearing it. We've been getting lost in the flawless, natural ebb and flow we have.

He rises quickly and shoots an apologetic, frantic look my way. He pulls his phone out of his pocket and actually exits my room to answer. His steps down the stairs muffle his "Hello" into the phone.

The girlfriend. It's got to be.

I rise from the floor, for once not feeling so torn up about it. The news isn't shocking any longer. It's instead this thing I've been forced to get used to. That includes the pain shooting out like little bolts of lightning from my heart. It's not that I like it, or that I'm okay with it; it's more that it's something I've come to terms with, or at least I'm trying to.

I grab the items from the floor that we were talking about: my panda stuffed animal he won me at the fair on our first date, the necklace I made in the art class that I failed because apparently jewelry wasn't included in the semester's final assignment, and the mood ring CeeCee gave me as a best friend present when we both got PE together sophomore year.

I toss the objects back onto my vanity, glancing at my bed, thinking maybe I do feel better about sleeping up here now.

I smile, thinking that at least that was worth the day.

I head back downstairs to see Caiden pacing my living room, talking into the phone.

"No, I'm sorry… it's not like that. It isn't. We're just friends… No, I'm not working today. I know I said I'd call, but I lost track of time… I know, sweetie. I didn't realize you were gonna surprise me."

It's then that Caiden sees me standing on the stairs, his eyes going wide.

I want to tell him to take the conversation outside. I have at least that much self-respect. Just because I can endure the pain, doesn't mean I willingly sacrifice myself to the heartbreak gods. Nope.

"I gotta go. I'm on my way. Sorry I wasn't there. See you soon. Bye."

His eyes are piercing as they pin me to the spot the moment he hangs up. I can't tell if they are pleading, or apologetic, or downright heated. I give him a shrug.

We have to be okay, don't we? I mean, I won't throw away an entire day of progress between us just because his girlfriend called. We were actually being normal.

"It's totally fine," I blurt out.

"But it's not," he says, moving his free hand to tug that bottom lip again, which has me licking mine. This is when I look away. *Get a grip.*

I trot down the stairs and scoot past him to the front door. We both know from his conversation that he has to leave.

"Your girlfriend back in town?" I ask, trying to be as sincere as possible.

He moves slowly toward the door. "Yeah, she is. She wasn't supposed to be here for a few days, but I guess she came home early to surprise me."

"How cute."

"Haileey…"

I wave my hand between us, dismissing it, although I'm mentally clawing at a sense of calm as I try to reply steadily, "Ya know, besides dealing with you and your ridiculousness last night, I really appreciate you stopping by today."

He's mute as he watches me. The silence rattles my nerves, so I keep rambling. "I mean, I think I needed the help, and I'm glad you were the one. Just, uh—*thanks.*"

Taking a small step forward, putting us dangerously close in what seems to be *his* comfort zone that is somehow morphing into mine, too, he lifts his hand to my chin, forcing me to look up at him. "I'm glad I came, too. I know things are shitty, but I'm always here for you. I'm just trying to figure this all out and do the right thing." He sighs. "And I don't know what that is. I wish I didn't have to go."

I shake my head and reply, "That's not my problem, Caiden." The words slip out of my mouth so eerily calm that I think I deserve an academy award for my performance. I can't take it when he makes it about the choices *he* has to make when I'm here just trying to survive. I'm screaming on the inside.

Caiden's lips twitch remorsefully. He closes the distance to press a chaste kiss against my forehead before saying, "Please tell me you're not going to sleep on the couch tonight."

"I won't be sleeping on the couch tonight," I confirm, smiling just enough to show him that I like the fact he's not arguing with me.

He grins. "Good."

He releases my chin and leaves to apparently go do the *right thing*. Whatever that means.

10

———

Standing behind the diner counter, I bend my body to the right to stretch my spine. It's so tweaked from sleeping on the couch, which I hate to admit I still slept on the night before. I did in fact walk into my old bedroom and consider sleeping there. However, after staring at the walls with old memories and the floor now decorated with new ones, I decided the progress I'd made that day was good enough and fell asleep on the couch.

In case we need to do a system check: yes, I'm still a mess.

"CeeCee, does this town have a chiropractor, or am I still so in the middle of nowhere, I'd have to go to Denver for that?"

She directs a disapproving stare and huff my way as she leans against the counter during the after-lunch lull. "Caiden was supposed to convince you to sleep in an actual bed. I'm really losing faith in that boy."

Damn her.

I straighten up, rolling my eyes. "Could you at least try to hide your shameful master plans from me? Coercing Caiden to come to my house is not something I want to be able to pin blame on. It'd be nice if I could go on pretending that my friends aren't all betting against me."

A small giggle escapes her as she goes back to picking at her nails. "On the contrary, we just want you to be okay. For the most part you're yourself, but don't think it's going unnoticed that you're carrying a pretty heavy weight on those peckish shoulders of yours. Speaking of, eat a burger, will you?" She jabs her finger into my gut, making me laugh. "Anyway, I know that oaf is probably part of this weight, but we all know he's the only one who can fix this and you—I mean. Not you. That's not what I mean. He just—"

I release a long breath while bending forward again to stretch my back. "This is what I'm talking about. Some things you just don't need to say, Cee."

My mind tailspins to memories of yesterday afternoon and how ridiculously unfortunate it is that CeeCee is right. Caiden is a remedy that can't be replaced.

Have I mentioned I'm not only a mess, but also an utter walking disaster?

What I thought sounded like her joining giggles is suddenly choked off. "Hailey, why don't you just call it a day?"

I stand up straight, worried I took my playfulness too far. "No—no, sorry. I didn't mean it in a mean way. I was kidding. Scold me as much as you want. How about I go make sure everyone has coffee?" CeeCee's brows furrow with pained confusion, and I can't help but laugh. "What? Is everything okay?"

Her eyes dart over my shoulder and then back to me. "Nothing. I think maybe you should just go home. You're tired, and you obviously need some rest. Here, let me show you the side door, have you—"

"Why are you being so weird? Did I do something wrong?" I ask, moving past her toward the coffee pot while tightening my apron.

"Hailey, just do yourself a favor and go home." This time it's a stern demand.

I swivel around, totally confused by the 180-degree change in mood. "Did I make a mistake? I'll fix it," I say, concerned, almost whining, not wanting to ruin the only place that doesn't make me feel batshit crazy.

She shakes her head as her lips are pressed into a hard line.

Then the sound of two dings from the diner door signal why she was trying to get me to leave.

CeeCee gasps, "I'll get it."

I shake my head, examining the sprite couple entering, not denying for one second that Caiden and Kristen look good together, but what are they doing here?

I can do this, can't I?

I wipe my mind of Caiden being my life remedy because right now, the sight before me only causes a sore throb in my chest.

I shouldn't look into us hanging out the day before. We're just friends, and he was being as loyal as he could. I should be thankful and not lie to myself regarding him helping me cope with the loss of my mom. It's not in my best interest to put emotions, want, and need into a situation that might not have any of those, at all.

I pull in a deep breath and whisper, "Stop trying to protect me, Cee. I can handle this. Oh, and next time, just tell me the jackass is at the door."

She forces a smile. "But the fact is, you don't have to deal with him *and her*. Let me get this table, Hail."

"It's fine," I retort as I walk over, smiling, which is a little harder to do than I expected as I pull two menus from the podium.

"Hi there. Table for two?"

Caiden's eyes widen at the sight of me, and I wonder if it has anything to do with him doing *the right thing*. Pretty sure it doesn't. His eyes dart erratically over my body, and I try for another pull of oxygen.

Maybe I'm being the weird one? I have to consider that as

an option, right? This is just how things are now. I tell myself to get over it. He's not mine. He's hers. I need to respect that. *He* needs to respect that.

I pull my attention away from him, noticing Kristen doesn't seem as perky as she was when I first met her. Her eyes look a bit stale as they slide to mine, although her tight smile is polite.

"Yes, please," she hums, "guess it makes sense we'd be seeing you here eventually, huh? So much makes sense now." She mumbles that last bit before speaking up again. "I've been missing the pie around here, but for some reason I haven't been able to get Caiden to bring me."

I nod, realizing that not caring is a non-option. My eyes immediately fall to Caiden's hand holding hers.

I'm totally okay with this. *Gulp.*

Maybe I should have let CeeCee handle this. It's another moment I could have let my pride take the hit and my heart get a rest.

I force a smile. "Glad you could come back."

I'm the worst actress known to mankind, because I'm pretty sure I said that through gritted teeth.

As I walk them to a table, this experience has me missing the anonymity of LA.

Of course, Caiden would avoid taking his girlfriend to the diner. I wouldn't want to see me either if I were him or her. However, there's an edge to this interaction I can't quite place my finger on.

"Here you go."

I place the menus down on the table and watch them shimmy in, sitting opposite of each other.

"Anything to drink?" I ask, pulling out my pad of paper.

They don't look up, and I swear Caiden's going to speak, but Kristen beats him to the punch. She folds the menu closed, places it back on the table, and replies with a sigh. "Ya know? We'll just take two coffees and two pies. I don't think we'll be staying too long."

I see Caiden flinch, but I don't bother giving him my attention.

I nod. "Okay, coming right up. I'll be right back."

I don't make it three paces before they begin mindlessly bickering. That's when I hear Kristen whisper, *"Why won't you talk to me?"* and Caiden's reply of, *"Not here."* And then her frustrated huff of, *"I see what's going on."*

I'm frantic when I get to the kitchen, and I pretend not to notice CeeCee peeking from behind the fryer.

I might even huff and puff as I place two pieces of pie with whipped cream on a tray and move to get the coffee.

"Is everything okay?" CeeCee chirps a little too pleasantly as she comes to my side.

Clank. Clink. The sound of ceramic coffee mugs and plates clamor as I anxiously prepare the order.

"Fine. Everything is fine. I just wish I could figure out what's going on. It's all awkward turtle out there."

"She doesn't really know," CeeCee exclaims firmly but quietly.

Clank... crash...

The mug slips from my hand and breaks on the tile floor. CeeCee rushes to pick up the shards of broken ceramic, and I'm still frozen to the spot.

"I'm sorry, Cee, I should get that." I bend down to help, but her hand is on my shoulder pushing me back.

She's at least smiling. "I got it." It's a firm *do-not-argue-with-me* tone.

I'm pretty sure I know what her earlier words meant, but I need to hear her say it.

"What do you mean she doesn't know?"

She lifts a dainty shoulder. "Kristen doesn't know you and Caiden dated, or the history. I mean, she knows we all grew up together and you and Caid were close, but she has no idea how close."

If I didn't think this whole heartbreak thing could sting

any more.

Is that why tensions are high?

CeeCee must read my face as she shakes her head. "Stop thinking whatever you're thinking."

"Then why not mention it? Us, I mean. Don't you think it's sort of strange that he wouldn't tell his girlfriend the truth about the girl he previously dated?"

"Why? So she could realize she'd never live up to the girl he's loved since he was in the third grade? So he would have to explain the initials tattooed on his arm? He was trying to save her the heartache, yet at the same time, make it easier for him to talk about you." I release a huff and roll my eyes before she continues. "Kristen's kind of new in town, and he didn't want to not be able to talk about you. If she knew you were his ex-girlfriend, he'd probably never be able to gush about you. None of us agreed to it at first, but we also weren't willing to avoid the topic when it came to you, so we just went with it. Please cut the guy some slack. He's struggling, too, ya know?"

"He loves her, so it doesn't matter."

Her brows scrunch together mockingly. "I'm sure he does in his own way, but do you really think he's ever stopped loving you?"

"You're not helping, Cee. I know you think you're doing the right thing, but I need you to stop. It might seem crazy to you, but I want him to be happy, and if Kristen makes him happy, I want him to stay with her." I sigh. "I'm going to leave all over again. No one seems to remember that part. I'm a ticking time bomb of heartache for him. I may be hurting now, but it'll be nothing like the collateral damage I could leave when the time comes. It'd be the same pain all over again if you keep carrying on like this."

She doesn't like this answer. I can tell by the puckering of her lips, like she just tasted something sour.

"It's okay, Cee. I'll be fine. We'll all be fine. Just let me and Caiden deal with this mess on our own. Sure, it sucks, but it's fine. I'll be fine. I'm fine."

Fine. Fine. Fine.

I place two new cups of coffee on the tray and lift it to get my order moving as I try to shimmy past her.

"Do you still love him?" CeeCee asks, and she almost says it too loud.

I turn around to look at her, and her eyes are demanding and sincere, glowing and wide. They reflect that she knows the truth I can't utter out loud.

I clench my jaw and turn back around, leaving her without the answer that she already knows.

Damn this town.

Saying those words, or not saying them, was harder than I thought. With each step I try to remind myself that Caiden is not the reason I'm here. I don't want to fume over the fact that he never told the truth about us. I just don't want to care.

When I step up to the booth, an eerie layer of discomfort comes over us, and I can't tell who put it there or where it's coming from. Maybe it's because "Ms. Brunette Sunshine" isn't smiling anymore. She might actually be flinging a bit of intensity at me through her hazel eyes, but they also look red and tired.

I place the plate in front of her and sneak a glare at Caiden, though he may not know why, but I'm torn away seconds later.

"—This isn't right," she says as she points to the whipped cream. The tone feels like a jab, but I shake my reflexive need to be defensive.

"Excuse me?" I ask, taking a large gulp of air, confused by Caiden's flat stare pinned on her from across the table.

"This pie," she sneers, and the waitress in me detects her frustration, but I can't tell if it's personal or if it really has to do with her pie. "I can't have whipped cream. Your mom knew how I liked it. I don't know why I assumed you would."

Pow.

Why does hearing the word *mom* from her mouth feel like

a form of ammunition. I want to be nice, hell, I even want to care for Kristen's side in all this, but in that moment I can't. It's as if she purposefully nicked my Achilles' heel.

I stumble a bit, her words knocking me off balance. "Uh—"

"Kristen. That's enough." Caiden finally speaks, and I know that tone.

"What?" she says shamelessly through her own defying look.

This argument is surely between the two of them, but why do I feel so heavily involved?

This burn is new. This burn hurts.

I grab her plate and leave.

It's too much. I decided. I drop off the plate on the counter before running to the back office, collapsing into a chair, needing... needing—I don't know what I need.

CeeCee enters moments later, and although her flailing arms mean she cares, she only overwhelms me more.

"So, can I at least admit I didn't know she was coming?"

I shake my head, thrown by the statement, but remember that being the queen of gossip usually involves knowing the whereabouts of your best friend's ex-boyfriend's new-ish-but-not-really girlfriend.

"Cee, relax. No need to defend the situation."

"What was that about?"

"Apparently I don't know Kristen's fucking pie order."

CeeCee can't seem to hold back the mocking curve to her lip when she hears me curse. Kill me now.

"She mentioned my mom. It felt weird." I sigh, my head falling into my hands.

"She what?"

I shrug. "It doesn't matter. It's stupid. I just wish I didn't feel like such a stranger in a place that's supposed to be home. Especially now, since apparently my entire backstory has been hidden away."

"Stop. It's not like that. It's just Kristen. She's not blind, ya know? It's hard not to notice when you and Caiden are in the same room." She lifts an apologetic shoulder before going on. "But let them handle it."

I stand, shaking my head. "Do me a favor and get the girl a new piece of pie. I think I'm going to take you up on leaving."

I'm about to move past her, but her guilty grin of gritted teeth stops me.

"Soo… I guess this would be a really bad time for me to mention that Gabe just stopped by to see you?"

"CEE-CEEEE!" I screech.

"Bad timing, I know—I know. I swear I didn't plan this situation this time."

"I can't deal with all this right now. It's too much. I repeat, TOO MUCH." The tone of my voice has reached a strange high-pitched squeak that could quite possibly break the sound barrier.

"Do you want me to find a way to get rid of him?"

I untie my apron and throw it at her face. "No. It's whatever."

"That's the spirit. I'll take care of your tables. I could accidentally drop pie onto Kristen's lap if you want."

I laugh, pausing to shoot her a sweet, *aw-you-shouldn't-have* pout. "You'd do that for me?"

"How do you people in LA respond, oh yeah—*Duh*. Of course, I would."

It's tempting to accept, but I have to remember that although tensions are high, no one should have to deal with the pain of an erratic heart, Kristen included. Ugh. I wish I didn't have a conscience. "I'll have to pass on the pie-spill."

I wave at her as I trail outside. I try to find a sense of relief in the string of giggles that involuntarily leaves my lips as I attempt to leave the chaos behind. I pull my hair tie free from my hair, running my fingers through the waves before stepping out of the kitchen.

I'm about to glance back at Caiden's table, but I'm a bit awestruck by Gabe's smile when he sees me.

Gosh, I want to like that smile. I want to like something new.

From behind his back, he pulls out a single orange wallflower. I was on the verge of smiling, but I falter at the sight of it.

"Hey, Hailey. I remember seeing these flowers in your hair growing up. It only seemed right to bring you one when I passed some on my way here."

I'd love the gesture if it wasn't the same type of flower that Caiden would get me in the mornings before school, or days on the lake. Little does Gabe know that Caiden was the one placing the flowers delicately in my hair all those years ago.

I shakily grab it from his hand. "Thank you," I whisper.

Kristen suddenly rushes blindly past us and out the door without a word. Whatever argument was going on at their table must not have gone well.

My eyes shoot to Caiden, who isn't rushing after her but power walking toward the door. His shoulder collides with Gabe's just enough to cause Gabe's footing to shift.

Although Gabe has said he doesn't want anything more to do with the drama-filled history anymore, he doesn't seem to hesitate when it comes to confrontation.

"You got a problem, Anderson?"

I cringe. Caiden almost makes it to the door. He swivels around and shrugs. "Why would I have a problem, Samuels?"

I twist my fingers around the delicate stem of the flower as I watch.

Gabe grins, and there's a hidden wickedness to it as he tilts his head. "You really want me to say it? Because I will."

Caiden releases a defeated huff… and I hate it. He knows he can't argue. He won't give an answer, just like I wouldn't give CeeCee one. Instead of darting his eyes to mine, they fall onto the orange flower in my hand.

He shakes his head as a way of responding before thrusting the diner door open to leave.

"Okay, so this wasn't supposed to go like that," Gabe says as he turns to me.

When my smile is weaker than I'd like, his falters. "It's okay," I reply, trying to recover. "Thank you for the flower. I do love them."

He presses his lips together into a hard line, his smile curious and probing. "It's kind of my way of saying sorry. Can I borrow you from work for a moment?"

His tone catches my attention. I want to tell him to take me away for the rest of the day.

"Sure. I was on my way out anyway."

He extends his hand out to me, and I place mine in his. Although his skin is warm and inviting, it feels foreign, but his firm hold is enough to have me hoping.

He pulls me outside to the parking lot, and there's one thing I can't ignore as we cross the tarmac. Caiden and Kristen are continuing their argument next to Caiden's truck. I don't dare look, but even fifty feet away, I can hear what they're saying as I trail behind Gabe.

"There's something you're not telling me. I can tell. It's the way you look at her."

"It's not what you think," Caiden replies, and his frustration is so clear that I can just imagine him tugging on that bottom lip.

"I think it's exactly what I think. Why won't you talk to me?"

With one final guttural sigh Caiden replies, *"This isn't working."*

It's the last thing I hear Caiden say before I hear a truck door and the screeching of tires as they leave the diner parking lot.

"Hailey…"

My head flies up, not realizing I was staring at the ground

in concentration as I eavesdropped, forgetting that I was holding Gabe's hand. I pull it free from his grasp as we make it to his dark gray SUV. My eyes widen curiously when I see through the window his vehicle filled to the brim with boxes.

"I know it's last minute and this makes me sort of a shithead. I'd hate to prove Caiden right in any way—"

"You're leaving?" I gasp. I'm jealous rather than upset.

He runs a hand through his hair, his smile sad and slight. "Uh… yeah. Last-minute change of plans. My sister has to be on campus at NYU earlier than we thought. I didn't want to rush the drive, and she has to be there in about a week."

"When are you leaving?"

He shrugs. "Um, tomorrow."

My brows scrunch together, and he actually lifts his hand to smooth out my forehead. I fight a smile. "I didn't plan any of this," he explains. "I also didn't plan on you coming into town and me being given this opportunity to try and win your heart. But let's be honest here, Hailey, that heart is behind a fortress."

"Is not!" I bark too defensively, and even I can't help but laugh at hearing my tone.

He tuts comically and leans forward. "Kiss me, then."

I laugh, shaking my head. "I don't remember you being this confident in high school."

"I'm kind of under a time crunch here, Hailey."

My lips twitch as I stare at his mouth anxiously. "You kiss me."

"As long as you say so."

He doesn't hesitate. He leans in that little bit to press his lips to mine. I allow his rough possession, and I feel terrible that I can feel his need to convince me. It's in his strokes. They tell me to give him a chance.

When Gabe pulls his lips from mine, we're both smiling, but it's his tiny huff that has the corner of my mouth twitching comically.

"Nothing?" he asks.

"Almost," I confess.

"Maybe I should try again?" He presses his lips against mine one more time, and I can't stop laughing as I peel myself away, pressing a palm against his firm chest. Our chortles wrap around each other next to the SUV that will whisk him away soon.

"Gabriel Samuels! You're persistent, I'll give you that."

"I'll admit, I knew I didn't have a chance, but I figured I had to try. At least I can say I kissed Hailey Elwood."

"Is that a thing? Because I promise you it isn't."

"In this town it is, trust me."

I roll my eyes, and he tugs at my arm playfully. "But Hailey, if you're ever in New York, I want you to call me. I'm serious." I grin at his cajoling tone, which causes his confidence to falter in a chuckle, as if he catches himself. "I mean, you never know. Maybe we'd have a chance in a different state."

"It's possible. How about we agree to be friends?"

He releases a long breath. "Okay, but I can't promise I won't try again someday."

I shrug. "By the time you see me, I hope you've found someone else. Someone who deserves you. I'm kind of a mess right now."

He tweaks a brow. "Can I speak openly as a friend then?"

"If you must," I reply, knowing exactly what's coming.

"It's Caiden, isn't it?"

Knowing Gabe will be hitting the road and onto a new path that probably won't be crossing mine anytime soon, I say, "It's lots of things. Caiden is just a variable my heart can't seem to shake."

"Write about it maybe?" He laughs.

"I tried!" I retort, as we share one final moment before we hug and say our goodbyes.

Oh God, I tried. I tried so damn hard.

11

I slam my notebook shut, needing to take a breather. My hand hurts from scribbling all evening. I could use my laptop, but it always feels more cathartic putting pen to paper.

Sometimes the words you have in your head are harder to get out than you expect. Also, it's hard to write a work of fiction when the words that are fighting to escape tell a story you lived; a story your heart guided; but a story your mind decided. How is it possible to write the next book, when the first one had a beginning, middle, and end, yet this one has yet to begin at all? I shake my head. I don't want it to be about me. I don't want it to be about the guy who made me choose, and I don't want it to be about the choices I made. Yet here I am, picking up the pieces right where the story left off.

Today provided for a lot of literary material, though I don't exactly know what I'm writing or where it's going. Who am I kidding? When I really break it down, today was a disaster, and maybe those many pages of notes reflect that. I'm hopeful that chaos can come off as beautiful.

I just wish the tornado that is my life would pass on through, or let's hope it whisks me away to Oz soon because I'm not sure how much more my sanity can take. The yellow brick road sounds a lot more appealing than PineCrest right about now.

Caiden's argument with his girlfriend is still ringing in my head, and I'm trying not to give it any clout. His white lies are not my problem, no matter how much they affect that beating life force inside my chest. I just hate that I'm the white lie.

Meow.

I roll my eyes at the sound. I'm one glass of wine into my night and not sure how much more patience I can muster this evening.

I examine my half-full glass, or half-empty glass, depending on your perspective. I'd rather not admit my current disposition.

Personally, I think I deserve a medal. I waited until well after sunset before doing anything with myself, which means drinking. It's the most appropriate thing I've done so far with my day. That, and saying my farewells to Gabe, who managed to escape town before me.

I try not to think of his phone number nestled sweetly in my phone, or the text message he sent when he hit the state line with his sister.

Meoooow.

I can only ignore that sound for so long before it transitions into a ghostlike shriek. I know from experience. I gulp down the last bit from my glass before placing it on the mantel and strolling to the screen door.

Soot, my furry love child, sits perched and perfect as he watches me approach, and if I'd commit completely to my insanity, I'd say his eyebrow is tweaked in such a way as to imply, *"Excuse me human, I'm waiting..."*

Wait, do cats even have eyebrows?

Someone admit me to an asylum, stat.

"C'mon, you rascal," I utter as I pull the door open.

Soot scurries inside and is quick to rub against my bare leg before strutting through the foyer. Even he can't soothe the itching unease that riddles my entire body.

I pull in a deep breath as I watch him make his way

around the room. He almost seems more at home than me, and I try not to be jealous of a cat.

He leaps onto the back of the couch, twerking his tail back and forth with each step before making it to the armrest. He jumps confidently from the couch onto the desk nestled in the corner, knocking a pile of papers over.

I don't even flinch. I just eye him and the mess now on the floor.

"Perfect. Just what I need." I shrug.

He doesn't care. He licks at his paws from the corner perch, as if acting like I did in fact deserve that.

"Did I ever tell you I'm not much of a cat person?"

Meow. He tilts his head to the side, stopping his licking to examine me mockingly.

"Yeah, and that I'm in the market for a new coat."

Soot throws his body onto the desk suddenly, and I hate how adorable it is.

Mew, he beckons.

"Does this act work on everyone else? Because I am by far harder to convince."

He rolls over again, letting out more *mews* as he stretches.

I roll my eyes. "I guess you're right. I'm the biggest pushover ever."

Caiden comes to mind as I approach Soot, scratching at his chin, igniting his purr.

"Don't tell anyone, especially Caiden, that I pander to your needs so quickly. Also, I'd like it if you kept our snuggles secret, too."

I rub at his belly, chuckling, because although sleeping on the couch is doing a number on my back, Soot has been curled in my arms most nights now.

Meoow.

I nod as if we just negotiated a merger. "Yeah, I agree. Let's be more productive. What do you suggest? Wait, don't answer that."

Meowww.

I grunt, eyeing the desk and the mess of papers shoved into the small shelves of the old wooden antique.

"But I don't really want to go through *her* stuff."

Soot stretches again, knocking another smaller pile to the floor.

"Okay—okay! Fine! I know I need to. First, more wine."

I grab for my glass off the mantel, and my childish stomps spook Soot, causing him to leap off the desk and wander the room.

"Sheesh," I mumble, until something on the floor catches my eye.

Caiden's name. Caiden's name scribbled over and over.

I place the glass next to me on the floor as I lean onto my knees to grab a tiny booklet peeking from the pile of papers.

It's my mother's checkbook.

Soot reappears, rubbing against my leg as he releases another *meow* and then nudges the small booklet in my hands.

It's a pad of checks, or I should say, used to be. The receipts that were written for who the checks were given to are the only pages left. My eyes go wide as I see only one name listed under every check number. *Caiden Anderson.* The amounts vary. Some as little as forty dollars to a check that's listed at five hundred dollars.

I stand, filling with an odd sort of rage. What is Caiden doing taking money from my mother? There seems so much more to this than meets the eye. As if this life in PineCrest didn't already hold so many secrets, this one feels like a blow to my gut.

I rise from the floor, flipping through the booklet. Nearly every page has his name on it. I fume, feeling my face heat irrationally. I stuff the booklet in my back pocket while sliding my hand frantically over the surfaces of the messy desk, carelessly knocking more papers to the floor, and I can hear my own shallow breath reverberating around me.

Water gathers in the corners of my eyes, and I don't know

why I'm so upset. It feels like betrayal. Was Caiden borrowing money from my mom and never going to tell me? I find another checkbook, this one in a leather case. This time fresh checks fill the front of this book, but I quickly turn to the back. Again, his name marks every lined receipt. I gasp when I see a check listed in the amount of eight hundred dollars.

"Oh my God."

I toss this one across the room while letting out a shriek of my own.

I've had it with not knowing. I've even had it with my mother and her secrets. She would never tell me she was giving her money away because I'm sure she knew I'd never approve. But I'm more furious at someone who was like a member of my family taking advantage of her. It's no secret she favored Caiden, but *money*, and all these checks? I demand to know why, and to make him accountable. Did he think he could get away with not telling me?

As if we don't have enough to work through.

This is the last straw for me.

I rush across the living room, grabbing for my car keys, and stomp out the door. I half hope this is the rage I need to let Caiden go, but my tears bewilder me. My frustration collides with confusion and anger as my body contorts with the need to have answers.

I deserve that much, don't I?

It doesn't take me long to figure out where Caiden is. I drive past his house to see that his truck isn't there and then drive to the only other place I can think of: the fire station.

Sure enough, his truck is among only two others sitting in the darkness in front.

I slam my car into park, feeling more at my wit's end with every mile I gain. I've lost it. I know it. I'm a heaping mess of missing my mother and possibly hating her—which was a place I never wanted to get to. All the while feeling the same for the stupid guy who's supposed to be there for me.

Life has never felt so foggy, and the only thing that feels clear is this burning anger that explodes deep in my gut.

Maybe it's this need to *feel* something. I'm in a constant state of trying to rein it all in. I won't anymore. I don't want to. I want to be mad, and being mad at Caiden feels right.

When I walk into the fire station dispatch office, my sneakers squeak on the linoleum floor, and I realize that Caiden might be sleeping upstairs with his crew.

Luckily, I see him leaning back in a chair, eyes resting closed, his arms folded over his stomach as his legs perch themselves atop the desk in front of him. Isn't he supposed to be working?

I stomp up to him and kick his boots off the desk. His body flings forward, and his eyes fly open as his arms jut out to avoid an oncoming fall. His palms fall flat onto the desk with a loud slap as he looks around frantically.

"What the hell!" he blurts out as he sees me fuming in front of him, tapping my toe furiously as I cross my arms over my chest. "Hailey, what are you doing?" he asks, just as annoyed.

His rugged face has my stomach doing a somersault, but anger and frustration win the battle over my nerves.

I pull my mother's checkbook from my back pocket and wave it in the air. "What have you been hiding, Caiden? Huh?"

He rises from his chair, smoothing out the navy button-down of his uniform, the sleeves rolled up to his elbows revealing his tattoos. I try getting a peek at my initials secretly woven into the art, but he's moving too quickly. His height suddenly feels intimidating when he greets me with the same seething intensity, but I'm not going to cower when it comes to this argument.

"What are you talking about?" he asks, running a nervous hand through his hair. I disregard the worn lines around his sizzling green eyes as they devour me in frustration and anger. I wonder what fuels his rage.

"My mom. I finally decided to go through some of her

things—"

"At eleven o'clock at night?" he cuts in.

My mouth bobs a bit. I didn't even consider the time. Is it really that late? Water pools in the corner of my eyes. I blink it back as quickly as it came. "I wasn't really. I just—it's tough sometimes going through Mom's things—" I shake my head, not liking the direction this is going. He's watching me like a wounded animal now. No, thanks. "Why was my mom writing you checks, Caiden? I was going through her desk and found her checkbook. Nearly all of them were made out to you!"

His face softens as he takes a step toward me. "I never once cashed any of them, don't worry."

I take a step back, confused by his endearing transition, practically fearful of it. It's as if he isn't fazed by the inquiry. I hate that the corner of his mouth crooking upward into a smirk has me losing my breath. I shake my head to get a grip.

"You didn't?" I ask. My hand nervously comes up to tug on a lock of my hair, and it's impossible to ignore my trembling, neurotic state.

He shakes his head. "Of course not. Your mom was as stubborn as you, and she just wrote the checks anyway. I told her she didn't have to pay me."

I stiffen with more confusion while I watch him take two more steps toward me. I try to move a step back again, but I bump into a desk.

He adds, "Hailey, are you okay?"

I'm anything but, and he knows it. I ignore his question.

"You act like I know why my mom was trying to pay you!" My voice begins to rise, and it feels good to shout, so I keep doing it. "Why the hell has my mom been writing you checks for years? Why would she do that? Why were you taking money from my mom? Why are you keeping all these secrets?" My words come out hot and fiery. I'm angry, but tears appear again, and this time I can't blink them back as they fall over the edge and drip down my cheeks.

The tears mean all the things I can't say. I wipe at them quickly, as if to hide their true meaning.

"Hailey, you've been gone a long time…" He gets choked up, too. His eyes dissect me as they always have, but they have a remorseful edge to them this time. He takes that final step, and I'm backed up against a desk, trapped. I couldn't move even if I wanted to. His hands slowly lift themselves up. I'm still clutching the checkbook close as if it's a shield. I hate that watching Caiden's emotions unfold puts me in a trance.

"Why Caiden? Why?" I beg. I'm pleading for something to make sense, because the only thing that seems to is the gravitational pull that appears between us.

"Your mom needed a lot of help around the house as she got older, so I would come around when I could to do things she couldn't, like yard work, handyman stuff, cleaning the gutters before the fall. Ya know? Things your dad used to do. She needed help, and I wasn't gonna let her do it on her own. She started to feel bad and wanted to pay me for the work or the supplies I would get." He pauses to chuckle, his eyes searing me with cherishing intensity, causing only more liquid to pool in mine. He loved her as much as I did. "I never once cashed a single check she gave me. Never. She'd get as mad as you are at me now. She'd shout and scream at me to take her money. I couldn't. I wouldn't."

"You did all that for her?" I whimper, and I wish I could sound stronger, more resilient. The way I want so desperately to be, but I'm breaking down.

He smiles, and I swear the edge to his mouth causes my knees to buckle.

"… And for you," he replies quietly, as if hoping I wouldn't hear.

Unfortunately, his words only echo and bounce off the walls of my skull until I commit his tone, his look, and those words to memory. I savor them when I shouldn't.

His hands finally make it to my face. I attempt to turn away, but his grasp is firm, holding my jaw steady, forcing my eyes to stay pinned to his.

His touch is too much. It confuses me more than this new revelation. My words come out erratic and unfiltered. "Why didn't she tell me you were doing that? I can't stop it. I'm mad at her—" I blubber, the salty tears spilling over my lips as I lean into his touch. His strong hands feel like home in an instant, even if they're rougher than I remember. The light stroke of his thumb against my cheek has my eyelids fluttering while I'm utterly enthralled by his stare.

"Don't you dare be mad at her, Hailey. Don't. Be mad at me. ME. I'd rather you be mad at me forever than hold anything against your mom. It's hard to understand, but know that she never wanted to distract you from your big dreams. She loved you too much. Especially because she would never let you get distracted by something like me. And think of it this way, just as much as you didn't want to tell her you needed her help, she didn't want to tell you that she needed yours. Never for one moment think she kept things from you to hurt you. She just wanted to keep things level. She wanted you focused. All she ever wanted was for you to fulfill your dream, because she knew from personal experience how important that is. She opened the diner for that exact reason. She may not have originally agreed to you leaving like the rest of us, but regardless, she was proud."

"B-but you were there for her, and I wasn't. She never let me be there. I wanted to be there. I wanted—I loved her—I can't—"

"And she knew that. She read your book, Hailey. It was obvious how much you loved your mom, just as obvious as how much you loved me," he blurts, and as if he can't help himself, his lips crash into mine. I don't even see it coming. I don't even get a chance to argue.

I've stared at his mouth so many times since seeing him in the bar that first night, wondering if things would ever be the same, wondering if I would ever get over my curiosity if his lips would meet mine with the same fervor they had when we were nineteen.

They absolutely do.

His mouth caresses mine while his thumbs swipe over my cheeks, wiping at the tears. I'm shocked by the whole experience, but my lips greet his with a sense of familiarity and desperate passion as our mouths reacquaint themselves with each other.

I drop the checkbook, my hands pressing flat against his chest, sliding up his shoulders, loving the feeling of every hard line. His heartbeat beneath my fingertips feels like a rapid-booming bass drum that sends mine into a tailspin of frantic beats, too.

When his tongue dips into my mouth, my hands reflexively move to tangle themselves in his hair. His body presses against mine, pushing mine back, forcing me to sit atop the desk as he continues to take that small extra step to place himself between my legs.

In that instant, I have never craved anything, or anyone, so much in my entire life.

He tastes of cinnamon coffee, and my tongue wants to taste all of him. It twists around his as a quiet groan escapes him.

His right hand slides down the length of my body, igniting a tingling trail in its wake until he takes a firm grip of my thigh. All I can do is bring him as close as possible, anchoring him to me as he hitches my leg around his waist.

How did I get here? Where am I again?

RING. RING. RING. "PineCrest station, small brush fire reported on Walnut Avenue. Reportedly, the Shelton family playing with illegal fireworks again. Blaze seemingly under control at this time. Officer's Barton and Garcia will be on scene to assist."

The 911 call is deafening over the loudspeaker.

He doesn't leap away from me but freezes instead. His lips stop stroking mine, and his eyes slowly open. It's as if he doesn't know how he got here, either. I can feel each of his muscles tense against me, one by one, as he processes the situation. I can even feel the gulp of his throat with his lips still pressed to mine, and his tight exhale.

Personally, I can't breathe.

The sounds of heavy footsteps can be heard on the floor above us as his crew (and presumably some of our friends), wake up to handle the emergency call.

He peels himself away as another ring echoes off the station walls as a reminder. His eyes are wide, round... terrified.

He takes three steps back, his arms rising defensively. He whispers, "Shit-shit-shit."

I'm petrified. My lips are swollen from his assault. My eyes examine his tangled mess of hair, knowing my hands are the cause, and then I absorb the gut-wrenching look in his eyes.

He thinks this was a mistake.

Another visible gulp as his Adam's apple bobs in his throat.

I can't stop my frantic heart, and I've lost my ability to speak. I've lost the ability to process *anything*.

He turns slowly to me, running an apologetic hand through his hair.

"I'm so sorry, Hailey. I have to go to work."

What?

He leaves without another word or an apologetic smile, just a look of fear. And what's worse is, I understand that fear. I understand it way too well.

He runs down the hallway, grabbing his jacket and gear hanging on the wall before disappearing in the garage where the truck is. I guess duty calls when you're the only emergency response team in a small town, but still.

I touch my swollen lips as if to prove to myself that I didn't make up what just happened. The tears that he had previously stopped are now back in full force as silent streams fall down my cheeks.

His look said it all. It was wrong, no matter how right it might have felt.

He has a girlfriend, and let's be honest, I'm so emotionally unavailable, it's ridiculous.

I can't imagine this has anything to do with him doing *the right thing.*

12

It's been four days.

Four days since Caiden kissed me, and four days since I've committed myself to being a recluse.

I've turned to my literary heroes on this one, and they all seem to approve.

At first, this seemed like a great idea. However, I can't say it's done anything for my writing, which is one of the most annoying parts of this situation.

Oh, and the fact that Caiden kissed me. That's pretty infuriating.

I banished CeeCee from bothering me in my writing cave, and I almost miss her misplaced optimism. She wanted answers as to why I didn't want her around, and I was too terrified to open my mouth because I know the truth wants to seep out.

I pace my porch, walking circles around my house, trying to find a purpose. My eyes continuously peek up toward the road whenever I hear a car.

I may have forbidden CeeCee from entering, but I've not had any contact with Caiden to tell him to leave me alone, not that I would.

I thought maybe he'd show up to explain himself, but he

hasn't. We've always been two people fighting for the last word. This silence is awkward. He must know that there's no use in explaining, I guess. What could he say? What would I want him to say?

This is just one of the many plot twists in my life.

The sizzle he left on my lips still burns so much that I can't seem to focus.

Damn him. Damn this town. Damn everything.

Meow.

Not now, Soot.

I stop at the front of the house, looking out onto the road, hoping for a sign, but my ringing cell phone distracts me.

I walk back into the living room, grabbing for it, and see CeeCee's name flashing on the screen. It was only a matter of time until she couldn't hold herself back.

I grit my teeth when my phone buzzes in my hands right after it finishes ringing. CeeCee isn't known to back down or be ignored. Hell, she can barely follow directions. I'm surprised she hasn't shown up on my doorstep already.

The text message she sent after the call vibrates again.

> I don't know why you're ignoring me, but if you're not at the bonfire tonight to explain yourself I'm going to be very very very upset.

I groan, tossing my phone against the couch so I can rub my temples. I don't want to go, but I know I can't skip it. That'll only cause more questions. I don't need a Brandon interrogation along with a CeeCee one. Good God, what if they decide to question me together? No, thanks.

I decide not to text CeeCee back. Maybe it's rude, but I'm not in the mood for nice, either. Not today.

Regardless, I spend the afternoon trying to choose something to wear, because I'm going to this party whether I like it or not.

In PineCrest, it's just bad manners to not show up to a bonfire party.

Damn this town… for the umpteenth time.

I roll my eyes.

Meow.

"Soot, would you stop!"

My feet crunch on the dry leaves and pine needles when I exit my car and wander toward the glow of the bonfire, pulling in that deep, necessary gust of oxygen. I don't really know what I'm walking into, but I at least know I could use a friendly face. I'm not sure the recluse life suits me.

I smooth my hands over my summer dress, the floral pattern feeling appropriate for the evening as I enter the crowd, avoiding stares while trying to seek out my friends.

I try to bask in the party buzz, and there's a sense of home and nostalgia that lies here.

This is when I see CeeCee standing, surprisingly, by herself near the fire. Though she's staring absentmindedly into the flames, she senses me coming before I can announce myself, turning toward me. I approach her with an apologetic grimace. I deserve her returning glare.

"So," she hums disapprovingly. "I'm glad to see you decided to join us tonight. Ya know, you're almost as bad as Caiden."

I'm thankful for the darkness, because my face gets hotter by the second, and I'd like to put the blame on the giant bonfire, but I know that isn't the case.

I may deserve the sass, but Caiden is the last person I want to be compared to right now.

"Am I?" I sigh.

Her eyes dart to the right, glancing across the party, and

Brandon is there, standing with Caiden. It throws me off balance, but I catch myself a second later as I shuffle up to stand up straight next to CeeCee, my mouth going dry.

After thinking I'd see Caiden in the days that passed since he kissed me, I'm stunned to have his eyes pinned on me so heavily from a distance.

I tear my stare away, annoyed. He's not allowed to give me that puppy dog look. No way.

Though, I do take note that Brandon is pretty much as far away from CeeCee as possible while still managing to be within the boundaries of the party. His own carefully crafted grimace says a lot, and the fact that he's refusing to look our way.

When CeeCee turns back to me, her glare has shifted into a frown. I may have my own shit going on, but I'm sure she does, too.

"You okay, Cee?"

"Me and Brandon broke up."

I raise an inquisitive brow. "I thought you said you two weren't together?"

She snorts.

Convinced by the sad creases around her mouth, and the entirely unfair, glowing, cat-like stare on me from across the party, I'm compelled to confess my secret, if she'll confess hers.

"Hey?" I reach out to touch her arm. She lifts her chin slowly to meet my eyes, and she looks as lost as I feel. I shouldn't find comfort in it, but I do.

"I think it's about time we have girl talk. Like, real girl talk."

"Are you going to tell me why you've been ignoring me?"

"Are you going to tell me how you really feel about Brandon?" I shoot back.

She nods.

"Then yes, but booze first."

She smiles as we link arms to find a bottle before we reveal our secrets, just like old times.

That's when I realize she's been hiding an empty bottle of beer as she says, "I've got a head start. You better catch up."

"On it."

Unfortunately, this journey requires us to get dangerously close to Caiden and Brandon. It's an entirely awkward experience when you overhear one of the guys punch the other as he says, "Dude, stop staring. You're supposed to have my back tonight. What the hell is going on with you?" and you know the person he's talking to is Caiden.

I don't hear a response, but only because I'm too terrified to hear one. In a haphazard attempt at being efficient, I just grab for the entire bottle of whiskey and make a run for it. I know John, the host of this party, would be annoyed, but I think at this point I have a damn good reason to take it. I still try to hide it as we scurry away, me with the bottle and CeeCee with red solo cups.

"I can't believe you just took the whole bottle." CeeCee giggles.

I shrug. "It's because Caiden won't stop staring, and I was scared he was going to open his mouth or something."

She waits until we get to the opposite end of the party, turning our backs on the crowd so we feel at least a little secluded. "Something must have happened between you two. You don't normally ignore my calls or texts."

I unscrew the bottle and take a swig from it. I enjoy the burn so much that I take another one right after.

This only ignites more of CeeCee's laughter, surely at my expense. "That bad, huh?" she asks.

I wipe the corner of my mouth with my arm. "You first. I need a moment before talking about it."

She nods, pulling the bottle from my hand, and pours some into her cup. "See, I'm a lady."

"Uh huh," I laugh as I shift gears, lifting my cup so she

can pour some into mine. "I didn't think about getting a mixer for our drinks."

"We'll be just fine."

I wait for her to take her first gulp, and she cringes, letting out a quiet gag before shaking it off. "Yowzers. Okay, I'm good..."

"So, you and Brandon aren't together?"

She hums. "You were right before. We weren't really boyfriend and girlfriend, I guess, but it was starting to feel that way. It's not what I want."

She takes another large gulp, and I do the same.

"Are you sure it's not what you want?"

She sighs. "No."

I don't have a response for that even if I do think she's full of it. Who am I to give advice when I can't figure out what I want?

"He really hurt me, Hailey. He hurt me over and over after that, too, even if I have no right to be mad, and even though he's gotten better. Much better, really, but I can't seem to forget him cheating. He dated after that, too, once we were officially done. He tried not to flaunt it, but it's near impossible for Brandon not to be a smug bastard. That's until he realized how much I was hurting. Caiden did do some good, even though he pushed Brandon to fuck around in the first place. Caiden told him how much seeing him with other girls was killing me. Unfortunately, that made him realize I was still in love with him."

"Isn't that a good thing? Or at least it could be?"

She shakes her head. "It should be, but it isn't. It took us a long time to be able to be in the same room with one another, but once we could, it helped the friendship dynamics. Our group was finally able to pull back together. It took almost a year, but ya know, it was too easy for us to get comfortable, me and Brandon, that is. We'd fool around, I'd regret it, or he would, but I was the one who could never commit."

"Did he want you to commit?"

"At first he did, but then he'd take anything he could get and stopped asking about getting back together. I liked it that way. I was too scared to make us official, because if I did, it would give him the power to break me." She releases a sad sigh. "What am I saying? I'm still like that, Hails. He scares the shit out of me. You've seen how he is. He could cheat on me again. I don't trust him. I'm scared."

"Cee, you can't think like that. Trust me when I say I understand this fear, but any idiot can see that Brandon wants to do right by you."

She grunts, gurgling through another large sip. "I know. He's really good at that part. He confronted me yesterday about what we were doing. I admitted we were getting *too* comfortable this round. I was staying over too much, he was texting me in the mornings and at night, and it was like we were teens all over again. He started making assumptions and expected me to do things with him. That's when he asked what we were doing."

"What did you say?"

"I asked him what he wanted."

"And?"

She shrugs. "He told me he wanted to make us official, that he wanted to take us to the next level. He was ready to bring us back to where we once were."

When a sad laugh escapes her before she goes on, I already know what's coming. "Poor guy." She sniffs. "I told him it was over. We can't do it anymore. That whatever he thinks we have, we don't. It hurt so much to lie."

My chest deflates. Her words remind me of when I told Caiden to let me go, but at least my words were warranted.

"Cee, you're miserable over it, aren't you?" She nods. "Then why not give it the chance that it deserves even though I know you're scared? You're upset now anyway. At least if you give it a try, you'll be happy. Brandon is an idiot, but he's not one to make the same mistake twice. Love is a risk. You just gotta take the leap."

She smiles, and I really adore the dopey edges to it as she turns to me. "He's so mad at me right now."

"I'd probably be mad at you, too."

She laughs. "Yeah, me too-too."

I laugh, taking a larger gulp, wanting to catch up with her drunken state as soon as possible. I can't tell whether it will help me feel less, or whether it'll amplify everything squirming through my very existence.

"I think you need to give Brandon a chance."

"I'm not ready, but I don't want to lose him, either."

"Maybe that's what you need to tell him. That you want to be able to give you two a chance, but you have to take it at a snail's pace. He'd at least prefer to hear that rather than a lie, like you don't want him. C'mon Cee, you're smarter than that."

"Huh, well, maybe… it's up for debate. What if I don't even want to try?"

I shrug. "Then you need to move on."

Her shoulders slump, but she nods her head as if she understands. I finish off what's left in my cup, grabbing for the bottle from her hands.

As I pour a fresh cup, I feel a fuzzy buzz travel to my fingertips, and I'm hopeful for a numbing remedy. That is, until CeeCee speaks. "What about you, Hails? You ever move on?"

My shrug is a reflex. "I tried. I'm trying… uh, I am."

Her giggle turns into a snort as she says, "Riiiight. That was convincing."

I turn around to glance at the party. The hum is at a welcomingly loud level, everyone seems preoccupied, and Brandon and Caiden are nowhere in sight. This is a comforting fact.

I need to say it. The truth is eating me alive.

"He kissed me, CeeCee. He's ruined everything."

She chokes on her current sip. "He did what?"

My brows pull together as I process what I've said. "But I think it was an accident."

"Wait. What-the-fuck. Hold the phone. He did what?"

"I will not repeat it, because if I do I might cry, or throw up, and you really don't want either."

"That boy. He needs to get his shit together."

I shake my head. "It's been this push-and-pull between us since I got back. But I told him to let me go. I told him to leave me alone. I may have even told him that whatever he thinks we have, we don't anymore. It was for the safety of the life he's living. Kristen makes him happy, even if I want to hate her. God, she's so annoyingly perfect, and I still consider pulling her pretty hair out every time I see her. It's irrational."

"You've always been a bit erratic, but we love you for it. Plus, that'd be a show I'd totally pay for."

I laugh an honest-to-goodness laugh, and it feels so good. "Caiden and I have at least been finding that level of friendship we used to have. I did miss that part. I just wish my heart wasn't so involved."

"How could it not be?"

"I guess you're right. It doesn't matter, though—"

"Oh, are we back to the *it doesn't matter* thing again?"

I grumble, taking another sip, and before I can form some sort of rebuttal, she adds, "What did you feel when he kissed you?"

This is when I forget how to breathe again. "Everything."

She tuts her understanding, but for once it doesn't sound patronizing. "What are you going to do?"

"Nothing. Absolutely nothing. Actually, I'm kind of pissed off about it. Caiden and I haven't even talked about it, but I guess there's nothing to say other than *oops*."

"*Oops*? What the...? Hailey. You're being ridiculous."

"Maybe I am, and I know you hate the response, but: Nothing. Fucking. Matters. I'm leaving. I'm going to figure out what to do with my mom's ashes, probably put you in charge of the diner, and get the fuck out of town. I don't take steps back, CeeCee. I only move forward, and Caiden is something I can't figure out, and because of that, I feel like it's safe to assume he's not a good idea." Displeasure thrums through my body, rattling me as I expel angrily, "He has a girlfriend. I'm not a home-wrecker. He's the one who needs to keep himself sane while I'm in town."

"You don't mean all that."

I drop my empty cup, letting my head fall into my hands as I reply, "I do. I can't take being here much longer!"

"Not to change subjects, but are you seriously putting me in charge of the diner? I'm kind of getting choked up here."

Another cathartic laugh escapes me, muffled by my hands as I peel them away. "Yeah, I am."

She giggles, nodding and grinning. "Okay, topic for a different time. Back to Caiden."

I sigh. "We don't have to talk about it anymore. I really only wanted to confess what happened, not that I need anything solved. I just felt like I needed to tell someone."

"Well, now it makes sense why he's been acting so weird the past few days. He's kept very much to himself."

I'm tempted to tell her about the circumstances of the kiss, and how he just ran off, but I don't. I've said what I needed to say, and if everything I've said to her so far is true, then the details really don't matter.

"You date anyone while living in California? I've never asked you that."

I press my lips into a hard line. They squirm under the pressure as I watch her.

"Well...?" she chides, her rising eyebrow telling me she's damn curious.

"Lots, actually."

"Slut."

I shrug, even if it's not true, or maybe it is. Wait, no it isn't. "I was just trying to do that whole moving on thing."

"Did it work?"

"Obviously not," I guffaw, thinking more whiskey is the only answer that makes sense this evening. I lean down to grab my cup, but I get distracted when I hear my name being shouted from across the party.

I turn around to find a face I didn't consider seeing even though we were just talking about her.

Kristen is stomping toward me, and the angelic, sweet-looking girl I had met no longer seems real. She looks pissed off.

Terror and a bit of embarrassment riddles its way up my spine, because whatever that look means, I think I might actually deserve it. This is exactly what I didn't want.

"HAILEY!"

I gulp at Kristen's shout, shaking out my shoulders, feeling the need to brace myself.

Gosh, I'm so tired. "Yeah?"

With Kristen still a good twenty feet away, and CeeCee pretty drunk by now, Cee hiccups, "You totally should have let me spill pie on her."

I want to laugh. I want to love her for still being my best friend after all these chaotic years, but I'm defeated, and all I can do is release an exhausted sigh, waiting for Kristen to berate me. She must know about the kiss. It's the only thing I can think of.

That's when I see it coming before everyone who's now watching does, and I do nothing to stop it.

Kristen flings the contents of her drink onto my face, the sticky blue liquid splashing over my cheeks and down my dress.

I hear gasps, and even the rushed footsteps of CeeCee against the dry leaves of the forest floor behind me.

Before opening my eyes, I raise my hand to stop CeeCee. I'm grateful she'd be so willing to fight for me, but I can fight my own battles, and let's be honest, if I wanted to destroy Kristen, I would, but I don't.

"That's what you get!" She tosses her cup on the ground as I wipe my eyes of the syrupy gunk, the smell of vodka singeing my nostrils.

"Why did you even come back? Why don't you just go home! You're ruining it for everyone here! Things were better when you were gone!"

I know I might have said that exact thing to CeeCee, but hearing it out loud, in front of all these people, confirming it, stings something nasty.

I would never confess that my stomach feels like it just erupted in ulcers, but I claw at my soaked clothes where the pain bubbles.

"Forget it. I understand..." My words trail off pathetically.

Normally, I'd be up in arms, but I don't have it in me. Not with this fight. Although, I don't know how to end this. I can't say the truth. Not in front of everyone at the party. I wish I could tell her that I believe I did deserve her drink in my face.

When Caiden kissed me days ago, when I stomped into the station in a rage, and then he left me vulnerable and confused, I knew it would be my secret to bear. He's done a good job being smart enough to ignore me. I didn't realize it until now, but I'm sure it was to keep people like Kristen from getting hurt. Yet, here I am, messing it all up anyway.

"Are we done?" I ask, and I know it's rude, but I want to leave. I want to run. I glance back and see not only CeeCee, but now Brandon and Cameron gathering behind me. It's sweet they'd come to my defense, but who does Kristen have? She's from out of town. Aren't these her friends, too? I don't want any part of this.

I need to do something, anything, but the moment I throw my hands up as if to signal my defeat, to throw up my white flag and walk away, she lifts up her other hand. I didn't realize that she was holding anything else, but there it is. Its worn cover, tattered edges, and tens of tabbed post-it notes glow in the shadows of the bonfire. She has Caiden's copy of my book.

I go wide-eyed. I assumed that book was something he kept secret. I know nothing of the idiosyncrasies of his new life.

"What is this, Hailey? Huh? Why does Caiden keep carrying this around?"

"I-I…" I babble. No matter how hard I try, I still get so anxious and embarrassed when it comes to those damn 98,452 words all strung together to somehow describe my previous existence. That damn book. It's made me and ruined me.

"He carries it around like a fucking Bible!" She shakes the book. She hates the book. She hates me. "Why does he do that, Hailey! Caiden mopes around reading this like the fucking *Da Vinci Code*."

Brandon has the gall to snicker behind me. It causes Kristen to lose her temper, and the sound collides with her drunken slurs as she shouts, "Fuck this! You've messed up everything!"

I can see tears welling up in her eyes. They glisten in the firelight, and I want to tell her I want to cry, too. I want to tell her I never wanted any of this. That this is the exact thing I feared. I try to pull in a deep breath.

It's just a stupid book about a stupid boy. I'm about to explain that exact thought, but she spits out, "Fuck you, Hailey!"

She turns with her arm raised, frantically shaking the book, and it becomes clear what she intends to do as she takes two deliberate steps toward the blazing bonfire.

My heart clenches. I know it's only a material object that could be replaced, but for some reason my heart clings to those specific pages, and those scattered highlights, and the messy notes drawn in the margins. That book she holds is as much Caiden's as it is mine now. I clench my jaw. There's nothing I can do about what she plans, and even if I tried, it'd give me away. It would show everyone I care. I blink back my own tears.

"Do something…" is whispered behind me, and all I know is, it's one of my boys who says it. How would any of them know the importance of the damn thing? Maybe I'm the fool in this situation.

I clench my eyes shut before she lets go of the book, but it's CeeCee's small gasp that has them springing open just as quickly.

I'm shocked to see Caiden standing before me. Where did he come from? His looming frame towers over Kristen's, and it's easy for his long arm to capture Kristen's wrist before she lets go of the book into the fire.

I watch Kristen's lips bob silently. She's caught in something she apparently isn't supposed to do.

Caiden brings down her hand slowly. They're staring at each other, nearly nose to nose. His face is stoic but furious. He slips the book out of her trembling hand, and I watch as he nonchalantly tucks it into the back of his jeans as if the gesture comes as second nature.

"I'm so sorry, Caiden," I hear Kristen whisper.

My heart is thumping out of my chest, and this time I'm absolutely positive I want to cry. No matter how angry he is, and how apologetic she looks, it still feels too intimate for me to witness. I don't care that this is an argument about my book. It still reminds me of their carefree smiles on the dance floor of the fair. They're lovers. They're close.

Caiden mumbles something I can't decipher, and I notice the tenseness around the party beginning to calm as everyone carries on with chitchat and beer pong. Yet I'm still watching, and it feels rude, like I'm intruding. I have to turn away.

I know I'm out in the forest, and the oxygen runs free here, but I still feel suffocated.

This is when I run. Again.

13

I turn onto my back on my blanket nestled among the tall grass while raising my hands up toward the sunshine. I stretch out my cramped fingers and wrists as I pull in a deep breath, enjoying my secluded secret space for the fifth day in a row. I should have thought of this solution sooner.

Before, I was waiting for someone to show up on my doorstep to give me answers. Now, I just want to disappear.

I must admit, something good came out of the emotional tragedy that occurred at the party: my creative juices have been flowing ever since.

I've calmed myself since the third-worst night of my life. The first night being leaving Caiden in PineCrest when I was nineteen. The second, when I heard my mother had passed away. Now the third would be witnessing Caiden and his girlfriend argue over a book I wrote about us.

I close my eyes at this thought. Even though I'm alone in a field, hidden away by the tall grass, and I can hear the babbling of a stream not too far away, I still manage to feel utterly embarrassed.

I'm thankful I have this secret place to retreat to. It didn't cross my mind to come here until I needed it. Kind of like the Room of Requirement in *Harry Potter*, except instead of it magically appearing, I pulled my rusty bike from the garage and rode it to the only spot that's never done me wrong in a time of need.

My shrieking phone to the right of my head startles me in the outdoor silence. I hurriedly grab for it, not wanting to send off any sounds into the valley to alert anyone to where I am.

If I wasn't so exhausted with rolling my eyes, I'd roll my eyes at me.

I answer, excited to see a name that doesn't spark a history of hysterical madness. My agent. "Janet! How are you?"

"I miss you. Where's my book?"

I laugh. "Do you miss me? Or do you really just need something to do?"

"I can say both, right?"

"You sound more caffeinated than usual."

"Well, I've switched over to five-hour-energy. I'm glad you noticed. How's the book coming along?"

I stretch out my right hand again. I've been tirelessly writing all day, and my hand is feeling the burn.

"Good, actually. I mean, I still need to kind of pull the story together, but I'm at least writing a lot."

"That's music to my ears. Are you ready to send me some chapters?"

"Eh, not yet." I pause, thinking I need to figure myself out before really figuring the story out. I hate how art imitates life sometimes. "But soon. I promise you, soon."

"How's herding sheep?"

I laugh loudly, rolling over onto my stomach. "You've just officially proven you have absolutely no idea what I mean when I say I'm in Colorado."

"So, it's not like *Little House on the Prairie*?"

"No."

"You don't herd sheep?"

"No."

"But there are horses?" she hums questioningly.

I laugh. "I guess."

"Okay, so I know something. Are there roguish men riding around shirtless on these horses?"

"We really need to get you to stop reading so many Harlequin novels, Janet. They're gonna do you in."

"So, you're saying no, there aren't? Well then, fat chance you'll ever get me to visit."

"I'll find a way, just you wait."

"Unless you're baiting me with a shirtless man and a new manuscript, then I say game on."

I laugh, remembering that my life in Los Angeles is so disconnected from what I have here, and it has me aching for it. "Jeez. I miss you."

"Finally, you admit it. I've been waiting." She pauses, humming over a thought. "Are you okay? I feel like I hear a little sadness in your voice."

"Does anything get past you?"

"Call it a gift. Now, what's going on? What about lover boy?"

I debate whether to divulge the whole story, but I know I don't want to. I'm not ready to, nor do I have the energy. Running away these past five days has given me a sense of solace, but it hasn't solved anything. With that in mind, I don't think I could find the words to make Janet understand. "It's complicated."

"Of course it is."

"I wish it wasn't."

"From what you've told me, there was no way to avoid complicated. How's that volatile chemistry working out?"

"We've combusted, and it ain't pretty." I sigh. "I'm working on it."

"Are you sure you're okay? I'm getting concerned."

"It's fine," I reply, even though it's not. "Something happened a few days ago, and I'm worried I'm messing things up being here. I don't want to screw up his life."

Her sigh matches mine. "Then maybe it's time to come

home. Ya know? I haven't had anyone to drink wine and watch reruns of *Sex and the City* with."

"No? What about Bethany in the foreign rights department? She was supposed to be my go-to replacement while I herd sheep," I joke.

"Yeah, well, that didn't work out when she caught me and Patrick getting coffee the other day. She's definitely not talking to me right now."

"JANET!" I shriek. "I thought we talked about you *not* calling him back?"

"I was looking to add a little spice, and maybe something a little dangerous to my life. See, this is why it's a good thing you come back. I need you to stop me from doing stupid things, like flirting with a co-worker's ex-boyfriends."

"You're a piece of work. But maybe you're right. It might be a good time for me to head back."

"—Hailey?"

I leap at the sound of a male voice from behind and squeal as I do. When my eyes collide with blazing green eyes and a serious frown as we acknowledge each other, I can't think straight. How did Caiden find me? His eyes are bright in the sunshine, and my whole body is on red-alert as my chest constricts.

From the phone I hear an identical shriek followed by, "I know you're mad I went out with Bethany's ex, but she'll have to forgive me eventually—"

"No, Janet. I, uh, gotta go."

Caiden is standing at the foot of my blanket in the tall grass next to my rusty bike. His eyes are glued to me, and I can't look away.

"Why?" she asks.

Really, Janet.

"Someone just appeared. I have to get off the phone."

"Oh-my-God, is it lover boy? Don't forget to write everything down—"

I hang up my phone.

"Caiden," I whisper, hating that his maroon v-neck stretches over his chest so annoyingly well, and that his hands stuffed into his tight dark blue jeans are overwhelmingly distracting. Don't even get me started on those beautiful forearms.

"Hailey," he whispers back.

I shake my head, baffled by his presence. "How did you find me?" is the only thing I can think of.

He lifts his right hand from his pocket to pull something from behind him. My book.

I release a breath of relief, knowing that it still exists. It had crossed my mind that maybe the book wasn't going to make it out alive. I gulp down the guilt the thought gives me. I should not be attached to that particular copy of my book, but I so am.

He waves it back and forth, and the corner of his mouth finally lifts into a smirk, softening the high tension. "This. It's like a treasure map if you know how to use it right."

Dammit, I can't fight my smile.

"Actually," he says going on. "I would've been here sooner, but it took me a bit of time to figure it out. I tried going to your house first, nearly every day, and then to the diner, but no matter what time I looked in those places, you were nowhere to be found."

I nod as if to confirm *mission accomplished*. "That's persistent, even for you."

"Yeah, tell me about it. Especially when every time I walked into the diner, CeeCee wasn't afraid to yell at me and make a scene."

"Remind me to give her the Best Friend of the Millennium award."

The lifted corner to his mouth falls. "Can I join you?"

I look around, my surrounding view blinded by the tall grass. I shake my head, and even though that means '*absolutely not, you can't sit with me,*' he takes it upon himself to climb onto the blanket beside me.

"I still don't understand how you found me."

I turn over on my side to look at him and hate how boyish he looks lying flat on his stomach, biting his bottom lip as he thumbs through my book, the sunshine glinting off his hair, reminding me of summers spent in this exact spot.

I refocus on what's in his hands, blinking a few times in disbelief as I watch all the highlights and tabs flutter by as he riffs through the book.

I turn over on my stomach, unable to take my eyes off of him. It's the most bizarre thing to witness, because he's so diligent and full of concentration when he focuses his attention on the book. My heart swells, and I wish it would stop.

"Here," he says. His index finger lands on chapter fourteen that I know all too well, making my face heat. I can't define how I should feel about being near him right now. I think on reflex I want to be mad, but my instinct is to cozy up to what home really feels like.

Interrupting my dissection, he continues, "I really should've thought of this first when you weren't home the first day. I should've realized you were hiding on purpose."

"I am not," I lie.

He raises a brow, dramatically looking from left to right. "This is practically your own personal fort. This was *our* place."

I shake my head. "No, you're mistaken. It was always *my* place, but you were lucky enough to be invited to this location. Invite only, you see."

He chuckles, his eyes dropping to my open notebook in front of me.

"Are you writing?"

I gasp, scrambling to shut it. "A little bit, but it's nothing."

He hums, and the silence hangs for longer than I want it to.

"Is there a reason you're here, Caiden?"

"I needed to see you."

My heart revs hard, because I want so much more than those five words. "Well, now you've seen me. What's up?"

His lips squirm. "Are you leaving town? I mean, I don't mean to intrude, but I overheard—"

"Actually, Caid, that's exactly what you're doing. Intruding. I mean, look around. I'm literally trying not to be discovered. The only more obvious thing would be me crawling into a cave."

He grunts, rolling his eyes. "Can we be serious for two seconds?"

"What makes you think we're never serious?"

"Because we're scared, and you especially, like to hide behind your well-crafted sarcasm."

"You think my sarcasm is well-crafted?" I gloat.

He releases another sigh, waving his book for dramatic effect again. "I think there's a lot of proof in here. You've captured us and your sarcasm really well."

"I think I'd like to be proud of that."

"Are you done?"

"Not even close."

"Hailey, be serious!"

"WHY? So, you can hurt me more?"

He's stunned into silence, and this time I don't let my stare leave his. I shoot him as much intensity as I can muster. Yeah, maybe I do use my sarcasm as a safety net, but can he blame me for that?

"I don't want to hurt you," he exhales, gathering his bearings. "I never wanted to hurt you. If I have, it's been completely accidental, but I know that doesn't make it right. You're not the only one who's hurting, either."

It's starting to feel like we have this conversation on replay. I don't fight my responding grumble as I roll over onto my back, closing my eyes. "Yeah, I get it, Caid. Is this the part where you tell me you're sorry again? I'll just go ahead and file that one away next to the other many apologies you've given me since I came back."

"I broke up with Kristen."

I think one would assume that my normal reaction would be to at least open my eyes. But we are so far from normal. So, on the contrary, I clench them shut tighter. Fear weasels its way into my gut, combined with heart-thumping anticipation and heartbreak. I don't know why his words terrify me, but they do.

My eyes are shut so tight that the corner of one squeezes out a tear that manages to make a run for it, rolling down my cheek, revealing way too much.

I don't see it coming because I can't see anything, but his hand comes up to my face, wiping away the rogue droplet. His fingertips are calloused but gentle, as if he might cherish me. When he lifts his fingers, my skin burns mournfully at the loss of his touch.

"Hailey…" he says, my name trailing off in that tone that begs my nerves to calm.

"Hm?"

"What are you thinking?"

"I'm trying not to think." I focus on the lukewarm sunshine from above as it hits midday, trying to bask in how good it feels against my skin, but Caiden keeps talking, and my eyes won't open.

"I'm really sorry for what happened at the bonfire."

I release a slow breath. He goes on to say, "When I knew you were coming back, I didn't know what to do. I was as scared as you were, but like you had made it very clear to me on the lake, I figured I should just try to carry on as usual until the dust settled. I didn't realize how seeing you would make me feel. I thought I had buried it away, but I was wrong. I know it might not mean much, but before you got here, I was already having problems with my relationship. Kristen made me happy, sure—"

"Caiden, please just stop."

"No, you're going to listen to this whether you like it or not. Out of everything that has happened since you planted your feet back here, you need to know the truth."

I open my eyes, turning my head to face him. He has my full attention now. I want nothing more than the truth, because everything up to this point has felt so convoluted and cloudy.

"Kristen was a good girlfriend, but like I mentioned, it was easy for me because I only saw her every other week or so because she lived in Denver. Her dad was a developer buying up property around town, so her time was split up between home in the city and in PineCrest helping her parents for work. I liked that. I needed the space and distance to function. Since the relationship had that, it had me thinking I could date again." He sighs, adding almost remorsefully, "You're kind of an impossible girl to get over, Hails."

The right corner of my mouth twitches, and I swear he stares at it like he wants to kiss it. "My relationship with her was gradual but *nice,* and I was content, but then all of a sudden, a year had gone by. Time seemed to zoom by, and when I really thought about it, it felt like nothing remarkable was happening for me to notice. I felt like I was just going through the motions. I panicked, I think. There was some sort of looming pressure I couldn't define. I liked Kristen, and it felt like because I had invested so much into the relationship already, I wanted to do right by her. She deserved that. So I kept going. I wanted to be better. I wanted to fall in love again. I wanted to convince myself I was capable of living a life without you."

I open my mouth to interrupt, but shocking me, his hand lifts back up to my face, covering my mouth. "Nuh-uh. For once I need you to let me finish."

He doesn't peel his hand away until he feels my smile. I hate my body's obvious betrayal so I try to switch it back into a foreboding frown when he lifts his hand away. Which must not be convincing, because he shakes his head with a soft chuckle.

"She started coming back to her parents place to see me more, and oddly our relationship started getting worse. We argued more. I was on edge, and I had no idea why, because I thought I was trying hard to make it work. I wanted to love her. There were way more good days than bad, but the bad ones weighed heavy. That started about three months ago. I kept thinking it was just a *me* problem, and that this suffocating feeling would go away. So, I kept giving in to all her demands. She didn't make me miserable. She made me happy, but it was still... flat. I don't know how else to describe it, but I thought that this was as good as it gets. What I—what *we* had, Hailey—me and you—I had convinced myself that we were some sort of anomaly. I considered myself lucky I got to have that sort of happiness, and I was prepared to settle after that, because nothing could come close, right? At least nothing that I had experienced. So, I was willing to make it work with Kristen because what we had was good, even if it wasn't great." He pauses to release a heavy, almost pleasantly miserable sigh. "But that's until I saw you again. Suddenly, everything changed."

"What changed?" My voice cracks because my throat is dry, and I can't believe what I'm hearing. I lick my lips, waiting for his reply.

"I felt the same as I did years ago. You kicked up the ashes that was my heart, and it scared me at first—okay, no— it terrified me. I thought that feeling didn't exist anymore because I hadn't felt it in so long. I shook it off at first, trying to keep things in perspective, but it only got harder."

God, I know how true that statement is, and I can't help myself as the words find a way to escape. "It did only get harder."

"Kristen could sense it, too. It wasn't fair to her, but there was a lot to deal with." He absentmindedly thumbs through the worn copy of my book before tossing it in front of him on the blanket. Maybe he has a love/hate relationship with it, too.

This possible fact, I adore.

"It had been almost a year since I picked up your book. After dealing with the loss of your mom, and still fighting the emotional battle of that, all of a sudden, word flew fast that Hailey Elwood was back in town. By fast, I mean Brandon called me when he was on his way to your house. I pretty much hung up on him and started rereading your book. I got through it in one night. It felt sadistic, but it had all the pieces I think I was missing. It's nostalgia, ya know? Your mom is in your book as much as us, and even our friends. I liked the refresher, but at the same time I asked myself what the fuck I was doing. I hadn't even seen you yet, and I was in a frenzy. After a day of panic, I started remembering how angry I was at you for leaving, but it suddenly felt misplaced, and then I didn't know how to feel. Which I think was worse than being angry or sad. I knew at that point I had to see you just to figure out what to feel. That's why I showed up at the bar unannounced that night. I couldn't take it. At first, I thought I'd hide out until you left town, but it started to feel like such an idiot move to miss the opportunity to lay my eyes on you, especially since I kept thinking I made up what I felt for you in my head."

I'm stunned. It's like he's plucking my own feelings from my brain. He must see the recognition, because he smiles before continuing.

"Dammit Hailey, when I saw you, I wanted you so bad." He pauses to let out a chuckle. "It was actually a little infuriating to realize through my wonder how I really felt about you, that I wanted you more than I wanted anything else. I was even mad at myself all over again for not waiting for you."

He makes it a point to focus his eyes on me, casting a lure into my soul without even trying, and catching. "I knew I had to keep life in perspective, and as time went on and I kept pushing myself to the limit, you made it abundantly clear that we each have separate lives, and I had to remember that I was trying to make my relationship work. Even if it was excruciating, I tried to do what you said. I shifted gears, trying to focus on Kristen again, but dammit, I had ADHD when it came to her. I was obviously distracted... by you. She noticed. That sucked because I didn't want anyone to get hurt, either. She didn't deserve that." He pauses, gulping down his thought. "You or Kristen, so I trekked forward. Trying to salvage what I had built. It didn't work. When you showed up tear-stained and angry at the fire station over your mom, I've never been so compelled to comfort someone in my entire life. I'm not the most nurturing guy, but my lips never wanted to soothe anyone so badly. Maybe it was selfish. Maybe I wanted to soothe your sadness as much as I wanted to soothe my pain. It hurt, holding myself back from you. The moment I said *fuck it* and let it all go to kiss you, I've never felt so alive in my entire life. This is when I valued time. The past year blindly raced by without me realizing it, but I never wanted time to go more slowly than in that moment when I finally had you."

I can feel my heart running a marathon in my chest as I try to hide my shallow breaths while I stay latched onto every word. I'm a hurricane of emotions, and my heart is trying to keep up with the adrenaline, and my mind is just trying to pick a direction to go. The roundness to his eyes as he finishes his story beckons me on a deep level that ignites every neuron in my being to spark. My body is all spontaneous combustion and natural disaster. All I know is, I have to remember to breathe.

"I know I panicked and ran off, but it was terrifying to realize what that meant, and that I had a lot to handle if I wanted to even give us the slightest chance. Do you understand what I'm saying, Hailey?" He gets serious, his eyes reeling me in. "That kiss was game over for me. I had to find a way back to you." He pauses again, watching me marinate in his words. My eyes flutter closed as I do just that, soaking it in. They don't open until he adds, "...but I wanted to do it without the destruction. Kristen started making that really impossible, but that was my fault, too."

I perk up, unable to restrain myself. "You lied to her about me."

He winces. "But I confessed everything in the end," he says crisply. "It might not make it right, but I made sure to tell her what you mean to me. What you were to me. I did it delicately, and in a way for her to understand. She is, of course, mad as hell. She's upset I lied, which I deserve. It doesn't make sense, but when I met her she was already a more fragile person than I was used to. Her knowing that the last girl I dated was the girl I'd known since I could walk was going to bring out all of her insecurities. That's a lot to compete with. I also wanted to be able to talk about you. I never wanted anyone to put boundaries on me being so proud of you. Her not knowing made it easier, even if it made it wrong. I don't know how to explain it."

He grumbles, running a frustrated hand through his hair. "I had figured out early on I was going to have to break it off with Kristen. I just wanted to try and make a clean break, but I kind of lost my mind after I kissed you. I also knew you were going to find a way to run, and all I could do was turn to the book for answers. This is when my clean break idea became impossible. I know why Kristen wanted to destroy that book. She could see the way I looked at you, the way I was suddenly avoiding the topic of you, and she caught me reading your book a few times up until the bonfire. She also figured out you were important to me, and I don't have that many important people in my life. She crossed the line when she attacked you and tried to burn the only possession I really care about. She lost it at the bonfire, but as angry as I am at her for that, I don't blame her. It's my fault. It wasn't pretty that night, but our relationship was over fairly quickly after that. She tried apologizing. I told her to stop. She slept at her parents' house, and I showed up the next morning to break it off. That's when I went to your house to find you."

I release a long huff, needing to turn away. "It's not that easy, Caid—"

"Don't you think I know that? Gimme some credit here. I wasn't knocking on your door for you to take me back—" He pauses, causing my eyes to lift nonchalantly to his. He gifts me a wry smirk with a ridiculously handsome raise of his eyebrow. "Well, maybe I was kind of hoping for that, but I knew you wouldn't. I knew—I know we can't fix everything with one gust of wind. I wanted to find you to finally tell you everything I'm telling you now. I'm exhausted with holding everything back. That's never been our style."

My chest deflates, and I can feel that honest rev of my heart as it wins the battle over my mind. I'm pretty sure my brain would prefer me to jump on the soonest plane out of here, but my heart is practically begging me to stay. This is when I give in, and the release becomes this liberating unwinding that begins at the base of my spine and spirals up to my neck, and my head falls slack, turning to look at him. He's smiling when he sees it happen, and I worry I'm as physically readable as my damn book.

I watch the delicate bob of his throat as he says, "I know it's a lot to take in, but this is what I've been working through. I wanted to apologize. To tell you how sorry I am for what Kristen did. That I'm sorry for how things got out of hand, and that nothing has felt more right than kissing you, even if it had been five years since our last one. It still feels the same. I would never give that up now that I know its value."

I'm caught. Utterly caught, and there's no escaping. His words are so deadly serious yet laced with such overwhelming sincerity that my heart can't fathom how to approach it. It just thumps incoherently loudly, but on principle, I shake my head and smile. "How did you think I'd take this story and these apologies, Caiden? Because it's a lot."

He shrugs. "It didn't matter what you would have done, or what you'll say, because it doesn't change the fact that what I've said is true. I'm not going to give you up anymore. I'm not going to tell myself I can't have you. It's unfair to me, and it's unfair to you. We've earned this, don't you think?"

I laugh, flinging my hands up to my face to muffle my manic giggles.

"Are you seriously laughing at me right now?"

Through even more laughter I reply, "Nope, not at all."

"How is it possible I became the more mature one?"

"You're not," I sputter. I still can't stop laughing, and I know I'm losing my mind. I won't look at him as my giggles relentlessly escape me in mad bursts as I stare at the clear blue sky, thanking the heavens and cursing them for the beautiful insanity unfolding.

"What would it take for you to take me seriously?"

What's funny is, I do take him seriously. More seriously than the air that's fighting hard to make it into my lungs. More serious than the sun shining above me. More serious than the glow in his eyes, but I can't seem to form words.

That becomes especially impossible when I feel the dusting of his fingertips over the bare skin of my shoulder. My laughter chokes off into a gasp.

Suddenly, not only can I not breathe, but I can no longer think. My teeth clamp down on my bottom lip, stopping any sound from escaping as my chin falls to my right. I watch, ridiculously enthralled, as he attempts to convince me of something he seems to think needs to be taken seriously when all he had to do was be patient. But I don't stop it. I enjoy the fact that I'm tingling everywhere.

He lifts his eyes, peeking up through his long lashes to gloat in my sudden silence before he starts his seemingly innocent assault to the nerve endings on my body. Sparks of electricity form when his fingers slip under the strap of my tank top, pushing it over my shoulder, before he leans in to place a kiss on my heated skin. That's when the electricity trails right to my heart.

He's still watching me carefully, and I do the same to him

as he peppers three soft, chaste kisses to my skin before saying. "Glad to see I have your full attention now."

"You always have my full attention."

He wrinkles his nose, and it's the most adorably hot thing I've ever seen. I get distracted when he places a very mature kiss against my collarbone this time. "I don't think so. It seems like this was a really successful way to get it, though"

As much as I want his lips to go on a little adventure over the hills and valleys of my body, I pull in the deep breath my body has been fighting for as I say his name in a trailing reprimand, "Caiden…"

He pauses, reading my tone, but smirks triumphantly nonetheless. "Yes?"

"You've made your point, but there's something I need to say, too."

This is what gets *his* attention. He lifts his chin more earnestly, and his eyes hint at a bit of worry.

"It's not that easy. I don't know what you want out of this, but let's not forget you broke up with your girlfriend just days ago."

He shakes his head, cutting me off with, "I know what you're thinking. I understand you're not just going to fall back into my arms."

"Then what is this? What are you doing? Teasing me?"

He smirks, licking his bottom lip smugly. "Kind of."

"Caiden!"

"Okay! It's also because I can't help myself. Is it crazy I want to make us work? I want to give us a chance. What do you want?"

I'm rendered speechless again. I have to take a moment to gather my thoughts that are thoroughly scattered across this blanket right now. He's asking me to admit out loud what I've been secretly trying not to want since seeing him. As terrifying as it is, and as stupid as it might be, the only relevant fact here is that this is about honesty. He's laid it all out there for me, and because of this, it compels me to do the same.

My breaths are shaky as I commit to the idea, stuttering my response. "I-I want to... *try*."

When I say it, even though I mean it with every fiber in my body, the risk is still there in the foundation of the statement. What we want comes with a lot of danger that we both might not bounce back from, but after years of feeling so empty, and suddenly weeks of feeling so alive, I can't think of anything more worth it, even if there's a ticking clock. So, I choose not to think about it until I have to.

"But Caiden, this isn't instant."

He nods in agreement. "I don't want to do instant."

"I can't just give you my heart again." I pause, knowing that he already has it whether I like it or not. "I think we need to start fresh. I don't want to jump into anything. I need time to figure you out, and I think you need time to figure *you* out. I'm not the one coming out of a relationship, and although we come with heaps of ridiculous history, and I know I'm not a rebound, I don't want this to be easy."

"But you're still willing to try?"

I nod, submitting to my shell-shocked agreement, biting my lip so hard it might bleed.

"Plus, I doubt you'd ever make anything easy for me," he adds.

I smile, and when the corners of my mouth reach ear-to-ear, a weight lifts from my shoulders and floats away with the passing breeze.

"This is almost mature of us." He chuckles.

"Some might say stupid, but I like your glass-half-full attitude."

He laughs, and it thrums through my body in one deliciously sweet rumble that reaches my fingers and toes.

"I'm going to prove to you that what we're doing isn't close to stupid." He pauses and lifts his hand to tug on his bottom lip, which has me licking mine. "I'm going to do something, but you have to trust me."

I gulp down his words, because when Caiden says *you have to trust me* it usually comes with something that I have to brace myself for in the most heart-thumping way. Which brings my thoughts back to him mentioning chapter 14 and using it as a treasure map.

"Caiden, those are the same words you said in this very spot."

He smiles wide, the corners of his mouth perching high on his scruffy cheekbones. "I remember very clearly. You did trust me that night, and I trusted you. Losing our virginity to each other under the stars that summer is a pretty damn good memory, if I recall."

I blush. "For the most part."

"Well, memorable enough for you to write about."

This time I blush crimson, and there's no denying the fact that is exactly what chapter 14 is all about. "Touché"

He snickers, sitting up enough to lean over my body. "This time my intentions are more innocent... kind of. Hold still, or they won't be."

I want to tell him how silly it is for him to say that when I'm currently petrified to the spot as I watch him sit up. I worry his mouth is going to move to my lips, and then I feel awkward when I'm disappointed they don't. Instead, he shifts his body lower as he perches himself over the lower half of my torso. I watch, intrigued and anxious when he lowers his face close to a very private part of my body. Shocking me further, he lifts his hands to the right side of my hip, lifting the shirt upward with one, and the hem of my jeans down just an inch with the other, revealing his initials that mark my skin as permanently as his presence in my heart.

I watch him lower his face farther and restrain my breathy sigh when I feel his lips touch down on the sensitive skin where the ink sits. He brushes his lips over the writing a few times for good measure, as if sealing his kiss before lifting his head enough to look at me.

"This is a promise, Hailey. I'm going to make everything

right, you'll see. That kiss is me promising you that this is it for us, and we're going to make it this time. And we'll start from the beginning. I'm going to prove to you that I'm ready, and you're going to do the same for me."

There's no stopping it now, and I can't tell if this is me stepping back into the past, or putting effort into a future, but it doesn't matter anymore. This moment is everything.

"Now, let me woo you," he adds.

"It's not that easy—"

"—What did I just say? Wooing. It's happening."

I roll my eyes, but we both can't seem to stop smiling.

14

———

"Stop looking at me like that, Brandon."

"I just don't understand," he asks, seemingly baffled, with a deliberate eyebrow raise as he sips from his beer bottle.

He's leaning against the wall next to the digital jukebox in the bar. My original plan was to come over here and choose some music as a way to put distance between me and the pool table surrounded by my friends. Specifically, so I could avoid Brandon's judgmental eyes. However, because he and CeeCee still aren't talking, he followed me like a puppy.

On any normal day, or at least before Caiden and I talked, I might have welcomed Brandon's dopey need to be around another human, but currently I'm afraid to speak. I lack filters and self-control right now.

Even if Caiden and I decided that we aren't going to tell anyone about giving "us" a fresh start like two strangers, it's been tough being tight-lipped about it.

In the days that have passed, it's been hard to fight my smitten smile, but even harder avoiding CeeCee's probing questions when she calls. All I could do to get her off my back was agreeing to go out tonight. So, here I am.

I'm sure if I did say something about Caiden to her, there would be a shit-show of words from my friends—not necessarily good or bad, more like gossipy and hilarious at my expense. Yeah, I'm not ready for that.

Actually, I'm not sure how it's all going to unfold either, so I might as well try and just—how does the saying go? Oh yeah, "go with the flow."

Do I even know how to do that?

"What's there to understand?" I groan, flipping through the digital display of 70s rock bands.

"Why are you smiling so much and smiling *like that*? It's weird. Stop being weird." He points the tip of his beer at me, but this time it's accusatory. "I could have sworn I dropped you off as a sobbing disaster a week ago."

"I've recovered," I huff, trying my damnedest not to shoot him the intense glare I'm currently giving Pink Floyd.

"You're hiding something."

I shrug. Mouth filter or not, there's no use hiding something like this from Brandon. This I know.

"What if I am?"

"Baby Bird… tell me."

I lift my stare from the jukebox and grab for his beer, taking a sip without permission before replying with, "You're just going to have to wait and see." *Like me.*

I was going to give his beer back to him, but my own words cause a thrum of nerves to roll through my body. Instead, I wave the bottle at him. "Can I have the rest of this?"

His squirrelly smile under his hipster mustache has me muffling a laugh before he snatches his beer back. "I need it more than you."

I give a very unladylike grunt and swivel the opposite direction. Music will have to wait. Liquid courage first.

My body flails as I slam into a rock wall of muscle. Someone's hands are quick to catch me as I stumble.

I'm on the verge of stuttering an apology until I realize the man I walked into has killer green eyes and a wicked curve to his smile that makes me want to kiss it and punch it all at the same time.

"Oh sorry, Miss," Caiden says, watching my apologetic shock transition into beguiled curiosity.

"Caiden, I—"

"—I don't think we've met before. Your name is?"

I laugh, watching his hand jut out for a handshake. Leave it to the bastard to take our talk literally.

I shake my head, staring at his hand, making sure I give his tattoos a diligent glance, too, before I reach for it. The beautiful idiot.

"Oh, we haven't met. My name is Hailey. You are?"

"Caiden." He smiles wide, and I hate what it does to me. Especially when I combine it with the purposefully gentle squeeze of my hand in his, which causes electricity to shoot up my arm and spark my own glorious smile.

I'm so in for it.

We are so in for it.

Brandon, who I almost forgot is standing there, sighs loudly, seemingly unamused as he pushes himself off the wall. "You two are so fucking weird sometimes," he says before walking back to the bar to grab another beer.

"Caiden," I hum, playing with his name on my lips, and I swear you'd think I wielded magic by the way my voice catches his attention as he stares back. As much as I love having his attention like this, a giggle escapes me, because I can't take him seriously. I lift my hand up, pressing my palm against his chest. He's too close. I push him, causing him to take a step back, and pull my hand away. "Okay, you can cut the act now. I don't think I can handle much more."

He's smiling, his lips twitching as he nods his agreement. "What are you drinking?"

I shrug. "You don't have to—"

"What are you drinking?" he repeats.

I shake my head. I'm not ready to play the battle of stubborn wills this early on in the game. "A beer will do."

I turn away and walk back toward my friends before he's left for the bar. I think it's safe to say, and safe for me, to take

Caiden in small doses.

I release a long exhale as I reappear at the pool table and notice CeeCee on one end and Brandon on the other. They're not-so-secretly eyeing each other from across the room.

When I'm standing between them, I garner both of their attention and their simultaneous glare which demands I choose between them. I sigh, shaking my head at both, and walk toward CeeCee, who needs me more than Brandon does. He's got the boys. The girls need to unite.

I ignore the huff from Brandon as I walk over to CeeCee.

"I knew I liked you for a reason," she says.

"Stop. Don't gloat. It's unfair to make me choose. I don't like being in the middle of it. I thought having you two publicly fondling each other was uncomfortable, but I think I might actually prefer that over" —I wave my hand flippantly in the air— "whatever it is that's going on here."

She huffs, shooting me a sad, probing glare. "Well, tell me how you really feel, Hails."

"No, don't take it badly. I just, I don't know how to fix this dynamic."

She shrugs, sipping her drink. "Brandon and I will bounce back. We always do." Her sad resolve makes me want to fix things, but she continues. "Where's your drink? We've been here twenty minutes, and you don't have a drink in your hand. There's something very wrong with this picture."

As if on cue, Caiden appears handing me a beer, gifting me a mischievous smile.

I wish he'd stop staring at me like he wants to make me into a meal. It's more obvious than I think he wants it to be. Plus, it's totally not part of our plan.

I grab for the beer, now distracted from my current conversation to reply, "Thank you."

Caiden stands there, lulling for a moment, and that's when I peek over his shoulder to see Brandon, Cameron, and Tyler looking in our direction like we're from another planet.

"Caiden, go hang out with your friends," I sigh, trying to control the PineCrest Armageddon that could ensue if he doesn't.

He sips his beer nonchalantly, turning his burly body in the direction of his boys.

Brandon capitalizes on it. "Dude, what the fuck?" he says over the music with both arms raised from the other side of the pool table.

Caiden grins, shrugging, before turning back to me.

"Could you be a little more discreet?" I give him a stern look, but it does nothing to his stupid smile.

CeeCee screeches into our conversation, her hand coming between Caiden and me, slapping both our chests as she flails her hand left to right a few times.

"Uhhh, did I miss something here?"

I shake my head, pursing my lips and closing my eyes to gain some sense of balance and backbone before I reply with, "No, nothing. Everything's fine."

It's CeeCee's high-pitched huff that has my eyes re-opening. "I chewed this guy a new one in the name of best friends, and you're here openly flirting with the same guy, who has a *girlfriend*."

I wince. Maybe I deserve that because I was so harsh about her and Brandon, or maybe it's because my flash flood of tears at the bonfire were painful to witness as a best friend. Regardless, I don't know what to say.

"I don't have a girlfriend," sounds from Mister Brilliant.

I groan, wiping the nervous drops of sweat forming on my brow while trying to figure out how my heart can beat so frantically while still managing to tremble. I just keep my mouth shut and take a large pull of my beer, enjoying the chill down my throat that finds a way to soothe the volcano of nerves forming inside me.

"You what?" CeeCee screeches in disbelief. Her eyes should be on Caiden. It's his news, not mine. But unfortunately, they are penetrating blue orbs of comical frustration, coming at me like an avalanche falling over a cliff of freckles.

I shrug, and she hates it.

"Hailey Lynn Elwood. What. The. Fuck."

I shake my head, totally baffled by the response, and I laugh. "Why are you mad at me?"

"You knew?"

I shrug again. She scowls.

"I knew for, like, a minute. Can you please give Caiden the twenty questions? This is Caiden's news, not mine."

Instead of giving Caiden her attention, she takes a step forward, purposefully wedging her body between Caiden and me. We both flinch in confusion, taking a step back.

CeeCee raises her hand, and Brandon is quick to notice as he says to her from across the room, "You trying to get my attention now, princess?"

She rolls her eyes, "Shut up and come here."

He shakes his head. "Not until you apologize."

I perk up at this, especially when CeeCee's cheeks burn bright red. She tries shaking it off. "This isn't about us. You're going to want to hear this. Caiden broke up with Kristen."

Brandon smiles triumphantly as he trails over with newfound interest. He waves at Cameron and Tyler, who are laughing behind him, to follow.

This is not at all how I wanted this to be unraveled.

"Baby Bird, this is the secret you were keeping?"

I can't stay tight-lipped any longer. "You've all lost your minds. How the hell is this *my* secret?"

A light must turn on in Caiden's thick skull, because finally he speaks. "This isn't a big deal."

I wish I could say he sounds convincing, but the stupid smile he can't seem to shake is too incriminating.

CeeCee and Brandon speak in unison. "*The fuck it isn't.*"

I laugh again, finding my sense of balance in the humor of the situation as I quip, "I'm happy to see this situation is what could bring you two back together."

They glare at me, and I love it. Caiden laughs, too.

Brandon shakes his head. "You got jokes?"

"For you Brandon boy, I got tons."

Both of our mouths squirm, holding back laughter. I know he (and CeeCee) wouldn't want their relationship so publicly talked about, but he asked for it.

He changes tack, turning away from me and back to Caiden. "Dude. We're bros. Hailey gets back into town, and you two suddenly start sharing secrets again?"

Caiden shakes his head. "It's not like that. You saw the disaster at the bonfire, and you know the shit that was going down before. The relationship was over before Kristen went AWOL. I did what we both needed."

I cringe, because I will never get used to it when Caiden refers to him and his (now) ex-girlfriend as *we*.

"You sure about that? I was wondering what it was gonna take," Brandon replies.

I peek over at CeeCee, who has the decency to gift me a best friend look of: *Huh, ain't that curious?*

Caiden squares his shoulders uncomfortably. "Yeah well, we finally reached a breaking point."

Brandon boldly jabs a finger into Caiden's shoulder. I'm sure it's supposed to be playful, but these two tend to get a bit alpha when they talk about things that might involve their *feelings*. It's almost cute, in that caveman sort of way.

"I just didn't think you had the balls to do it, since she took your balls months ago."

"Well," Caiden grunts, his patience wearing thin as he replies through clenched teeth. "I grew my balls back, now fuck off."

Brandon enjoys the moment too much to let it go. His shoulders shake as he releases a slew of burly chuckles at Caiden's expense. For a moment I worry, but then my own laughter emerges, because, well—it's funny.

I laugh. I squeal. I may even snort. That's when CeeCee

joins in.

I wish I didn't think Caiden looks so beautiful angry, but he does. A beautiful idiot with thick furrowing brows, piercing jade depths, and an adorable grimace.

I reach out to touch his tattooed arm to calm him even though I'm still laughing.

His skin feels as hot as his anger, but it at least gets him to turn to face me. "Caiden," I sigh, "C'mon. He's messing with you. It's nothing new."

His eyes fall to my hand touching him, and I can feel his body let go of that tension that's wound so tight.

Brandon hums as he takes in the scene. "I guess it was just a matter of time."

We must be so obvious, and now I don't know what feels appropriate. Thinking about it makes me feel bad for Kristen, even if I don't like her, but it's hard for me to wrap my head around the feeling. I pull my hand away.

It's Caiden's reflexive sigh that has me understanding he feels the same.

"There's nothing going on," I blurt out to all of my favorite people. "We're just friends."

CeeCee is back in a flash. "Who are you trying to convince here?"

There's no winning with these people, just as I predicted.

My optimistic attitude is on the brink of vanishing, and I get real with my friends, because if I don't, there's no hope for any of us.

"Hey!" erupts from me.

Chuckles, giggles, and chatter stop, and CeeCee even manages to soften the anger that lines her face.

"Baby Bird" is uttered swiftly, as if the almighty Brandon is the one who notices my frustration, or maybe he's being apologetic.

"Do me a favor, guys," I ask. "Give us some space. Nothing is going on. You're right: Caiden just broke it off with," I gulp down her name as I say it, and it goes down like a sour Skittle, my face puckering, "*Kristen*. Can we have a little compassion here? Maybe even a little time? I can only take so much. You want things to be good? Then I suggest you let this go and stop giving us a hard time, all right? We're taking this… slow."

CeeCee's hand collides with Brandon's chest, and I swear he smiles. They're so weird. "Let it go, Brandon. I think it's for the best," she says.

They stroll away almost like they like each other again, and I cross my fingers at the thought.

I exhale, lifting my stare to find that Caiden's eyes haven't moved from mine.

"Stop it," I snap, forcing myself to turn away.

"You care about me."

I shake my head, fighting off a laugh through squirming lips again. "Nope. No, I don't."

I notice from across the room that CeeCee and Brandon have gone back to bickering. I think that might be them getting back to normal. *The sick games we play.*

"You care about me a lot," Caiden quips smugly.

"I don't know where you got that idea. Maybe you're confused with the fact that I have a reputation to keep now."

He rolls his eyes. "How could I forget you're famous now."

My gut bubbles when I hear that term, and I worry he already knows how much it makes me uncomfortable. I'm losing my footing fast. My cheeks heat. I try to be clever and go with it. Although, I can't form words, so I just nod.

He leans on one foot, tilting his head curiously, seeing right through me. "Doesn't that mean I'm famous, too?"

"No, it doesn't."

"It totally should. Aren't they making a movie out of our book?"

My brows pucker tightly, and my nerves dissipate into something more comical. I fight a smile. "Did you just say *our* book?"

He nonchalantly drinks from his beer as he nods.

"It's *my* book," I exclaim.

He shakes his head, admonishing me with a smirk. "They should cast me as the lead in the movie, don't you think? It only seems appropriate."

"You actually don't look anything like the character," I chide. Not having the character resemble him was a purposeful tactic.

He snorts. "I think they'd make an exception."

I roll my eyes. "Are you done?"

He laughs victoriously, winning a battle against my nerves, and takes a confident step closer. My palm flies up to his chest. I hesitate, which wasn't my plan. I stare at my hand flat against his sternum. I wiggle my fingers a bit, loving how warm and hard he feels.

My eyes fling themselves up to see Caiden staring at my hand with a well-crafted smile. *Bastard.*

I find the discipline to push him away.

"You need to keep your distance for now."

"Sorry, I'm working on it."

A tiny, barely-there whimper of displeasure escapes me, and luckily it goes unnoticed.

The idea of him actively trying to stay away feels so… unproductive. I remind myself that it needs to be this way even though I'm having a hard time remembering why when he's watching me so closely.

I pull in a leveling breath. "I'm going to walk away now."

"If you must."

I scoot around his rigid frame, and I notice him being a bit stunned by my resistance to his… charm? I'm not sure I'd call it that.

Gosh, I think I'm going to need something stronger than beer.

With this in mind, I walk straight to the bar and wave at

the burly gentleman wiping down the counter.

"Nice seeing you in here rather than the diner, sweet pea."

I smile at the gentleman known as Hal Yates who I've known since I was a kid, like everyone else here. Last I heard, his wife passed away a few years back. He's been passing through the diner pretty frequently since I've been waitressing there. He tips well, even though I tell him not to.

"How's business, Hal? Looks like you've got a crowd tonight. I should have brought you pie!"

He nods, looking around while tapping his belly. "I'll hold off on the pie for now. For me, it's the regular crowd for a Friday night."

I nod, too, acting like I understand. I've been here a few weeks now, and I don't necessarily feel like I fit in like I used to. I'm still trying to catch up.

His croaky voice pulls me back as he says, "You a regular now?"

I turn my head to look back at my friends. For the first time, the sight looks normal, even with our older age. The boys and CeeCee huddle in the corner, all arm to arm like a little family. Caiden seems to be in the middle of telling a story, and I think it's the most relaxed I've seen him since I got back. When the corners of his mouth lift high as he releases a loud laugh, I don't know why the inside of my chest tightly writhes with a combination of gleeful hope and foreboding terror. Caiden looks up and catches me staring. I blush, turning away to shoot Hal a crooked, mournful smile and ignore his question. "I'll take a gin and tonic please, make it a double."

Hal nods, but I get the feeling he's agreeing to something else entirely as he silently makes my drink.

"On the house, sweet pea. Can't say your mom would approve of me mentioning this, but just so you know, that was her favorite drink."

My cheeks heat, and I grin. "Really?"

"She'd also never like me to admit how often she might have been in here."

I go wide-eyed, eager for a new type of information I have yet to encounter until now. "No way? Can't say I'm that surprised. I guess we were never the churchgoing family."

He laughs, and it feels like a mini-accomplishment.

I grab for my drink, take a tight sip, liking my reflexive smile powered by curiosity. "My mom ever soft on anyone, Hal? She ever, I don't know, date? Or have friends I didn't know about?"

He stumbles, pausing a beat, just enough to cause a giggle to spurt from my lips, especially when he can't do anything to hide his own reddening cheeks.

"Can't say I knew anything about that."

I nod, taking a longer sip this time. I don't want to push it. Hal is a proud man, and I won't mess with him in his own bar, but I'm pretty sure I know enough to feel satisfied. Maybe my mom was a flirt. It'd give us something in common.

"This town teaches me something new every day, I swear."

He shrugs, rubbing at his weathered face and grey stubble. "Sometimes it ain't just the town, it's the people, Hailey Elwood."

"What does that mean?" I say, taking a bigger pull of my drink before placing it onto the bar.

He raises his brow, scolding me. "It means that although roots are important, sometimes it's the people that teach you the things you need. Sometimes, putting your focus on a place, rather than its inhabitants, can distract you from what's really important."

I sigh, regaining my center as I smile. "I can see why my mother would like you, Hal."

He laughs, deep and thunderous as he shakes his head, waving a hand at me. "Get outta here…"

Before he can reveal more scarlet color to his jolly cheeks he walks away, releasing deep laughter as he saunters down the bar to get someone a beer.

I finish the rest of my drink, leaving the glass, and do my best to contain my goofy grin as I walk back toward my friends with a rejuvenated sense of self, the hope winning the battle against the fear, which is always the best feeling.

As I take long strides, I lift my head to catch Caiden's eyes already on me as he hugs his beer to his chest. He's supposed to be listening to Cameron, who's explaining how he thinks Olivia Humbolt has the hots for him as I approach.

Usually, I'd roll my eyes at him, but mine are currently being pulled in by the green tractor beam in front of me.

CeeCee, who I didn't see standing next to Cam, nudges me with her hip as I come to a stop, pulling my stare away.

She leans in to whisper, "You look happy, Hails."

I shrug. "I think I am."

"That's the best news I've heard from you in ages." She pauses, licking her lips before adding in an even quieter voice so no one can hear, "I'm sorry I freaked out on you about Caiden. You two are—"

I wave my hand, cutting her off, replying in the same low tone, "We are nothing."

"Hailey…"

I peer up at the rough-and-tumble voice that's suddenly beckoning me, interrupting my conversation with CeeCee. I worry I'm not going to be able to hide how my joints have turned into jello.

"Yes, Caiden?" I reply.

"Can I talk to you outside?" he asks.

I feel the eyes of all my friends on me like hot fire. I don't care what they might be thinking, but it doesn't mean I have the confidence to speak, so I nod.

Caiden makes it a point to shimmy past me, not asking anything of me, not his hand or touch, but merely to follow—and I do.

When I turn around, CeeCee says this time loud enough for everyone to hear, "It sure don't look like nothin'."

I have half a mind to react, but I don't. I follow Caiden

out the door, not turning to see my friends gawking, which I know they are.

When I reach the outside, the evening hits me like a refreshing wave. I close my eyes and halt my feet just so I can bask in it, the silence being half of the feeling of rejuvenation.

I hear boots crunching on the gravel in front of me. My eyes spring open.

Caiden is there, bobbing on his boots, finally offering his hand to me.

I squint at it. "What happened to keeping your distance?"

He shrugs. "I'm working on it," he repeats but doesn't pull his hand back.

Without having the bar as an audience, I grin, grabbing for it.

I want to ask him how this is so easy for him. How he can ask me for a moment or reach out for my hand so easily? How does he find the confidence to do these tiny things that I'm still struggling with? After talking about taking things slow, me letting him woo me, and him explaining his previous relationship, I'm still on edge. I'm still so cautious.

"Relax, Hails."

We make it to the back of his truck when he yanks at my hand, pulling me to him.

"You're so tense," he adds.

"Of course, I am. You terrify me." My teeth come down hard on my bottom lip, and I curse gin for breaking my mouth filter.

He smiles, the twist of his brow saying something more. "Don't you think I should be the terrified one?"

My chest constricts, and he must notice because he pulls us further into the shadows between his truck and Brandon's. He pushes me against his truck as he says, "Stop thinking so hard; it's not healthy."

"Did you just tell me thinking isn't healthy?"

He towers over me, giving off that effortless closeness as

he leans in. "With you? Yeah. When I watch you think, I worry I'm going to see a nerve burst, right" —he lifts his large hand to my face, pressing his index finger in the center of my forehead— "here. You think too much." His hand hovers and then smooths over my face, cupping my jaw to lift my eyes to look at him.

"How is this so easy for you?" I sigh, loving the feeling of his hand against me.

He shrugs, humming as his lips twitch adoringly. "You don't get it. You're the only thing that comes easy to me."

I grin. Actually, I want to cry from happiness at hearing those words. An overwhelming sense of understanding washes over me.

"Ya know," he continues. "I used to be easy for you, too."

"I know. You still are. I'm just trying to resist it."

"Don't. Please don't."

I sigh dopily. My resistance is merely a shield, and he knows it. A shield that's ridiculously exhausting to keep up at all times.

"Okay," I reply, letting my shoulders slump. I worry that Caiden could ask me to do anything and I wouldn't have the power to turn him down anymore.

He smiles victoriously, and I stare at his beautiful mouth as the corners lift. I remember how rough yet soothing his lips felt against mine, even after all these years.

"Do you want to kiss me, Hailey?"

My eyes spring to his. "Maybe."

He leans in. "Me, too."

I giggle, and he mirrors it with a chuckle of his own. His humid breath fans over my face, sending tingles right down to my core, and I'm having a hard time defining what my reality is because this teeters on surreal.

"Caiden, we were going to take things slow."

"Life is short, and I'm sick of wasting time, aren't you?" he retorts.

I understand so completely.

Exhilarated by his words, I bite down on my bottom lip and take a playful step to the side, trying to find home in the effortless side that Caiden used to give me—still gives me.

I pull in a deep inhale, the smell of pine and Caiden's smoky cologne making for a blissfully heady cocktail, and all I want is to drop the wall I built so fiercely around my heart.

The left corner of his mouth rises as he watches me, crumbling my caution, telling me he remembers this game, and that I'm finally willing to let go. It causes my heart to flutter.

Will we always be kids? God, I hope so. I didn't think that would be something I wanted so badly.

"Don't run," he chides while blowing out a less than calm breath that gets my blood pumping.

I grin, my lips puckering together to try and contain it as I take another deliberate step away from him.

"Hailey…" he hums. He also takes a step forward, preparing his start, knowing where this is going. I lick my bottom lip. His black boots crunch on the gravel. The low sound of music vibrates through the walls of the bar. I love that we're alone, and we have this moment. It's always easier when it's just us.

This is what I missed. We've always been goofy idiots. We were playmates as much as we were best friends and lovers. We played games that no one cared to understand, and that's just the way we liked it.

I don't remember the last time I felt this free.

This time when I turn around and run, it's not in fear. I welcome the chase, but I'm more eager about being caught.

Tag, you're it.

A shriek of a laugh escapes me when I don't make it three steps before his hands are on my hips, swinging me back. Next thing I know, I'm being playfully flung back against his truck.

The sound of the wind being knocked out of me emerges in the form of a skirting giggle, but everything below my waist clenches tight when Caiden's eyes pin me to the spot, and I'm put into a silent trance, my lips twitching anxiously.

He leans in, his humid breath skimming over my mouth again, fanning that fire burning inside me. The curve to his lips tells me he's enjoying this, but that look in his eye is deadly serious. I try that whole breathing thing I'm not so good at when he's around.

"You always did suck at that game," he whispers.

He leans in a little bit closer, and I'm ready for my rebuttal, but his laughter interrupts me. "Hailey, can you do me a favor and just shut up for once?"

My brows pull together. "What, why?"

His lips crashing against mine. His smile against my newly formed one as his lips find a rhythm with mine is the happiest I've been in a long while. I could drink him in forever.

He tastes like a welcome bout of homesickness. The kind that makes me realize that homesickness isn't a place, but a person. This is the moment I don't feel so lost anymore. I'm home because he's home. It's the most insane epiphany I've ever had.

My arms involuntarily lift, wrapping around his neck, pulling his body closer. His hard, lean frame presses against the length of mine, sending a carnal thrill through my body. His hands lift, making a deliberate, electric trail down the nape of my neck, over my shoulders, down my torso to take a firm grip on my hip bones. My nerves spark erratically at his touch, especially when I can feel just a couple fingers make contact with a bit of bare skin above my skirt.

His tongue dips into my mouth, and I don't try to contain my whimper as my fingers find a way to tangle into his hair, anchoring his mouth to mine.

This moment is precious to me because there's nothing holding us back anymore. I try to cherish it, but the good things only last so long, and if you have friends like mine, they wouldn't allow it.

A loud, long, drawn-out whistle comes from the bar. We

pull away, out of breath and totally caught.

"Slow, my ass!" Brandon shouts from the doorway, dragging a reluctant CeeCee behind him, which can't be a good thing, but my mind is somewhere else entirely.

I feel a little twinge of anger that my moment with Caiden's lips was cut short by my oaf of a friend, and lucky for me the feeling must be mutual.

"Do you always have to be an asshole?" Caiden shouts.

"Yes. It's how I keep your shit in line. You two should take it easy," he reprimands.

"As if you know anything about taking things easy!" Caiden shoots back.

A tight huff squeaks out of CeeCee from behind Brandon as if in agreement, and that's when it becomes clear that she's an unwilling hostage. I'd focus on that, but what's worse is, I hate that part of me agrees with what Brandon said about us.

I step away from Caiden, who tries grabbing for my hand, but I slither away as I walk into the openness of the parking lot. His groan of annoyance is most definitely heard.

"What are you doing, Brandon?" I shout back, smoothing out my clothes as I do.

"Taking Cee home," he responds. "And don't worry, we're both going home sexually frustrated as all hell." I try not to laugh but fail as it comes off as a snort. "She drank too much, and I think she's had enough, trust me. Just doing my duty and dropping her off before she makes more of a scene."

She shrugs, not necessarily fighting his words. I tilt my head to the right, peeking at her disposition, judging her tweaked hip and arms crossed over her chest in annoyance even though she hasn't budged from Brandon's side. I hate how CeeCee always has to play hard to get. It has me almost feeling bad for Brandon. Almost.

I roll my eyes at the whole scene. "I don't know how you can stand there and lecture Caiden on relationship logistics when all of us are so fucked up."

All four of us release a loud, pent-up burst of laughter I didn't know my words would ignite. Maybe some things are truer than others, and this is proof. We're all so out of our minds when it comes to love that it's hilarious at this point.

Brandon lets his laughter trail off in an exhausted sigh. "Well, Cameron is still convinced Olivia is trying to get into his pants, so he's inside still trying to get her to come home with him."

Caiden comes up to stand beside me, rubbing at his swollen lips as he says, "Sounds like Olivia is the one that isn't so convinced."

"You got that right."

"I'm going to take Hailey home, too."

I look at him with wide eyes. This is news to me.

Brandon nods, waving a flippant hand at us. "Whatever."

Both boys whisk off their reluctant dates, me included.

CeeCee keeps barking at Brandon when he tries to open the truck door for her, and I keep eyeing Caiden with a suspicious glare as I climb into his truck without his help.

Brandon and Caiden just laugh at their own private joke, while I try to hide how anxious I am now that I've taken down my shield when it comes to Caiden Anderson.

When Caiden's truck comes to a stop in my driveway, I want to say something clever, or even funny, but I'm too rattled by the silence that filled our drive from the bar to here. He hasn't even touched me, which feels odd because he pretty much devoured me like I was his last meal on death row approximately fifteen minutes ago.

"Why'd you do that?" I ask, wincing because I know he can't read my mind and figure out what the hell I mean. Also, that wasn't remotely clever.

He turns off his truck and turns toward me. I think he's

smirking.

"Do what?" he asks, and I come to the conclusion he's most definitely smirking at me from that tone.

"Touch me?" I question.

There's a longer pause than I expect. "Do you want me to touch you?"

"I meant during the drive. You didn't even try to touch me, not even my hand."

"Hailey, what do you want?" I hate the curious hum in his tone. This is all a game to him.

I huff. He will not make me into a plaything. Not when it comes to this. "You're messing with me now, and I don't appreciate it. But funny, since you're asking, I think I want you to drive yourself back home now."

I start climbing out of his truck, and I can hear his laughter.

He's already coming up behind me as I approach the porch steps. "Hailey, I'm sorry. You make it too easy for me sometimes. I didn't touch you because I thought you wanted some space. I'm trying to read this for what it is. I'm trying to pace myself."

I turn around, nodding. "I understand that. That kiss was just—"

"—Tilted my world on its axis? Yeah. I'm actually trying to rationalize it at the moment. That's why maybe even I need some space. You know what I mean? I want you, all of you, but in the right way, like we talked about."

I sigh, laughing as I remember something, feeling like the ridiculous one. "This reminds me of when I was the one trying to convince you we should lose our virginity to each other."

He takes a confident step forward, putting us nearly chest to chest. His presence overwhelms me when he gets this confidence that pulls the rug from underneath me. I lose my breath.

"Does this mean you're trying to get me in your bed,

Hailey Elwood?"

I'm thankful for the darkness as I turn crimson. I shake my head violently, totally embarrassed. "Get your head outta the gutter. No-no-no. What I meant by that was, I'm always the one in the end who has a hard time not rushing things. It's just funny to realize that you've always been the person to rein me in, even though you're generally crazier."

"You think I'm crazy?"

"Err—kind of. You know what I mean? You were always the more adventurous one, and here I am trying my hardest to play this the right way but failing."

"How can you not see that you're the adventurous one out of the two of us? I'll take that I'm crazy at times, and sometimes irrational, but damn Hailey, can't you see you're the most fearless person in this town?"

I release a happy sigh and close my eyes briefly, soaking in the moment. "Sometimes I forget how much faith you've always had in me, even if you didn't follow me to Los Angeles."

His arms come around to hug me close. I lean my cheek against his chest and breathe him in. I think what I've said must have struck a chord. We stand in silence after that. It lasts so long, I worry maybe I've said the wrong thing.

"Can I tuck you in?" erupts from Caiden, banishing the worry. I release a cathartic giggle at the question.

"Tuck me in?" I ask, pulling away, shaking my head. "You're cute, but no. Maybe it's best you kiss me goodnight and go on your way."

I turn around, knowing that the moment isn't over. If I could, I'd never want the night to end. I've challenged Caiden in my most favorite way, and he's never been one to back down.

Sure enough, I can hear him behind me as I approach my front door.

His clunky boots hit my porch, and I'm waiting for his rebuttal as I pull my keys from my pocket. I want Caiden to tuck me in, but the battle is lost when out of nowhere a skirting meow rounds the corner of the porch as Soot comes into view. He runs up to Caiden, rubbing himself all over his leg.

I'm baffled at the animal who's unceremoniously taking my moment away. "He never does that to me, and I feed him. Obviously, he loves you more."

Caiden's smug grin glows in the moonlight. He leans down to grab for the cat, the animal appearing miniature in his arms when he brings him up to his chest. My knees wobble.

As if knowing my kryptonite, he lifts the cat to his face, shamelessly rubbing the cute creature against his scruff, their eyes matching green. Good God, it's body-liquefyingly adorable.

"Wanna let me in now?" Caiden asks, rubbing his face with equal affection against the feline.

"You're kidding me right now?" I pant.

"Aren't we cute?" he chides with a deep timbre to his voice that has a bizarre way of complimenting the scene before me.

I sigh, squinting at this guy and his cat. The tables have turned, and I've lost my footing.

My brain has lost its reason for its existence as I reply, "Fine."

I open my door, and it isn't until I see my suitcase sitting in the living room where I left it that I realize I was too caught up in my gooey moment with Caiden to remember one thing.

"You're kidding me, right?" Caiden blurts as he walks in, noticing the same thing as me. "I thought we agreed you were sleeping in your bed?"

I shrug, feeling caught. "I couldn't."

His thick brows pull together as he shoots me a look of concerned disapproval. He places Soot onto the floor and closes the door behind him.

I pout when he turns around. "Don't be mad at me."

He growls with an exasperated sigh. "I'm not mad—well,

maybe a little. Hailey, I just thought..." He pauses to scratch the back of his head as if to think of a way to approach this. "I thought we were past this. I thought we made progress. I want to believe you're doing okay. This has me worried."

I blink back the sudden water that appears at the edges of my eyes when I try to reply with, "We did make progress, and I am okay."

He extends his hand out, and I know what he's going to do. I shake my head.

"Hailey, take my hand."

"I don't want to sleep up there, Caiden. Don't do this."

"Trust me."

I grit my teeth when he says that. "This isn't about trust. Please don't make this about me and you."

"I know it's not. Remember how you mentioned all that faith I have in you? Well, c'mon. I know you can do it."

I blink more furiously to keep the tears at bay, trying to figure out how the night took such a turn. Before I can lift a hand to my eyes to wipe the overflow away, I'm suddenly being thrown over a shoulder. I yelp, not seeing it coming.

"Caiden! No!"

He doesn't reply, but instead starts stomping upstairs with me slung over his shoulder.

"Caiden, I can't!" I shout, trying to squirm out of his arms, but he's a solid piece of man, unmoving and stubborn.

He bursts through my closed bedroom door, the stale sweet smell hitting me. He doesn't turn the light on, but slowly puts me down on my feet in front of him.

Before I can get words out, his lips crash to mine, his hands fiercely grabbing for my face, anchoring my mouth to his, as if he fears I'll pull away. I would never.

I don't care about words when his lips are against mine. Not when I've lost so much valuable time when it comes to us. I hum a sweet moan as my tears subside and my body calms.

His tongue dips into my mouth for a taste, then dances over my bottom lip before he pulls away, leaving me out of breath.

"I'm going to tuck you in, Hails."

My face still in his grasp, I try to shake my head in disagreement. "I don't want to sleep here alone," I reply more pathetically than I'd like.

"Who says I'm going anywhere?"

My breath catches in my throat. "We agreed on slow," I gasp, even though my heart thumps with the need for him to be close.

He kisses the tip of my nose, then places a chaste kiss against my lips before replying with, "And who said you're getting into my pants tonight?"

I laugh, but it comes out as a croak when clashing with my emotional state.

"I'm here for you. We'll do this together, okay?"

With the wall I've built nearly obliterated now, I exhale the words, "Together sounds nice."

The corners of his mouth lift under his thick scruff. He releases my face to trail his hands heavily down my body until reaching the button of my skirt.

I continue to hold my breath as I watch him. He releases the button with a half-smile, letting the fabric pool at my feet. His eyes stay pinned to mine, as if to say the moment isn't about how badly he might want my body, but simply about *me*. I want to cry all over again, but for an entirely different reason now.

I lick my lips when I feel his hands come to the hem of my tank top, and he lets his fingers loiter against the skin above my panties before pulling the tight material up and over my head.

I'm in just my black lacy bra and black boy-short underwear. I've never been one for sexy, but I'd be lying if I didn't admit I might have actually matched this pair of underwear just in case Caiden might see it.

This time he lets his eyes drop down, and his vision

sizzles down the length of my body. I smile, glad for the darkness, because I'm sure I'm blushing everywhere.

"Your turn," I whisper.

I lift my hand to his jeans, unbuttoning them and pushing them over his strong, narrow hips, trying to keep my limbs from shaking.

When his jeans pool at his feet, I don't hesitate in grabbing for his shirt, but I make sure when I move to lift it over his head that my thumbs drag over the surface of his skin until it's off.

Surprising him, I take his shirt and pull it over my body. It hangs baggily over me, but the warmth from it against my skin calms me.

I can hear his tight, short chuckle of appreciation once I have it on. It isn't until then that he leans in, presses an adoring kiss against my lips, and says, "You're beautiful."

We climb into bed, tangle our arms and legs around each other, and fall asleep under the same covers we did five years ago.

Together never felt so good.

15

My eyes flicker open. I can't figure out what's woken me up, and I can't remember where I am. I should be startled, but I'm more stunned, distracted by what's directly above me as I'm lying on my back.

I squint, examining the chipped paint on the off-white ceiling, and its familiarity pings my well-being. The recognition sends a shiver through me when I connect the chipped paint to the many evenings I'd spent in my childhood bedroom throwing a softball at the ceiling as I waited for Caiden to come to my window.

My chin falls to the left, trying to put the pieces together. Caiden. He's here.

My eyes widen in disbelief. I have to admit, in the years I spent away from home, my nightmares usually started out like this. Normally, they'd be dreams, but the cruelty of the situation would hit hard when a much more baby-faced Caiden would evaporate from my imagination to reveal nothing but darkness; then I'd wake up in a cold sweat of homesickness. So I keep blinking at him, waiting for that moment, but his eyes flicker open and catch me staring.

The right corner of his mouth lifts. "Morning," he whispers gruffly.

I'm too enthralled by the color of his eyes in the early

sunshine to respond, and instead my hand rises of its own accord. My fingertips dance up and over the thick scruff of his jaw. His full smile forms as he watches me in awe.

My fingers trail into his bedhead of hair. I'm so stunned he's here lying in bed with me and staring at me like I'm his world, when I thought I'd never get a moment like this ever again.

I'm still terrified I'm dreaming and that he'll disappear, so I lean in, not wanting to wake up, wanting to savor what I have as much as possible, even if I made it all up in my head.

I press my lips to his, feeling their warmth and their gentle caress against mine as my eyes sink closed.

His hand curves over my hip, his grip tightening against my overheated skin under the blanket.

He pulls away with a delightful hum as he says, "Well, that's a first."

"What are you talking about?"

"You kissed me." His hand gently squeezes at my hip again, sending a thrill to every neuron in my body.

I shake my head. "What? We've already kissed since I came back."

"Yeah, but I've always kissed *you*. This time you kissed *me* first."

He tweaks a brow, and I have a hard time containing my giggles. Leave it to him to keep track of that.

"I guess I never realized. Sorry."

He nods, tutting as he licks his bottom lip. "You could make it up to me?"

"Clever you." And I don't hesitate. I don't want to hesitate anymore. I close the distance between us to kiss him again, and this time I'm met with unrestrained fervor.

His lips coax mine open, and his tongue explores my mouth, tasting me. I match him for every stroke and release a moan when his hand on my hip pulls me roughly against him, aligning our bodies together in one heated mess.

A crashing wave of a sensory overload washes over me.

The smell of my sugary room, the woody scent of his skin, and the soft, worn cotton of the sheets against the exposed parts of my body, with the addition of his frantic mouth all makes for a delicious concoction that my breathy gasps can barely keep up with.

His low growl when his tongue strokes over mine ignites a frenzy. My hands slide down his neck and over his shoulders, enjoying the feeling of his bare skin, my fingers digging into the hard flesh of his biceps as he pushes me onto my back again, pressing my body into the bed with his.

He whispers, "Hailey," when he takes a second to pull in a tiny, leveling breath before his mouth is back on mine. My body buzzes when it absorbs that deep, pleading tone in the form of my name on his lips.

His mouth moves down the nape of my neck, leaving a burning trail in its wake as his right hand moves under his shirt that I'm wearing, smoothing up over the skin of my torso.

I've never felt so alive. I can feel every neuron pulsing in sync with my rapid heartbeat. I want him closer. I want him everywhere. For a second, I consider I'm dreaming again because I can't remember when I felt this good.

My legs wrap around his hips, pulling him into me, and I can feel the hardness of his erection against the apex of my thighs.

He pulls away to release an exasperated breath, pushing his hips in harder, rubbing himself against my throbbing core as he rests his head between my shirted breasts. His panting breaths come out as deep grunts.

"Caiden," I finally whisper back.

He lifts his chin to reveal his firecracker eyes, the gold in the green, brighter and more fiery than I've ever seen them.

"Hailey, I..."

The sounds of vibrating bass and tires coming over my gravel driveway float through the window above my desk.

"No!" Caiden says instead of finishing his sentence.

"Goddammit, no..."

His hips press into mine in urgency as he releases an exasperated breath, burying his face into my shoulder.

When I hear a high-pitched giggle outside once the sound of music stops, and the rush of grinding gravel as a vehicle comes to a stop, I groan with him.

"What are they doing here?" escapes me.

He lifts his chin up, his eyes heated and frustrated. He pushes himself forward until his lips are feather-like against mine, and I can't tell what I find more erotic: his hard body against me or the teasing anticipation of his lips against my mouth.

"Let's just not answer the door." He brushes his lips against mine from side to side, delicately trying to convince me.

"You know that won't work."

"I don't want to wait. Not for this." This time he crashes his lips hard and unforgiving against my mouth.

I moan in unison with the sound of the doorbell.

"Caiden," I try to whisper, but it comes out muddled and whiney.

His gruff laugh is what I hear in response as he pulls away saying, "Don't say no."

I shake my head, gathering my wits. I'm pulling in that deep breath, hoping for clarity, but Caiden surrounds me. He's my atmosphere in this little bubble of us, and I love it, but I try for logic.

"Maybe we should, *um*, take it easy."

His eyes burn flatly as he stares back. "You don't mean that."

I release a wry smile at his obvious disappointment. I place flat palms on his bare shoulders, pushing him off and onto his back, switching places as I climb onto his hips, straddling him, trying to desperately ignore his hard-on rubbing against where I want it.

"Please tell me this is where we pick up where we left

off?" he asks, his large hands still cradling me at the waist.

"Caiden," I sigh again. I'm trying to reprimand him, but when he's sitting up, putting us nose-to-nose, I know I've failed.

"If you keep saying my name like that, I won't let you win."

Ding-dong

I want him so badly, and when I watch the corner of his mouth rise, I know I'm all too obvious. I want to be the stronger one here, but I'm starting to question my grip. It's a battle of wills, and the push and pull is messing with my head.

"Have it your way, Hails," Caiden replies in defeat, reading my face. He doesn't bother kissing me again before he lifts me easily off his hips, plopping me unceremoniously onto the bed as he swings his legs over the edge of the mattress.

He groans as he readjusts his dark grey briefs, but it doesn't stop me thinking he's handling this battle better than I thought, because now I'm the one pouting.

He stands, and I'm thrown when I scan his burly form stretched out in the bright sunshine, and his thick muscles are defined as clear as the day outside, leaving nothing to the imagination when he's only wearing snug boxer briefs. I didn't have the night or the proper lighting to give my admiring justice.

Ding-doooong.

"Hailey?"

"Hm." I'm so sexually frustrated and mesmerized by the deep V of his hips that I don't bother looking up. "What?"

"You're wearing my shirt."

My eyes try peeling away his briefs with imaginary telekinetic powers, but when the elastic doesn't budge and the silence hangs too long, I lift my stare to see him grinning smugly. Yup, I'm definitely not winning.

"So what?" I reply.

"Would you like me to go answer your door like this?"

He's trying to push my buttons, but the idea ignites something else entirely. A mischievous smile of my own appears, and I know how to regain my footing. I scoot off the bed, pulling his shirt off in one move, tossing it at his chest.

"Here."

I bend down to grab for my shirt and skirt from last night. When I rise, his eyes trail over my body, following all the curves and dips until he meets my eyes. I widen my grin.

"So, this is how it's going to be?" he says.

I nod, pulling my shirt over my head. "Yup."

"Game on."

I shake my head, giggling, and slip my skirt over my hips. "This isn't a game, Caiden. This is about doing the right thing." I turn around and try making my way to the bedroom door.

"Me being inside you isn't the right thing?"

I stop dead in my tracks and stumble when I reach the doorframe, grabbing for it before I fall. I turn my chin to look at him. He clicks his tongue triumphantly, knowing exactly what he's doing.

His eyes dare me to tempt him again. My libido and my psyche can't handle that option at the moment. Not with words like that.

It's not like I didn't know Caiden has a dirty mouth, because my eighteen-year-old self surely remembers those moments, but I somehow forgot about it among his supposed *wooing*.

I grumble and feign annoyance, and maybe stomp my foot ever so slightly. "You're totally not playing fair now."

"I thought you said it wasn't a game?"

"Argh!" I roll my eyes and try pulling myself together. I give up this time. "Please, just clothe yourself!"

One point: Caiden. Zero: Hailey.

I walk out into the hallway, whispering frustrated gibberish to myself as I trot down the stairs,

"Only because you asked so nicely!" he shouts back.

"Stop it!" I have a hard time hiding my laugh as we bicker.

"Never!"

I reach the door giggling like a loon, and not managing to contain the laughter as I swing it open. I wonder if I look like a lunatic or a hormonal mess. Either one would be accurate.

CeeCee and Brandon stand there perplexed on my doorstep. This time my giggles turn into relentless laughter, and apparently still feeding off my sparring with Caiden, I speak. "Well, looks like you two made up."

I'd pin CeeCee as the one with endless sass, but it's Brandon who grunts, moving past me as he says, "Hardly."

My laughs cease when I catch sight of a defeated CeeCee still standing before me.

"We're better than his tone implies," she replies quietly.

"Are you sure?"

She shrugs. "I did what you said. He has a hard time with the taking it slow thing, but accepted the answer for what it is. I told him I can't be official just yet, but I'm more open now."

"I don't know if that's exactly what I told you to do, but at least there's some honesty somewhere in there."

"As much honesty as I can muster."

I wave her inside, and she marches in. Brandon is walking out of the kitchen when I turn around.

"What are you doing?" I ask him.

He smiles genuinely this time. "Are you busy?" he asks, his eyes darting toward the stairs.

"No," I shoot back, placing my hands on my hips.

"Where's Caiden?"

I swallow a dry gulp and shrug.

"Hailey, his frickin' truck is in your driveway."

"It's not what you think." I shake my head back and forth, admonishing him. I would never be able to explain how hard it was for me to climb into my old bed, and how Caiden's arms simply held me all night, making it possible for me to sleep soundly. Nope, Brandon would never understand that. He's not so good at the emotional thing, from what I can tell.

A thundering of footsteps from above catches our attention. Caiden appears, walking down the stairs, and I squint suspiciously when I watch him pulling on his shirt as he's walking. Couldn't he have done that in my room?

"Looks like you two have a problem with *slow,* too," CeeCee quips.

"Stop it. He stayed the night, but nothing happened. I swear."

"Yeah, right," she replies with an eye roll.

I wish I was lying because what's the point in actually making us take things slow when I get ridiculed for not doing it anyway.

I make eye contact with Caiden's thoroughly unamused stare as he lets out a sigh of confirmation once he makes it to the living room.

Brandon walks over to him, slapping him hard on the shoulder triumphantly, apparently reading the moment for the truth as he says, "Welcome to crazy town of the sexually frustrated. It's not a happy place, man. It's a level of purgatory they didn't tell us about."

Caiden fights a smile. He's definitely listening to Brandon, but his eyes are searing me to the spot.

With fuming embarrassment and publicly known sexual frustration, I walk into the kitchen with no real purpose. CeeCee quickly follows.

"Cee, what are you doing here? Not that I'm not pleased." I pause, gritting my teeth, wondering what mischief I might be getting into if she hadn't appeared with Brandon, but continue on. "I just wasn't expecting you two."

"Did we interrupt?" she asks, reading the puckering of my face.

I sigh, leaning toward the doorway to see Brandon and Caiden in deep conversation on my couch, with Brandon leading the conversation in a low, undecipherable tone. If they're speaking freely, then I can.

I swivel around and walk to the opposite side of the kitchen island to face CeeCee.

"Kind of, but it's okay. We need to pace ourselves."

She laughs, shaking her head. "What's there to pace?"

I shrug. "I just need it. I've been overwhelmed since the moment I stepped back into this town, and now that things seem to be, I don't know, situating themselves, I need time to readjust. Can't I take my time with this?"

"Sure, I guess. I just assumed that with all the time that's already passed, you'd be ready to just *do it*, already."

"For the love of God, please tell me you don't mean sex, because that sounds ridiculous. Please be more insightful."

She laughs, and I wish she'd keep it down. "It's exactly what I mean, because it does sound ridiculous. I just think that if you want it, what does it matter now? We're not teenagers anymore, we're adults."

I stare at her, blinking a few times, annoyingly dumfounded. "Stop being right."

"Nope." She smirks.

"Maybe I just want to drag out the game," I confess.

This time she grins. "Well then, that's different. I approve of the tease."

"You would," I hum.

Her glee flatlines into a sarcastic glare. "That's not funny."

"Oh, it's definitely funny." My lips squirm, feeling good that we've both made jabs, but I pull myself together. "You sure you're okay?"

"Yes. Baby steps and, how did you describe it? *Pacing.* I'm trying, Hails. I really am, but there doesn't seem to be any winning with Brandon right now."

"The dude is impatient. You can't blame him."

She releases a long sigh. "This is why today is important."

"What's today?"

"Gang hang out."

"That sounds like crime is involved."

She laughs. "Only if you want it to. What I mean is, me, you and all the boys head to the shore for the day, and s'mores and beer a night."

My chest tenses, thinking of the last party I was at, but she catches it before my panic sets in. "Only *us*, Hailey. No one else. Just us, Brandon, Caiden, Cameron and Tyler. We need some gang time, don't you think?"

My nod is reflexive and giddy. "I would so love that."

"I was hoping you would."

Brandon strolls into the kitchen, rigid but smiling, and Caiden follows, but he looks languid and kind of dopey under that thick layer of scruff, that if my memory serves right, holds two barely-there dimples.

"We're heading out," Brandon says.

CeeCee perks up. "What? Where?"

"I'm gonna ride with Caiden to his house, and we'll meet you and Hailey at the spot. Cam and Tyler are already there. They just texted me."

CeeCee opens her mouth but quickly shuts it. I understand her struggle. She wants more but can't seem to muster what that is exactly. That was me less than a week ago. Poor girl.

"Okay," she breathes out, her eyes locked onto Brandon, who doesn't waver as he stares right back.

I have to give Brandon some credit underneath his brute demeanor at times, because as if he can read CeeCee's struggle he adds, "I'll be quick, okay?"

This calms her, and she nods.

Brandon doesn't waste another second wallowing in their obvious torture. He turns around to leave, but he has to move around Caiden, who is staring at me like an idiot.

Brandon jabs him in the chest. "Come on, you love-struck fucker. I can't wait around for you."

Caiden manages a chortle of laughter as Brandon shimmies by and heads out of the house.

CeeCee fiddles in her seat as her eyes dart between Caiden and me. I catch her smile, and although my heart swells while stuck in the middle, I so badly want simple, but this will never be simple between Caiden and me. I hate that I kind of love the beautiful chaos that seems to manifest between us, like static electricity, and he isn't even officially my boyfriend yet.

"Do you two need a minute?" she chirps.

I shake my head, but Caiden stalks over. He doesn't seem to care that CeeCee is five feet away, or how we're supposed to try and keep a leveled amount of distance.

"You going to kiss me goodbye?" he hums.

I shake my head, pursing my lips to fight the annoying smile that wants to break through my face. "Nope."

He takes another step, closing the distance between us, forcing me to look up at him.

"Are you sure?" he goads.

"Yep."

"Hailey, kiss me."

"Why do you ask when you're not going to let me win anyway?"

"I think I've been fair enough this morning."

CeeCee stifles a giggle, but I can't look away. I feel the lava flow of heat to my cheeks.

"Fine."

I stand up on my tiptoes and press a kiss to his lips, but he catches me off guard by crashing his mouth into mine. He takes no prisoners, and in a flash he's coaxed my mouth open, dipping his tongue in for a cruel, quick taste, pressing one last possessive stroke against my lips before pulling away.

I'm out of breath within a nanosecond, my eyes heated and my body in a frenzy when I look up, feigning anger. "Was that entirely necessary?"

"Yep."

He grins, turns around, doesn't say another word, and clonks his way out of my kitchen and out of the house to join Brandon.

CeeCee giggles. "You let me know how *pacing* things goes for you, yeah?"

I've got more of a skip to my step than usual as I hop out of CeeCee's Jeep, and I'm keeping the reasons why to myself, although CeeCee's tiny smirks as she watches me tells me she's probably figured it out. Aren't I allowed to be filled with a little bit of smitten hopefulness? Can't my friends let me have that?

That might be one of the things I wish had changed. We might have *grown up*, but I don't think we've really *grown up*.

As I come over the small hill, I'm greeted with the sparkling horizon of the lake mid-summer. The air is thick, teetering on humid as we walk through the fading woods, and I pull in a deep breath, liking that pine smell freshly diving into my lungs this late afternoon.

As I stroll toward our secret spot on the shore, Cameron is already barreling toward me from the sand.

"Hailey, where have you been all my life!?"

I'm in such a good mood, I meet him in stride and leap into his hug. "Where's my beer?"

"Did I ever tell you you're my favorite? Beer is right this way."

He swings me around once before letting my feet back onto the ground, keeping an arm around me as we walk.

"Funny thing, Hails, it seems you and Caiden have matching smiles this afternoon. Coincidence?" He smiles dopily, too, beer surely fueling it.

I laugh, turning my head completely to face my friend, his

shirtless form showing off his heavily tattooed chest, though his arms are free of ink, the opposite of Caiden. I'm a bit stunned by the deep intricacies of ink and lettering.

"You checking me out now, Hailey?"

I laugh again, snorting. "You wish—"

Ring. Ring. Ring.

How dare my phone interrupt my dealings of potentially well-crafted insults.

As I pull my phone out of my jean shorts, Cameron adds smugly, "Oh, I forgot, you're kind of taken now. Better be on your best behavior, huh? You can't be ogling the hot guys on the lake, ya know?" He takes a swig from the beer can I didn't know he was holding while shooting me a wink.

"You're ridiculous," I quip before answering the phone. "Hey, Janet."

"Who's Janet?" he interrupts, eyebrows wiggling. "Is she one of your friends in California?"

I try shoving the idiot away, but he bungees back as I reply, "She's my literary agent, now go away—Janet, you there?"

Cameron is bouncing around me like a puppy looking for a treat as I try to make my way to our friends. I can't stop laughing.

Janet answers, "Who's that?"

I press my palm against Cameron's face while saying into the phone, "My friend Cameron."

As if by some absurd form of coincidence wielded by hormonal pixie dust, I hear in unison from my phone and from the frenzied friend in heat in front of me, "*Is he/she hot?*"

"What the fuck," I whisper, leading into a hysterical laughing fit. I choose to respond to Janet. "Well, Cameron's not your type. He's not shirtless riding a noble steed or anything."

"... But I'm at least shirtless! One out of two ain't bad!" Cameron shouts.

Janet squeals into the phone, "Alert the damn town. Someone get him a horse, stat."

I groan, rolling my eyes, finally seeing light at the end of the tunnel when I see Caiden sitting on a fallen log, seemingly distracted as he talks to Tyler, shirtless himself.

"Janet, you're absurd. I gotta go."

I've switched from loud and rambunctious to breathy and waif-like in a nanosecond, not looking to see where Cameron ran off to.

"I was kidding," she replies. "But seriously, is he hot?"

"Spare me," I chortle. "I'm serious, though. I have to go. I don't mean to answer and then cut the phone call short. I— uh—just walked into something."

"Huh," she tuts knowingly, but refrains from saying what's really on her mind. "No worries. Just... call me back when you get a free moment. It's kinda important."

"I will. Bye, Janet."

"And ya know, enjoy your time there..."

The trailing off of her sentence doesn't sit well with me, but I shake it off. Then it almost leaves my mind immediately because Caiden notices me, his eyes seemingly smiling in recognition.

"Hailey?" Janet questions.

"Hm?"

Caiden rises from his seat, making his way toward me, my heart revving hard in my chest, like a car about to take off at the finish line.

"Just call me, okay?"

"You know I will."

"Sooner than later."

"Of course."

"You're distracted."

"There's a shirtless guy in front of me," I add quickly before Caiden can hear. "And not Cam," I'm sure to make clear.

She sighs, which I don't expect. My brows pull together

at hearing it, and the smile on Caiden's face fades.

"Just call me. Bye, Hailey. Miss you."

"Miss you, too."

She hangs up, and so do I. I place my phone back into my shorts pocket. My eyes drop to the mixture of dirt and sand at the shore's edge.

Caiden's fingertips meet my chin, lifting my face up.

"Everything okay?"

"Everything is perfect." When the words leave my lips, I don't completely mean them. My body involuntarily flings itself into Caiden's arms, seeking some sense of gravity. My arms wrap around his neck, breathing his skin in when I nuzzle into him.

I had originally wanted to keep us platonic this afternoon, keeping our distance and only allowing little touches here or there, but for some reason, my body rumbles with the need for his in a way to remedy my troubled soul and overly cautious mind.

I pull in a deep breath, letting the thoughts of my phone call with Janet dissipate and fade away.

He squeezes me close. "Can I kiss you?"

I snort, finally feeling like my feet are back to being planted. I pull away, releasing my grasp, but he tugs me harder. "That's kind of you to ask."

"So, the answer is yes?" I shake my head. "This is so not fun."

I laugh, trying to step out of his grasp, but am met with resistance even when he lets me go. His fingers drag heavily into the light, holey material of the sweater that's covering my bikini-suited body. I grab for his wrists, peeling him away completely. "Settle down, Sparky."

"Baby Bird, cut the man some slack. He's been blue-balled for years over you."

I hadn't realized Brandon had managed to get away and notice everyone else. He's perched on the open flatbed of his truck, Tyler and Cameron sitting in lawn chairs in front, while CeeCee is cackling over the joke as she situates the grill.

"I refuse to believe he was blue-balled. The person I think who's blue-balled is *you*."

Brandon's face falls flat while everyone starts cracking up.

"That was a low blow, Hails," he says, feigning pain, placing his hand over his heart.

"You mean, no *blow* at all," Cameron adds, slapping his knee.

"That joke only kind of works." I move around Caiden, hating that I can't look him in the eye with the mention of blue balls. I can't help but think of how he's been in a relationship and how it's impossible he's been celibate.

Caiden trails close behind, whispering, "He's being an idiot, and you know it."

I shrug. I so badly don't want to care. "It's water under the bridge and all that, Caid. What do I care?"

"Are you just saying that?"

"No, I mean it. What do I care?" I repeat. "We lived different lives, remember?"

"Not anymore, we don't."

My brow twitches, and a siren goes off in my brain, because I want to tell him, *"but we actually still do,"* but my teeth come down on my bottom lip, holding it back.

"Hamburger, Hailey?" CeeCee shouts from the grill.

Caiden raises his hand up to my face again, smoothing out the skin between my eyes. "There you go again, thinking too hard."

I smile, trying to find something easier to stare at, but unfortunately, my eyes only drop to his bare chest, the speckling of hair doing nothing to hide the burly but lean muscular lines of his chest and abdomen. I like that his chest is free of ink and his arms are packed full of scenes of nature. It just looks so good on him.

"You try and act like a lady, calm and controlled, but I

know you're not even close," he says, catching me in something as his fingertips scratch over that defined "v" on the right side of his hips.

I shake my head. "You probably shouldn't walk around not wearing a shirt, then."

"That so?"

I lift the left corner of my mouth, smirking in a way that I know Caiden will see as challenging. I reach for my shorts, unbuttoning them, his eyes dropping to my hands.

"You need help with that?"

"You wish."

"You know I do."

I cluck my tongue, rolling my eyes as I let the material drop to my feet. I bend down, grabbing for them, and shove them at his chest. He begrudgingly takes hold of them as I let them go.

I reach for the edge of my sweater, swiftly lifting it over my head, wielding this black bikini with a lot more confidence than the last time.

"Hailey," he groans, "totally unfair."

I toss my sweater at him and walk away, making sure to swing my hips more deliberately as I stroll toward CeeCee.

I strut past Brandon and the boys, and I hear Brandon chortle quietly to Cam, "He's totally blue-balled. Women are cruel, man."

"Preach, brother, preach," Cam barks back.

CeeCee is grinning as she flips a burger on the grill, shaking her head at me. "You're just as bad as the boys, you know that?"

"Of course I do. It only feels fair."

"I guess." She laughs. "I must admit, I do enjoy seeing the guy suffer for once."

"Me, too," I grin, leaning down to open the ice chest, grabbing for a beer. That is, until a hand comes down fairly hard on my ass.

"Eep!" I squeal, barely managing to keep a grip on a beer can as I stand. "Caiden!"

"That's for teasing me." He grins, winking, before turning to CeeCee who looks as happy as I feel, even though I might be rubbing over my stinging bum. "Burgers ready yet?"

"Caiden Anderson!" I reprimand. I won't let it go.

"Yes, sweet, sweet, frustrating, Hailey? Want me to kiss it better?"

I'm blushing beet red, especially when CeeCee's incessant high-pitch giggles are barely being muffled by her hand.

I grab for his arm, tugging him to turn around so he's facing me. "You are making such a scene in front of our friends."

He shrugs, reaching for my beer can, and opens it for me before handing it back. "You don't think they know what's going on? You don't think they know how badly I want you?"

I gulp down his words, grabbing for my beer. He smiles knowingly. The jerk.

"It might do us both some good, Hailey, if we actually just live in the reality of the situation. Might save us from the stress."

"Oh, you have this all figured out now?"

He nods, leaning in, and I think he's going to kiss me, but he doesn't, and I hate that he doesn't. He places a sweet peck of a kiss on the tip of my nose.

"I have it more figured out than you, I think."

I smile, but it's sadder than I intend it to be. "You actually have no idea how right you are."

He releases a long breath that matches my remorseful smile, and I wonder if we're thinking the exact same thing. Which is, *Can we keep this?* And, *Is time our enemy?*

He grabs for my hand, tangling his fingers around mine, which I willingly accept.

"That's my girl. C'mon, let's go take a seat with our friends."

He tries turning around, but with his hand in mine, I yank him back.

"Hail—"

I cut him off, kissing him on the lips. Not for too long, but enough to ignite that waiting wick of my heart that sizzles a trail to my core. I pull away, feeling that gravitational pull all over again, grounding me.

"I feel better now."

He smiles smugly. "Good."

I think we just made progress on something I didn't know we needed to work on.

I've had the most incredible day so far, and I'm annoyed for not allowing a day like this to happen sooner. But I guess it had to happen this way.

We all had to work for this somehow. From dealing with my mom to finding the balance among friends, and oddly enough, to me finding out there's no way I could stop loving Caiden Anderson if I tried.

Life is ridiculous that way. Life just won't allow our heart to let some people go.

I walk to the edge of the lake, tugging on my sweater as I lift my leg to dip a toe in the slow, lapping waves. My senses take surprising comfort in the brisk cold of the water, reminding me of the bitter cold of the ocean on the west coast. I think about the crashing waves in Santa Monica, a fairly short drive from my apartment in Los Angeles.

The popular beach area is a place I'd frequent for jogs or a simple stroll on the sand. I always wondered why I head there when I'm in need of clarity when it actually never gives it to me.

I tried so many times, hoping the ocean would someday make me as happy as everyone else who is drawn to it.

I know why it didn't now.

With my eyes pinned to the lakeshore, I'm able to count almost ten beats before the retreating wave makes an effortless crawl back to the sand without a care in the world. My whole body finds a home in the sight, because it's a reflection of what this place gives me, and why I love it here.

While I was gone, I tried the ocean in hopes for that same calm, but never got it. I must have been seeking this familiarity in the turbulence of the ocean, in hopes the sea would smooth out and soothe the homesickness I didn't know I was suffering from. Instead, the water thrashed against the sand and surfers under the sunshine and had a funny way of reflecting my emotions inside me, even if I didn't realize it.

Now I'm here, and it just makes sense. Everything makes so much sense.

Strong arms come around my waist, spooking me out of my thoughts, and a deep baritone spills over me like thick, warm molasses. "What are you thinking? Please tell me it's good."

I should probably tell Caiden he needs to take a step back. We've been doing so well today, but I lose the ability to use my mouth when his nose nudges my head to the side and he places a kiss behind my ear.

"Hm" is all I got.

"Nice sunset, huh?"

I blink open my eyes and see the sun resting just above the tree line, glowing purple as it gets closer to the horizon, the purple blending into a bluish-green with the trees, and it's stunning.

"Beautiful, actually."

"I'm sure it has nothing on those California sunsets, though."

"You'd be surprised what PineCrest has over LA"

The corner of his mouth twitches and I realize he thinks I mean *him,* and I let him think it. He wouldn't be wrong, even if I don't confirm it out loud.

263

"Walk with me?"

I look over his shoulder to see Cameron and Tyler helping with logs from Brandon's truck. Brandon is busy looking at CeeCee like she's his world as he speaks, but the good part is, she's smiling as she listens, and even if it's slight, I know they're making progress, bit by bit.

The group is on the verge of lighting our small fire for a night of storytelling, laughter, and drinks, and us stealing away for a little doesn't feel like a crime.

"Walk where?" I ask.

He shakes his head. "Stupid question."

He starts his strides up the shore, grabbing for my hand, tugging me after him.

I don't bother giving my friends a heads-up where we're disappearing, because I know it would come with a dose of cajoling embarrassment.

I trail after him, keeping a solid grip on my smile. I stare at his hand wrapped securely around mine. My eyes dance over his tattooed hand, the rockabilly typography reminding me that I want so badly to know what the letters on his knuckles say.

My eyes are happily distracted when we come up to *our* tree, the same one we spent many days and nights at as kids. Then I remember our last argument here just weeks ago. Telling him to *let me go* seems like such a far-fetched idea now.

He releases me, not when we've reached the tree, but instead when we get to the dry sand in front of the water. He plops himself down and pats the space next to him.

I smile, scanning the surroundings for a brief second to take it in. *Serene.* It's the only word that does it justice.

"You look... good, Hailey," tumbles gently out of Caiden's mouth, drawing my vision to his.

I nod, because I'm guessing he means my carefree state.

I clumsily take the seat he's offered. Maybe I'm a bit

giddy because I've had a few beers, but my gut tells me I'm just happy I get Caiden to myself for the first time since this morning.

I exhale. "I get you to myself, finally."

Caiden doesn't reveal full-toothy grins often, but when he does, it's such a win. He lifts his hand, tugging on his bottom lip, and he's so distractingly handsome. Growing up did him good. The lines of his face and body are so much more defined, just like the soul they hold.

"Why do you think I stole you away? I was getting bored of Cameron and Tyler arguing over who gets dibs on Olivia Humbolt. It's obvious that girl wants nothing to do with either of them. Plus, Cameron's been stupidly looking at you in that bathing suit of yours."

"That's why I put this sweater over it. He doesn't mean any harm. He's just been drinking." I purse my lips, trying to hide the smile I get when I get a hint of Caiden's jealousy.

"Can't really blame him, though."

I exhale, chuckling quietly, but my resolve is sincere. "Ya know, I'm glad I'm here with you, Caid. I just feel like I should tell you that. Life is filled with all these funny moments, and time is precious, and I just want you to know that. I need you to know that."

"What's gotten into you?" He laughs, leaning in. I think he's going to kiss me, but his hands reach for something else entirely.

Apparently moved by my words, or growing impatient, he grabs for my waist, lifting me onto him. My legs straddle his thighs while my hands take a firm grip of his biceps, needing to steady myself.

"Caiden," I shriek through a giggle, but I'm not moving. No way.

He raises both of his hands to my face, cradling it as he examines me. "It's sort of unbelievable, isn't it? How far we've come?"

I nod, a mixture of sadness and happiness twisting around

my heart, giving it a gentle squeeze in my chest, because sure, we've made it far, but where the hell are we going?

I peel his hands from my face, holding them between us, finally giving me a moment to examine his knuckles.

"What do these tattoos say? I've been wondering."

I lift them both, and the moment the two words become recognizable, a single word on each hand, he says it out loud.

"Stay true."

My face heats when I look up to see Caiden's eyes on me, hooded, serious, and heavy.

"Stay true," I repeat back. "Any special significance?"

His short huff of a chuckle brushes against my face. "Of course. It's always been about you, you know that? No matter how hard I tried."

I sit up straighter, comfortable on the perch of his lap. I tilt my head to examine his stern look, but there's a bit of apprehension behind that deep green glimmer.

I really love the way Caiden looks at me. He cares what I think.

He continues, "I got trees and the forest, and all these picturesque places tattooed on my body, and then I realized that all these places were special to me because they were places that meant something to *us*. It's funny really, to know that all the things you love were because of another person. It's annoying, actually," he says playfully.

I grit my teeth. He laughs, leaning close enough to place a chaste kiss on my lips before pulling away.

"Even those words, *stay true*. I got them to be a reminder to stay true to who I am, to what I need, to follow my heart. The problem is, Hails, you rule those, too. I tried for the longest time to pretend it wasn't true. I repressed the fact for so long, begging for some other purpose—which totally contradicted the words. Then..." He sighs. "It all comes back to that moment I saw you in the bar, or maybe when I kissed you in the station. It was game over. If I didn't push myself to have you, then those words wouldn't mean shit. *Stay true* means staying true to myself and *you.* "

He releases a long breath, as if he's just revealed a secret. The corner of my mouth lifts when I catch his transition into caution, watching me process his explanation. His large hands are still being held by mine, my thumb tracing over the word *Stay*.

I want to say something, but words don't feel powerful enough. It's ironic since I'm a writer, but with him in front of me, my legs wrapped around him, my skin over-sensitized and slick with the summer evening, the sun nearly gone over the horizon, and my heart trying to find a way to beat out of my chest, I do the only thing that seems appropriate.

I lift his hand slowly upward. I watch the slow, apprehensive bob of his Adam's apple in his throat as I bring his knuckles to my lips, kissing each letter lightly.

When I'm done with his knuckles, I lift his arm higher and pepper kisses over the tattoo on his forearm, tracing my lips over my hidden initials among the woods that remind him of us.

I hear a quiet groan leave Caiden before he pulls his arm out of my grasp so he can grab my face, pulling my mouth to his. It teeters on frantic, his lips nearly bruising mine. I wrap my arms around his neck. I choose Caiden over oxygen as I pull him as close as possible, pressing my lips into his.

His tongue coaxes my mouth open, diligently tasting me.

I breathe him in, soak in him, devour him, focusing and loving how every synapse in my body is on the verge of short-circuiting when his hands trail heavily down my chest, over my thin sweater, stopping at my hips, pressing me harder into his, feeling his erection against my throbbing core.

The feeling it elicits is almost too much, making my mind fuzzy with need as I pull away in a tight gasp, keeping us nose-to-nose.

"Caiden," I groan, knowing I don't want to budge, but I ache for more, and wonder if this is one of those moments I should slow down.

"Don't you dare think right now, Hailey Elwood."

I giggle, shaking my head, the tip of my nose delicately rubbing against his, fighting logic, love, and lust. "Playing hard to get is getting... hard," I sigh.

With the night sky reflecting off the surface of the lake as the only source of light, I can still see the shadows of Caiden's smile as it stretches across his face triumphantly.

"Why make us both suffer, then?" he replies.

"I don't know," I chide. "Seems like the right thing to do. I thought you'd be the one suffering, though, not me."

He laughs. "Don't stop kissing me, Hailey. You know you want this as much as me, and that's okay..."

"See, now you're not playing fair, because I don't follow orders, Caid—"

His lips cut me off. The brash contact is exactly what my body needs more of. His mouth presses hard into mine.

"You are so difficult," he says between our lips.

A skirting giggle escapes me between his possessive capture of my mouth. I meet him for every lapping stroke as my tongue dips into his, eager for more.

We are definitely breaking the boundaries, but I don't care anymore.

"Why do you make me beg?" he whispers as he pulls his lips away from mine to begin a trail down my neck.

"Because I can. I can't let you think this'll be easy," I breathe out.

His fingers dig into the flesh of my thighs as he squeezes. "I think you just like to drive me crazy."

"That, too," I hum, reveling in the smooth drag of his lips over my collarbone.

I wrap my arms around his neck. Looking over his shoulder, I note that the glow of the bonfire is far off in the distance on the shoreline. My eyes sink to a close, absorbing the sound of the lapping lake waves and the feeling of

Caiden's lips trailing back up to my own.

My mouth is eager for their return. I press mine to his frantically. His returning growl is one that rocks my insides, shooting quivers down my legs. As if his hands can sense it, they slowly drag upward. My core throbs for him to get closer with each slow inch. I teasingly press my hips into his. He releases another groan.

"Hailey..." he whispers, his sentence trailing off against my lips. "It's like we're seventeen all over again."

"Who says you're going to make it to home base on the shore, Caiden Anderson?" I smile against his mouth.

His hands against my thighs rise with fevered determination suddenly as he takes a good hard grip of my ass, pushing me into the bulge of his swim trunks.

"I do." He grins as he slides the sandpaper scuff of his chin across my jaw before placing a kiss on my thumping pulse point.

My hips reflexively press themselves into his. An explosion of need rips through me. It's as if he just tapped into the deepest corner of my psyche: a carnal need buried among the memories I tried forgetting, but that was always there, waiting to be unleashed.

"Tell me you want me, Hailey, so I know I'm doing the right thing."

I grab for his face, crashing my lips to his, pressing into him, my body and soul seeking relief in so many different ways.

"I want it. I want you," I mumble through rushed kisses.

A moan of approval escapes him as his fingers hook under the strings of my bathing suit bottom.

I dip my tongue into his mouth, tasting him, devouring him in a way that screams more *need* than want.

I can feel his fingers fumbling for the strings, until I feel a gentle pull on the bikini, and I've never been more thankful for their structure when the fabric falls from my body.

His large hand curves over my sex, and I'm so riled up, I

push myself into his palm, his fingers trailing between my folds to the opening of my sex, teasing the entrance at first before slipping one, then two fingers inside.

I buck against his hand, my body drenching his fingers.

"Holy shit," he groans against my mouth, starting an in and out rhythm with his hands as he says, "I've wanted you so bad, for so fucking long."

My hands drag down his chest, trying to keep my goal in sight while keeping a leash on the rampant pleasure rolling through me. I reach the waistband of his swim trunks, unbuttoning them, not hesitating a second before slipping my hand inside, getting a hold on his hard cock, dragging my hand up and down the shaft in sync with his fingers inside me.

"I need you," I breathe against his mouth, my thumb working the tip of his length.

He huffs out a frustrated breath and pulls away, his eyes in a frenzy and his hips bucking into my hand. "I don't have a condom."

My skin feels on fire, and I can already feel a light sheen of sweat over my body with the evening humidity.

"I'm on the pill," I sigh. "I've never been with anyone without a condom."

"Neither have I." He pauses to groan, my grip on his cock gently tightening. "But that's a lie. Technically, we both have."

His hand inside me pulls out, sliding up and down my sensitive folds, rubbing at my clit, and I'm nearly on the brink.

"Huh?"

"We made some risky decisions when we were kids. Impatient meetings on the shore, kind of like this one, where we didn't use one."

I giggle, pressing my lips to his, remembering all those blissful terrible decisions. I was on the pill then, but I wasn't the most diligent at taking them every day like I am now. I like the idea of Caiden being the only person I've ever been with without a condom.

"C'mon, Caiden. I want you inside me."

"Some things never change," he chides, lifting my hips above his before slowly lowering me, my body taking him in one swift move.

I let his name roll out of my mouth in sinful happiness: "Caiden..."

"Fuck, I love it when you say my name."

He fills me to the brink, and my body pulses around him.

Caiden grabs for the edge of my sweater, pulling it off my body, leaving me in just my bathing suit top. He digs his fingers into either side of my hips. We stay still, just savoring the fill as our bodies acclimate to the tight space, but it makes my head dizzy.

"You have to move, or I'm going to go insane," he growls, his lips dragging up my jaw, his eyes closed, and his breathing heavy.

I smile, pressing my lips into his, tangling my fingers tightly into his hair, anchoring him to my mouth as my hips begin to rise and fall, quickly speeding up with his strong hands guiding me.

Our shallow breaths and the sound of our bodies coming together are the only noises twisting around the tones of the soft waves and gentle breeze.

I'm hot everywhere, my body buzzing and tingling, my legs trembling, my thoughts blurring as our hips find a rhythm that ignites that earth-shattering spark in my core. The fiery feeling starts pulsing and pulsing, and I forget how to breathe as we groan against each other's mouths in fevered need.

"I love you so much," he says, his lips nearly bruising mine to convince me, and the pleasure and pain of it is euphoric.

"I love you, too," slips from me easily, and although I know I should have kept those words a little more protected, and that I should be a little more cautious with them, it doesn't matter when we both release a vision-blurring orgasm. I forget myself, seeing stars, and letting out another groan of his name, and dammit, another *I love you.*

Whether I like to believe it or not, nothing has ever been truer, and also so terrifying.

16

———

Ring. Ring. Ring.

It's been an interesting few days, to say the least. So much so that if you told me I would be managing Caiden, chaos, my childhood home, and avoiding responsibilities, I might have keeled over in the downright maniacal laughter of insanity. Yet here I am, living the unforeseeable.

Ring. Ring. Ring.

I blink a few times, staring blankly into space as I stand in my old bedroom, trying to pretend my phone isn't ringing, glowing with a name I'm not ready to face.

This would be the "avoiding responsibilities" part.

I scan my room, nodding my approval at the tousled bedcovers and the suitcase on the floor. I've almost grown comfortable with this space. I slept in my own bed one out of the three nights Caiden hasn't been here.

Hey, that's progress in my world.

My ringing phone finally stops and beeps ten seconds later, signaling a voicemail. It echoes ominously through the summer night.

I release a long grunt of self-disapproval into the silence.

I've been avoiding Janet. I never called her back that day on the lake, and that's her second call today. She's relentless when she wants to be, and I keep telling myself I'll call her in the morning. We're on day three now, and it's not getting any easier. Eventually, I know I'll have to face the music.

Maybe I'm overreacting.

Maybe she just wants my notes.

Or maybe it's something else entirely.

Possibly something inevitable and awful that I'm not ready for.

Whatever it is, it's just going to have to wait. Currently, I'm a little more nearsighted than usual.

Trying to keep my distance from Caiden since making us official on the shore of the lake has been incredibly difficult. I'm still trying this whole *pacing ourselves* thing. That night, we walked back to our friends, hand in hand and continually kissed under the glow of the bonfire that night.

For the first time since I came back, our friends stopped teasing us then. They let us be. Which, funnily enough, is what makes Caiden and me feel official, but I'd be lying if I said it doesn't have me a little on edge.

The only thing that's keeping this relationship—if that's what this is—normal, rather than us acting like frantic, horny teenagers who need to be with each other every second, is the fact that he has a job, which reminds me I have one, too.

His shifts at the station run in chunks of twelve hours, and I found out he has some catching up to do since he's (apparently) already taken so much time off since I hit town. This is something he reluctantly admitted.

He explained he had been leaving work early most days just to avoid me at the diner or passing shifts to Tyler so he could pop up at a bonfire party I was at, or once to make love to me on the shore.

Even alone I blush at the memory, feeling tingly all over just thinking about it.

All those times Caiden had to shift his schedule to accommodate our ridiculousness, it did not make his bosses very happy. I get sheepish over the chaos I caused just by appearing, even though the outcome's been worth it.

Now, Caiden has to rectify all that time off before the fire chief gets even more pissed off at him. Apparently the words, "Anderson, she better have a fucking magical pussy for you to be taking all this time off of work," were uttered, to the hilarious amusement of Brandon and the gang at the station.

I cringe thinking about the fire chief blurting something like that. Men can be pigs.

But I miss *my* pig.

It's been three days since I last saw Caiden, but he's sent a slew of text messages while he's been working.

Unfortunately, as punishment, the fire chief sent Caiden and Brandon a couple of towns over to help out with a brush fire, which made him not only busy, but entirely out of reach.

It gave me an odd sense of worry I've never encountered before when it came to his safety. I've never needed to think or feel that way unless it was about my mom. To know Caiden was out fighting a fire I could see updates about on the news had me anxious and stressed. Luckily his text message earlier reported he was safe, unharmed, and on his way home to me.

However, now that his safety is confirmed, I realize that I needed the breather. A time to think freely without Caiden infiltrating my psyche. I probably should refocus my sights and goals.

What do I want? And w*hat do I need?*

Neither of which I'm sure of anymore, but I tell myself I don't need to figure those things out just yet.

I do know I've been productive at least one way in the lulls of wandering thoughts. I've been scribbling notes and sometimes even entire chapters. This, I should be proud of.

Let me begrudgingly admit that Caiden inspires a lot. His lips, his touch, and his words all seem to be an excellent foundation for creativity. Who am I kidding, this guy *is* my first novel.

My lips twitch at the thought, knowing I'd never admit that out loud to him.

However, here I am, stumbling into a delightful way to stretch the first novel into a second.

A sequel. How am I supposed to write it when I haven't finished living it yet?

I like the idea of writing a continuation of the fictional happy ending that I used to wish for. Writing it was the easiest way to cope with the heartbreak all those years ago. I got to write my *what-if* ending. Now, here I am living it.

Enter head spin here.

Though, the real-life version is a second chance romance, and the heroine has no idea what the hell she's doing.

By the way, *I'm* the heroine of this real-life novel.

I'm about to face-palm at the thought, but my ringing phone distracts me.

I glare at the blinking electronic, knowing that two calls in a span of ten minutes can no longer be ignored. I grab for it, hands shaking.

"Janet, hi," I breathe out.

"You're avoiding me," she deadpans.

I bite back a smile. Always the straight shooter. "Okay, maybe a little."

"Please tell me it's for a good reason."

"I've written the first five chapters!" I squeal. It does feel good to tell someone, but I also hope this excuse will act as currency in exchange for some forgiveness (and time).

"Eep!" she replies with equal glee, and it feels good to be understood in this way. "That's great! Do you feel comfortable with me reading them so I can see where your head is at?"

"Actually, if it's okay, Id like to gather my thoughts a bit on it. I feel scatterbrained, but I'm excited. There's a lot of inspiration swirling around here in town. But I swear it's nearly done to send over."

"Oh-oh, is that *happiness* I hear in your voice, Hailey?"

"Maybe..."

"Well, holy shit, seems like you got Lover Boy back?"

I roll my eyes. "Maybe," I repeat crisply, not so eager to feed into her.

"Bullshit. You're back to bumping-and-grinding with Mountain Man, aren't you?"

"Janet, I'm not fucking a yeti. You make it sound so primal."

She laughs, cackling into the phone. "I crack myself up, really. I'm reading another client's manuscript right now, and she's got some serious lumbersexual going on. Made me think of you and your sexual conquest."

I snort. "At some point we need to get you to have a life outside of novels, and out of other people's business."

She giggles again, and I wonder if she's already dipped into a bottle of wine tonight. I peer at the time, knowing with the two hour time difference it'd be nearing six o'clock for her.

"I will at some point. There's always a new book to pitch and a new deal to barter."

"I'm going to find you your own romantic hero. You need a real one."

"Write me one, how about that?"

"Whatever, I'm working on it. Maybe the next project, I'll take your perfect man into consideration for a plot."

"Speaking of next projects..." she hums, and the off-tune sound irks me.

I'm silent, waiting for her to go on, my heart picking up pace, and I wish I could figure out why.

"Was my segue too obvious?" she asks. I can picture her eyes scrunching together under her black-rimmed glasses in pleading embarrassment.

"Just spit it out. What's my next project, oh mighty one?"

"How about that movie that's going to be made about *your* book? That feels like it should be on your radar."

My face empties of color. It makes sense. It's time now for that to start happening. I signed on for that three months ago already.

"Okay..." I pull in a quick breath, knowing that this is

inevitable, but maybe I can bide my time. Stretch this out. Ease into a solution. Figure out what this means for me and Caiden.

"When does this start?" I ask, trying not to sound as desperate as the frantic, vibrating heartbeats that are wreaking havoc in my chest.

"You need to come home for a while, and as soon as possible, really—"

"Don't do this, Janet. Give me a couple more weeks," I blurt out, feeling a giant crack forming beneath me as my world shifts like two tectonic plates coming apart.

She sighs, and I know she hates doing this. "I wish I could. What do you want me to say, Hailey? This is a business as much as this is your dream. Life requires you to play the part to the brand that you are now."

I snort, running a hand through my hair. "I hate when you call me a brand."

"You know how I hate coddling, and I know how much you hate being coddled. They need you here to help with the screenplay and for some press. Don't make me hold your hand. I get it. You're tied up with Lover Boy—"

"It's more than that!" I spit out.

"Is it?" she questions.

This is the Janet I love to hate. The one who makes the publishing industry into the corporate monster I wish it wasn't. She's all for hearts and flowers, but when it comes to getting shit done, she's a hardass when she wants to be—or when she needs to be. Which, regrettably, makes her an awesome agent.

"You became a brand the moment you hit the *New York Times*, and the moment you signed the movie deal contract. The studio needs you present for interviews. People are dying to hear what you have to say about casting choices and how much creative say you get with the screenplay. We'll need to run through everyth—"

"Janet, please..." I plead, needing her to stop talking. She lets the silence hang, and I soak in it for the time being, using it to pull myself together. "...I can't leave right now. Things are barely falling into place. It's not just Caiden; it's the diner, too. I need more time. If I go, when can I come back?"

More silence. This time it's unwelcome.

"Janet?"

"I don't know," rushes through the phone.

"You don't know?" I repeat back.

"I know this is hard, but this is also your career. I can't give you an end date, but I know it *will* die down at some point. A couple months, maybe? The diner can survive without you for a bit."

I've barely been away from Caiden three days since getting him back, and now we're talking months of long distance. But at least I know CeeCee can run the diner.

How will I explain this?

I notice the trembles have reached my fingertips.

Tink.

My brows twitch when I hear the sound, but Janet's words drag me back to the phone call.

"You can't drop everything you have going on here in LA, Hailey. There are contracts you signed and people needing your direction now. You know I'm all for the recluse lifestyle you love, but that's got to be put on hold for now. You have obligations here, and they're not going to go away. They're relying on you."

"I can't leave Caiden. I need more time," comes out gawky and awkward.

"Sure, you can," she tries sweetly, as if patronizing a child, which causes my blood to boil. "I can give you a few more days, maybe five at most, but I need you back home. He'll understand. You two spent five years away from each other. Maybe with a few months apart, you'll be inspired to complete the sequel."

This puts me over the edge, and those nerves collide with an irrational anger. I can't stop myself as I shake my head and respond the way that I know is so wrong, but nothing feels fair.

279

It never does.

"—I'm going to have to call you later!"

I hang up on her, tossing the phone onto my bed as if the damned thing burned me. I'm fuming, my face hot, my chest heaving.

Clink-clink.

She was trying to be light-hearted about the situation, but anything that involves Caiden is anything but light-hearted. No, it's always *heavy-sledge-hammer-hearted* when it comes to him.

Normally, I would have laughed at her attempt, but I can't, not with this, not when I just got him back.

Five days at most? What am I going to do? Why couldn't I be given more time to enjoy what it's like to have Caiden here in PineCrest, living carefree?

Clunk-clink.

My phone starts ringing again, and I know it's going to be Janet trying to apologize, but it's me who needs to cool off. I'll call her back in the morning when I've collected my thoughts. I swear I will.

I shake out my limbs, more distracted by a very distinct sound. It's familiar in a surreal way, and I need it to distract me from my waiting reality across the country.

I blink a few times as I approach my window, hoping I'm not making those sounds up in my head.

Clunk-tink.

My eyes flicker to the window, knowing that I definitely just saw something hit the glass. My heart is beating an intense dub-step remix at what that sound means. And I need it more than ever.

Clunk-clank.

That's most definitely the nostalgic sound of my romantic hero throwing rocks at my window. My heart twists, pulses, and clenches, knowing I want to run into his arms for comfort, but also considers running in the opposite direction in search of safety from the hurricane of heartbreak that could ensue.

Logic doesn't win this battle. Love does, and I worry how long it can hold out in this war.

"Caiden, you're crazy," I whisper as I reach for my window, unlocking the latch.

Tink-clunk.

I allow a grin, and the simple joy it gives me is indescribable. As I absorb the feeling, the word 'grin' doesn't feel good enough to describe the smile that splits my face in half as I fling myself at the window in an attempt to lift it open.

The damn thing probably hasn't been opened in years. My first shove only causes a bleak squeak to emerge from the worn wooden frame. I'm annoyed and overly eager, teetering on manic. I need this moment more than I need anything else. I need *him*.

I shove the window upward again, my palms digging into the wood, trying to lift it, and it still only squeaks its resistance, but doesn't open.

Clink.

I'm fuming at this point, especially when I hear Soot smugly meow as he struts into my room, seemingly just to watch my struggle-fest.

"You think I'm funny, huh?"

The cat just plops himself on the floor in the middle of my room, as if to mock me more.

"I'm so not in the mood," I grumble. "I'm under a lot of stress right now, Soot."

And I need Caiden's mouth to make me feel better.

Clunk.

I leap at the sound, giving it my full attention, and give it a determined scowl. I shove at the window again, lifting with all my might. I relentlessly push and push, holding my breath until the squeak screams longingly and the swollen wood gives. It springs upward. I nearly fall out the window as I let out an exasperated breath of accomplishment. I can hear Soot swiftly running out of the room, apparently disappointed with my success.

"Hailey, what the hell?" echoes impatiently from below.

I'm practically hanging from my windowsill, but that stupid smile is back in a flash when I see Caiden on the grass staring at me in one of the most picturesque scenes from my youth I have replayed in my mind so many times.

Though this Caiden is broader, stronger, and has thick scruff that makes him into a man, his smirk and moon-lit eyes tell me he's the same. The same guy who never denied how crazy he was about me, like the way you would never deny the existence of gravity, or the wind. He would only ever shrug, as if his love for me was some infallible fact written in the stars.

It's a shame it took me leaving him to realize how precious that sort of love is.

"I can't believe you're throwing rocks at my window right now," I chide, forgetting my anger and choosing to live in the moment. "I have a front door, you know?" I feign an annoyed eyebrow raise, but he swiftly rejects it with a chuff.

"Oh, you love it, and you know it."

That I do.

He doesn't wait for my rebuttal because he's already scaling the side of my house, springing onto the oak tree with ease before making it to the gutters on the roof of the first floor.

This Caiden is also much stronger. Something that took seventeen-year-old Caiden ten minutes, took strapping twenty-four-year-old Caiden less than five minutes.

He makes it to my window, which I'm still leaning out of, and presses his lips to mine without warning before coming inside.

I hum dreamily at the contact, turning how my body feels into an audible sound.

He tastes of mint and coffee, and smells of charcoal and pine. I'm putty in his hands over the blissful sensory overload.

"How did you like my grand entrance?" he says against my lips.

I grab him by the collar of his work shirt and tug him inside while the sounds of his rounding chuckles escape him.

"Most definitely like old times," he quips as he slings a leg over the sill, and then the other before falling into me, his arms wrapping tightly around my waist.

I'd yank him into my bedroom just like this when I was a needy teen, more than him playing Romeo-through-yonder-window-breaks.

My hormones, when it came to Caiden in our youth, sometimes rivaled his. He was so much more patient than me. I wanted his pants off, and he wanted to kiss me stupid first.

Lucky for me, five years tests even the most patient man.

He stumbles into my room, pushing me back, tumbling us back onto my bed.

I release a yelp, pulling away to let out a string of laughter as he buries his head in my neck, kissing and nibbling over my pulse point, leaving a hot, sticky trail.

Before I know it, he's swung me over his body, perching me over his hips.

My hands drag over the thick navy linen of his shirt. "Did you just get back into town?"

I can't get over the look in his eyes, like he's just ended a hunger strike and he's about to have his first steak in months.

"Yeah, I did. To Brandon's dismay, I said no to a beer and dropped him-the-eff-off so I could come see you. I haven't even made it to my house yet. But guess where I dropped him off?"

I slide my hands down his torso, loving the sinewy feel as I shrug. "Where?"

"CeeCee's. He was livid, but they were texting constantly while we were away, so I knew she missed him. I just dropped his ass off at hers. Think she's gonna be pissed?" He wiggles his brows as his hands make contact with my thighs, gripping them near the knee.

"Was Brandon pissed?" I ask, loving how natural this feels and how much more I want. I swallow down my bubbling nerves, refusing to acknowledge them.

"I don't know. I drove off before he could cuss me out. I skidded off in the direction of your house, stranding him at hers. I'm a fucking genius," he exclaims.

I laugh a body-rattling laugh, the vibrations running a course through my body straight between my legs where my most private area is nestled nicely against Caiden's slowly hardening length.

"Are you playing matchmaker now?" I ask.

He sits up, curling his arm around my waist and smirking like he's won the Pulitzer. I'm so enthralled by the spark in his eyes when it's matched with his feral grip on my body, pressing me to him. "Nah. I was just sick of Brandon moping the past three days."

"Quite the Prince Charming you are."

His smug grin only grows, causing the butterflies in my gut to not only flutter, but rage for an escape, and it's hard for me to hold back my tiny gasp.

"Ya know what I love about summer?" he asks, changing tact, his tone turning gravelly and hot.

I tilt my head to the side as I feel his other hand greedily slide up the length of my bare thigh.

"What?" I ask.

"You in these tiny dresses."

"Oh really—"

Ring. Ring. Ring.

My phone rings somewhere nearby. I see the blinking light of my screen on the bed to the right. *Janet Martinez* flashes. I lean over to grab for it, hating and loving so many different things at once.

"Don't you dare answer that," he says, his hand reaching its goal of my panties, his fingers stroking over the damp fabric. Just like that, I push the thought of my agent and my career into the far reaches of my brain, giving myself up to the tiny pressure he puts against the most sensitive part of my body. I turn my phone off and toss it onto the floor.

"Caiden, I—"

"—Nope." He kisses the spot below my ear while sliding his fingers under the flimsy underwear, stroking me, petting me like you would to soothe a pain, but it only causes a throbbing need to ignite there, colliding with my unease. It wins the battle seamlessly before bouncing the unease away to a dark corner of my psyche to be dealt with at a different time.

I focus on Caiden. He makes me want to cherish this tiny moment. It's mine. Caiden. All of it. I refuse to let time get the best of me like it always has. Even if the choices I made, or have to make, will come sooner or later. What happens if I just pretend that time doesn't exist? What if only Caiden and I exist?

"I love you, Caid."

His lips crash into mine as he twists our bodies back around, one arm around my waist, the other cupped against my sex as he flips me over and presses me back into the bed. He pulls the arm around my waist away to curve his hand around my jaw, anchoring my stare to his as he says, "And I love *you*, but ..."

His pause ignites a mini-panic as my whole-body tenses. "But what?"

He chuckles, completely oblivious to the unease that's sitting like seeds in my gut, waiting to grow and bloom when the time is wrong and inappropriate.

Caiden kisses a trail down the nape of my neck, over the curve of my breasts, biting at the hem of my clothing that covers them before dragging his nose down my torso as his hands push up my dress.

"... *But* we need to get you out of these clothes. They're obviously causing you discomfort."

I giggle, releasing the tension, knowing I'm being absurd. I lift my hands to his head, raking my fingers through his thick hair.

"Is that so?" I ask while he rubs his scruffy chin back and forth over my bare stomach, igniting my lust and dissolving my worry into oblivion.

"Oh, yes. It's too tight, I think. It's the friction." He pulls away as if to examine it.

He nods as he says, "Yep, the friction it has against your skin could cause a fire or something."

I roll my eyes as I fight back a smile. "Well, thank goodness I have a fireman on hand to help, though I think this fireman needs to work on his *wooing*."

He pulls my dress off, leaving me in just my bra and panties before perching his chin on my tummy as he grins something magnificent. "This fireman knows how to *woo*." He takes a firm grip of my thigh, his fingertips digging deliciously into my flesh.

I shake my head, fighting back my squirming. "He could work on it. Although, at least he's good with his hands."

A humid huff of his laughter hits my skin. He scoots up my body, putting us nose to nose.

"I missed you," he whispers, as if it's a secret.

Hearing it makes me happier than I thought it would. He's relit the furnace to my heart and turned up the heat. I wish I knew how to wrap my mind around it.

It's weird when you realize you were never as happy as you could have been.

Water unexpectedly pricks at the corner of my eyes. "I missed you, too," I whisper back.

"Whoa there, what's wrong?" he asks, noticing the emotions I wish I could hide.

I shake off the tears, banishing them. I lick my lips and lift a heavy shoulder. "I'm just scared."

"Scared of what?"

It's such a good question, and I try for the most honest answer.

"That this isn't going to last forever."

He shakes his head, a hint of anger hiding under the furrowing of his brow as he sits up on his knees. Then he untucks his work shirt from his pants and pulls it off his body, tossing the garment across the room and giving me a 20/20 view of his chiseled chest.

He lays his body on top of mine, kissing a trail across my collarbone and up my neck until he reaches my lips. He kisses me hard, bruising even, as his lips dance with mine, his mouth only content when I moan against his.

He pulls away. "I'd never let anything get in the way of our forever. We worked too damn hard for it."

I exhale, making sure that every bit of tension, sadness, frustration, anger, resentment, *everything*, comes out with that gust of breath.

I grab for his shoulders, pulling him to me. "I need you," is the last thing I say before crashing my mouth onto his.

It's his groan that satisfies me, fueling me forward. My lips coax his open, tasting him, devouring him, using him as a remedy to my worries, and feeling the instant cure.

I drag my hands down his chest, my fingers pressing into his muscle, loving his soft skin over the hard muscle until I reach his pants.

I unbuckle his belt, then push his pants and underwear over his perfect hips. He kicks his clothes off and presses his hips into mine. His hard length presses into my core against the damp fabric of my panties.

"I missed you so fucking much," he breathes out. "I can't live without you. I need you. I need this body..." He moves his mouth to my breasts, kissing over the soft skin as he reaches behind me to unhook my bra, pulling it off me. He places more tingling kisses over my sensitive buds, working his tongue around each before placing his face to mine. "... And this mind." He presses a heart-wrenchingly sweet kiss against my forehead.

There's so much I want to say, and so much I wish I

could say, but words aren't enough right now.

I kiss him like my life depends on it.

Both of his hands trail down either side of my torso until they hook into my panties, pulling them off achingly slowly.

"You've always liked to test my patience," I moan against his lapping lips, and his laughter against my mouth ignites an electric current that matches the one that sparks when the head of his cock presses into the opening of my sex.

He pulls an inch away, a smug grin on his handsome face. "Tell me you need me again," he demands.

My lips twitch, fighting back a smile. I nibble on my bottom lip, basking in the fact there are no barriers between us. His naked body against mine, matching smiles and goading looks that speak of lust and love. He'd never believe me if I told him, but he's my equal in ways he might never understand. The yin to my yang, the Bonnie to my Clyde, the peanut butter to my jelly.

I don't have any shame in feeding into him. "I need you, right now and forever."

He doesn't hesitate, pressing himself inside me in unison with his lips slamming into mine. He fills me to the brink. I lift my hips to his and arch my back.

Our heavy breaths and groans move in blissful sync as he quickens his rhythm against my hips, hitting in me that achingly sweet spot, making my knees tremble. His frantic need and dwindling patience are evident with each swing of his hips into mine. I hook my legs around him, digging my nails into his lower back, pulling him harder into me, loving how consumed I feel. His lips drink me in, his body around me, his hips smacking into mine over and over, driving out my fears, fueling my rising need, and igniting that carnal climb as he goes faster and faster.

He buries his face into the crook of my neck, nipping at the skin. His breaths are shallow, and all I can do is groan every time his hips make contact with mine.

I can feel it: that tidal wave that's gathering between my legs as he hits that spot inside me that no one else has.

My fingers dig harder into his flesh, dragging up his broad back, loving the slickness that's appeared on his skin and the sound of his groans in my ear.

The wave builds, and I can't fight it much longer. "I love you" comes out in a sigh before I bite into his shoulder, releasing a moan that rumbles through me as my body clenches tight around him.

His relentless rhythm drives my orgasm on and on, until I can only see stars. His body trembles as he rolls through his own release, and I love that every muscle in his body tenses against me as he says my name over and over again and tells me he loves me, too.

His body collapses against me, and all I want to do is bring him closer.

My legs, hooked around his hips, hug him close. He shifts his body so he can press a possessive kiss against my mouth, then to my nose, and to each cheek before he says, "I don't want to move. Can I just fall asleep right here inside you?"

I giggle, and he laughs. I comb my fingers through his hair and curve them around his jaw, pulling his face to mine for another kiss, loving his ridiculousness, his annoying charm, and those bright green eyes that own me.

He places one last adorable kiss against the tip of my nose before he pulls out and rolls over onto the bed next to me. He brings me close like you would your favorite stuffed animal. A smile peeks through my lips as I find my place curled around his body, placing my head in the crook of his neck, fitting like perfect puzzle pieces.

His eyelids are heavy, fluttering as they fight prolonged blinks, and I know he's had an incredibly long few days.

I lay my palm against his chest, feeling the rise and fall between each of his breaths, knowing I'm going to lose him to sleep at any moment.

A tight squeeze of his arm around me and one last

affectionate kiss against my forehead tell me I'm right.

I tap my fingers against his chest, lightly back and forth, counting the seconds between each exhale. Everything feels so calm, even though I know a storm is coming.

His body fidgets slightly as if he's fighting against sleep.

I lift up my chin, knowing he needs the rest, and press a kiss to the corner of his mouth. "G'night, Caiden," I whisper.

When his breaths are long and deep, I know he's fallen asleep to the light brushes of my fingertips sliding back and forth, acting like a metronome to his thoughts.

He whispers two barely-there words that I'm sure he doesn't mean to say out loud, but I wonder if the things you say right before you fall asleep hold the truth you can't say out loud?

"Don't go," he exhales before falling into a deep hum of sleep, my fingertips matching the rhythm of his breaths.

If only it were that easy, I think, though I know he probably only meant it in response to my goodnight.

It's sometimes terrifying how in tune a person can be with your biggest fears without even knowing it, even if it's by accident.

17

I toss my still-vibrating phone into my apron pocket, eyeing the clock on the wall. Janet has been relentless this morning, but I guess she's unleashing her war games in order to get hold of me since I unceremoniously hung up on her last night. I wouldn't put it past her to enlist the powers of Google to find the number to the diner soon.

It's eleven a.m. here, which means it's nine a.m. for her. Even that's a little early for her to make calls. She's never been a morning person, but maybe she didn't sleep much last night, like me.

I keep trying to focus on better things, but it's proving more difficult than I'd like.

I walk out of the back office, and CeeCee's standing at the counter pinching the bridge of her nose, apparently still trying to wrap her head around the life breakdown I gave her of my morning.

"So, what do you mean you snuck out?" CeeCee harps as I pace the back area of the diner. "That's *your* house. I don't think I've ever heard of a girl sneaking out of her *own* house, let alone sneaking out to go to a job she isn't actually scheduled for. I thought you and Caiden were doing amazing?"

My hands fly up to my face, rubbing my eyes until I see stars. "We are! We're doing more than amazing." *Almost too amazing. Is that a thing?* I sigh. "I just… need some space."

CeeCee's eyebrows angle upward. "What? Five years wasn't enough space for you?"

I cringe. My eyes water. I deserve that. "It's more than that. It's… complicated."

She huffs, and when I look up, she's walking away. She doesn't care to deal with me anymore.

"CeeCee!"

"No."

No? I trail after her as she speed walks back into the office. My heart hurts. I don't want to feel like this on all ends. I keep wondering when I'll stop feeling so much stress from all angles, but nothing seems to be letting up. When do I get to breathe?

When I enter the back office, she moves around me to shut the door.

"You're making me sick," she says, shaking her head. "Like, physically sick. I keep puking."

"I'm making you puke?" I ask, confused.

"Yeah, this nauseous back-and-forth." She pauses, clicking her tongue and rolling her eyes. "Okay, maybe Brandon's the reason, too. He's driving me crazy. Too much stress. This is just making it worse. No one I know can seem to keep it together." She places both palms on the desk as she releases a long exhale. "When will we figure out this whole life thing, Hails? It only seems to get harder."

I remember I'm not the only one going through a lot right now.

"It's the million-dollar question, isn't it?" I lean back on the desk space next to her, slouching as I release my own exasperated sigh, letting my mind trail itself to an epiphany. "Ya know, I think it's why I write. So I can try and connect to this reality I'm supposed to navigate. Turns out, I don't know shit."

CeeCee laughs, hard. The high-pitched squeal, a mixture

of sweet midwestern girl and glee, reminds me of simpler times when all we were worried about was whether we'd get kissed under the bleachers after football games.

Damn, I miss those days.

Rumbling hums through the diner, and my stomach bottoms out.

I peer to my right to see CeeCee eying me like a hawk.

We both know what that sound means without looking at the clock. *Must be lunchtime.*

I consider running, but running now would give too much away and show what little backbone I actually have.

We both rise from the desk and move swiftly to the breakfast bar as the rumbling comes to a stop.

I swing my vision to the window, and it's crazy how I involuntarily melt at the sight of Caiden hopping out of Brandon's truck.

Caiden will have this effect on me until the end of time.

His shirt still looks rumpled from the evening it spent on my bedroom floor, and his hair is still tousled from my fingers running through it constantly last night. Little did he know it was awe and worry that made me so fidgety.

I thought when I left this town all those years ago, that agony was the worst I'd ever feel, but right now, it's giving it a run for its money. I want it all. I want the career. I want Caiden. I want Los Angeles, but I also want PineCrest.

Staring at Caiden, I'm pleading with the cosmos for a happy medium because letting go seems so ridiculous, but my brain can't fathom a solution.

"You know you gotta talk to him, right? Like, this isn't a decision you get to make on your own."

I frown at CeeCee, wishing what she said made sense. If only this situation was fair.

The jingling bells of the double doors sound as Caiden, Brandon, and Cameron stroll inside. Caiden is like a magnet polarized to my existence. We make eye contact as he shoots me his crooked smile and beelines for me as the boys take a seat at a booth.

"Hey Hails," he says, gravelly and wonderful. "Is everything okay?"

Huh? I shake my head. I realize I'm frowning.

"Yeah, I'm fine," I stutter, leaning over the counter and pleased that he returns the gesture, putting us almost nose to nose.

As much as I fear everything, the need to be near him is one I can't ignore. Even among the chaos, he always seems like the answer. It's another tumbling guilty thought, and I so want to feel the opposite when it comes to being madly in love with him.

Instead of pulling away like my brain tells me I should, I press a kiss to his lips. I can tell he finds it surprising by the slight flinch, but he's quick to catch up by gifting me a few lapping strokes of his lips against mine. It puts my guilt at bay, and I want to tell him everything. My worries and fears, my hopes and dreams, but the words don't leave my lips when he pulls away.

He's all dimples and a dopey smile but seems to remember himself as he furrows his brows curiously, as if to question how he got so sidetracked.

"Well, you had me worried for a sec. You did kinda leave me hanging this morning. I was surprised when I didn't wake up to you next to me. The note was cute, but did you have to leave so early for the diner?"

I swallow the truth that wants to come out and shrug. "Sorry, I forgot I had to open, and you looked too cute to wake up."

He squints.

"What?" I ask.

"Nothing. Just had to double check. I missed you, that's all."

I smile. "I'll make it up to you somehow."

He clicks his tongue smugly, and I want to pretend a little

longer that we're perfect. I want to imagine that I could make it up to him with a night in, a home-cooked meal, and something sexy on underneath my clothes. It's such a simple fantasy that it's bizarre that it'd be so hard to achieve.

"Promise?"

My stomach bottoms out. "I'll try my best."

He nods. "I'm gonna head to the table, but just a heads-up, the gang's getting drinks tonight at O'Sullivans."

"When does the gang *not* go to O'Sullivans nowadays?"

"How else would we deal with the women in this town?" He winks.

I grab a dishtowel off the counter and toss it at him as I restrain my laughter. "Get out of here before you make more of an ass of yourself."

Caiden grabs for the string of my apron, pulling me into a surprise kiss. His humid breath tangles around mine, and so do his chuckles.

"Whatever, you love me and you know it," he says as he pulls away.

I can barely stand and thank the heavens for the counter that's holding me up. "Unfortunately."

It's the most honest thing I've said all morning. He shoots me a wink before heading back to the table with our friends. Brandon lets out a low whistle as Caiden takes a seat in the booth, and I'm sure I'm as red as a tomato.

I take a moment longer to fantasize about Caiden and the simplistically wonderful life we could have, letting it trail from sexy rendezvous from the diner to the fire station, and then back to my house where we'd make a life together, maybe someday having a family of our own. It sure does sound like a novel in my head. I wonder if people actually get happily ever afters. If I don't, will CeeCee and Brandon? Or what about my mom? Was she happy? Did she choose right every time? How did she know?

"Ya know, at least your mother had some manners."

I blink a few times before I realize the voice comes from

my reality and not some cruel joke within my daydream.

"Excuse me?" I ask as I make eye contact with a woman I've never seen before. Her straight, shoulder-length brown hair that curves around her petite face and her pastel polo shirt and slacks don't fit PineCrest, but more a summer in the Hamptons, and even though I don't know her, there's something uncomfortably familiar about her.

"We've never met, but I had hoped your mother might have taught you all the qualities we loved her for. Her kindness and compassion, and her lack of drama," the woman sneers.

"Excuse me?" I babble again, my heart managing to plunge itself into my stomach and water to gather at the corner of my eyes. How could this stranger nick my Achilles' heel in a matter of seconds? What right does a stranger have to sling such words about my mom? I'm an open wound, and she's pouring salt on it.

"My name is Eva Palmer. Kristen Palmer's mother. We own a few stores around town. You would know that, but you've been gone a long time."

The blush that filled my cheeks drains as I lock my stare with Caiden's ex-girlfriend's mom. I can't seem to move my lips. I was ready to unleash my anger, but I've lost any sense of self.

"I've heard things here and there, how you damage people with your selfishness. I mean, it wasn't explained to me that way. But I connected the dots from what Kristen's told me about Caiden's past relationship, and how you left your mother alone. My daughter told me what has unfolded since you arrived. Was it your plan to do it all over again? Come and destroy lives for your own entertainment?"

"Ma'am, I'm sorry for what happened between your daughter and Caiden, but I—"

"No, spare me. I don't understand why someone who thought they were better than this town would come back, and instead of focusing on mourning her mother's death, would break up a perfectly happy couple. This town is rattled by your appearance. Isn't it obvious? I'm just trying to figure out why you're still here. Is it for some self-fulfilling prophecy to make a buck on another book? These are people's lives you're messing with, Hailey. Not characters in one of your smutty novels."

A tremble slithers up my back, and I want to defend myself, but I don't have it in me. She's nailed all my fears in one decadent speech. And as a mother, she has every right to stand up for her daughter. Who am I? My mother's dead. I question my own reasons for being here.

"It's not like that ma'am," I mumble with my chin down. "I'm sorry for the stress I've caused your family. That wasn't my intention."

"At least your mother taught you how to apologize."

She's so eerily calm, it's terrifying. I shuffle back a step, worried I'm about to fall over. My spine has disappeared, and my joints feel nonexistent.

It isn't until I hear the sounds of heavy boots on linoleum that I manage to lift my chin.

Caiden's red in the face as he rushes to intervene. I can't tell if it's in embarrassment or the need to save me.

"—Eva, what do you think you're doing?" erupts from a very pissed off Caiden.

The woman slowly turns as if she expected this very thing. Her smile is slight and carefree. She shrugs and lifts a well-manicured hand to Caiden's forearm.

"Caiden, my dear. It's nothing. Just putting in my two cents, that's all. It's my right as a mother, you know?" She pauses, licking her thin, frosted pink lips, as if debating what to do next. "Kristen misses you. We all miss you, but honestly, I thought you had a little more class than how this situation played out. When you've managed to knock some sense back into yourself, don't hesitate to stop by the house." She doesn't bat an eye my way and instead gently squeezes his arm before walking away without a goodbye or an apology. "We miss our normal life. The one with you in it. This town could use a bit of normal," she hums as the door closes behind her.

I'm empty of everything. Instead of feeling a rapid heartbeat within my ribcage, I feel hollow, my skin drained of color and my lungs empty of oxygen. I think for the first time I actually might know what numb feels like.

When shockingly warm hands reach for my ice-cold cheek, I flinch.

"Hailey..."

My glazed-over eyes swing to Caiden's, and I only want one thing. "I have to go."

He shakes his head and reaches for my hand, but I take a step back away from the counter. His eyes dart all over my body, looking for answers that I don't have. "Don't be like that, Hails. I'm sorry she did that. She didn't have the right—"

"Yes she did, Caid. I... I... need a moment."

"Let me take you home. Let's talk this out."

A sad twitch occurs at the corner of my mouth. It's a sweet thing to say, but there's nothing to talk about. I pull the knot on my apron free and take it off, placing it on the counter.

Everyone is staring: CeeCee from the kitchen, Brandon and Cameron at the booth looking uncharacteristically stunned, and all the patrons who look wide-eyed and ready to tell the juiciest gossip to their neighbor.

The hum of Elvis in the background isn't enough to cover the awkward aura filling the diner, and the best remedy I can fathom is removing the problem: me.

I walk around the breakfast bar, smoothing out my tank top and skinny jeans, focusing on breathing in and out.

Caiden's ready to follow me out, trailing after me like a concerned mother hen, but I'm not in the mood for sympathy. Not when it comes to my mom, or how I broke up a relationship or interrupted the lives of PineCrest.

I just want to be left alone. I want to feel some sense of control. I haven't felt it since I stepped foot in this town, and today's fiasco is confirmation that I may never get it.

I turn around to place a heavy palm against Caiden's chest, stopping him. "I'm fine. You and I both know you can't miss any more work, and I could use some air."

"You're not fine."

"Don't tell me what I'm feeling," comes out sharper than I'd like, and Caiden slams his mouth shut, befuddled. "Things are just complicated, Caid."

"Please let me be there for you."

I want to tell him I don't need him, but it'd be the biggest lie I've ever told, so instead, I gift him a tight smile, stand up on my tiptoes and place a kiss on his lips, and another on his stubbly chin, and one more for good measure on the tip of his perfect nose.

"I'll see you tonight, okay?"

He releases a pent-up breath that signals his defeat. "I love you," he exhales.

"I love you, too."

I'm about to walk away but remember that I left my phone in my apron pocket. I lean back over the counter to grab it, the silence somehow emanating into a thick layer of static fog with all eyes still on me, but most importantly, a heavy emerald stare that's trying to read me. But I've rebuilt the emotional wall I've mastered in the past five years. I didn't think it would be so easy to build back up once Caiden and this town seemingly made it crumble just by existing, but now I think I need that protective wall more than ever.

I swivel around before I head out the door to absorb one more vision of Caiden. I smile, he smiles back, and it's satisfying enough to have me ready to depart.

It's all so strange and uncomfortable, but so necessary, and unfortunately none of us has to like it. It doesn't matter, though. Caiden doesn't stop me as he tugs on his bottom lip while he watches me leave, and CeeCee doesn't utter a sound even though she's the only one who knows my agony, and Brandon simply looks confused as hell.

The answer to CeeCee's question earlier suddenly comes to me:

Life never gets easier. Ever.

I grab for a pen as I pass the hostess podium, scribbling the thought down on the back of my hand so I'll remember to put it into my notes.

I wish my mom was here. She'd be able to knock some sense into me. She could help me figure out the rights and the wrongs. She'd probably tell me I should've stood up for myself. But my mom's *not* here, and I feel like a shell of myself.

It's funny how one call from last night could have a snowball effect on my life. It's one blow to my well-being after another. All I keep thinking is, it'll just take one more call to set it all right again.

As I exit the diner and the humid summer hits my skin, I stick the pen into my pocket and grab for my phone to dial Janet's number. I barely get two rings in before I hear, "It's about fucking time, Hailey."

Yeah, I guess it is. My time is up.

18

I'm sweating bullets when I enter through the swinging door of the bar. The buzz inside makes me feel more claustrophobic than I'd like, the murmurs and music seemingly sucking the oxygen from the room. I try counting to ten in my head to calm my nerves, but all I can manage is counting days, like how I've only been here twenty-seven days, possibly eight hours, twenty-four minutes, and thirteen seconds… fourteen, fifteen, sixteen…

Deep breaths.

How can I crash and burn so quickly? I'm a glorified drama mini-series. I've managed coming back to greet my heartbreak, break up relationships, rekindle a romance, to ruining it all in record time.

The worst part about it is, I knew this is what was going to happen. I knew the potential destruction I could cause. Mrs. Palmer's voice resonates in my head, and it's terrifying. I'm selfish. I'm cruel. I thirst for a type of love I don't deserve, and in the end it's better to crawl back to my cave on the west coast.

My call with Janet today proved it.

I shift from counting minutes and days to counting my steps. It takes five steps inside before I see Caiden fast approaching. My heart flutters involuntarily. I'm sure he's been watching the door since he arrived, waiting for me to get here.

I wouldn't say I ignored Caiden today since our awkward diner departure, but I definitely was slower to respond to him. I'd wait an hour instead of minutes to answer text messages. And as I watch him make his way to me, I can tell his steps are cautious. I've put him on edge, and I don't blame the guy.

My eyes drop to the orange flower in his hand. I blush, and I'm thrilled that the smile on my face appears so naturally.

"Is that my favorite flower?" I ask when he's stopped in front of me.

He wets his lips as his eyes drag shamelessly from my head all the way down to my toes. I hate and love that Caiden looks at me with such fresh eyes every time we see each other. A girl deserves to know this feeling, and I highly recommend never letting something like this go, unless you absolutely have to. Like me.

Lifting the flower up, I realize what he's about to do.

"Yes, it is," he replies. "I give these to you. Only me."

A shocking giggle escapes me. How is it I forget how good laughing feels? It's a natural remedy that soothes my woes, even if it's brief.

"Only you?" I ask, feeding into Caiden's rare, but oh so hilarious jealousy that I don't remember seeing so clearly since I was eighteen, over the same boy's attention at that.

"Gabe Samuels is an idiot. He knows better than to touch my girl, but it doesn't matter now, does it?"

I shake my head back and forth, letting my smile grow into a full-blown grin as Caiden moves to place the flower behind my ear.

I blink back the water that wants to fill my eyes, because regardless of how cute this moment is, I've already sealed our fate.

"What's wrong?" he asks.

I choke out a laugh, wiping at the corner of my eyes.

"You're just so annoyingly perfect sometimes."

He laughs, and I so badly want to laugh with the same zest, but my laughs are sadder, driven by something much darker. My life has a soundtrack of a ticking clock which seems to echo in my brain and somehow still overtakes the loud sounds of indie rock and roll blaring through the bar.

Caiden leans down to kiss me, and goddammit he tastes so good. *Too good.* If I had my way, I'd let him kiss me stupid right here in front of everyone. Normally I would, but today's not a normal day.

Today's D-Day.

My insides plummet with my growing nerves, and I pull away. I've never pulled away before.

Instead of calling me out on it, he just stares at me blankly, watching me like you would a cornered animal. I try to fake a smile, but I haven't been able to shake that numb feeling since the diner.

In a panic, I turn away, and what's weirder is, he lets me. It's what I think I should want him to do: to give me that free pass out of the situation; to be a master avoider; to give me a moment to pull myself together. But of course, that's actually not what I want at all.

Tonight, I'm no longer driven by love, and instead it's fear that fuels each step. Me, myself, and I know that if Caiden were to make me accountable for even just a moment, my personal Armageddon would unfold.

I keep thinking I can pretend a little longer. Savor his sweetness. Bask in his endless *I love you*'s, but it's all a lie. I just don't know when I'll have the guts to confess what I've done. But it's becoming clear the floor is crumbling beneath me. I've never been a good actress. That's why I'm a writer. I can't help but write truths, even if I label them fiction.

Trying my best, I plaster on a smile as I walk up to my group of friends in their normal spot. CeeCee is clutching a drink as she makes fun of Brandon taking a shot at a game of pool, while Cameron looks on, hiding his snickers behind his cue, and Tyler is trying to pick up the cute brunette watching in the back.

I envy their routine. They get drinks together, gather at the same lunch spots together, and share nearly everything.

My life in LA has its routine if you consider morning coffee and traffic, but it's still erratic. I rarely see the same people, and my conversations vary from obscenely emotional storytelling to mundane complaints that never matter. You'd think I'd like the variations, but as I stare at my friends, I love that they have this closeness and hold it so dear. I'm reminded that they let me back in so easily.

I've never felt so ungrateful in my entire life.

"Cee, I need a drink. Let's get a drink."

She swivels around, not realizing I was behind her. Her short, pale pink dress twirls beautifully as she turns to face me.

"Is Hailey Elwood finally speaking a language I can understand?"

I nod, needing that drink more than she knows.

A firm hand smooths over my hips from behind, giving my flesh a gentle squeeze of admiration before moving to take hold of my hand. Caiden's warmth is unmistakable. His skin against mine always feels like a blanket fresh out of the dryer.

"I'll grab us a drink!" CeeCee chirps.

I still haven't looked at Caiden. I give his hand a tense squeeze back but slowly slip away from him.

"Hailey?" I hear, but the deep tone is barely audible over the music.

I pretend I don't hear it and instead trail behind CeeCee to the bar.

"Is everything okay?" she asks as she hails a bartender.

I nod my head a little too violently. "Yeah. Fine. I'm just, ya know…"

"… Neurotic as hell tonight?"

I purse my lips into a smile. "I guess."

"Have you talked to Caiden yet?" She turns back to the

bar. "Two beers please, and also two shots of tequila!"

I don't argue.

"Um, no I haven't, but I will."

"When?" she asks, tapping bright red fingernails on the bar.

"Soon," I retort.

"How soon?" she persists.

"Knock it off, CeeCee. Not tonight, or I might just explode."

She goes wide-eyed a second. "Sorry… are you on edge because of Kristen's mom earlier today? I can't believe she did that."

Drinks appear at the bar as my mouth goes dry. "It certainly didn't help the situation. Are we doing shots or what?"

Her brows furrow over her bright eyes and her nose wrinkles as she watches me. "Well, don't take it out on me, 'kay?"

I exhale. "I'm sorry. I'm trying to figure out how to handle this."

She grabs for the shots, but her movements are slow as she hands one to me. "Did something else happen today? Something you're not telling me?"

I shrug and grab for the beer as I attempt a sandpaper gulp, eager to wet my palate and relax. How could she know? *Because I'm terrible at playing pretend.* "Everything is fine. Why would you say that?"

"Something's different, but I can't tell what. I've never known you to let someone get to you so much, if it's Kristen's mom that's bothering you so much."

"She's for sure the icing on this shit cupcake I'm currently living."

CeeCee's furrowing brow turns angular in annoyance. "We can't be that bad, can we, Hails? We're all pretty much family here, and Caiden can't keep his eyes or hands off of you. Life could be worse."

"Can it?" I blurt out more sharply than I'd like.

"What's that supposed to mean?"

I shake my head, regretting everything at once. "Nothing. Let's drink."

CeeCee's enthusiasm from before has subsided as we take the shots in one quick gulp.

She slams the glass onto the bar, hissing out the fumes as she turns to me. "Ya know, I'm just going to let this weird, bitchy side of you slide because I know you're all sorts of confused, but I think it's probably more important for me to say that I'm here for you if you need anything."

The gravity of guilt is quick to reappear inside my guts. *Dammit, I'm going to miss her, too.*

"Sorry, Cee. I just need to drown it all out tonight. Is that something you can understand?"

Her smirk is sadder than normal. "I can totally understand that."

We grab for our pints and head back to the boys.

I stretch out my fingers, feeling the buzz thrumming through my limbs and beg for my nerves to subside, eager for the alcohol to take effect.

"Drinking tonight, Hailey?" sounds as I approach the pool table. The harsh, judgmental tone is impossible to ignore.

Caiden grabs my nearly half-empty glass from my hands and places it on a table. My brows pull together. "So what?" I huff at him.

"It's never been your thing, so I thought I'd ask."

"How could you possibly know what my *thing* is anymore, Caiden?"

His eyes heat with annoyance, and I'm stunned by my misplaced question and tone. "I used to be your thing. Am I still? Because I'm starting to question a lot of things tonight."

My sassy look falters as he redirects the conversation to a topic I'm not ready for. I reach for the orange flower in my hair, absentmindedly fiddling with the petals as I take in the sight of Caiden and try to figure out an answer to his question. Of course, the real answer is, he's the *only* thing I'm into and always have been, but I don't want to feed into the façade anymore. I won't be able to keep it for very much longer. I change tack, trying for alcohol and sarcasm as my only way out. "I think I need more drinks to handle tonight."

I try moving around Caiden, but I figure out quickly there seems to be a fine line between walking as if you're calm and collected versus sprinting for an escape. My steps come out like frantic shuffles as my boots skid against the worn wood floor, because I'm trying to act normal, but the guilty dead weight of my feet isn't helping.

I'm losing my mind. This is what the situation is doing to me. It's turning me into a lunatic.

I don't make it three feet away from our friends before I'm stopped. Caiden's hand on my forearm gives a tight squeeze. I think it's supposed to strike a sense of urgency, but I'm pining for him to comfort me. Although, how could he possibly know that when I'm acting like a raging bitch of deflect and ignore?

"You're not making sense. You're acting weird."

"That's a subjective opinion. What you don't realize is that I am, in fact, very strange. I'm sorry I didn't send you the memo—"

"You're doing what you always do," he grunts.

"Excuse me?" I lick my lips, knowing my nerves are officially going to get the best of me.

"You're avoiding. You do this every time, even before you left. You can't smart-ass your way out of this one, Hailey. Not with me. You owe it to me. To us."

I grit my teeth to fight back my defensive sob. Can he not make me feel so predictable, please?

"Fine."

"Then tell me what you're not saying… what you're afraid to say. Obviously, there's something on your mind."

It's a dare, and I've brought him to this point.

My bottom lip trembles without my permission, and I glance around at all the people. Our friends and some strangers, and the music in the background only amplifies my anxiety, as if *Nirvana* really needs to become the soundtrack to my demise.

"In front of all these people?" I whisper.

He shrugs, and it hurts, the motion sending a venomous burn through my veins, but I've done this, haven't I? This is all my doing. I've made him angry. And an angry Caiden has a way of mastering *indifference* like a frickin' champ. He wields it like passive poisonous darts, with each effortless shrug and drag of his glowing eyes, and it stings.

"If you're ready to be serious, let's take this outside."

Now the question is, am I ready to be serious?

I swallow down my bubbling guilt barreling up my throat and nod. He leads the way with heavy, determined steps. I ignore my friends' open gawks. Even CeeCee is stunned as she watches Caiden and me leave. I wish I could explain.

I've forgotten how to breathe, and I keep thinking going outside will help, but instead the sticky humidity that hits my skin suffocates me more.

Caiden doesn't speak for a whole minute, as if hoping I'll speak first or that the silence might give something away, but instead I just keep averting my eyes. I choose to stare at the endless darkness encasing the trees around us, thinking about how we were in this same spot when I saw him for the first time after five years of worrying he was just a figment of my imagination.

Now things are *too real*.

"Why are you acting like this? One moment we're good, and then suddenly we're not. Does this have to do with earlier?"

I snort. "It's everything." I wave a flippant hand, my patience vanishing, expecting him to understand, but all he can do is watch me pace in the middle of the dirt parking lot.

"Everything? I can't keep track, Hailey. You're driving me nuts. One minute you want me; the next minute you don't. Then everything's the problem. But I guess that makes sense, because you can't seem to look any of our friends in the eye, and you sure as hell can't stand looking at me longer than one second."

I come to a halt facing away from him, proving his point. "I don't want it to be this way. I promise you that, at least."

"Would you fucking look at me when you talk to me? Don't I deserve that much? What the hell is going on? You're being cryptic."

My boots drag slowly on the gravel as I turn to look at him. "Caiden, I'm freaking out, okay? It's… I'm… so fucked up." I have half a mind to add, *We're so fucked up*, but it's probably too honest.

He pauses a beat, his eyes glowing with confusion as he dissects me. "Let me help you. Please Hailey, talk to me. I feel like I'm losing you, and I don't know how to keep a grip on us."

A sob unleashes itself from my mouth, and Caiden is at my side in a second. I must look crazy. I throw myself willingly into his encompassing arms that hold me close.

"You have no idea how much I wish you could fix this," I reply.

He presses a kiss to the top of my head. "Talk to me, Hails. I love you. Let me love you, for fuck's sake. You always think you have to deal with things alone, but you don't have to this time," he pleads.

I bury my nose into his chest, pulling in a deep breath as I squeeze at a fistful of his flannel shirt. "Take me home first, Caid."

Treating me like a delicate china doll, he doesn't argue, as if words might break me. He wouldn't be wrong, either. He simply slides his hand into the front of my jeans to grab my keys and takes the lead.

The ease with which he takes care of me is wonderful. I

clutch his hand tightly as he walks me to my rental. He opens the door for me and helps me inside. He even presses a sweet kiss against my damp cheek before saying, "It's going to be okay," and closes the door.

He's bliss wrapped in tattoos and scruff, no matter how wrong his words are.

I try not to cry on the drive home, and he doesn't try to get me to speak. Good, because I'm trying to find the words to say to him when I have to reveal the truth, and I've got nothing.

I'm a writer. I should be able to find the best way to frame our own romantic tragedy for him to understand, but every time I try to, it never seems to make sense, and I doubt saying it out loud will help.

He's going to hate me by the end of the night. It's inevitable.

We pull into my driveway, and the clear summer night is ominous with the full moon hanging over the pines.

Does the full moon appear to signal the end, or is it supposed to signal a fresh start?

I want to write the question down in my notebook as I enter through the squeaky wooden door into my living room.

The permanent smell of apple and cinnamon makes me nauseous as I try for a deep breath. I can't help but think how disappointed my mom would be with me today, and it's such an awful thought that a sniffle escapes.

My steps stop in the doorway of the kitchen. I hear the front door shut behind me and can feel Caiden's presence fill the living room.

I turn around sharply to catch him staring. He's absentmindedly playing with his perfect bottom lip as he cautiously takes in the situation, and I don't have it in me any longer now that we're alone. I break.

"I'm leaving," I blurt out, and although a pins-and-needles feeling appears in my shoulders, a heavy weight is also lifted.

He releases his lip, his hands falling to his sides.

"What?" he asks, as if I didn't just shout it out into the silence.

"I'm leaving back to LA, Caiden."

"When?" he asks, stunned.

"In two days."

"What? And you're telling me now?"

"I just found out today." I withhold the fact that Janet offered to give me another week. At the time of the phone call, I just wanted to disappear and not be such a nuisance to this town, but now with Caiden standing in front of me, I wish I had accepted. Doesn't matter now. The plane ticket has already been booked, to my agent's excitement.

He pauses a beat, as if trying to delicately calculate the situation. Maybe now he can see why I said I was so fucked up earlier.

"Okay…" he exhales. "So, you're gone for a bit. So what? When do you come back?" he questions.

"I don't know." Can hearts tremble? Because mine is. I can feel all those tiny fractures that marked my heart from years ago reappearing with each second that passes between us as he puts the pieces of the situation together.

"You don't know?" he repeats, and I can sense his anger surfacing. I think I'd prefer his anger over everything else. Anger is easier to handle, and also easier to get over. "What does that mean?"

"It means, I don't know if I'm ever coming back. I've been trying to figure out how to tell you—"

"Well fuck, Hailey, you've barely given us forty-eight hours to figure it out."

I bite back a sob. "There's nothing to figure out."

His face falls with the realization of what I'm doing. "Are

you saying it's over between us? After everything?"

I shrug, my face puckering with the sadness it's trying to fight. "I don't know."

"That's not an acceptable answer. I'm not going to let you go this easy this time. You can't make this decision without me." His voice rises an octave, and it sends a shiver down my spine.

Where are my words when I need them?

He continues as he takes a step toward me. "Don't be so rash about this."

"Come with me?" I whisper desperately, even though I already know the answer.

He shakes his head, befuddled with the request. "Hailey… I can't. Not permanently. I want to be there for you. You know I'm your biggest fan, but don't do this. Don't drop this life you fit into so perfectly."

I shake my head, hating the way he's worded it. "Nothing is perfect, Caiden. The decision's been made. My work is in LA. I can't guarantee when I'll be back, and I'd hate myself if I allowed you to hold yourself back because of me."

"You holding me back?" he guffaws. "It sounds more like I'd be holding you back, and you're just cutting your losses. If that's the real reason, then say the truth!"

"That's not the reason," I gasp. "I want you, Caiden. I want you with me all the time. You make me better, but the fact of the matter is, I have obligations in California that I can't get out of. There's a high probability with the book and the movie I won't be able to leave for months, maybe even a year. A weekend here or there might be all I can offer, and I don't think that's enough, and those are things I can't even guarantee. I've signed contracts and made promises to a lot of important people—"

"More important than me?"

I choke back another sob. "That's not fair."

"Don't you dare tell me what's fair."

"I don't want to have to do this. Please know this is literally the worst decision I've had to make. I don't have a choice."

"Yes, you do. You can't just leave. Stay here in PineCrest with me where you belong," he says, his words shaking with more and more confusion.

"I was never going to stay," I reply, and I wish I didn't say it with such a nonchalant shrug, because it only sparks Caiden's temper.

His boot stomps on the worn area rug of the living room, the hollow thump echoing in the silence. I wince.

"Then why did you come back? I mean, really, Hailey. What was the point? That's it for us, then? You get to make this decision without talking to me? You didn't even give us a chance. I think I deserve that much. You can't just spring this on me." He's pleading now, and it makes my body ache to hear his desperation.

"I shouldn't have let us get this far. I'm so sorry, Caiden, I—"

"Are you kidding me right now? You can't honestly ask me to believe that you're just *sorry you let it get this far*. Let's talk about accountability now. You knew what you were walking into. Hell, even I knew what the possibilities were when I found out you'd be heading back into town. Can't say I didn't want it, even if I knew it was wrong. We're all curious about the what-ifs, but I refuse to believe that you thought you could come back here to take care of your mom's stuff and not be pulled back into what we have. You're not stupid. We both know that you came back because you wanted it, even if you were scared."

He's out of breath, heaving in a long inhale of oxygen as his grimace softens into a disappointed frown while his hands run through his messy hair. "It doesn't have to be one or the other. We're not nineteen anymore. There's got to be a gray area. Why can't you just stay here and write? I've seen your notes and journals hanging around. You've been pecking away at it. You could be perfectly happy here."

How is it that in the last five years I've felt misunderstood? That no one got who I was when it came to the inner workings of my melodramatic heart and irrational musings of impossible happily ever afters? I would be desperate for a connection, to look someone in the eyes who said they got who I was.

I never imagined that the moment I'd get it would be now, here, and from piercing green depths that are finding the truths that I don't want people to see. It's horribly ironic, and annoyingly refreshing.

My mouth bobs, seeking out a word to get a proverbial grip on, but I can't keep it together, not when Caiden gets it only too well.

"I'm sorry. I wish it was that simple," I cry. I rub my face, pressing my fingers into my eyes until I see stars, blocking out the view of Caiden, whose frown feels like a flesh-eating bacteria burning into my heart. "I love you, you know? I love you so much it hurts. But the facts are, I worked too hard to lose my momentum with the book thing. You have to know that. Look at how much I've sacrificed to get where I am. I have to stick it out in Los Angeles. I don't want to hurt you. And you just implied you'd never leave PineCrest. Your life is here, right? Tell me where this gray area is? Because right now, I'm seeing a lot of black and white. Can't you see how much I'm suffering? I don't want it to be this way. Maybe you're right. I was curious, but this is the exact danger that I knew could ensue. This is my fault. Just like before. I knew falling for you again was a possibility, and I also knew if it happened that I'd destroy the both of us in one stupidly beautiful firework. Ya know, when the chaos is so pretty, you can't help but just watch it burn before it dissolves with the stars into oblivion? That's us, on the brink of oblivion. It's addicting."

I pull my hands away from my face, my fingertips damp,

confirming that I can't stop the tears. I let them stream down my cheeks. I give in. I accept them. I show them to Caiden. I allow him to see me.

Caiden's endless eyes absorb me. They twitch infinitesimally as he takes three steps toward me, closing the distance between us. He grabs for my face with both hands, holding me at my jaw, lifting my watering eyes to his. Leaning down, he places sweet kisses against the wet streams rolling over my cheeks over and over again until they slow, and his mouth finally moves to mine.

He's like a life mask. His lips on mine breathe life into me, as if I've been spending too much time at high elevation or in the depths of the ocean.

My arms reach for him, wrapping around his perfect hips, my hands dipping into the back pockets of his jeans.

He pulls away, speaking inches away from my lips. "Don't we get to try for the sequel, Hails? Even if it was just pretend in your first book, we still kind of made it. What about book two?"

I'm crying and I can't stop. "Not all books have happy endings."

It's the saddest thing I've ever admitted.

He sighs, his eyes darting all over my face. We've finally reached an impasse. This sad, solemn understanding that sometimes love isn't enough. He's not going to move, and I'm not going to stay. Regardless of everything we've talked about since I got here. It's the same problem from five years ago. We expected too much from each other. Hindsight is 20/20. We should have known better.

"Caiden, kiss me more."

He pouts, his brows pulling together as he says, "But it won't change anything."

"I know, but it doesn't mean I still don't need you. It's selfish and stupid, but I do, and I'm sorry."

His thumbs smooth over my cheeks, wiping away the stream of tears. "I hate you," he says out loud. The sad crook to the corner of his mouth is a confirmation that it's a flat out lie.

I sniffle and offer my own sad smile. "I hate you, too. Does that help make this any easier?"

He shakes his head, and I swear I see his eyes water just a bit. "Nope. Not at all."

So here we are, trying to make our reality bearable. Soothing it with an outright contradiction to our actual feelings is all that we have left, and I'm thankful for it. He could run, kick me to the curb and abandon me, all of which I deserve. But instead, gluttons for punishment, we pretend a little longer even though we both know the truth. We're pathetic.

Pulling and pushing, he presses me against the wall next to the stairs. I whimper as he crashes his lips to mine, and it only takes seconds before his mouth picks up the pace, frantically searching for a solution we both so desperately want.

He lifts me off the ground, carrying me upstairs to my bedroom, his mouth not once taking a chance on words.

His rushed kisses that meet my lips feel like a little bit of everything in one firecracker of a touch. It's a punishment, an apology, and worst of all, a goodbye. He knows what I'm going to do because we've been here before. There might even be a dash of hope in each possessive stroke, and I savor it, licking over his lips, and whisper his name, wishing things were just... different.

But his kiss tells me this is it. There was a lot less talking than I anticipated. Maybe it's because we had a similar conversation when we were nineteen. Why rehash the past? Instead, we take advantage of the time we have left, because life isn't fair, and love is cruel.

He takes me to my bedroom, and we make love over and over again.

In the briefest silences when dawn is approaching, we giggle together like the sunrise isn't the start to our demise.

Sometimes a lie feels nice, but lies never last long, especially in PineCrest.

19

Entering the airport feels more like I'm about to depart on a NASA space mission rather than a flight across the U.S.

I guess PineCrest always managed to feel like the only place that grounded me, and LA more like outer space anyway. Not to mention, the point of no return.

I rub at my tired, swollen eyes, feeling my sanity slipping. I've spent more time crying in the past twenty-four hours than I have in my entire life. It's as if everything I've been holding in since the death of my mom and then having to walk away from Caiden *again* came crashing down on me all in one tidal wave of tears last night as I sat in the living room staring at my mother's urn, pleading for her to talk to me, to tell me how to be better.

I can't tell if leaving will ever fix me. Right now, it feels like the opposite, but I tell myself all artists are broken in some way. I just hope I produce beautiful things in this tortured chaos.

The only thing I do know is that I have to leave if I'm choosing to continue with my dream, but it's feeling less satisfying by the second as I stroll through the hallways of Denver International Airport.

As I make my way to the plane, I realize it's a staggering possibility that this might be my last trip to PineCrest. It makes my insides ache.

It doesn't take a rocket scientist to figure out that I've officially lost the only reasons that would have me coming back. I'd fly CeeCee out if I had to and manage the diner via phone or email if need be. That's at least how I explained it to her in between my sobs while we chatted on the phone, and all the while she tried to tell me it'd all be okay.

And although I adore CeeCee, my two real reasons for staying are my mom and Caiden. My mom is gone, and Caiden might as well be. He's not dead to me, far from it, but I wouldn't be shocked if I was to him. It's just one of the things we do to keep our hearts safe. We confine our tragedies to something like death because then we can go through its phases like functioning adults. First, it's anger, then denial, grief, depression, and finally acceptance before moving on.

For me? I tend to like to suffer, and apparently, I also have a problem with letting go.

Everything about what I'm doing feels wrong, but it's logic that tells me this is what I need. However, I've never been a fan of rationality. I don't think that's what's gotten me this far. These impossible dreams, like writing, take more risk than logic. I keep trying to figure out why I'm latching onto it now.

Regardless, during the three-hour drive here I dissected my predicament and analyzed the facts. Of course, it's not like I didn't want Caiden and me to work; it's that we can't. Time didn't help us, which is a shame. You'd think we'd have it all figured out within five years. Quite the contrary. There's no room for us to compromise when our lives are rooted in completely different places. At least this was all something I repeated like a mantra on my drive from PineCrest to Denver, replaying the argument Caiden and I had in my living room over and over again and how he gave in. He let me go.

I dropped off my rental car with bizarre satisfaction and disdain. It felt drenched in my three-hour thoughts and memories of a town I'm not sure I should hold onto. It was the only thing I've been happy to rid myself of so far.

Even from drop-off to the security gate I toyed with wanting to stay, not able to shake this daunting feeling. Do I run as fast as I can to the west coast just so I can take a hot shower in my own apartment and wash myself of this once and for all? I guess that's the only thing I can do, or at least it feels like it. I put one foot in front of the other, even if it hurts.

This whole debacle has made one thing clear to me, though: life is entirely unfair.

Losing people you love should not fall under the practicality of life. It doesn't seem right, whether I'm talking about my mom or Caiden.

Waking up alone yesterday morning felt exceptionally cruel. I haven't slept since.

My body deflates and my eyes droop with exhaustion as I plop into a seat at Gate 23 waiting for the announcement to board the flight that will help my indecision because it'll give me a point of no return.

I reach into my sweatshirt pocket to grab the now very worn note that was left on my nightstand yesterday morning.

I slump as I stare, tugging at a ragged, unwashed strand of my hair as I read the five words over and over again:

I will always love you.

That's it. No signature or endearment, just this irrefutable fact in Caiden's chicken scratch handwriting.

Why isn't love enough? I'll add it to my list of reasons why life isn't fair.

It doesn't change the fact that I can't stop staring at the note. I suck in a breath, accepting my awful fate, and consider something absurd.

Maybe I should frame the note when I get home. It can hold the inspiration for novels to come, and also remind me that at least I felt this for real *once*.

It's both sadistic and sad.

I stuff it back into my pocket, hating and loving the damn thing at once, noting that's how I tend to feel about Caiden, too.

I turn to my carryon luggage, squinting at it, and think about my mother's ashes tucked away inside.

"Mom, I'm scared. What if what I'm doing is wrong? What if it's not worth it? I should have stayed home all those years ago. I'd never know this pain. I might actually be happy," I whisper, hoping no one hears me losing my mind.

My eyes sink closed, trying to grasp onto memories of the joy I felt when I snagged my book deal or the moment it hit number one on the *New York Times*, and how I rushed to call my mom. I try to remember why it was worth it.

I want to think that my mom would say it all was. That as long as it was something I worked hard for and wanted, then it's fine.

My lips twitch at a far-off memory in my teens, leaning over the breakfast bar of the diner, staring at my mother's rosy cheeks and silvery blonde hair as she'd say, "C'mon, Hailey. You can't have your pie and eat it, too," as she'd slide me a fresh piece from the kitchen.

I can't have it all. Ain't that a shame.

Mom, I miss you.

My eyes fly open when two women take a seat in the chairs behind me, jabbering away.

If sitting at the gate is this bad for my brain, I can't imagine what my two-hour flight will be like. I figure stocking up on as many obnoxious, mundane, vanity-infused magazines as possible is the best way to go to distract myself.

I'm about to get up from my seat, but the woman behind me catches my attention as I hear the ruffling of pages. A book is tossed from the girl directly behind me onto her friend's lap to my left.

"Here. I got you the book I've been telling you about."

I try not to fidget, but I can't help it when I lift my chin just enough to catch a glimpse of my very own novel. Its pristine trade-paperback size with the glossy movie poster cover stares back at me.

I never did love its flashy makeover, which feels like some annoying self-fulfilled prophecy. I've grown with that book. There was a time when I and that book were both rough around the edges, but look at us now.

I get the urge to move. I should remove myself from this situation. I'm too raw to witness what might be said, but no matter, I continue to listen in as my heart picks up pace.

"So, is this going to be a perfect beach read, then?" the girl asks. "I need a really good love story. I'm such a sucker for them and need something like that right now."

Don't we all...

"You won't be disappointed." Her friend squeals with excitement that makes me smile as I try to keep my stare forward. "It's more than love, it's like, I don't know, fate! The *feels*, oh God, the *feels*. I hear it's going to be a movie. You can't go wrong with this book. It totally helped me through my breakup with Zack. Why can't book love be real love? Ya know?"

"I know, right?" her friend chirps as she flips through the pages. "Maybe it's unfair for books to make these unrealistic expectations, but I don't care. I need some sort of hope."

My blood churns hot and thick as heat rushes to my face while I try not to get emotional over a stranger's conversation I shouldn't be listening to. But I can't help myself as I lean my head back to get a better look at my book and a better listen, but my stupid head bumps into the girl behind me.

Thunk.

"Whoa?" the girl says out loud as she leans forward to avoid more injury.

I twist my back around, rubbing at my scalp. *Ow.*

I'm twitchy and excited, but also a little manic as I say, "Ya know, love like that *does* exist. I'm just an idiot."

"Excuse me?" the one clutching my book says as she gives me a baffled, green-eyed expression. It strangely reminds me of Caiden, and I realize everything at once.

"I'm sorry. I know it sounds crazy, but I couldn't help myself." I point at the book in her hands, squinting in disbelief at it, feeling foolish and amazed. "I'd know about that whole *love* thing. Don't give up hope, and if you find that love, don't be an idiot like me. Hold on to it and never let go."

Both women exchange looks of confusion. I must look like I escaped from the nearest insane asylum. That is, until the bump-on-the-head girl snatches the book from her friend's hands, flipping it over to the back cover.

"Oh my God, you're Hailey Elwood."

I cringe as I catch a glimpse of my author bio. "I hate that photo they put on the back of the book," I retort as I start to rise from my seat, suddenly frantic to leave, flooded with all the reasons I wrote the book in the first place and what it's taught me now.

"So, it is you, right?"

I shrug, grabbing for the handle of my luggage. "Yeah, it is."

"I loved your book! Can you please sign it for me?"

I grin, shaking my head as I glance at the time. "*Shit*— oops, sorry. This'll have to be super quick. I think I just realized I have to go get the guy that made that book into a reality. Thanks for inspiring me not to make the same mistake all over again."

Both girls squeal as I grab for the pen in one of their hands, flipping to the cover page to write "Stay True" and sign my name.

I hope they understand its meaning, but I'm not sure they'll ever grasp how much they've managed to help me with something so seemingly insignificant. Sometimes an epiphany comes in the strangest, simplest forms.

I'm scrambling to leave with a polite smile. "I'm sorry, I really have to go now. I'm glad you enjoyed the book, and I hope your friend does, too!"

My feet sprint in the opposite direction, and all I can hear are the fading giggles of girls and the squeaking wheels of my carryon on the airport floor.

I'm grinning, but I'm also crying as I retrace my steps back to the loading area. Security is a breeze when you exit, but my carryon gets dragged and flips over every time I attempt a turn or pick up the pace.

I grunt as I pull my carryon upright as I rush through glass double doors to the pavement.

This part isn't so easy. I'm still three hours away from PineCrest. I'll have to rent another car and hope I don't get a speeding ticket.

I'm cursing myself as I approach Rent-A-Car, wondering what Caiden might be doing right now. Is he back at the station? At the diner? The bar? Is he thinking of me?

I grunt, wishing things could be fixed instantly. I can't just call him, can I? I need to tell him I made a mistake. I need to tell him that I don't care what I have to do, I'll do anything to keep him.

I pull out my phone, my eyes darting from the line at the counter to my finger hovering over his name, wondering what my plan of action should be.

A familiar rumble vibrates through the loading area behind me, and my heart shudders with it.

I wipe at my eyes as I swivel around, stunned at the sight of Brandon's truck pulling up onto the curb, spooking a couple people twenty feet away.

I nearly drop my phone, loving and hating how perfect Caiden Anderson is all over again as he appears, hopping out of the truck.

Couldn't I be the hero this time?

Of course, he's going to show up. He's so perfect, he'd take the blame to make this right.

It takes less than fifteen seconds for him to see me on the

other side, petrified to the spot, staring back at him as if he was a mirage.

He doesn't hesitate. He closes the truck door and runs to me, as if he's afraid I'll be the one heading the other direction.

Stopping three feet in front of me, he starts frantically talking, "I should—"

"NO, I need to talk." I feel like an idiot. I would literally do everything I can to make this work, even if I lose the movie deal right now, no matter how much I fought for it. I'd find a way to fix it later, because there's not going to be another chance for Caiden and me. I pause, absorbing the way he watches me with that funny dimpled smirk. "I can't believe you're here right now."

He releases a pent-up breath. "Why aren't you on your plane right now?"

"Because I was about to run back to you."

His smirk grows into a full-blown grin. He bashfully points at himself as he says, "For me?"

I nod. "I was being selfish."

"We both were. I don't know how we managed to replay history, but I haven't been able to shake this feeling, Hails. There has to be a way. I'd rather do what it takes to make us work and make the mistakes along the way if it meant I got to give us a chance. It'd be worth it."

My shell-shocked look transitions into laughter. We've always been more of a dramedy than a contemporary romance. It's no wonder I was able to write a book about us. We're a hot mess of ridiculous.

I shake my head in disbelief, licking my lips, tasting salty tears, thankful that we both had similar epiphanies.

"I need to tell you something," I sniffle through more tight giggles, reaching out to grab his hand, fiddling with his fingers to calm my nerves and to confirm he's really here. "Want to know how I knew whatever I was feeling was real? It's going to sound stupid."

Caiden looks at me with a satisfied crook to his lips. My

nerves are too caught up in the moment as I stare at our hands, the words excitedly leaving my lips. "I was sitting at the gate, anxious to get on the plane because I wouldn't be able to back out at that point. While trying to sit still, trying to figure out why everything felt so wrong, I overheard a couple of women talking. One of them was recommending a book to her friend. It happened to be MY—*our* book." I pause to witness Caiden's lips squirm at my first out-loud acknowledgment that the book is in fact about us. It fuels me forward with a bit of giddiness brewing in my veins.

"She was gushing about it and how it helped her, and her friend said she wished love in books was like that in real life. See, what I'm trying to say is, here I was sitting in the airport terrified to make a choice because I didn't know which one was right. And When I overheard those women talking, something just *clicked*. It lit me up from the inside. I realized that the story I wrote was worth telling... *our* story. Not just to me, but to other people. At first, it terrified me, but it was also exhilarating. I always knew people liked my book, but the reason why never dawned on me. Hearing them say those things was like this confirmation of what I had been trying to pinpoint." I pause, pulling in a breath, squaring my shoulders as I lock my stare with Caiden's.

"That I love you, and how I was making the same mistake I did before. You're what makes the choices and dreams worth it. I wouldn't have made any of it without you. I wrote the book with us in mind, and I used it to capture how we impacted each other, and readers feel it; they must. People believe in our story, but there's a key ingredient that makes the difference. It's *the ending* they connect with. It's that last chapter that makes the book worth reading. People love the story, and the happily ever after... that I made up! Although most of the book is based in truth, the most fictional part is the end. We didn't get our happily ever after... and here I was, eavesdropping on a conversation, on the verge of throwing away the possibility of finally getting to have *that* happy ending. I'd be a fool to let that go."

"But we can have that now," Caiden whispers.

"I don't know what it'll take, Caiden, and I think I'm at the same point as you. I don't think I care what it takes anymore as long as I get to have you. It all sounds so crazy."

"It is crazy." He chuckles as his hand squeezes mine.

"Caid, I don't think I want to live in LA if you're not there, but I have to be there for the movie. There has to be a way to slice up our time while I finish, no matter how long it takes, even if it's a year. We can work on it, on us. I want to find the balance. That is, if you're willing to work through my insane schedule for a while. It won't be easy. You're needy. I'm needy. It'll be tough."

He blinks a few times, absorbing my words. "Are you saying you'd be willing to make PineCrest your home base?"

I gulp down my nerves but can't fight my reflexive smile as I exhale my honest answer of, "Yes. LA will always be there. You're right, I can write here, and I can always travel to LA, even if it means longer than I'd like for work, but I want to be here with you. You're worth it. It's because of you my dream was able to happen. And if anything, I need you for inspiration."

Caiden huffs, trying to hide his smirk. "You're so terrible at being serious." His hand grabs softly for my sweatshirt and yanks me forward, causing me to stumble into his chest. I can't fight how much I want to be near him. I wrap my arms around him and breathe in his charcoal pine smell.

"I love you, Hailey. Now, let's go or we'll miss our flight."

I pull back to flash my own look of shock. "Wait, what were we just talking about? I said I'd stay for you."

He presses a placating kiss to the tip of my nose. "This is your dream, babe. I'm not going to let you throw that away for me. Just because we agreed we'd make this work doesn't mean I wouldn't be willing to sink to groveling to my boss for a couple weeks off so I could support my girl."

"Grovel?" I squeal excitedly.

"*Grovel*," he confirms. "And I'm on kitchen duty at the station for a month after I get back."

"You groveled for me?"

He rolls his eyes. "Don't ruin the moment, Hailey."

I laugh, grab for the collar of his shirt, and pull him into a kiss, knowing that not only do we finally get our happily ever after, but I'll write us a sequel, too.

THE END

ABOUT THE AUTHOR

Alex Rosa lives in Los Angeles, California. By day she's a Digital Marketing Manager, by night a writer of swoon-worthy books, and somewhere in between she's also 1/2 of the podcast Book Babes and Bubbles.

With nearly ten years of writing experience, she has published five novels, including the Tryst Series with Intermix, Penguin Random House's digital imprint.

A pop culture fanatic, cemetery creeper, and self-proclaimed nerd, she's always following her favorite fandoms, the latest foodie finds, or picking her next city excursion or outdoor undertaking.

Her obsessions are on the brink of bizarre, but that's just the way she likes it.

www.alexrosa.org
Instagram.com/oh_alex
Facebook.com/author.arosa
Twitter.com/oh_alexrosa

Other Titles by Alex Rosa:

Tryst
Entangled
Rash Decisions
Fahrenheit
Emotionally Compromised

CPSIA information can be obtained
at www.ICGtesting.com
Printed in the USA
BVHW031125051020
590310BV00001B/32